What the critics are saying

"A romantica anthology with three powerful stories that could give a reader testosterone overload, EQUINOX fits the bill with a 'Capital T.' With sexy heroes and strong heroines, EQUINOX is definitely not to be missed... The sex scenes are graphic in nature and hot enough to burn the fingertips. Ms. Kingston, Ms. Harper, and Ms. Windsor certainly have a way with the written word." - *Jordan Moon, The Word on Romance*

"One of the best things...I liked about this Anthology by these talented authors was the fact that different genres were focused upon. Thanks to Ms. Kingston we take an exciting journey back in history, Ms. Harper shared with us a journey of time travel....past and present coming together and Ms. Windsor captivates us with her interesting speculations for the future! Each shines with their stories and they all know how to enthrall, thrill and put a spell on their readers. WARNING: reading all three stories at once, leads to testosterone overload...but it is a pleasure!!" - *Tracey West, The Road to Romance*

"EQUINOX is an erotica anthology of stories connected by spring's ritual celebrations. Lots of amazing men—and even more amazing sex—await readers who want to spend their nights with these tales of passion." - *Cindy Whitesel, Romantic Times*

"Equinox is a fun exploration of the fertility festivals that have always played a role in the celebration of spring. All three stories are unique and should appeal to lovers of the paranormal... Equinox gives the reader a nice mixture of subgenres of romantica, historical to time travel to futuristic. I look forward to future anthologies of this nature." - *Nicole La Folle, Timeless Tales*

Discover for yourself why readers can't get enough of the multiple award-winning publisher Ellora's Cave. Whether you prefer e-books or paperbacks, be sure to visit EC on the web at www.ellorascave.com for an erotic reading experience that will leave you breathless.

www.ellorascave.com

EQUINOX
An Ellora's Cave publication, 2003

Ellora's Cave Publishing, Inc.
PO Box 787
Hudson, OH 44236-0787

ISBN # 184360745X

ISBN MS Reader (LIT) ISBN # 1-84360-444-2
Other available formats (no ISBNs are assigned):
Adobe (PDF), Rocketbook (RB), Mobipocket (PRC) & HTML

EQUINOX edited by Allie McKnight, Martha Punches, and Ann Richardson.
Cover art by Bryan Keeler.

EQUINOX

Walpurgis Night

by Katherine Kingston

Night of Fire

by Vonna Harper

Handle with Care

by Annie Windsor

WALPURGIS NIGHT

Katherine Kingston

Chapter One

Flames roared up toward the dark sky as the townspeople tossed bits of wood onto the burning heap. Lit by its radiance, the facades of buildings became collages of bright splashes riven by shafts of deep shadow. The town itself melded into a patchwork of bright and dark, the contrasts starker and more mysterious when lit by the blaze rather than daylight. People gathered around the fire, passing wineskins and pastries. Musicians played a lively tune and a few hearty souls danced. The bonfire celebrated the equinox, the change of seasons when light overtook darkness for possession of the day.

Fianna huddled in the darkest shadow she could find, wishing she could disappear completely. Not far from where she stood, her friends and acquaintances ate, drank, laughed, danced, flirted, kissed, whispered to each other, and occasionally went off in pairs, giggling and stroking each other. Part of her envied them their simple happiness.

Of a sudden, some of the merriment died away and the crowd quieted as they looked down the road. Fianna leaned out to see what caused their unease, and then stared in surprise herself. Three men approached the town square. They were tall, young, fair, clad in leather and linen, and wearing swords at their sides. Norsemen.

As they drew close enough for the fire to illuminate their faces, she recognized the man in the center as Henrik, the son of Hjallmar, the leader of the band that had settled not far from the town. Though everyone had flown into a panic at their arrival, they had settled again quickly when the group made no demands on the town or the people save that they'd claimed a portion of land for grazing their animals and planting their crops.

The town still kept an uneasy eye on the Norse settlement, but so far the occasional relations between the two had been peaceful. A few Norse stragglers had visited before, and some remained, becoming part of the community, but this was the first time a group had arrived together and appeared ready to stay.

Like everyone else gathered there, Fianna wondered what drew the newcomers to the celebration. Though the Norsemen rarely showed much emotion, their current demeanor didn't suggest they were looking for either battle or business. Perhaps simple curiosity had brought them.

Despite their stern expressions, they were a handsome group of young men. All were strong, well muscled, and carried themselves with confidence and pride. Henrik walked in the middle, the obvious leader of the trio. He was taller than the others, and his hair glowed like molten gold where the firelight played on it.

In her fascination with the visitors, Fianna took a step away from the shadows where she'd been hiding, and thus betrayed herself to the view of another group of young men who'd been watching and searching for her.

Her heart contracted and fell in on itself when she heard Artur yell, "There she is. The witch. This night she'll have to take one of us."

She turned to see Jerrod, the miller's son, Artur, apprentice blacksmith, and Keovan, a merchant, running toward her. She looked around for room to run, but she knew it was futile.

They surrounded her. She fingered the hilt of her dagger, which hung in a leather sheath from her girdle, but in truth she dared not use it. Though her mother had promised it would help protect her, it couldn't assist her in this. Those irritating young men had the right of it, that on this night one of them could claim her services. Perhaps all of them could claim her.

The firelight flickered on their leering faces, delineating Artur's profile, cruelly outlining his receding chin, and glinting off Keovan's perpetually runny nose.

"Who will it be?" Jerrod added. "Tonight you must choose one of us."

It was so, and that was just the reason she'd tried to remain out of sight. She would have hidden in Marla's home had she not suspected they would search the place for her. In fact, they were so intent on having her, they'd have searched every building in town and the surrounding hills. She'd gambled that by staying near the center of activity, but concealed in shadows, she might remain hidden. One small lapse of attention had overset the plan.

"Choose, witch," they taunted her. "Or perhaps you prefer to be truly branded witch and face the fire."

She glanced at the bonfire and tried to keep the terror from showing too clearly on her face. Surely there was some other way. Fianna let her gaze roam around the square, watching the gathered crowds. Evidently they'd decided the Norsemen posed no threat. Most had resumed their revelry, laughing, dancing, and flirting.

She spotted the Norsemen not far away. Someone had passed them a wineskin, and one of the three was drinking from it. A wild idea formed in her head.

"Choose me and I'll make you roar and scream with delight," Jerrod promised, drawing her attention back to her tormentors.

"I have the equipment of a bull and I'll fill you properly," Artur boasted.

Keovan couldn't match his companion's physical assets and attempted a different form of persuasion. "I've a gold chain brought from the east that can be yours, do you go with me this night," he offered.

Fianna glanced at each one and then at the others in the square. The leader of the Norsemen glanced her way and met her eyes briefly, but he clearly decided their doings were none of his concern.

"I've made my choice," Fianna announced to the group. All three stared at her. She glanced at each in turn, then shifted her gaze away from them.

"Him," she said, pointing to the leader of the Norsemen.

While Artur, Jerrod, and Keovan still stared blankly at her, she pushed past them and walked toward the visitors.

The Norsemen's eyebrows all rose in surprise as she approached them. Fianna ignored all but the man in the middle, keeping her gaze locked with his as she neared. "You are my choice," she said to him, making the words loud enough to be heard by the small group of men following her as well as those in front.

"You're Henrik," she said to him. "Nay?"

"Aye, lady," he acknowledged. "And you are?"

"Fianna."

"Ah. And for what purpose do you choose me?"

This close to him, she had to look up to see his face. His expression remained so shuttered she read nothing in it, nor did his tone reveal any emotion save mild curiosity.

"To be my...companion for the night." She wasn't sure what word to use that he would understand. She wasn't sure she wanted to use any word at all. As she faced this stern, intimidatingly large, strong man, Fianna asked herself whether this had been a good idea. It got her out of the reach of Jerrod and his fellows, but it might leave her in an even more dangerous situation.

"Your companion?" Henrik scanned the square, taking in the revelers, his gaze coming to rest on one couple all but undressing each other in the street. The woman's leg was over the man's bent knee, and one of his hands rested high on her thigh while the other pushed aside her bodice so he could reach her breast. The woman, meanwhile, had both hands pressed against his chest under his shirt.

While he stared, Fianna wondered what she'd do if he turned her down. She supposed she would have to choose one of the group that still stood behind her, waiting to see how this would play out.

"Why do you ask this of me?" Suspicion almost overwhelmed the curiosity in his tone.

"You are a man," she answered. "I am a woman. And on this night it is said that all must pay homage to the spirits that control the fertility of the land." She wasn't sure how much he understood of her language.

When he commented, "And you think I'm the best of the choices you have," she decided it wouldn't be wise to underestimate him.

He looked at the group of ardent suitors standing behind her, and his face softened a fraction out of its hard set. "You don't know what you risk with me."

She puzzled at that. "Nay. But I know what I risk with others."

His eyebrows flicked upward. He leaned forward to whisper to her. "You cannot know how I prefer to enjoy a woman."

"Nay, that I do not," she admitted. "What should I know?"

His expression grew darker. "I do not prefer it quick. Or gentle. I like women who will give everything to me, and accept all I want to do to them. Think you, you can do this? Or are you wishing to change your choice?"

"Do your women survive their time with you?"

He laughed suddenly. "Usually. In truth, none have died of the things I do with them, though I've seen a few swoon. Most seem quite pleased and satisfied with our time together. Not all can satisfy me, however."

She looked at him. He thought he was frightening her. And she should be heeding his warning. But along with the fear was something else. Her stomach did odd little flip-flops, while a frisson of excitement settled hard and heavy in her loins. "I will

Katherine Kingston

do my best, though I can make no promises until I know more of what you want."

"'Tis just for this night?"

"This one night only," she assured him.

He stared hard into her eyes, as though trying to read her will. "You interest me, Fianna. I will accept your offer."

Fianna let out a long sigh, though she wondered if relief was truly the proper reaction. She just knew that if she had to give herself to one man, this was the one who seemed most appealing. Oddly, his words about his possibly unusual preferences made the prospect of time with him more appealing rather than less.

He said a few words in his own language to his companions. One of those two laughed hard and struck him on the back. The other looked suspicious. A brief argument between that one and Henrik ended with the man pronouncing something she couldn't understand. She could read the tone, however, and he'd clearly said something on the order of, "On your own head be it."

Henrik's companions moved away to leave him alone with her. The man glared at Jerrod, Artur, and Keovan until they, also, got the message and retreated. Then he bent his stare on her again.

Fianna studied his face, trying to decide how worried she should be. His features were strong, from the straight, gold eyebrows to the firm, jutting chin outlined by a neatly clipped golden beard. In the firelight she couldn't tell the color of his eyes, only that they were light. A bit of satisfaction had leeched into his otherwise set expression.

"So, lady," he said, "What do we now?"

"We go some place private."

"Know you such a place nearby?"

She nodded. "My quarters. I share a home with Marla, the midwife, but I have my own room."

14

"Let us go then." He took a torch from one of the many stands holding them and nodded for her to direct him.

The house was quiet and dark. Marla was probably with Master Cooper at his place. They'd been lovers for years, though Marla refused to marry him, claiming she was content with her living arrangements as they were.

Fianna lit a lamp and carried it back to her private room. Henrik put the torch into a stand, then glanced around the room. She wondered what he thought of her very spare quarters, but she didn't ask and he volunteered no opinion. He paid little attention to it in any case. His gaze returned to her and stayed there. She blushed when he looked slowly down her body. She hoped her shape pleased him. Most men seemed to consider her attractive, but the Norsemen might have different notions of beauty.

Fianna had no idea what to do next, what he might expect of her, so she waited for him to make the first move. Henrik unbuckled his belt and slid the sheath holding his sword off it, laid both aside, and then removed his leather vest and shirt.

She let out a gasp of pure wonder as she stared at the most beautiful masculine chest she'd ever seen. Broad shoulders narrowed gradually down to a slim waist and hard, flat belly. A thin mat of gold hair lay over the strong muscles below his throat, with the dark buds of nipples protruding from it. The lovely flesh almost demanded she touch it, but something in his expression prevented her from reaching out.

"Have you done this before?" he asked.

"Aye. Once or twice."

"No more than that?" He sounded incredulous.

"No more."

"Did you take pleasure from it?"

She drew a deep breath and let it out slowly. She hated to be found wanting, but neither did she wish to lie to him. "Nay, in truth, I found little, though I'm told it should be pleasurable."

"So it should," he agreed. "And you will get pleasure from it with me. But you must first agree that I am your master in this and you will do all I say without hesitation or question." He stopped and drew a breath. "I warned you my needs and desires were different. This I ask of you, that you agree I am your lord for this night and you must obey all orders or face my punishment for the failure." His harsh expression softened. "I know it is not easy for one of your spirit to submit yourself to another's will. But I believe I can show you the way to greater pleasure than you've ever known."

The demand left her breathless and confused, while his promise set off that funny feeling in her stomach.

"Fianna?" he prompted. "Do you agree?"

"If I don't?"

"I'll put my clothes back on and go. But I'll stay out of sight so those men will believe I'm with you still."

She was stunned by that bit of proposed gallantry. But she hadn't been clear about her question and tried to clarify. "Nay. I mean if I agree and then I don't follow orders? How would you punish me?" she asked.

"Ah." A gleam lit his eyes. "What do you suppose I should do?"

The heat rose in her cheeks, so she must be blushing. A vivid image had come into her mind, and she wasn't sure whether it fascinated or terrified her. It depended on how much she trusted him. But—he had asked.

"I know not," she said, hoping she wasn't making a terrible mistake. "What were you thinking?"

He stared hard at her as though he tried to read her mind through her eyes. "Perhaps I'll spank your bottom until it glows pink. Or possibly I'll use my belt, doubled over. Which frightens you more?"

She sucked in a sharp breath, but she wasn't sure whether the twisting feeling in her stomach was dismay or excitement. "The belt," she whispered.

He nodded. "Do you agree, then?"

"But you didn't—"

"And I will not. You know enough to make your decision."

How could she be so thrilled and so terrified at the same time? But when she looked at him, stared into his eyes, she knew he wouldn't hurt her. And she knew she wanted this more than she'd ever wanted anything with a man before. Even so, she had a hard time making herself say it. "Aye," she finally managed to choke out.

For the first time a real smile washed across his face. It transformed his features, turning him into a breathtakingly handsome man. Her heart hammered in her chest.

"Good," he said. "Very good. Take off your dress. Slowly."

Fianna drew a deep breath to calm herself before she pulled the ribbons that fastened her dress at the neck. She slipped it down off her shoulders and let it fall to the floor. She wore nothing beneath it.

His breath caught in his throat. "You're beautiful. Come to me."

She walked toward him, all too aware of how her breasts bounced as she moved. Her woman's parts between her legs felt swollen and heavy.

When she was close enough, he reached out with both hands, which he put on either side of her face, running the palms across her cheeks until he could bury his fingers in her hair. His hands were strong and callused, but their clasp was careful, his strength moderated to avoid hurting her.

Henrik leaned over and fitted his mouth over hers. Shocking tingles sparked from the place where his lips touched hers. She'd never guessed it could feel like that. Then he ran his tongue over her lips and nudged them apart. When he invaded her mouth, it sent a jolt through her entire body that she felt right down to her toes. She moaned deep in her throat. Heat began to burn inside and spread through her.

He put a hand behind her head to steady her as he began to kiss his way across her cheek to her ear. His tongue caressed the tender skin around the ear and he blew gently into it. After retracing the path and kissing his way to the other ear and back, he began to move down along her jaw to her throat.

Her breath moved in and out on hard pants as the fire he roused in her grew.

His hands shifted their grip, sliding down from her head to rest on either side of her chest. His thumbs slid inward until they brushed the undersides of her breasts. She was jolted again by shards of sensation tearing through her from the contact. Nothing had ever made her feel this before, certainly not her few encounters with males of the town. His fingers left trails of heated skin wherever he touched.

Henrik released her for a moment while he moved back to sit on the one chair in the room, a bare, straight-backed thing that groaned and creaked when he moved. He settled himself as comfortably as he could get on it, then pulled her to him, lifted her onto his lap, straddling his legs, and slid her forward. In that position her legs were separated and her quim pressed hard against the fabric that barely contained his straining cock. Fianna felt it throbbing against her. He closed his eyes for a moment, and his breath came in loud, stretched pants until he adjusted to the contact.

It was almost obscenely delicious to be so intimately close to him. Feeling greatly daring, she reached up and brushed a hand against his face, running it down his cheek and along the neat, golden beard. With a finger, she traced the outline of his lips. He opened his mouth and sucked the tip of her finger inside. A thrill chased its way up and down her spine as the heat flowed through the finger and flooded her body.

His hands moved around her and cupped her breasts. Henrik squeezed them gently, pushed them together and up, testing their weight and firmness.

When he brushed fingers across her nipples, the sensation hit her like a lightning bolt. Tiny knife-thrusts of pure pleasure lanced her repeatedly. For long moments he did naught but play with those sensitive tips, stroking and flicking them until she was near to sobbing with the pleasure. She'd had no idea her body had such capacity for delight.

Now the heat was gathering in her loins and a pressure started to mount. She knew not what it might be leading to, but there was a need there, a need only he could answer.

Fianna looped her arms around his neck to hold herself upright. She'd thought his touches brought ecstasy, but then he dipped his head and ran his tongue over the tip of one breast. A small shriek tore from her. It felt as though a flaming brand had been set to her, and she was blazing, burning up with the unbearable heat of it. Henrik looked up at her with lazy, gleaming eyes, smiling in satisfaction as she moaned and writhed.

He drew the entire nipple into his mouth, tongue circling and flicking at it while his lips sucked. She bounced up and down and wriggled against him, the pleasure so great she couldn't keep still. He repeated the action with the other breast, then moved back and forth between them. Fianna heard herself sobbing out loud.

Henrik's teeth scraped over the nipple in his mouth, and then he bit down on it, lightly at first, but gradually increasing the pressure until pain mingled with the pleasure. But it was a deliciously exciting sensation that mixed the various aches so thoroughly she couldn't tell where the pleasure ended and the pain began, and it hardly mattered anyway. She groaned loudly and buried her hands in his soft, silky hair, holding onto hanks of it, pulling on them when he transferred his attention to the other breast, biting down on that nipple until he brought her to the brink of screaming with an agonizing excitement and ecstasy. She'd never have guessed pain could feel so sweet.

He released the nipple from the clutch of his teeth and soothed it with the tip of his tongue. Tears burned her eyes from the amazing combination of sensations. He stopped, watching her, and flicked away a drop of moisture that slid down her cheek. He bent forward and kissed her mouth hungrily. She pressed her chest against his, loving the way the hairs rasped against her sensitized nipples. He felt so wonderfully hard and solid, but he held her so carefully and used just as much of his strength as needed.

She was shocked and felt bereft when he suddenly lifted her off his lap again and set her on her feet. Her legs felt so shaky she wondered they held her up at all.

"Take off my boots," he ordered.

After a moment of surprise, she knelt in front of him, removed his fur-lined boots, and stroked his feet. He permitted it for a moment, then stood up.

"Now remove my leggings," he said. When she reached for the laces, he put a hand on her arm to stop her. "Without using your hands."

Fianna looked up at him, taking in the gleam in his light eyes. So…a challenge. She let her eyes slide down his long body to his waist, then lower. The laces on either hip and at his waist were key. Fortunately all were tied in bows at the top rather than knotted. If they were loosened, the leggings would slide down and off. She went to her knees again at his left side and grabbed the end of one lace in her teeth. A gentle tug undid the bow. She used her mouth again to loosen the top of the crosshatched lacing. She slid around to his other side and repeated the process. Which left just the laces in the center.

She knew what to do. But her mouth would be so close to him, an intimacy she could barely imagine with a man she barely knew. Still, this was also the most exciting thing that had ever happened to her. She leaned forward and nuzzled her face into his belly until she could take the lace between her teeth. A deep breath of the leather of his leggings and his male scent made her pulse race again.

A quick tug on the lace released the bow. The leggings began to slide down his body, but the leather caught on the tip of his erect cock. Fianna took another deep breath and leaned forward again. This time she grasped the leather itself between her teeth and lifted it off the jutting flesh, then let it drop to the floor.

She stared at him. It might be rude, it might not be wise, but she couldn't help it. Henrik was, simply, the most extraordinary man she'd ever seen. His cock, longer than her hand, stood out from his body, thick and straight. The soft sacs of his balls hung between legs that were long, strongly muscled and nicely shaped.

"Very good," he said, complimenting her efforts to undress him. "Now, kiss my cock."

Her breath caught in her throat and a wave of dizziness passed quickly. She put a hand on the floor to steady herself. She couldn't conceive of touching him that way. The idea paralyzed her.

"Fianna, I said to kiss my cock." His words had a hard, dangerous edge.

She heard it but couldn't make herself move.

"Fianna," he repeated.

"I cannot," she said. "I've never…I've never even touched a man there."

"Are you refusing my order?" he asked.

"I don't want to refuse, but I…"

He bent down, took her arm, and drew her to her feet. "I warned you what would happen if you disobeyed an order, did I not?"

Chapter Two

She stared into his eyes, now the color of cold steel. She drew a harsh breath. "Aye."

"This can stop now, if you wish," he said.

Her heart clenched and a lump formed in her throat that made it difficult to speak. "Nay, I don't wish to stop."

She was sure the look on his face was relief, but he said, "Then you need to be persuaded to do as I tell you?"

"Perhaps," she admitted.

"Are you sure? You know what I'll do."

He asked more than one question with those words, and Fianna thought about all of them before she answered. "Aye."

He nodded. "Stand still," he said, stepping back away from her. "Do not move."

She didn't move, but she watched him pick up the leather belt he'd removed earlier. She watched him double it over and hold one end. Then he was behind her and she couldn't see it anymore.

She heard the swish of air as it swung and the crack when the leather smacked against the flesh of her bottom, printing a streak of pain across it. The shock of it as much as the sting made her cry out. He hadn't really struck very hard, she realized, but the leather was heavy and it did burn.

She was more prepared for the next smack and was able to swallow her outcry. He spanked her five or six more times, until her bottom stung fiercely and she could no longer stifle a moan.

But, like the sensation when he'd bitten her nipples, the sting washed through her system and transmuted into something just the opposite of pain. The burn went straight to her womb and settled hot and heavy between her legs. It was a deliciously agonizing feeling.

"Are you ready to obey me?" he asked.

"I...I think not," she said. She looked at his face. His expression was neither angry nor unhappy, but watchful, intent, and even a bit joyful. She had a sudden realization. This was a kind of a game. Serious in its way, but not serious in the manner of things that really mattered — life and death, illness and injury. She could stop it whenever she wished. He wouldn't hurt her anymore than she wanted to be hurt. But he hoped she could meet his enjoyment of this different way of giving and taking love and was pleased by her responses so far. She'd joined him in a strange and different sort of mating. She admitted to herself that so far she was enjoying it just as much as he was. "Nay, not yet," she reaffirmed.

The leather spanked down a bit harder. The pain was bright, fierce, almost overwhelming, and she moaned softly. As it faded, though, it became a deeper burn that fed the pressure of need within her. Five more whacks each stoked the fire within and without, until she was awash in sensation. The next one struck low down, at the crease between bottom and thighs, and it stung far worse than any of the others. She squealed and reached back to massage the blazing flesh.

"No more," she said. "Please, no more. I'll do whatever you ask."

"Well enough, then." He put the belt back with the sword sheath before he came back and stood in front of her. "On your knees, now, and kiss my cock."

She dropped to her knees, leaned forward, bracing herself by holding onto his hips, and pressed her lips to the hard shaft about midway along its length. He tasted a little salty and very male. After moving her mouth a bit over him, she hesitated, unsure what to do next.

"Put your tongue on it," he directed. When she'd done so, he added, "Lick up and down, from the base to the tip and back."

It felt strange and exhilarating to touch him so intimately, to hear his breath come faster and harder, to feel him getting tenser and harder. His cock was a thing of wonder to her. The skin was soft and smooth, though it felt very thin, over the hard length of it. The bulbous tip was even smoother, with skin as soft as a baby's. He groaned as her tongue reached the small opening in the tip and explored.

She worked back down. When she reached the base, she started up again. He caught a sharp breath in his throat and put a hand on her head to stop her.

"No more for now," he said. "Your tongue is so skillful, you'll have me exploding beforetimes."

Fianna was absurdly pleased by the compliment. Henrik drew her to her feet, wrapped his arms around her to pull her close against him and kissed her on the mouth. He prized open her lips and explored the inside with his tongue. She met him and tangled her own tongue with his, stroking until she was burning up with the heat pouring through her.

Mouths still meshed together, he urged her backward until they reached the feather-stuffed mat that was her bed. He released her and then eased her down until she lay on the bed looking up at him. He knelt on the floor beside her.

His hands played with her breasts, his fingers stroking, tweaking, rolling, pinching her nipples until she was moaning and the pressure of need built in her loins to throbbing intensity.

One of his hands slipped off her breast and slid downwards, across her stomach and abdomen to her legs. He rubbed up and down her thighs. His fingers slid around to the inside. She sobbed and slid her legs apart, not sure exactly what she wanted from him, but confident that he would know.

A smile slid across his stern face at that sign of trust. His hands stilled for a moment, and he moved back to where he could kiss her again. He placed a series of tender kisses on her temple, cheek, and lips before he shifted again and gently nudged her legs even farther apart.

Henrik's first touch on the sensitive nether lips of her woman's parts made her jump and squeal. The tingles running from his touch washed her in a pleasure beyond any imagining. He continued to stroke gently back and forth, up and down, and she felt herself swelling, opening, almost weeping for his touch. He pushed a little deeper, a little harder. His fingers rubbed across a spot at the center of her quim and her back arched with the intensity of the feeling it brought. From then on, he concentrated his attention on that spot. His stroking built the pressure in her to burning, white-hot heat. It grew and grew until she knew she couldn't contain it much longer.

Then he gave the spot a harder tweak, a firmer brush, and all at once that contained need burst in a shattering explosion of pleasure. Spasms that pulled her body tight and then released it jolted through her. Every nerve was suffused with delight while her body bounced in a rhythm of release that took her to far reaches of experience. Like waves washing onto shore, the spasms rolled and rippled through her body, built, and broke, time and again. He continued to stroke her lightly, provoking more outbursts, while she jumped and thrashed. There could be nothing more exalting under heaven.

It was amazing. It was rapturous, delightful, astonishing, and yet, it was incomplete. Something more was needed to finish it properly. This time she had a sense of exactly what was wanted.

"Come into me," Fianna begged him as the spasms began to abate. "I need you inside to finish it off."

"Not so quickly. It needs a bit more attention from you to ready it for that work," he demanded, looking down at his cock in a way that left no doubt what he meant.

It looked perfectly ready, jutting out, long and thick, from his body. But he moved closer and she wrapped her hand around it, marveling at the contrast between the hardness of the rod and the softness of the skin over it. She let her fingers travel up and down, caressing it until he was moaning and gasping. With her other hand she cupped the balls beneath, kneading them gently. They filled her palm.

She found a sensitive ridge just below the tip by noting the way his eyes tightened and fists clenched when she ran her finger along it. Henrik could tolerate only a few minutes of her stroking before he straightened and moved over her. He positioned himself between her legs and looked to be sure she was ready for him.

At her nod, he pushed forward, past the entrance. As she'd had so few other encounters, her passage was still tight, unused to this exercise. He was also larger than either of the other two men she'd lain with. It stung for a minute or so, but he allowed her time to adjust.

Henrik began to move in and out, sliding in deeper, waiting a moment, then pulling out, only to push in even farther. The pressure inside roused again, causing her to tighten around him. She wound her arms around his shoulders and dug her fingers into his back. He began to move faster, kissing her as he plunged into her.

He felt so good, his skin smooth where her fingers stroked, his hair like finest silk, his body hard yet yielding. His kisses set her every nerve aflame. His chest hair tickled her nipples when he bent to match his mouth to hers.

The need mounted as he moved within. He filled her so completely, so thrillingly. Fianna jumped and her inner muscles tightened a little more each time he pushed in. His breath came harder and louder. The rhythm grew faster, frantic, desperate. Finally she felt it go again, felt the world spin away from her as her body released the built-up tension in spasms of ecstasy. Dimly she heard him make an inchoate, roaring sound and his tense body shuddered with the force of his coming.

It was delightful beyond telling, beyond anything she might have imagined. Spasms of pure pleasure rolled through her body, convulsing her. She rolled with them, drifting on the sea of joy, drowning in the thrill of it, until it finally began to fade, letting her slide gently back into herself.

For a few minutes the only sounds were their moans and sighs. They lay together, arms wrapped around each other, drifting on the aftermath of the most intense pleasure Fianna had ever felt.

She wanted to remain just like that forever, joined with him in that most elemental way. But eventually Henrik rolled off her, stretching out close beside her on the narrow mat. He put one arm under her neck and shifted until his side lay touching hers from chest to feet. She turned so she angled toward him and could see his face.

"That was amazing," she told him reaching out with a finger to brush his lips. "I had no idea it could be that way."

His smile was beautiful. "It has never been like that for me before, either," he said. "I've had good times before. But not like this. No one has understood so well or wanted it the way you did. No one. Ever." He ran a hand through her dark, wavy hair and wound a strand around his finger. "Fianna...Why do they call you 'witch'?"

She wasn't sure she wanted to tell him. She knew not what the Norse believed, and thus how he might react to it. But she had never been good at dissembling and didn't want to do it with this man. If he was appalled or discouraged, it were better she knew it now, before anything more developed between them.

"I am one, in a way," she admitted. "My mother was half-fae and I inherited some of her blood, though I am much more human. I work with Marla, who is a healer as well as a midwife, and I know as much as she does now about the body and about herbs and potions. But sometimes... I know other things. Things not discovered in any ordinary way. On occasion I realize— through the use of some other sense—what is ailing a body and how it might be fixed. Not always. Not even most of the time, but often enough. The people here have seen it often enough, but understand it not, so they label me 'witch'."

He didn't recoil or let go the lock of hair he toyed with. "You use this gift you have for the benefit of those here in town."

"Aye. But anything beyond their understanding frightens people. And where there is power, it can be used to harm as well as heal."

His fingers stilled for a moment and his eyes narrowed. "Of course. But those young men chase you and dare your wrath."

"Aye, but they're young. And they know I want to continue to live in peace here, so I wouldn't dare harm them."

"What will you do about them? They'll not give up their pursuit of you. That you chose me for tonight might be yet more incentive for them."

She sighed. "I suppose eventually I'll have to choose one of them to wed. But I'll not concern myself with that tonight. Tonight is for us."

The wonderful smile lit his face again. "Then let us not waste it."

He kissed her, and stroked her, petted, licked, and sucked her into another explosive climax before he entered and spilled his seed into her yet again.

* * * * *

Lying together afterward, she dared to ask him, "Are your people settling here permanently or just staying for a while?"

"Our town grows and becomes more solid by the day. My father will stay here with these people. The land is fertile and supports rich herds. We've no quarrel with our neighbors and seek peace among us."

"Your father will stay...but you will not?"

He hesitated for a moment. "My brother has been off...adventuring. He's due to return any day. When he comes back, he can remain with my father while I go off to seek my fortune. I've been waiting my chance for a long while."

She dared not let him know how that news crushed her heart. She had no right to feel it so. One night was all she'd asked, and he was giving her much more than she could have expected. They were all but strangers and so it would remain. Why, then, did the news he'd be gone soon leave her feeling so bereft? She'd likely not see him again after this night ended, but she would have a memory she'd treasure always.

Perhaps he had some of the same feelings. Their third and last coupling of the evening had an almost frantic energy about it, as though he needed all the touching and loving they could manage between them to store for future consideration. When it was over, he held her again, and this time they fell asleep in each other's arms.

The first light of dawn woke them. They didn't speak as they dressed, but before he left, he pulled her into his arms and kissed her thoroughly. Then he drew back and stared at her as though memorizing her face. She would never forget his.

"I'll carry the memory of this night with me as I sail the seas and walk across new lands," he promised her. "I'll warm myself with it on cold nights and fill long hours alone with dreams of you."

"I won't forget either," she agreed. "And if you have time before you go, come to me again."

He didn't answer that. He would make no promises he couldn't keep.

Chapter Three

Fianna wasn't surprised when he didn't come to her again. For a week after their night together she went around in a daze of hope and longing. She'd never wanted anything so badly as she wanted another night, many more nights, with him. She even thought about going to him. But good sense prevailed. If he'd wanted more of her, he would have come. He knew she was willing.

After two weeks, the hope faded, though the longing didn't. She didn't allow herself to mourn or grieve. With the arrival of early spring, there was much to do. The small herb garden behind Marla's house needed to be turned over and enriched to ready it for planting. The perennial bed needed weeds removed before they choked the emerging young plants. Cool weather herbs had to be gathered from the woods and prepared. Work kept the painful thoughts at bay.

For a while the work—and the possibility that the Norseman would return—kept her importunate would-be suitors at bay. Not for long, though. They soon realized the Norseman was no longer about, that he had returned to his own people and didn't watch over her, so Fianna had to resume being careful to avoid them. The effort was doomed to eventual failure, but she had avoided thinking too hard about it, so she wasn't prepared when they did catch up with her.

She was returning from delivering a poultice to an elderly woman who suffered from sores that refused to heal when she spotted the three of them coming out of a building. She ducked behind the nearest wall when she saw them, but she wasn't quick enough to avoid their notice.

She turned to run when she heard one of them shout, "Look who's out wandering around by herself! The witch must be looking for something!" The young man's tone suggested he knew what she sought and he was just the man to provide it.

Rushing past a donkey-cart and woman leading a cow, Fianna turned into a narrow alley between the wooden side of the tavern and the public stable. They saw and followed. Fianna quickly realized her mistake in leaving the more open and populated part of town.

Behind the tavern, rolling pastureland spread to the hills in the northwest. The road going that way wasn't far and travelers passed along it. No help for her, though. A scream wouldn't be heard at such a distance, even if there were any chance someone might investigate it.

Her pursuers were gaining on her. Her breath came in ragged pants and a stitch in her side made running agony. Two of the three young men following her had the advantage of longer legs and more time spent in physical activity. She had no chance of outrunning them to any place she might expect to get help. There were few of those in any case.

Minutes later, before she could manage to wend her way back into the main part of town, they caught up with her. An arm snaked around her from behind, holding her fast against a hard body. For a while she just hung in his hold, too winded even to struggle. Then her captor twisted her around to face him.

Jerrod, the miller's son, leered at her with narrowed dark eyes. "Where's your Norse lover now, witch?"

His companion, Artur, gibed at her, "He didn't stay around for more of you, did he? What say you to us now, witch? No Norseman to dally with now. He was a pretty toy to play with for a while, but you need someone to be your man. As you've refused all of us to now, 'tis obvious you've no comprehension of what we offer. It seems you need a sample from us, as you were so willing to accept it from him. We'll teach you what you're missing, whether you will it or no. You'll take all of us."

"I'll take none of you willingly," she answered, still struggling to catch her breath. "And I promise you will all regret it do you force me." She tried to work her hand down to pull the dagger her mother had given her from its sheath.

"Brave words," Artur said. "Yet I wager we shall have you begging us for more before we finish." He saw her fingers creeping toward the leather sheath at her side, and forestalled her effort. He got to the dagger before she did and drew it from its case. He studied it, while the third man huffed up beside them and latched onto one of her arms. Even so, she continued to try to wriggle away from the men's hold.

Fear tightened her throat and sent waves of icy coldness down her body. Her stomach clenched as nausea roiled through it. She would not show it. "You'd best plan to kill me when you're done, and even then I'll haunt your dreams and make your nights a torment," she promised them.

For a moment the men paused, but they couldn't back off now without losing face in front of the others. A month ago, they wouldn't have dared do this, but her choice of the Norseman had rubbed them on the raw and pushed them into proving something, though whether to her or themselves, she couldn't guess.

Fianna found herself abruptly tossed to the ground and stretched out, with one man holding her arms above her head and another holding her ankles. Jerrod released one leg long enough to flip her skirts up, revealing her knees and thighs.

"Nay. Wait," Artur warned. He knelt over her with the dagger poised. The slanting rays of the late afternoon sun glinted off the silver blade and set the red jewel in the hilt burning. For a moment she thought he meant to cut her with it, but then he inserted the blade under the top of her dress and began to slice down through the material.

The fabric parted and fell away from her. She shivered in the chill fall air as her breasts and then her belly were left naked to the kiss of the wind and the lecherous, leering eyes of her captors.

Chapter Four

She closed her eyes, praying to whatever deities might be listening that something would happen to spare her this. Even so, when rescue did come, she barely believed it.

She felt the thunder of hoof beats through the ground before she saw or heard anything else. Her captors were so fascinated by her naked body, they failed to notice even when the sound of approaching horses became audible. By the time they looked up and prepared to fight, it was too late.

The leader of the group of horsemen surveyed the scene quickly and gave them all a disdainful glare. He didn't even bother to draw the sword strapped to his side. Fianna pulled the remains of her clothes back over her body as soon as the men released her hands, but she still colored when Henrik stared at her.

"I regret that I interrupt your recreation," he said to her tormentors. "But I have need of the lady's services."

Fianna couldn't help staring at him. In sunlight, the man's handsome face, straight carriage, and a natural air of command made him even more striking. His expression, though, was tight and hard, promising no kindness, very different from the way he'd looked the last time she'd seen him. What had happened to rouse that fierce glare? A frisson of unease crawled up her spine, and she shook despite her efforts to remain still.

The three men who'd been her late captors stirred.

"She's no lady," Jerrod said. "She's a witch."

"We have need of her services as well," Artur protested at the same time. "And were about to avail ourselves of them. You've had your time with her. Give us an hour and then come back and get her."

Henrik's expression showed no change. "I know what she is. I cannot wait for you to finish this business." He turned to her. "I need you to come with me," the man stated.

"Why?" Fianna asked. Was it possible that he did want her—enough to take her this way? The Norse raiders were notorious for their sexual appetites and for taking what they wanted whenever they wanted. Still, Hjallmar and his son, Henrik, had been restrained and had even intervened in a case where a woman had been forcibly taken from her family by one of his men. And he would surely know that even now he had only to ask to get her to come to him.

Artur protested, "The lady doesn't want to go with you."

He had read her hesitancy correctly, but he misjudged the strength of her hatred for them and what they'd tried to do.

Henrik threw Artur another disdainful look and then ignored him, focusing his attention on Fianna. He watched her struggle to hold her dress together for a minute, then reached up, removed his own cloak, and tossed it to her. Fianna wrapped it around herself, grateful for both the coverage and the warmth. She'd begun to shiver with reaction as much as the chill. The garment bore the remembered scent of the man.

"Come with me," Henrik repeated, and it wasn't an invitation.

Fianna shrugged, trying not to let the hope rouse. "Why do you want me?"

"We need a healer."

She wasn't disappointed. No reason she should have expected anything else. It was a struggle to keep her emotions in check and her face blank. She nodded. "Then it would be wise to let me collect some things before we go."

Henrik considered that for a moment. "So be it."

She nodded. Her late tormentors stood watching the interchange. Artur still held her dagger. He didn't protest or resist when she walked over to him, took it out of his hand, and replaced it in the sheath at her side.

Two of Henrik's men dismounted and came to her. She turned away and started to lead the way on foot, but one of them put a hand on her shoulder. "Ride," he said, firmly. "Come."

Sensing that they would brook no refusal, Fianna went with them to the group, looking for a riderless horse. She was shocked when the two men on foot suddenly took her and lifted her onto the back of Henrik's mount, without giving her any warning or time to prepare. They ignored her shriek of surprise.

Her companion turned his horse. Fianna gasped and put an arm around his waist to steady herself, but was able to relax a bit when the horse settled into an easy walk. She didn't move her arm, though. Her hand rested against his flat stomach, and there was something both soothing and exciting about the contact. Although his shoulders were broad and substantial, his waist was much leaner. Beneath the leather jerkin, she felt the play of hard muscle there. She didn't look back, but she felt the glares of her late captors following her as they left the area.

The party of five horsemen drew considerable attention riding through the small village. People stepped aside, stopped, stared, and pointed, muttering among themselves. Neither Henrik nor any of his party paid notice to it. Instead he led the group to her cottage.

Marla heard the clatter and came outside to peer at the arrivals. Her expression changed from alarm to puzzlement when she saw Fianna being assisted from the horse by one of the Norsemen. "What is happening?" she asked as Fianna approached. The woman's gaze swung back and forth between the grim-faced horsemen and her young friend.

"Come inside with me." Fianna took the older woman's arm. "I need to pack a bag. They need a healer."

"Ah. And did they ask you?"

"Nay, but I haven't been coerced, either. Indeed they rescued me in a sense." She told Marla about the men who'd nearly raped her.

The woman sighed. "I've spoken to Tom Miller about his son before, but he will not curb him. Those boys will not give up easily and will cause you more grief. Girl, you must find someone who can protect you or settle on one of them. That is the Jarl's son you shared horse with, no? The one who companioned you on the equinox night."

"Aye, but harbor not any romantic notions concerning him."

"He has no wife here, I'm told."

"He's a Norseman."

"And a strong man. Well-favored, also. You could do worse."

"I could not do it at all. Why should he have any interest in me but for a pleasant night's dalliance?"

"For the same reason those other young men do, Fianna. I know you have no vanity yourself, but your looks will draw men. Perhaps even that young Viking, do you exert yourself but a bit. You cannot go on as you've been doing. It might be better for you to find some other place to settle if you will not have one of the men here."

"Nay, I know," Fianna admitted, as she pulled off the ruined dress and slid a fresh one over her head. "They might well have killed me after using me this afternoon. I don't want to leave here, Marla. Where would I go? What would you do without me to help you? I am needed here." She tied the ribbons on the dress and set her girdle with the leather sheath back over it. Then she gathered a cloth bag and began to choose what she might need.

"I'll survive, dear," Marla said, handing her pouches of herbs to put into slots in the cloth bag Fianna was loading. "And so will most in this village, if you do leave."

A growing rumble of voices and tromp of feet swelled into a commotion outside. Fianna wondered if the Norsemen were having an argument with people from the town. That wasn't it, though, as she learned moments later, when three of the town elders, followed by assorted others, crowded into the main room of Marla's home.

Alfred, the most prosperous and influential merchant in town, stepped to the front of the group and stared at her. Fianna spied Keovan lurking behind several of the older men.

Alfred watched her for a moment longer. "The situation grows intolerable," he informed her. "Long have you been a disruptive influence with your arrogant refusal to choose any man in town to partner you. Too much like your mother, you are. You have come close to inciting some of the young men of this town to violence. Just today, I understand, there was trouble. You're disrupting too many lives, Fianna, Eislinn's daughter. This cannot continue."

The man paused and looked around the room as though waiting for someone to contradict him.

"I agree," Fianna answered. "Three men nearly forced me this afternoon. They need to be warned that such behavior is not tolerated."

Alfred looked surprised but recovered. "I'll be speaking to them about it," he promised. "But there is an argument that your refusal to take any of them continues to injure and wound them, inciting them to uncharacteristic acts. This cannot go on. You, Fianna, must do your part to stop it."

"And that part is?" she asked.

"You must marry. And soon. I'll not tell you whom to choose, but I declare this. You have until the eve of May Day, the night the Norsemen celebrate Walpurgis, to make your choice. Have you not agreed to wed with some man, you'll have to leave the village that night and not return, on pain of death."

For the first time his expression showed some distress. "I do not like having to pronounce this doom or force you to this," he said. "But the need for peace in the town compels me to it. You must decide whose suit to accept and cease tormenting the young men of this town."

Alfred looked at her. "Do you understand what you must do?"

She stared back at him. "Aye," she answered on a sighing breath. "Because they cannot control themselves as reasonable men are normally expected to do, I must sacrifice my freedom to live my life as I would. This is a strange justice."

He had the grace to look abashed. "It is perhaps not entirely fair to you," he admitted. He drew a breath and his face hardened. "It is nonetheless necessary. You are a woman, and so must be subject to a man. That is how it must be."

"I see," she agreed, wanting to argue further, yet recognizing the futility of it.

"Very well. We'll await your decision." The man nodded to her and to Marla, then turned to leave, signaling that the others should go with him.

Marla's face showed compassion when she turned to Fianna. "I'm sorry it has come to this for you. I know there are few good choices."

Fianna shrugged and resumed packing her bag of medicines. "I suppose I could agree to marry Jerrod or Artur or Keovan. Not a one of them thrills me, but I could reach accommodation with one, I suppose. I know not how to choose among them, though."

"There are other possibilities, no?"

Fianna shrugged. "Walter, the blacksmith's apprentice. He's slow, but strong enough."

"My cow's smarter than Walter. And he's too young anyway."

"I'm sure I could get a proposal from Densley, the old Cooper."

Marla shook her head. "Too old. He's doddering. He'd fall over dead from the shock did you make a move toward him."

Fianna sighed, closed up the bag and hung it on her shoulder. "I'll think on it." She glanced outside and saw the

Norsemen still waited there. "I know not what exactly the Norsemen want of me so I cannot say how long 'twill take."

"Take care of yourself," Marla said.

Fianna nodded to her and went back outside. Two Norsemen approached the door but stopped when they saw her emerge. Again they accompanied her to their leader's horse and helped her mount behind him.

She strained to get a better look at Henrik's face in the brief moments before she was raised up to the horse, searching for the warm, caring lover she'd known. His strong features were set in a stern expression that didn't soften as he watched her. His blue-gray eyes were cool, the arched brows drawn into a scowl. No hint of warmth or sympathy showed in that handsome face.

Fianna shivered when she settled into place behind him. The blond hair that hung to his shoulders rippled with gold highlights in the sunshine, clean and tangle-free. The scent of leather was mixed with a hint of soap and something potently masculine coming from him. That smell set her senses ablaze with memory. Yet something had changed since last she had seen him, to set the sternness so firmly in place on his features. Or perhaps he just dared not show any sympathy or kindness to her, lest it be taken for weakness by the men he commanded.

The trip didn't take long, thank goodness, since she was far from comfortable in that position. The Norsemen's settlement was only a short distance from her town. She'd never been there before, however, and looked around curiously as the party rode into the center of a grouping of ten or so houses. Two of them were very long buildings built of wood, raised off the ground on enormous poles, with straw-thatched roofs. The others were smaller versions of the longhouses, scattered in a rough half-circle around an open area where children played and people gathered to talk.

A small crowd of men and boys emerged from one of the longhouses to meet them. Several boys took charge of the horses as the men dismounted. The same two who'd helped her onto the horse assisted her off as well, and supported her when her legs wobbled a bit.

Henrik ignored her and turned immediately toward one of the smaller buildings. Her companions moved to follow, still holding her arms, so she went with them.

Enough light flowed in the window openings of the house to let her see clearly the interior. In one corner an older man sat, whittling on a piece of wood. He wore an intimidating frown. She'd seen Hjallmar only once before, but despite the greater years, the resemblance Henrik bore him was clear. A woman stirred a pot hung over the fire on that wall, releasing an aroma that reminded Fianna she hadn't eaten for a while. She doubted they would offer her food. At least not right away, and not if the mission they'd summoned her for could be accomplished quickly.

Henrik went over to the old man, bowed toward him, then folded himself onto a low stool and began talking. Fianna knew only a few words of the Norse tongue, and none of them helped her distinguish what they were saying. But more than once they turned to look at her. The old man argued and waved a hand in a way that showed he wasn't happy. Finally, though, they seemed to come to an agreement.

Henrik stood. As he turned toward her, he drew his sword from its scabbard and pointed it at her.

Fianna couldn't move. Shock held her firmly in place at first, then the realization that she could do little about the situation. If he wanted to kill her, there was little she could do to prevent it. Better she face him with courage than with sniveling pleas or cowering fear, though she had no idea why this was happening.

Man and sword advanced on her until the point was no more than an inch from her breast. She looked up and met his light eyes. Fierce emotion blazed there, but it wasn't anger or hatred.

She held his gaze as she asked, "Why?"

He ignored her question. "Turn around," he said.

Fianna debated refusing but couldn't see anything to gain by it. She turned. He was suddenly beside her, the sword pointed down. With his left hand, he took her arm and led her to a panel that walled off about a third of the building into a separate room. Henrik pushed aside a length of cloth draped over the opening into it, and waited for her to go in.

A rough mat covered in linen cloths covered nearly half the floor space. A man lay stretched out on it. Pain drew his face into harsh lines and printed dark shadows under his sunken eyes. His hair would have been the same bright golden blond as Henrik's save that it was matted with sweat and mud. In fact, when healthy, she suspected the man would look quite a lot like Henrik. But he was far from healthy. His skin looked grayish, and his breath gasped in and out too loudly.

"What's wrong with him?" Fianna asked. She began to understand why they'd brought her here.

Suddenly the sword came up, and its point came to rest against her breast. "You will heal him," Henrik said.

"I'll try," Fianna answered, "but even I can only —"

"You heal him or you die."

Chapter Five

She met his steely, blue-gray eyes and refused to look away from his demanding gaze. For several quiet, tense moments they stared at each other. She searched for the lover she'd known and found naught of that one. Instead she saw a pain so deep and cruel clawing at him, it could only find outlet in this way.

Finally Fianna said, "Your threats are useless. I'll give him my best efforts as a healer. I do that for all I treat. But I cannot guarantee it will be enough to save him. I cannot heal all." She stepped back and turned away, to face the sick man. "What is wrong with him?" She went to her knees and put a hand on the man's forehead. His flesh felt hot and was coated with sweat.

Henrik sighed, set his sword down on a table, and knelt beside her. "He was injured in a raid. The wound was stitched and appeared to be healing, but then it started to swell and he became ill. They brought him back here." He lifted the man's tunic and removed the dressing from a wound in his shoulder.

Fianna drew in a sharp breath. A cut ran along the top of his shoulder then angled down across his chest. It had been stitched, but it wasn't healing cleanly. The skin all around the wound was swollen, and red streaks radiated from the area. She muttered a quick prayer under her breath, since she feared it would take a miracle to save him.

"This will not be easy," she said to Henrik. "I'll need hot water and cloth, as much of both as you can find."

He nodded and went to give the orders. She was checking over the sick man's body to be sure there weren't any other injuries she didn't know about when he returned. "How long ago was he wounded?" she asked.

"Four days past." For the first time his stoicism slipped and Fianna got a glimpse of how much he cared about the patient and how much it was costing him not to show it. His hands clenched into involuntary fists and his entire body tensed with evident frustration.

"Your brother?" she asked him.

He nodded. "Ranulf."

She looked at Henrik again. "This will be difficult. The wound must be opened again, to allow the ill humors to drain from it."

He shut his eyes for a moment and drew a harsh breath. "It will heal him?"

"It may. If the ill humors haven't taken too strong a hold on him. I'll need someone to help me."

"I'll help. What need you?"

She looked at him, meeting his eyes again. For the first time since his unexpected rescue of her earlier, she felt she really saw the man rather than the image of invincible power he tried to convey. The shadowy depths of his light blue eyes betrayed the pain and fear he hadn't allowed to show before.

"This won't be pleasant," she warned.

"Tell me what to do."

Before she could answer, the woman who'd been tending the pot earlier pushed the hanging cloth aside and brought in a bucket of steaming water along with a pile of clean linen. She set both down hastily and left. Before she could go, Fianna called to her, "Wait. I need a brazier with lit charcoal and some cool water as well."

The woman gave her a blank stare, then turned to listen to Henrik as he translated. She nodded and left again.

While waiting for her return, Fianna removed the dressings and began to clean the area around the wound. The young man on the mat groaned once or twice but otherwise gave no indication he was aware of what she did.

The woman returned with the brazier and set it on the floor, then left and came back with the cool water.

Fianna pulled her mother's dagger from its sheath. Henrik's eyes flashed and he moved toward his sword.

"I won't harm him," she said. "I told you I must reopen the wound."

He drew a long breath, nodded, and returned to his position kneeling by his brother's head.

Fianna held the dagger, warming it between her hands, her right palm over the red stone in the hilt. She remembered her mother's words about it when she'd given it to Fianna.

The dagger is a gift of the fae, her mother had told her. *'Tis bespelled in ways I cannot explain to you. It can heal as well as harm, but you must set your will to its action.* That had been shortly before her mother had gone away three years earlier, disappearing into the mists beyond the mountains. Fianna moved the dagger so she held it by the tip of the hilt and the very end of the blade. She stared into the red stone, willing it to the healing of this very ill young man.

After a minute or two, her thoughts turned back to her mother. The woman had warned Fianna for some time that she would have to leave, but Fianna had never believed it would happen. Until the day she found her mother lying still and pale on her cot. When Fianna roused her, her mother had kissed her and said, *I was waiting for you to return. I have no more time. You know my mother was of the fae and my father a mortal man. My time in this realm was no more than borrowed and is now at an end. I grieve to have to leave you, my love, but if I stay I'll fade away to naught. As it is I've nearly o'erstayed my time. You have what I've taught you and my dagger for your protection. It should be enough.*

She went to the door and picked up the small pack laid there waiting. *One more thing, Fianna. One day you'll look into the dagger and see your fate. Act wisely on what you see.* She kissed her one last time before she walked out the door, heading for the mountains. Fianna didn't follow. Even if she caught up with her mother, she wouldn't find her.

Fianna willed herself to put those thoughts aside and concentrate on imparting her will for healing to the dagger. She folded one of the cloths and wrapped it around the hilt, shifted her grip, and plunged the blade into the flames spurting up from the brazier. She held it there long enough to heat the metal thoroughly.

When she pulled it out of the fire, Fianna let the edges of the cloth fall back far enough to reveal the red jewel again. She stared into it. The memory of her mother brought tears that obscured her vision, turning the heart of the jewel into a sea of swirling red. Yet tears couldn't account for what happened next.

In the depths of the stone, something more than just its red heart grew brighter and flared into sparks. Orange and yellow streaks ignited, flickered, and roared up into a blazing fire. Flames leapt high, higher than herself as she watched it. She could see no fuel for it, yet it seemed it needed none.

She gasped and almost dropped the dagger onto her patient. Her mother had said she'd see her fate in the stone someday. Was this to be how she would meet her end, then? Fire? Dear heavens, she hoped not.

Hoping to deny it and will it away, she closed her eyes. When she opened them, the flames still blazed in the jewel's red depths. But from the heart of that fire another image was forming. A face seemed to emerge from the flames, with hair of fire…Nay, not fire, a fiery shade of gold. A man's face, strong, handsome, with light eyes and…

Again she nearly lost her grip on the dagger. It had to be a trick of the light. Or a reflection. Perhaps he was standing behind her and his face reflected in the jewel… But, nay, he still knelt beside his brother's head, off to her left, staring at her with an expression of mingled alarm and confusion.

"Are you well?" he asked.

She shook herself. There was no time for fancy or speculation. A man's life was slipping away while she mooned over a vision. "Aye. I'm well," she answered. "I just had a moment of dizziness. It will pass."

She looked into the stone again, hoping it had all disappeared. But no, Henrik's face still stared out of the jewel at her, backed by fire. Was he, then, her fate, also? And what did that mean?

As one speculation chased after another in her brain, the images began to fade from the jewel, until she stared at nothing but the red center of the stone. She sighed and shook herself. There was work to do and she needed all her wits about her.

"You must hold him still while I do this," Fianna told Henrik.

His throat worked, his mouth pulled into a tight line, but he nodded and leaned over Ranulf. He put one hand across his brother's head and the other on the man's uninjured shoulder.

As she'd promised Henrik, the next few hours were far from pleasant. Ranulf screamed and tried to rise when she reopened the wound, but Henrik held him firmly. She let the wound drain, then set a cloth soaked in hot water over it to pull out as much of the ill humors as possible. In the meantime she sponged him down with cooler water to try to reduce his fever.

The light faded as they worked. The woman who'd brought the other things returned with candles and oil lamps to light the room. Fianna asked for more hot water and kept changing the cloths on Ranulf's shoulder, replacing each as it cooled. Eventually she felt the heated cloths had done all they could. She got a bottle and a jar from her bag and unstoppered the bottle.

"You'll have to hold him again," she warned Henrik. "It will sting when I pour this on the wound." He nodded and resumed his place, keeping his brother still, even when the stinging liquid washed over the damaged flesh, though Ranulf flinched and tried to roll away. Henrik watched in fascination as Fianna took another pot and spread the ointment from it over the injury.

The last thing to accomplish was re-stitching the wound. Mercifully Ranulf had lapsed into complete unconsciousness again by then. Though Henrik continued to hold him, Ranulf didn't move while she worked the needle in and out. When it was done, she knelt by his side a few minutes longer, watching the patient's face, praying quietly for his healing. She wasn't at all sure he would survive.

She put a shaky hand on his forehead. As long as the fever remained moderate, it was likely a good thing, but should his temperature spike too high, the outcome wouldn't be good.

"There's little more I can do for him right now." She glanced up at Henrik.

The man's pale face was drawn into a frown. "Will he live?" he asked.

She reached for a clean cloth, soaked it in the cool water, and bathed his face with it. "He's a strong man," she said, trying to reassure herself as well as Henrik. "And the wound itself is not so very serious. If the ill humors hadn't taken him so strongly, he'd have recovered from it quickly. If the Lord is merciful, we'll have driven back the poison far enough that his own body can overcome the rest."

"Is there no more we can do to help?"

"Keep him warm enough and cool enough," she answered. "Cool him down if the fever goes high. Try to get some nourishment in him. Wait. And pray."

Henrik stroked his brother's hair back from his face. "I've waited for so many things, for so long," he said, his voice quiet, reflective, sad. "I should be better at waiting than I am. Do they not say practice brings competence? If so I should be very good at patience. Yet I am not. I cannot but anticipate every coming moment and wish it were done and over with before it begins so I can move onto the next and thus get through them more quickly."

He sighed and laid a hand on the side of Ranulf's face. "Sleep, my brother, and may your body mend."

He got to his feet, though the movement lacked his usual grace as he was stiff from hours of kneeling. Exhaustion took its toll as well.

He reached down to draw Fianna to her feet. "Come and rest now that you've done all you might."

"Someone must stay with him and sponge him regularly," she protested. "And I need to be here if the fever spikes."

Henrik studied her face. She wondered if she looked as drawn and gray with fatigue as he did. "I'll get someone to stay with him."

He disappeared through the curtained exit and was gone for some time. When he returned, a woman in middle years followed him into the room. They had a long conversation in his language, and he pointed to the cloths and water twice. As he finished his instructions, the woman nodded and shooed him away.

Henrik put a hand on her arm to lead her though the curtain. "Riga will watch over him the rest of this night. I've told her what to do. She'll wake us should there be any change. I've also had a mat brought in and placed in the other room, so we can rest but be nearby should we be needed."

Fianna wondered at his use of the word "we." Did he plan to share the mat with her? But she was so far beyond exhausted it shouldn't matter that he'd be so near. She would sleep.

When they lay down together, she curled up facing the wall, but he put an arm out to draw her closer to him.

"Fianna?" he said as they lay in the darkness. "I regret I acted as I did earlier. Drawing my sword and threatening you. It was badly done."

"Why did you so then?"

"I didn't know if you…I feared you would be angry with me and refuse to come, or after I forced you to come, refuse to help him."

"Why would I not help him?"

He was silent for a moment. His breath sifted gently through the hair above her ear. "After the night we spent together, I didn't come back to you again."

"And you believed I'd be angry and refuse assistance because of that."

He sighed. "I think I should have known you better. But in truth, we did little talking that night, and so I cannot truly say I know you so well."

Fianna considered that. "Aye, that's so. Though I think I could say I knew something of your heart after that night."

"Without doubt, you're a better judge of people's hearts than I am."

"Then know this now. No matter how angry or disappointed I was that you failed to seek me out again, it would never have stopped me from doing all in my power to heal one who is sick or injured." She paused before she added, "In truth, I could not in fairness blame you. I chose you without giving you much choice, asking only that night. And you gave more generously than I deserved."

His laughter blew over her ear and the side of her face. "You think you gave me no choice that night? I could have easily said you nay, did it not suit me to answer your request. But I was intrigued by a woman so bold and beautiful. My curiosity as well as my manhood demanded I say aye."

"And your manhood and your curiosity being at once satisfied, you had no further need of me."

"Not so. You're one could inspire a lifetime of curiosity and desire. I have met none at all like you before in my life, and every part of me, from my head to my manhood, clamored to explore further what happens between us. But I should not do so. 'Tis not right I should do so."

"Nay?"

"Fianna, I told you. I thought you understood. I will be leaving here. I would have gone as soon as Ranulf returned, had he not come back in such condition. Even so, when he recovers and is able to take my place by our father's side, I'll be off. Knowing this, it didn't seem fair that I seek you out again, despite your kind invitation. I would not have you forming an attachment to me that would be cruelly sundered when I left. Were it not for that, I would have come to you every night since."

"My invitation was many things, but kindness played no part in it," she admitted. "This trip is important to you."

"I've waited half my life, it seems."

"Yet your brother has been gone on his adventure."

"Aye. And I tell myself I begrudge it not. Yet in some measure, I do. But now my time is near, should he live."

"And if he does not?"

He was silent so long she wondered if he'd answer or if he'd fallen asleep. His breath had not the regular rhythm of sleep, however, and after a while he said, "I would remain here. My father is not well. Age and exhaustion are on him. He needs someone vigorous and strong to maintain his order."

Fianna sighed. "I'll do all in my power to save Ranulf. More than that I cannot promise you."

"Nor do I ask it, despite my rash words earlier. I spoke out of my fear and frustration."

"I understand. It is done."

They were both quiet for some time. She thought he'd fallen asleep until he asked, "What was happening at your home this afternoon? Why did all those people come to you? Were they concerned that you were being taken against your will by us? Or did they seek your testimony against those young men who would have forced you?"

"None of those," she said. "They came to tell me I was disrupting the peace of the town by inciting lust in the young men. It was decreed I must choose one to marry."

"'Tis not your fault. True men need not force a woman to their will."

"Aye. But whether I am at fault or no bears little on the case. In the interests of peace, I must be wed. So I must choose one by the night of your Walpurgis feast."

"And if you do not?"

"Then I must leave the town, on pain of death."

He moved against her, apparently distressed by her answer. "That is harsh of them. Do they value you so little?"

"Not so high as their peace, it appears."

"You could leave and find others who value your services more."

"Aye. But I've been happy there, and they have need of me. I have no wish to leave."

"You have no longing to see more of this world? 'Tis a very large place, and I understand there are wonders to be found. I am eager to be off and begin discovering them myself."

"Nay. I want the comfort of a room of my own, my bed, my garden, and my work."

He touched her, ran a gentle hand through her hair. She got the feeling he wanted to offer comfort but knew not how. Finally he said, "I hope you can find your way to a solution that brings you peace."

That was the last she remembered of that night.

* * * * *

Fianna roused when the first light of dawn seeped through cracks around windows and doorways. She shifted and was momentarily surprised to feel another body moving against her back. When she rolled over, Henrik was awake and watching her.

She smiled and reached out to touch him. She ran her fingers through the tangled disarray of his blond hair, watching the lazy grin play across his face. That smile, worn for her, touched a place deep in her breast with a heat of longing and desire. But within moments his face darkened, and he looked toward the curtained-off partition.

Reminded of her purpose for being there, Fianna quickly scrambled up off the mat and went to the other room. Henrik was right behind her.

The woman, Riga, was wiping the cloth across Ranulf's forehead. She spoke to Henrik in Norse for several moments, and he commented or questioned in the same tongue. Fianna was reassured when Henrik didn't seem too upset or unhappy in response. Several times, though, as he looked toward his brother, worry shadowed his expression. Once he even closed his eyes briefly and expelled his breath on a long sigh. She found herself wishing she could pronounce some magic words to wipe that concern from his face and restore the smile from earlier.

Fianna touched Ranulf's forehead and throat. He felt warmer than he had the previous night and was still muttering, though she couldn't decipher the words. The pulse in his throat beat hard and fast.

"He stayed the same for most of the night," Henrik reported to her after he'd sent the other woman off to bed. "About an hour ago, he began to get worse. He started talking, but making no sense with it, and Riga thinks he has been getting warmer." His breath caught in his throat. "This is not good, is it?"

"It is not good, but not surprising either," she told him. "I didn't think I could get all the ill humors out of the wound. I pray we removed enough that his body can fight what remains."

"What should we do?"

"Sponge him off and try to keep his fever down. I have an infusion I'll make that will help with that. If he shows signs of chills, we must have more blankets to wrap him."

Henrik nodded. "I'll get more blankets."

While he was gone, Fianna dipped a cloth into the water and swabbed it over Ranulf's face and down his chest and arms. Like his brother, he was an impressively built man. In fact, if his face weren't so gray and drawn, his hair so shaggy and unkempt, he would look a great deal like Henrik.

Odd that she didn't have the same kind of reaction to him she had to Henrik. There was no tingle of excitement when she touched Ranulf, no frisson of longing for closer contact when she looked at him. He roused her pity and her concern as a patient but nothing more. In fact...

She froze, horrified by the thought that crossed her mind. It wasn't something she could wish for. It wasn't what she would want. But she couldn't deny it was there. If this man were to die, Henrik wouldn't go away. He wouldn't leave his father on his own, no matter how much he longed for travel and adventure. And if he were staying, he'd likely want to see more of her, maybe even provide her with an alternative to the men of the town.

Nay. She didn't want to think that way. He was her patient. She would do all in her power to save him, though she wasn't truly sure how much that was.

She drew out the dagger and held it over Ranulf with the blade parallel to the length of his body. She stared hard into the red jewel in the center until the wash of scarlet filled her vision to the exclusion of all else. She waited for the vision of flames or even the sight of Henrik, but it didn't happen.

After she'd looked into the jewel for some time, the red color began to swirl in a way she'd never seen before. The color seemed to flow in waves in an uneven, roughly circular way. She wondered if her sight were going odd, but couldn't tear her gaze away from the jewel. No vision came to her, but she thought a voice spoke inside her head, saying, "Choose."

Choose what? she asked silently.

"What you pray for."

What I pray for? I don't understand.

"What do you truly want for this man?"

That he live or die, mean you?

"The choice is yours."

Chapter Six

She felt as though someone had punched her in the stomach. This was no such responsibility she would want. Though she had to wonder if she just imagined the voice and the promise it implied. Perhaps it was just her imagination? But if it were so?

Temptation slashed a burning path into her gut. He was so very ill, so very close to death anyway. His passing would likely bring her what she wanted most in the world right now. She wouldn't have to do anything at all, in truth, save fail to pray for his life. She could gain so much by it.

But Henrik would lose so much. His dream of travel and adventure would be smashed. And clearly he cared much for his brother. Ranulf's death would bring Henrik terrible pain.

Fianna shut her eyes but she couldn't shut out the vision of her patient dying and what it would mean for her. Tears leaked from beneath her lids and traced burning streaks down her cheeks.

"Nay." She said that word aloud. *I cannot wish for his death. I'm a healer. Do I not give my best effort to help him recover, I lose more than a patient. I lose the most important part of what I am.*

She would lose her soul.

She placed the dagger back in its sheath, closed her eyes, and prayed to whatever gods might be listening for Ranulf's healing. When she heard Henrik speaking to someone in the next room, she wiped the tears off her face with the sleeve of her dress, and resumed sponging off the patient. He continued to mutter and occasionally writhed or flailed his arms.

Henrik came back into the room, bearing blankets, clean linen, and a bucket of water.

He knelt next to her. "How does he?"

"Holding on. I fear his fever is rising."

Henrik took the cloth from her. "I'll stay with him for a time. There's food, drink, water to wash with, and some fresh clothes for you in the other room."

Startled that he would think to do all that for her, she looked up at him. Shadows lurked in the depths of his light eyes, worry and concern for his brother, but there was also a hint of care and concern for her. It warmed her right down to her toes.

"I won't be long," she promised as she stood up.

No one else was in the other room, but a trencher bearing bread, fruit preserves, and strips of dried meat waited for her. The water in the pitcher was warm and bore a light rose fragrance. Fianna splashed it over her face and hands, used a cloth nearby to clean the rest of her body. It felt wonderfully refreshing. A plain, clean linen blouse and skirt hung over a chair. By drawing the ribbons on them tight, she was able to fit them to her body. Even the length was right. Someone had gone to a good bit of trouble on her behalf, and it wasn't hard to decide who it must have been.

His kindness and thought for her increased the guilt that unworthy thoughts about his brother had even entered her mind.

She thought more on that as she ate the food left for her. The Church taught that the devil was ever ready to pounce on one's weaknesses to tempt one to' evil. She'd never faced that sort of temptation before. Was it a weakness that she was coming to care for Henrik too strongly? Possibly, but she had to believe she could find strength there as well.

She ate quickly, only realizing how hungry she was when she began and could barely get the food to her mouth quickly enough. Once it was gone, she went back into the other room.

Henrik was swabbing Ranulf's face, while the man tossed and turned on the mat.

"We need fresh water and more fuel for the brazier," she told him.

Henrik nodded and went to get it. When he returned, she prepared an infusion of bark and herbs that was often effective in fighting fever and set it to heat. While the mix boiled over the brazier, she sponged Ranulf off yet again. When he suddenly started shivering, she wrapped a blanket around him.

"Why do we make him cold with the water then make him hot with blankets?" Henrik asked. "This is good for him?"

"We're not making him hot or cold. His body itself does that. We're trying to keep him from getting too hot or too cold. Those are not good for him. So when he gets too hot, we cool him off, and when he gets too chilled, we make him warm."

Henrik nodded. "That seems right."

Ranulf was being fairly calm for the moment, so Fianna used the time to change the dressing on his shoulder and inspect the wound. The swelling didn't look dangerous. The discoloration remained in the vicinity of the injury and didn't seem to be spreading. The red streaks radiating from it had gotten neither worse nor better. Before she put on a new bandage, she spread more of the salve she'd used yesterday on the wound. The recipe for both the salve and the infusion had come from Marla.

Henrik wrinkled his nose at the odor of the salve. "What is in that? It smells worse than the pig stocks."

"If I told you, you would not permit me to use it. 'Tis a healer's secret. But it is often helpful in preventing ill humors from gathering in a wound such as Ranulf has."

He looked dubious. "Your infusion smells almost as bad. Must all medicine reek to be effective?"

"Be glad you don't have to drink it. It tastes worse than it smells."

"It will truly help him?"

She heard the plea that underlay the question but wasn't sure how to respond. "These medicines are often helpful," she answered carefully. "But nothing can guarantee a cure."

Pain lanced through her when she saw the way he looked at his brother. The anguish in his face cut into her own heart. Clearly there was more here than just his wanting Ranulf to recover so he could go his own way. He cared desperately for this man he hadn't seen for so long. She wished there were something she could say or do to ease him.

She stood up, moved closer to him, and put a hand on his arm. When he turned toward her, she leaned into him and wrapped her arms around his waist. Her head rested against his chest.

For a moment, he just stood there, tense and unmoving. Then he sighed deeply, relaxing a bit out of his stiffness, and put his arms around her to hold her to him. His breath was ragged and uneven.

Her first reaction was a wave of tenderness, that he trusted her enough to reveal even this much of his pain and let her share it with him. But then, wrapped in his arms, tight against his body, a powerful tide of longing for more complete union suddenly surged through her, making her shake. Would it always be thus with this man? His mere touch sent ripples of awareness, like sparks snapping against her, all over her skin. Once he was gone from her life, would she continue to long for the sound of his voice, the way he looked at her?

He tipped back her head and kissed her, deeply, tenderly, hungrily, until her knees were unsteady, and all she wanted was to rip off clothes and impale herself on him. Would her body ever forget how he made the heat spread wildly through her, the way the pressure gathered in her loins when he held her?

Footsteps sounded from the other room, coming toward them. He released her when she moved back away.

The older man who'd been in the other room when they'd arrived the previous day pushed the curtain aside and peered in. Henrik said something to him in Norse and the man entered. His gaze focused on Ranulf. When he noted he was no better, the older man's shoulders slumped and his body tensed up. The questioning expression on his face turned to something harder and less readable, keeping his feelings shut inside.

He and Henrik exchanged words and glanced occasionally toward her. While they talked Fianna turned to the brazier and removed the small pot holding the boiling mixture to a clay plate set nearby for the purpose.

"Fianna?"

She turned to face Henrik.

"My father would like to make himself known to you and thank you for your care of Ranulf."

The older man nodded and came toward her, took her hand, and struggled to say her name, "Fee-ah-na."

She nodded and bowed her head, giving him the respect due his age.

He said something more to her in Norse.

"My father is Hjallmar, and he thanks you again for coming to care for his son," Henrik translated. "He also wishes me to convey his apologies for my rude treatment of you yesterday."

"Tell him there's naught to be concerned about," Fianna asked. "I understand you were unhappy and worried about your brother, and so acted in a way not normal for you."

She shot a glance at Henrik. "It was not normal, was it?"

He shrugged. "I am not very trusting of strangers."

"Except when she solicits you for a night of sex?"

"Perhaps especially so then."

"You didn't act like you were suspicious of me then."

"You may not have noticed how careful I was. Until I had you helpless in the throes of a need as strong as mine."

Henrik's father broke the tension building between them when he asked a question in Norse. He and Henrik spoke back and forth for a few minutes.

"He wants to know if there's aught he can do to help?" Henrik translated.

Fianna was about to say no, when she had a thought. "Tell him it might help if he would sit with Ranulf for a while and speak to him of how much he wants him to get better. Though it seems not so, Ranulf might be able to hear and understand, and it might serve to draw him back and encourage him to fight harder to recover."

Henrik relayed her suggestions to his father. The older man nodded and, with Henrik's help, settled on the floor beside the mat. He took his son's hand in his and began to speak, in a low, soothing, caring tone.

Fianna poured out some of the liquid infusion into a cup. "I have to get him to swallow some of this," she said to Henrik. "It tastes terrible and he'll resist. Can you help me get it into him?"

He nodded, but they waited while Hjallmar sat at his son's side and pleaded with him to keep fighting for life. Finally the old man sighed and stood up again. He spoke a few words to Henrik, nodded to her, and left.

"My father has things to attend to," Henrik said, "but he'll return after a while. He thanks you again for your efforts to save Ranulf."

Fianna nodded and held up the cup. "Ranulf needs to drink some of this."

Henrik lifted Ranulf's head and pushed in lightly on his cheeks, while Fianna carefully dribbled the liquid into his mouth. Ranulf grimaced and tried to pull away, but Henrik held him firmly. Henrik closed his brother's mouth when he tried to spit out the bad-tasting liquid, keeping his lips together until he swallowed. They repeated the process several times until Fianna was satisfied that enough of the infusion had gotten into the sick man.

For the rest of the morning and into the afternoon, they continued to try to keep Ranulf's temperature stable. She was pleased when half an hour or so after they'd fed him the infusion, his fever abated somewhat and he slept quietly for a while.

Henrik left her, saying he needed to take care of some business, but he sent a woman who spoke a little bit of her language to stay with her while he was gone. He asked that he be notified of any change in his absence.

The room seemed darker and emptier without him in it. She hoped it was merely that he was the only familiar person in this settlement of strangers, but she suspected that wasn't the case. Had this room been full of the townspeople she'd known all her life, his leaving it would still make it feel colder and lonelier. It disturbed her to consider how important he'd become to her in such a short period of time. She couldn't afford it.

Henrik returned briefly early in the afternoon to let her know there was food in the other room. He looked at his brother and nodded when he saw him sleeping quietly.

"Come with me," he said, looking at Fianna. "You need a rest. Erawyn can stay with Ranulf for a while. She'll let us know if there's any change."

Fianna debated, but her patient was resting quietly and there was little more she could do for him for a while. She let Henrik help her to her feet. As usual the sparks jumped between her flesh and his where they touched. Even with her worry for Ranulf, the pressure built in her loins just from looking at him.

They stopped to eat in the other room, where a tureen of an aromatic stew and several bowls waited. The food was as tasty as it was filling, but an even greater hunger was building in her as she watched Henrik. He ate with near, careful precision, and was unfailingly courteous, though he was also tense and worried.

When they were finished with the meal, he escorted her out of the building. Fianna blinked in the bright sunshine. Her eyes had difficulty adjusting to the light after so much time spent inside in the dimmer light. They made a quick trip across a piece of the open area at the center of the settlement, between two buildings to another one built some ways back from the rest of the houses.

"This is mine," Henrik told her with some pride as he ushered her through the door and into the structure. "I built it myself, though I spend more nights with my father than here. I've had need of a place where I could go and be alone to think and plan."

They were in a large center room that had a fire pit at the far side. Doors on either end, to her left and right, gave access to smaller rooms off this main one. The furniture wasn't elaborate or extensive, but what there was appeared well crafted.

As she was looking it over, he came up behind her and slid his arms around her, cupping her breasts in his palms.

"I want you so much I can scarce bear it," he said softly to her. His tone sounded more pained than joyful, however. "I know not if I should do anything about it, though. My brother is ill and may be dying. Is it right that we take pleasure while he suffers?"

Fianna considered it, though thinking was difficult with his hands caressing her breasts, making the heat gather in her loins. "I know not. But…if you were in his position, and he in yours, what would you tell him?"

His hands stilled. "I suppose I would tell him to go on. Life does not stop because I am ill. Why should my brother be miserable because I am? It benefits me not that he's grieving and unhappy."

Fianna turned within the circle of his arms to face him. She reached upward to place her hands on either side of his face, running her fingers into his hair, and kissed him.

"Then so shall we respect him," she said, "for I suspect you two are much alike."

The fire of excitement raced through her body, sparking an explosion of desire in her loins. Moisture gathered between her legs. He adjusted his hold on her, swung her up into his arms, and carried her through the door at the far left, into a room that held a bed big enough to accommodate two people easily. He set her down gently on it and began to remove her clothes. When she was bare to the waist he stopped to toy with her breasts.

"Your skin is like the finest silk," he said, while stroking and tweaking the nipples until she was squirming with desire. She lay back, and he leaned over her to use his tongue on one nipple while his fingers worked the other. He sucked the tip into his mouth with a hard pressure and rolled it around, working his tongue on it, scraping his teeth over it as he slowly released it. Then the other breast drew similar attentions.

She loosened the laces on his leggings enough to allow her to slip her hand inside and wrap it around his cock. She'd been aching to touch him for so long. He moaned deep in his throat as her fingers explored along its length, dipping into hollows and brushing along smooth, satiny flesh.

In a frenzy of need, he began rapidly stripping off vest, shirt, boots and leggings until he stood over her in naked, rampantly masculine glory. She reached out to cup the dangling sacs of his balls. The pair filled her hand. His breath caught on a sharp hitch when she squeezed and kneaded them. Her other hand circled his cock and rubbed up and down.

"You fit in my hands perfectly," she said to him.

"I fit perfectly elsewhere as well." He yanked off the rest of her clothes and pushed her legs apart. His fingers tested her readiness. When he realized she was moist and open for him, he lay over her and positioned himself. Their eyes met.

"Now," she begged. "Please. I need you."

With one hard thrust he pushed all the way in. For a moment it stung as she stretched to accommodate him, but when he began pumping in and out, the end of his cock seemed to find a place deep within her that sent piercing shafts of pleasure exploding inside. It built the pressure in her quickly to a point almost past bearing.

"You feel so good around me," he whispered to her, the words broken up by gasping breaths. "So hot and tight."

He thrust firmly and fast, filling and stroking her until she was strung so tight it was a wonder she didn't break. Then, with one strong, deep plunge he sent her spinning out of control into a universe of swirling colors and throbbing waves of pleasure washing through her. She drifted with it, plunging and bucking with the continuing spasms.

Henrik let out a loud groan as he spilled his seed into her.

They clung to each other in the aftermath, riding the continuing shocks and spurts of pleasure. Her breathing gradually slowed as the incredible peace spread through her. A wonderful sense of completion and connection made her cling to him. She clutched at him, bringing his torso right against hers.

"I wish we could stay this way forever," she told him. "Only with you have I known such pleasure. And such peace."

He kissed her gently before he rolled to the side. "Time will not cease its movement for us," he said on a long sigh. "And I fear what its march might bring us. But for now, rest."

He shifted her until she lay on her side, back to him, and he pulled her against his body, one of his arms under her neck, the other draped over her side so he could hold one breast. It felt remarkably safe, secure, and comfortable being sheltered in the crook of his big body that way. She quickly drifted off to sleep.

An hour or so later, they were awakened by someone banging on the door. Henrik rolled away and off the bed, dragged on a long nightshirt that hung to his knees and went to find out what was happening. Fianna heard a rapid-fire exchange in Norse. Suspecting the worst, she got up and began to dress.

Chapter Seven

Even before he said, "Ranulf is worse. They need you there," she knew from the expression on his face the news wasn't good.

She blinked as they rushed out into the mid-afternoon sun. Guilt washed over her that she'd been dallying with Henrik while Ranulf's condition deteriorated. But she couldn't have prevented it happening even had she been there. Still she hurried back to his bedside.

Ranulf's fever was definitely up, and he shifted restlessly on the mat. With the help of the Norse woman and Henrik, Fianna got more of the infusion into him, and for a while it seemed to help him rest. Just an hour or so after that, though, he was tossing and turning again, muttering and waving his arms. A touch on his face confirmed that the fever was continuing to rise.

It took the three of them holding onto him to keep Ranulf from twisting so much he tore open the wound. Occasionally he would cry out or shout out long strings of words, presumably in his own Norse tongue. Henrik knelt beside her and put his hands on his brother's shoulders.

Through the rest of the afternoon and into the evening, his condition deteriorated. The fever worsened. His periods of delirium became more frequent and more violent. They sponged him off and struggled to keep him cool, but sweat still gathered on his temples and chest. The beating of his heart raced, and his breathing became faster and more shallow.

Whenever she could, she tried to get him to swallow more of the infusion. Fianna didn't know how much of it could be safely given in any time period, but she thought it better to risk giving him too much than not enough. If he were dying anyway, she'd do all she knew to fight it.

She changed the dressing on his injured shoulder again. The wound was still draining, but there appeared to be no great increase of inflammation. For the rest of the time she could do naught but try to cool him when he was too hot, warm him when he shivered with chills and keep him from injuring himself when he flailed around in delirium.

Henrik stayed with her for the rest of the day, save when he went out to get fresh cloths, more water, or food. He brought her tea and cider and water for drinking. As darkness fell, he lit candles around the room. When she winced after kneeling too long in one position, he helped her shift and rubbed her shoulders and neck to relieve her tension. But his gaze went often to his brother and anguish pulled his expression into hard, pain-wracked lines.

Ranulf's ravings grew more noisy and his flailings more violent as the night went on. His temperature kept climbing despite her efforts to keep it down.

During one particularly restless interval, it took the two of them together to keep him from throwing himself off the mat. When Ranulf calmed again, Henrik turned to her and asked, "Should I get my father? Is this the end?"

Fianna debated and finally said, "Nay. Not yet." She sighed and added, "It may not be long, though."

Henrik looked dubious but accepted her word.

Riga, the woman who'd stayed with Ranulf the previous night, came in and asked if they would need her again. Through Henrik, Fianna told her that they would stay with him themselves.

For several more hours they worked over Ranulf, bathing him, holding him, feeding him as much of the infusion as they could get into him. She prayed again for his recovery, fearful that only a miracle could save him. Late that night, or perhaps it was in the early morning as Fianna had long since lost track of time, he had a prolonged spell of violent thrashing around that included screams and angry outbursts of hoarse yells. Henrik declined to translate his words.

They wrestled with him for what seemed a very long time, when he suddenly went limp in their arms and stopped moving completely. Henrik's eyes widened and his face went white. He looked up at Fianna.

Chapter Eight

Ranulf didn't appear to be breathing, but when she felt for his heartbeat, she could still feel the pulse of it. She leaned down to put an ear to his chest. Air still moved in and out. Sweat dappled his flesh, but that skin was cooling. Alarmed she felt for his heartbeat again, pressing her fingers to his throat to check the rhythm. It was stronger than she expected and steadier.

This might yet be the prelude to his sinking into a deep sleep from which he wouldn't awake, so she said nothing to Henrik either way. But he saw something in her face and knew that her hope for the outcome was rising. "He is better?" he asked.

"Aye. But do not rejoice over it yet. It might be an interval of peace before the fever attacks again."

It wasn't. Another hour later it became clear Ranulf was indeed improving. Though the fever didn't disappear completely, it was much lower, and he no longer had the periods of delirium.

Shortly before dawn, when the first rays of light began to wash away darkness, Ranulf opened his eyes and looked around. He saw her first and frowned. He said a few words that drew a shout of relieved laughter from Henrik.

Ranulf's gaze slewed far enough to the side to see his brother. A smile struggled to form on his face. They exchanged a few more words and both chuckled, though in Ranulf it was just a bare hiccup of amusement.

"What is the jest?" Fianna asked.

"He wondered if you were a Valkyrie or an angel. He wasn't sure, if he died in this land, which afterlife he'd find."

"You assured him I was neither."

"I told him you were both. But he wasn't in any afterlife."

Her heart did a strange little flip-flop at those words. She stared at Henrik, meeting his intent gaze, where the dawning haze of gratitude and joy lit his eyes. She wanted to go to him and throw herself into his arms. She wanted to feel him on her, around her, in her. He was a man like no other she'd ever met. She knew him well enough to know he felt the same, but this wasn't the time or place.

Ranulf looked at her. His eyes were more blue-green while Henrik's were blue-gray, but the resemblance between the two of them was even more pronounced with him awake and alert. He said something more and Henrik laughed again.

"He said he's sorry he's been asleep so long if he had you working on him."

The two men had a much longer exchange. By the end of it Ranulf appeared ready to fall asleep again. Fianna got him to drink a few sips of water before he did.

"We'll need meat broth for him for the next day or so, then some soft bread, porridge, and other light foods until he is able to sit up."

Henrik nodded. "I'll see to it. And I must tell my father." He stopped on his way to the door, turned, and came back to her. He drew her to her feet and kissed her. It was much quicker and lighter than either of them wanted, but better than naught under the circumstances. "I owe you thanks and more. Whatever my father's house can provide for you, you'll have. Ask what you will of us."

Fianna thought of the one request she wanted more than anything to make of him. She couldn't. It wouldn't be right to ask him to give up his dream to indulge hers. But, oh, how she wanted to beg him to stay. Stay here, stay with her. "I'll think on it," she said, instead.

He nodded and left. While Ranulf slept, she changed the dressing on the wound again. The redness and swelling around the injury had retreated. The red streaks radiating from it were fading. His fever remained mild.

The woman who'd been with him while they slept yesterday came in bearing a tray of food, which included breakfast for her and a cup of broth for Ranulf. Fianna ate the bread and meat enthusiastically. Ranulf woke again shortly after she finished. He spoke to her, but without Henrik to translate, she had no idea what he said.

"Can you understand me?" she asked in her language, spacing out the words to make them easier to understand.

His blank look and a shake of the head told her he didn't comprehend. She held up the cup of broth and made a drinking motion herself before she moved it toward him. He nodded and tried to push himself up. He looked surprised to find himself so weak he could barely move at all.

Fianna sat next to him and lifted his head so that it rested on her knees. She helped him take a few swallows of the broth before he turned away from it, indicating he'd had enough.

Henrik returned with his father and several other people following behind. There was much chatter, laughter, and excitement among them when they saw Ranulf was awake and lucid. Fianna backed away, giving them room to crowd around the patient.

"Tell them they must not stay too long and tire him out," she requested of Henrik. "He still needs rest to speed his recovery."

Henrik nodded. After speaking with a couple of the people present, he came back to her, took her arm, and nodded to the other room. Before they could leave, though, Henrik's father came over, took her hand, and pressed it to his cheek. He said a few words in Norse that she could tell were meant to convey his gratitude.

"Tell him I did only what is in me to do as a healer," she asked.

He nodded and passed that onto his father. The older man said something more and kissed her on the forehead.

"As I said earlier, you have but to ask whatever reward you will of him," Henrik translated.

"I am giving it thought," she said. When his father returned to the group crowding around the bed, she and Henrik escaped into the other room.

"You've eaten?" he asked. When she said she had, he said, "Come with me, then. We both need sleep. It was a hard night."

"Aye," she agreed. "But worth it."

"Very much so."

Fianna went with Henrik back to his home. Though his touch, as always, evoked that deep body hunger for him, she was too exhausted to do anything about it, and she suspected he must be, too. Still, it felt wonderful to rest with his body curled around hers, his arm under her neck, her back pressed against his chest. She slept deeply.

When she woke, he was already up. She didn't see him in the room, so she rose and got dressed. He wasn't in the large central room, either. Just as she was about to return to the house where Ranulf lay, he came back.

He smiled at her. "Ranulf continues to improve. He was complaining about the broth and saying he wanted real food."

"That's good, but do not let him go to it too quickly."

"I told them what you said about it."

"Good."

He was watching her with a lazy grin that held a wicked hint of mischief in its depths as well. "Did you rest well?" he asked.

"Aye. Very well."

"Would you like to take a steam bath?" He paused a moment and there was a hot promise in his tone and in his expression when he added, "With me."

"What is a steam bath? I've never heard of this."

"Nay. You Anglish know not how to get really clean. You'll like it."

"I'll try it."

The smile that spread over his face completely devastated her. He was so handsome, this Norseman, and so strong, loyal, and kind. He was so much all she'd want in a man, yet she couldn't lay claim to him. Still, she could treasure every moment with him and store up memories to cling to later.

Chapter Nine

He led her to a building that was some distance from the main settlement, near the shores of a swift-moving river. The structure had no windows and just one door. Smoke rose from an opening in the center of the roof. When they went inside, they were in a small anteroom that held a couple of benches and a series of pegs on the walls. A fresh set of clothes for each of them hung on the pegs. Another door led to the main part of the building.

"I had this prepared for us," Henrik said. "You undress here before you go in." He drew his leather vest off over his head and began to unlace his shirt. Fianna took off the borrowed clothes and hung them on pegs. She left her boots under a bench.

She hesitated, shy for a moment, before turning around to face him. In the dim light of the room, she could only just make out his shape, but it was beautiful. She wanted him so badly, it was a knife stabbing at her heart. He came toward her, took her hand, and led her to the door to the other room.

A blazing fire roared in a pit in the center of the small room, making it bright and very warm. Two rings of large stones circled the fire. Benches lined three walls. A row of buckets, filled to the brim with water, waited along the fourth wall. A stack of wood for the fire and a pile of cloths rested beside them. Henrik picked up a bucket and poured the water over the rocks, careful to keep it from flowing onto the fire. After two more, the room became so steamy Fianna felt droplets of moisture gathering on her skin. He led her to one of the benches.

"Sit for a minute and let it penetrate. You will feel relaxed."

"'Tis very warm." She wasn't sure how much of the heat came from her surroundings and how much was roused by her companion.

"So it should be," he said. "Warm is relaxing and inspiring."

"Warm is making me hot and…tense."

"It is? I'm disappointed."

She turned to stare at him. "How so?"

His grin was so full of mischief and wicked suggestion, it made her heart flutter and her pulse rate speed up. "I thought I made you hot and tense." He leaned over and kissed her, hard, deeply, dazzlingly.

"You set me on fire," she whispered against his lips. She put a hand on his chest, purely for the pleasure of feeling his slick, sleek skin.

After a minute or two, he drew away enough to let him pull her to him, lifted and turned her so that she ended up kneeling on the bench, straddling his lap, the hard length of his cock between them, pushing against her quim.

Watching his face as the contact worked its magic in arousing him delighted her. She still wondered at the amazing effect she could have on this tall, strong warrior, who preferred sex fierce and bold. In its way it was as astonishing to her as the times when she managed to know what ailed someone without having any idea how she knew. Both were mysteries that seemed to reveal something of the universe in their depths.

Henrik bent to lick her nipples, then began suckling them and scraping with his teeth. Need exploded within her, driving her into a frenzy of desire. Sensation washed through her as the mix of pleasure-pain from her breasts fired her blood. She moaned and gasped, then squealed even louder when he reached down between them and parted the folds of flesh pressed against his cock. His fingers invaded the cleft and began tickling the bud until she couldn't bear the need.

"Henrik!" She all but screamed his name. "'Tis…I need you. Please, please!" she begged.

He lifted her again, sliding her down over his cock, impaling her on its hard length. The feel of it within her was exquisite. She wrapped her arms around his neck as she began to pump herself up and down on it. Meanwhile he continued to tweak a nipple with one hand, while he stroked her quim with the other.

The tension built fast and hard with so much sensation flowing from various points on her body. She moaned and even cried in the frenzy of need as she bounced wildly on him, trying to milk every tingle. Every time she lowered herself it drove him deep into her body and pushed some magic point that throbbed with pleasure beyond bearing.

She heard him moaning as well and encouraging her. "Oh, gods, that's so good," he groaned in her ear. "Faster. I'm going to explode. Ahhhh."

They climaxed together, her release squeezing him and milking his seed in long, potent spasms. For long minutes, she was frozen on him, as the jolts of climax rolled through her over and over. She collapsed against him, still jumping with the aftershocks, holding tight to his neck as the glorious conclusion wound down.

When she was able to speak again, after she'd kissed him, and combed her fingers through his hair, she asked, "Is this a common part of a steam bath? No wonder 'tis so popular."

"Not usually," he said. "It was a special treat I arranged for you."

"And I'm very grateful. I don't know that I'll ever be able to bathe again without thinking of this."

He pushed her away from his shoulder so he could see her face. "'Tis not over yet. We have time to ourselves and many more things to explore. We have sated the sharpest of the need. We can be slower and more relaxed next time. I don't think you'll be truly clean, in any case, until I've licked over every inch of you."

"Every inch?"

"Perhaps not *every* inch. All the most important inches," he answered. He lifted her from his lap, set her back on the bench, stood up, and eased her down until she lay face-down, stretched out along the bench. "A rub on your back, though, will help you get in the right mood. I will not be rushed this time."

He threw more wood on the fire and splashed more water on the rocks. She looked up at him and said, "Before we start, I want a bargain. Whatever you do to me, I must be able to do the same to you."

His eyebrows lifted. "You would demand this from me?"

She drew a deep breath. "Aye."

He smiled. "So be it. This will be interesting."

"I certainly hope so."

He knelt beside the bench and began running his hands up and down her back, pushing and pressing in places. Initially she was surprised by the pressure he put on various muscles, the force he used in kneading some spots, but quickly realized how good it felt and how it helped relieve tightness in those areas. She sighed and reveled in the attention. His fingers seemed to know all the right places to touch and squeeze.

Eventually he moved down from her back along her buttocks. It changed the way she felt about what was happening, from being relaxed, to the beginnings of a new arousal. She liked the way his big hands worked her bottom, rubbing, tapping, patting. He stroked along her legs, tracing down to her feet and then back up. Her breath caught when his fingers ran up the insides of her thighs. Runnels of sensation tingled their way right up to her loins. The heaviness began to press again, and moisture that might not be sweat gathered between her legs.

He rolled her over. Fianna lay on the bench staring up at him. The dampness in the air darkened his blond hair and stood in small beads in his close-clipped beard. The heat made his skin pinker than usual, which contrasted nicely with the light blue-gray of his eyes. He was magnificent. She felt a heart-stopping thrill just in looking at him and wanted to wrap herself around him, hold him to her, and never let go.

He dipped his head. She thought he meant to kiss her, but instead he was fulfilling his promise from earlier to lick all over. His tongue circled her lips to start with, ran up along her temple, forehead, and down the other side, explored her cheeks and ears, then went down along her throat. She shivered in the heat as the touch sent ripples of pleasure along her nerves.

The most important inches came in for a great deal of attention. On each breast, he began at the outside of the mound, circled around it, then spiraled inward, making a slow, lazy, unbearably thrilling trip to the nipples. His tongue just skirted around the deep pink rims once or twice before he moved inward to lave the tips with concentrated attention. She was shuddering from the need and desire he'd roused by the time he finished with them.

Once her breasts had been treated thoroughly, his tongue glided downward again. Raspy and moist, it trailed a line of heat on her skin. He stopped at her navel to lick around the indent and probe into it with the tip. Then he continued down her abdomen to the crease of her legs. When he got there, he planted a kiss, but moved over to run his tongue along the front of one thigh.

She groaned as the tingles followed along the path his tongue traveled down her leg to her foot. When he lifted the foot and drew each toe individually into his mouth, she squealed and writhed. Who could have guessed that toes could feel so much? He set down the one foot and started on the other, sucking each toe into his mouth, and then when he'd attended each one, beginning a slow, nearly unbearable ascent to her hips. He reached the crease and planted another kiss there.

When he tried to nudge her legs apart to gain access to the most important inches of all, though, she had a wild, wicked idea, and resisted, refusing to let him move her.

"Part your legs," he demanded. The tone of his voice suggested he sensed her resistance presaged something else, and he would indulge her.

She shook her head no.

"You refuse?" he asked. "You know what will happen?"

She looked up at him, loving the way he understood what she wanted, and the fact that he so clearly wanted it as well. "I know."

He nodded and lifted her from the bench, flipped her over, and set her back down gently on her belly. "Do not move. I'll be back."

He was gone for a few minutes. When he returned he carried four or five slender branches, all three to four feet long, cut from a tree. She sucked in a sharp breath and wondered if she'd been so wise after all. She didn't believe he'd really hurt her, though.

She still cringed a bit when he stood over her holding one of those branches and brought it down on her bottom. The stroke was little more than a tap, however, that created a tiny sting. Five or six lashes later, the stinging was beginning to spread out along her entire bottom. It wasn't terribly painful, in truth—more of a pleasant burn that was doing its part to feed the heavy, throbbing need building in her loins.

After a few more, he stopped and asked, "Are you ready to obey me now?"

Fianna didn't have to think about it long. "Not yet."

His only answer was to swing the switch down on her bottom a little harder. Caught by surprise, she yelped when the sting was a bit harsher. Not unbearable, by any means, though. He paused and waited for her to object or ask to stop it.

When she didn't, he swung again. He followed that one with a long series of smacks starting at the top of her bottom, moving down to cover the surface, and then onto the backs of her thighs, delivering each stroke harder as he went. By the time he moved back up her thighs and was lashing her bottom again, it was beginning to burn in a way that bordered on unpleasant. But it was still feeding the growing fire in her.

Two more harsh strokes carved bright ribbons of pain across her rear. It was enough.

"Please," she said, "No more. I'll obey."

He nodded and dropped the branch. Fianna reached back and rubbed the flesh to dissipate the burning. Amazingly, though, the sting was working its way down in her loins and changing into...need. Her quim felt hot, moist, and heavy. She felt her heart beat in its pulsing pressure. She wanted to drag him down on top of her right then.

"Roll over now," he ordered. "And part your legs for me."

She did as he directed. Parting her legs meant letting them drop off the sides of the bench onto the floor. He shifted her toward the end of the bench, then he knelt on the floor at that end. For a minute all he did was stare at the feminine secrets she revealed to him in that open position.

Then he leaned over, put his hands beneath her bottom to lift it a bit, and brought his mouth down on her slit. The touch of his hands on the hot flesh sent fresh curls of fire swirling through her. She couldn't contain a small scream when his tongue brushed over her bud. It sent shockwaves of near unbearable pleasure careening through her system.

"Heavens, oh, heavens," she murmured. "'Tis taking me..."

She clutched the edges of the bench, her fingers almost digging into the wood as his tongue ran over her slit again and again. The pressure was building quickly, the fire growing hotter. Her head rolled from side to side and her body arched under his attention. She screamed again when his lips closed over the bud and drew it into his mouth. His greedy tongue probed at it. The sensations were wicked, wild, pleasure beyond reason, extravagant...He scraped his teeth over the bud then worked it faster with his tongue until she exploded with a release that had her bucking and jolting over and over.

It surged through her, carried her on clouds of pleasure to a sublime state of joy. Her body kept tensing and releasing, jerking repeatedly with the shocks. He continued to lick the bud and that provoked more spasms. She held the bench and floated on the pleasure for as long as she could. Finally, though, she could take no more and pushed away from his clever mouth.

She lay back on the bench, completely spent, totally relaxed, beyond any movement or even thought for the moment. Henrik came around and sat on the bench beside her, then lifted her until her head was against his chest. "Never have I met a woman who enjoyed exploring different sorts of pleasure as you do," he murmured to her. "Nor have I met one who exploded with her release as do you. Nor one as kind and willing to give her every effort to heal a sick man."

"The first two are testament to your skill as a lover who provokes such passion in me," she answered. "The third is merely the way I am and not true virtue."

"Why so?"

"Virtue is something one must work at. Giving all to heal someone is simply in my nature and so requires no great effort." She thought, though, of the decision she'd had to make between what she wanted and what her skill required of her. He would never know about that.

Henrik sighed and held her close. His heart beat strong and steady beneath her ear. "I call it virtue, nonetheless," he insisted.

She didn't answer. There was too much joy in just cuddling against him, sated and happy, for the moment. But then she felt his rampant cock jutting against her and recalled he hadn't had a second release as she had, which brought to mind the bargain they'd made earlier. "Earlier, you promised anything you did to me, so I could do to you as well," she reminded him.

He looked surprised and disconcerted for an instant, then nodded. "So I did."

A spurt of enthusiasm over the idea brought her up off the bench to stand in front of him and say, "Lie down on the bench, face down."

Chapter Ten

He frowned, but he did as she directed. For a minute Fianna could only survey his form from this new angle and delight in it. His back was strong, with broad, solid shoulders narrowing to a slim waist and sleek, muscular hips. She reached down and rubbed her hand along his back, feeling the play of the sinews under her fingers. As he'd done for her earlier, she began to massage and knead the muscles to ease him into greater comfort.

It seemed to work. Henrik sighed deeply and relaxed from his stiff position. He began to tense again, though when her hands moved down to stroke his buttocks. Though narrow compared to his chest, they were gracefully formed and just rounded enough to be intriguing. His legs were parted slightly, letting her see the backs of his balls. She ignored them for the moment, though, stroking down his legs. The muscles of his thighs were strong and solid, like the rest of him. He was truly an impressive man, this temporary lover of hers. Just touching him fired a possessive longing she'd never have guessed she'd ever feel about a man. She wanted to lay claim to him, to have him around always. Not just for sex, though. She liked being with him even when they weren't making love; she liked falling asleep in his arms, talking about their dreams and desires, working together. She also liked touching him, she decided as she ran her hands back up his body and buried them in his soft, silky hair.

"Roll over," she ordered him.

He complied without hesitation, turning his large frame over so that he looked up at her. His eyes held hints of laughter.

She bent over to kiss his face, much as he'd done with her earlier, licking his lips, temples, down along the line of beard to his ears, and then continuing the exploration with her tongue down his strong throat to his chest. There was a slight taste of salt on his damp skin that nonetheless tasted sweet to her. Her tongue tangled in the whirls of hair on his chest and scraped lightly across one masculine nipple. He drew in a sharp breath as she circled the hard bud, stopped there and closed her lips over it. She sucked and nipped at it before moving over to the other one. His heartbeat picked up speed and his breathing became faster under her loving attention. She loved watching his body jerk and knowing she could bring this big, strong man to such extremes.

She licked lower, running her tongue down his stomach, stopping to explore his belly button, then following the narrowing arrow of hair onto his abdomen. She skirted the length of his cock, though, and continued down one strong thigh and a long stretch of leg to his foot. He reared up with surprise when she kissed the end of each toe. She waited for him to say something, but he just smiled and lay back down.

She ran her tongue back up the inside of his leg to his knee, where she transferred her attention to the other leg and went down to the toes of the other foot. He made a strangled sound halfway between a gasp and a sob. The journey continued up the outside of his leg.

When she got to his hip, she settled her face between his thighs, halfway down to his knees, stuck her tongue between them and ran it up the insides of both thighs, stopping just short of his balls. His breath was coming in loud, gasping pants and his body jerked and tightened.

"Now spread your legs apart," she ordered him.

Playing along with the game, he dutifully refused.

Her pulse and breathing sped up. "You disobey me?" she asked. "You know the consequences."

He didn't answer. The lazy, wicked grin he threw her nearly ripped her heart out of her chest. It occurred to her that even if he left and never returned, she might never be able to have sex with a man again. Certainly it would never be like this with anyone else, and she feared he spoiled her for anything less.

She turned away to find the branches he'd left lying on the floor. She didn't want him to see the sudden spurt of tears in her eyes and wiped them away surreptitiously as she picked out the sturdiest switch on the pile.

"Roll over," she ordered him. Her voice sounded steady and forceful. She hoped no revealing shine lingered in her eyes.

He said nothing but did as she commanded.

Fianna admired the smooth skin and lean muscle of his buttocks. It seemed a shame to mark up such beauties with the switch. But curiosity and a sense of mischief won out. She raised the branch and brought it down but didn't try to put much force behind it. There was a small thwacking sound when it met flesh. He made no sound and didn't move. A very faint pink line showed on the skin.

The next time she struck just a little harder. Again he offered no reaction, but another light pink mark showed, the color spreading out a bit. She slapped the branch down several more times in succession. He never made a sound, and after a bit she realized, he wouldn't. He was a Norse warrior. She could whip him half to death and he wouldn't make a sound. Not that she wanted to do that. She didn't even care if she drew any reaction from him. She didn't want to hurt him, just to give him the same sort of different pleasure from it he'd brought to her. This was fun, unlike any experience she'd had before, this playing of the different sorts of games he seemed to enjoy as much as she did.

Four more swats, delivered a bit more sharply, drew low welts. She hoped she wasn't hurting him too much. Surely he would stop her if she was, but would it offend his warrior's pride to have to ask it?

She hesitated and lowered the switch. "Are you prepared to obey me now?" she asked.

He turned a burning gaze on her. "You haven't worked hard enough for it yet."

She sucked in a sharp breath and hoped she was up to the challenge he presented to her.

"So be it, then," she said and raised the branch.

She brought it down hard enough to elicit a disconcerting crack when it struck flesh. He didn't even grimace. She smacked again, harder. The next few strokes drew raised welts on his buttocks and thighs. Between the steamy atmosphere and the effort, sweat began to form on her temples. Five more hard lashes and he said, "I believe 'tis time for me to do as you ask."

She dropped the branch. "Do so, then."

He rolled over, barely suppressing a wince when his sore bottom touched the hard wood, and let his legs hang off either side of the bench. She sat on the end of the bench, straddling it, facing him, and reached down to touch him. His cock was full and thick.

Fianna leaned over and ran her tongue from the very base of it all the way to the tip in one long, slow swipe. His stoicism disappeared as his face tightened up, eyes squeezed shut, and tendons stood out on his neck. He groaned and muttered something in Norse.

"What is that?" she asked.

He drew in a breath. "You slay me so sweetly, my love."

"You're far from vanquished as yet, my hero."

She made another pass from base to tip, stopping to swirl her tongue around the thickness at several spots. He gasped and jumped. She licked over his balls until he moaned and wound his fingers in her hair. Then she moved up the length of his shaft and ran her tongue around the tip, probing into the small opening.

When she took the entire tip into her mouth and sucked on it gently he groaned in a way that sounded almost like a sob. The muscles of his thighs clenched hard beneath the hands she had resting on them.

"I cannot—" he groaned. "Cannot hold it much longer." He raised his head. "Your mouth or your quim?" he asked.

"Stay." She pushed down on his chest, then moved herself along the bench and lifted herself up enough to hover above him. Using her hand to guide it, she lowered herself onto his cock, impaling herself on him. She slid down until he was planted deep inside her. She was so hot and moist and ready for him, his cock slipped in easily.

They rocked together as he pushed up and she slid down on him. She liked this view. She liked being able to control the tempo of their movements and watching his face as the rhythm brought him pleasure and increasing tension.

Henrik reached up and tweaked the tips of her breasts. When she let herself down on him, it hit the spot deep inside that made her jump. The hot fire blazed within, needing him to quench it. She groaned as she bounced up and down faster and faster.

"Oh, Lord," she murmured. "Henrik. Love—" She screamed as he pinched a nipple hard at the same time his cock surged against her. It sent her over the edge in the spasms of release. She sobbed aloud as the heat exploded within her, sending repeated jolts through her body. He pushed into her two more times before the spasms of her release sucked him into spilling his seed.

The wonderful starbursts of pleasure kept firing off within her, launching her higher and higher into the oblivion of total ecstasy. For long minutes afterward, she did naught but sit there, clutching him within her body, disinclined to move or let him go. The pleasure softened and faded but left her peacefully spent.

She pulled herself off him and half collapsed to her knees by the side of the bench, her head pillowed on his stomach. He stroked her damp hair. They stayed that way for some time, content to be peaceful together, touching each other.

Eventually, though, he roused. She lifted her head and sighed. He stood up, went and picked something else up from a corner of the room. When he came back she saw he held a cake of soap.

"Now that we've sweated and licked all the dirt away, we use the soap to wash," he said. The note of humor in his voice told her he appreciated the mild irony of his words.

They used another bucket of water to soap themselves. Henrik poured water from the bucket over her hair and massaged the soap into it, careful to be sure none dripped forward into her eyes. The feel of his fingers rubbing at her scalp and slipping along the strands of her hair would have been arousing were she not already so sated.

She did the same for him, in turn, and found a different sort of satisfaction and intimacy in the task of soaping his hair. It roused again that possessive longing to have more of him than just these few stolen moments. She fought back the tears and won.

"Come now for the last part of the bath," he said, when she'd got his hair nicely full of lather. "The part that will make you feel refreshed."

He drew her to her feet and led her to the door, then out. She looked around, hoping no one could see them as they walked naked through the trees. They were alone, however, and she heard no sound of anyone else nearby. The cooler, drier air was a shock on her bare skin after the hot dampness of the sauna. It was naught compared with the shock when he led her along a path downhill to the river, and waded right in, dragging her with him.

"What are you doing?" she yelled at him as he pulled her along.

"This is the final step in getting truly clean," he said. "'Tis a shock at first, but get in it and you'll find it refreshing.

At the outset, at least, it wasn't refreshing at all; it was just cold. Her nipples tightened into pebbles and gooseflesh popped out all over her. She squealed as he plunged in, moving out in the water until he was up to his chest. He scooped up handfuls of water to rinse off his chest, then ducked his head in it to wash away the soap in his hair.

Fianna hesitated, but since she was already in the water, and had a head full of soapy hair, she followed his example. It was cold on her thighs, then on her belly and her breasts. It was cold on her shoulders and in her hair when she dipped it into the water to rinse off the soap.

"Now jump up and down a few times to get your blood moving," he advised. He held her hand and hopped with her, bobbing up and down in the water. After a few minutes she realized her body was adjusting to the water temperature and it wasn't too unpleasant. Still, she didn't object when he said it was time to go back.

They got out of the water and ran, hand in hand, up the hill back to the steam hut, laughing together like children, their wet hair streaming out behind them. They reached the hut and dressed quickly in the clean clothes left waiting for them. By the time she was dressed, Fianna had to admit that she did feel refreshed and revived in a way she rarely ever had. Perhaps the sauna and dip in the stream afterward accounted for part of that. It certainly wasn't all.

As they left, Henrik stopped and pulled her into his arms. He didn't kiss her or say anything, just stood, holding her against his body, her head cradled against his shoulder. Fianna didn't need words to hear all he tried to tell her of his gratitude, his joy in her company, his liking, his sadness, and his regret.

Tears began to form again but she held them back. She hadn't spent so much time fighting tears since the days following her mother's disappearance. And now she was faced with the loss of another she'd grown to care for. She drew a deep breath. She would have no regrets or sadness about this. The time with him had been a gift, and so she would regard it.

He sighed and let her go after a while. Hand in hand, they made their way back to the village and the hut where Ranulf lay.

As they neared the place, an uproar of arguing voices, tinged with some dismay, reached them. Fianna's stomach clenched as she wondered if Ranulf's condition had taken a turn for the worse while they were bathing. But surely someone would have come to tell them, had that been the case.

They had to push their way through a fair crowd of people to get to the room that held the patient and was the source of the disturbance. When they were finally close enough to see what was happening, she let out a long breath of relief.

Ranulf was awake, alert, and feeling sufficiently revived to want to get up and be about whatever business he thought needed his attention. Some of the group packed into the room attempted to keep him down. Others argued that he should be allowed to rise if he wished. At least, those were the impressions she got from the tone of the various interchanges in Norse.

Then Henrik said something loudly enough to be noticed by everyone. The room quieted and people turned in their direction. He spoke again and motioned toward the door. Fianna needed no translation for those words. A few people argued, but most did as he directed and filed out of the room. Ranulf said something to a couple of them as they left.

When they were alone in the room with just Ranulf, he and Henrik exchanged a few words, then Henrik said to her, "He says he feels strong enough to be up. Is this a good thing?"

"Let me look at his shoulder, and we'll see."

Ranulf lay quietly while she removed the bandage from the wound. He and Henrik exchanged a few words. The looks directed toward her suggested she was the subject of their conversation, but Henrik declined to translate.

Ranulf's injury looked significantly better than it had the previous time she'd changed the dressing. It no longer oozed so heavily, and the swelling and redness were much reduced. The red streaks radiating from it had disappeared, and even the discoloration from the bruising was fading. She put more salve and a fresh bandage on it and sat back, looking at her patient.

He watched her with a glint of amusement wrenchingly similar to a look she'd seen on Henrik's face. But then the grin faded and his expression grew serious. He said a few words to her.

Before Henrik translated, she guessed from the tone that he was offering thanks. Henrik confirmed it. "Ranulf knows you likely saved his life, and he offers you his gratitude."

"Tell him he is welcome. Healing is what I do."

Henrik conveyed that to his brother.

"He also wants to know if he can get up," Henrik added. "He says he is feeling much stronger."

"He needs to be careful of the shoulder, but if he has the strength, then I think it safe for him to get up. Let him try to sit up for a bit first, though."

As she anticipated, Ranulf experienced some difficulty just sitting up, even with his brother's assistance. As soon as he managed to get himself halfway upright, he swayed and turned very pale. Fortunately Henrik was prepared to catch him if he fainted. He didn't, but it was close. After a few gulps of air, Ranulf said something, and Henrik eased him back onto the mat.

"Tell him not to be too upset that it was so difficult this time," Fianna asked Henrik. "It will be easier next time, and by tomorrow he should be able to sit up for a little while."

As Henrik conveyed that information to Ranulf, a woman came into the room. She waited for Henrik to finish then spoke to him herself. Henrik nodded and answered, and Ranulf added something as well.

"My father requests we join him for a special meal to thank you," Henrik told her. "Ranulf said he'd like to rest for a while."

She nodded acceptance. Henrik escorted her to the largest of the longhouses in the settlement. On the way there, Fianna told him, "As Ranulf is recovering well, there is no need for me to stay here longer."

He didn't say anything for a moment. "It will be well into darkness before we finish tonight. Stay the night and I'll take you home tomorrow."

"Well enough."

"Fianna—" He stopped, both talking and walking. She halted with him, turning to look at him. She couldn't read all the expressions that chased across his face, but the pain and distress were obvious enough.

He drew a long breath and let it out slowly. "Never have I felt for a woman the way I feel for you. It makes it difficult for me to know what to do now. For most of my life, I've awaited this opportunity to go off and see the world, explore what it offers, and seek my fortune. Yet now that the time has arrived, a part of me would rather remain here with you. Even do I go, a piece of my heart will remain always with you. I'd ask you to wait for my return, yet I know you cannot do that. A choice is being forced upon you." He drew himself up as though bracing himself for an anticipated blow. "I know not..." He stopped for a moment before he said, "Do you ask it of me, I'll not go. I'll remain here and wed you myself."

The miserable tears were starting to collect in her eyes again. His face showed no expression now other than a stern resolve, but she knew what it had cost him to make the offer. She understood the depth of the sacrifice he offered to make, admired him for it, loved him for it. In truth she loved him for all the good things he was, this strong, honorable, intelligent man who struggled to do what was right, whatever the cost.

She desperately wanted to say the words, to ask him to remain with her. Her heart had never wanted anything more. She could imagine no greater happiness than sharing a lifetime with him. But because he was willing to be strong and noble, she owed it to him to be likewise.

Chapter Eleven

She straightened her back and drew a hard breath. "Nay," she answered. "Though I am grateful for your offer, and a part of me wants very much to say those words to you, yet will I not. You've told me how long you've waited for this chance to go exploring the world. Your heart yearns for it. Do you stay here at my request, you will never be completely happy. Always there will be something missing, and someday you'll begin to ask yourself what you might have lost for your loyalty to me. I would not be the cause of that. I love you too much to settle for a man who yearns for something else."

"My heart yearns for you, too," he answered. "It is being torn in half. I know not how to choose."

"I am choosing for you," she said. "The man I love now is not the one you will be in a few years, if your yearning for adventure and new sights be not assuaged."

His face tightened into an expression of pain. "I wish… You could wait for me here," he offered. "My father and my brother will shelter you and protect you."

She considered it for a moment, then shook her head. "Nay. It will do naught but cause disruption and possibly conflict between your village and mine. Should I return to town to serve someone who is ill, I'd do so under the shadow of death. Yet, did I not accede to someone's pleas for help, there would be anger and hard feelings about it. And should they learn that I'm here and yet unwed, I've no doubt Artur and the others will seek to capture and claim me."

He nodded slightly, then continued to stand there, watching her. The pain and conflict in his eyes was more than she could bear. She took his arm and turned him toward the longhouse. "It is settled. Do not tear yourself apart over it. You will go on your adventuring, and when you finally return, rich, sated, and ready to settle, if we're meant to be together, there will be a way."

She remembered the vision she'd seen in her dagger's jewel. In some way, he was her destiny. "There will be a way," she repeated, as much for herself as for him.

Use what you learn from the dagger wisely, her mother had told her. Why was wisdom so difficult and so unclear?

He nodded again and they went to the longhouse, where a crowd that surely comprised most of the settlement was already gathered and waiting. A round of cheering erupted and those who were seated stood as they entered the room.

A series of trestle tables were pushed together, end to end, to make one very long table that filled most of the space in the room. At the far end, Henrik's father waited. Two empty seats remained beside him at the head of the table. Henrik escorted her there and seated her in the middle place, where she would be between him and his father. The end of the table accommodated two people comfortably. Pressing her in between made it somewhat crowded, but neither of the men flanking her seemed to mind.

Servers carrying laden trays began delivering food. Each course of the many served that night were presented first to the three of them at the head and then passed on down the table. The quantity and variety of the offerings astonished her. They really had gone to considerable effort to make this meal a special thanks to her. At least three varieties of meats were offered, bowls of assorted vegetables, baskets of fragrant breads, and an assortment of fruits. Considering that it was spring, with no harvests yet in, they must have emptied some larders to accomplish this. She hoped no one would be short later as a result.

But to spurn anything would be to insult their efforts, so Fianna ate until she could hold no more without danger of exploding. Accompanying the food, pitchers of a strong-tasting, potent drink were passed around to fill the cups by each person's place.

When she asked Henrik about it, he told her, "'Tis mead, a drink of fermented honey. If you like it not, I can ask them to bring you water instead."

She sipped at it carefully. "Nay. It merely takes some adjusting to the taste, and the way it burns."

Much conversation and laughter occurred during the meal. Henrik translated some of the jests so she could share in their amusement, though in truth, many of them made little sense to her. Nonetheless she tried to smile and be gracious. With Henrik's help in translating, his father asked about her and the town, her family, how long she'd been a healer, and how she'd learned it.

He expressed sorrow to learn she had no parents or other relatives, then stunned her by telling her, through Henrik, that she must consider himself and his sons as her family. Should she ever be in need of anything, any help he could give, she must come to him. Fianna was touched by the obvious genuineness of the offer. There was some comfort in knowing she could believe in that promise and call on it if needed. She thanked him in turn for it.

The most difficult and most precious part of the evening, though, was being close to Henrik, talking with him, accepting morsels of food from him, watching him eat and drink. It might well be the last time she did so. Whatever the dagger might have shown, she had doubts she'd see him again after the morrow. She stored each view of him, each action, each expression, to be a comfort to her when he was no longer present. But otherwise she tried to bury the sorrow deep within. These people deserved better from her than morose acceptance of their hospitality.

She believed she succeeded, as no one seemed to notice anything amiss. Whenever she met a set of eyes around the table, the owner would smile at her, often saluting her with an upraised cup or piece of bread. She tried to acknowledge the greeting in like fashion.

The meal lasted far into the night, with courses being brought one at a time, and allowed to settle somewhat before the next appeared. By the time it ended, Fianna was so full she could barely move and so tired she could scarce keep her eyes open. She felt light-headed and dizzy as well, probably from the mead.

People finally began to rise and filter out. Henrik saw how sleepy she was getting and excused them both from the table, saying goodnight to his father. She was so woozy by then, she barely remembered making the trip from the longhouse to Henrik's home. Nor did she recall later how she'd gotten out of her clothes and into bed.

She woke in the morning with Henrik's arms around her and a feeling of dread anticipation hanging over her. This day she would leave and likely never see him again. Though he hadn't said when he would go, she imagined he wouldn't delay long now that his time had arrived. It was spring, as well—a good time for setting out on long journeys.

Before they rose, he held her and made long, slow, sweet love to her. As if he needed to memorize each inch of skin, each move, he stroked her up and down with infinite patience and gentleness, touching every sensitive spot, kissing her all over, until the need he could always rouse was screaming for unity with him. She stroked him as well, filling her senses with the feel of his flesh and hair, the scent of his body, the sound of his low moans of pleasure. She savored each one as a treasure to be guarded.

When he moved over her and filled her, she kept her eyes open, drinking in the sight of him as the exquisite pleasure tightened his features. She watched his face, hoarding the love she saw there. He slid into the final, stretched moments of highest tension before it let go with the release of his seed into her. Only then did she close her eyes. His last powerful stroke drove her over the edge as well, sending her to that soul-shattering place of jolting, shuddering joy.

Afterward they lay together quietly for a while. Neither of them wanted to move and end their final moments of private connection, but eventually the increasing light forced them into action.

They dressed quickly and broke their fast on warm porridge ladled from a large pot simmering in his father's house. Then the two young men who'd been with Henrik at the equinox festival arrived, dressed in riding gear and weapons. They'd brought Henrik's horse along with them.

Before they left, Ranulf emerged from the other room, standing shakily, a man and woman positioned on either side of him for support. With Henrik translating, he added his thanks and reiterated the promise for himself that she could at any time ask him for help and it would be granted. She kissed his cheek and warned him to take care and not try to do too much until he was stronger. Then she went outside with Henrik to the horses.

Fianna had an alarming moment of *déjà vu* when they lifted her onto the horse behind Henrik, but she wound her arms around him and held on tight all the way back to town. The trip didn't take nearly long enough.

Their journey through town to Marla's house again attracted attention, but no one followed them. When they reached the place, all of the men dismounted, but only Henrik accompanied her inside. Marla wasn't there, and Fianna was absurdly grateful since it gave them one last private moment for their farewells.

He drew her into his arms and kissed her, but only briefly. "I know not when I'll be setting out," he said, "but I hope it will be soon. Do not forget, though, if you have trouble or need anything, you can go to my father for protection."

"I won't forget," she promised. "I won't forget you either."

"Nor will I forget you. However far I sail, you will always ride with me in my heart."

"And you will have a home here in mine always."

He turned quickly and walked out the door. She watched him go directly to his horse, mount swiftly, and ride away.

Chapter Twelve

The days were long, the weeks endless. Time moved slowly through the next fortnight, as though it were a frozen river struggling toward the sea. Without Henrik her life seemed without purpose, without interest, without anything to hold her attention. She treated the sick and wounded, attended the dying, helped Marla with a difficult birth. None of it seemed to have the importance to her it held before. Where once this work had been the way she found value and purpose in life, now it seemed empty. Not that the intrinsic worth of her efforts had changed, but she had learned how much more there was to life. Having discovered the possibility of a soul-deep connection with another human being, its withdrawal left her with an aching hollowness inside.

And through it all ran the need to make a decision that would affect the course of the rest of her life. The choices were few and none of them excited her. Her thoughts continually turned to Henrik and what he might be doing at the time. She could almost picture him at the helm of his ship, sailing the waters, looking for new lands. She wondered what it felt like to be on a ship on the ocean.

She periodically ran into Artur, Jerrod, and Keovan, occasionally as a group, more often singly.

When she met them together, they glared at her but made no effort to stop or interfere. Clearly someone had warned them about their behavior and they'd taken the admonition to heart.

Each of the men sought her out on various occasions and attempted to woo her in their individual ways.

Jerrod boasted of his strength, his stamina, his future expectations of being important in the town. He wooed her with promises that he'd protect her from all dangers and build her a home that would make her the envy of every woman in town.

She thought of Henrik's size and strength, his ability to lead the men of his town. No one could ever protect her half as well as he could.

Artur reminded her again of the size of his equipment and swore he would satisfy her sexually as no other man could. Fianna fought down the temptation to laugh, but knowing it would be cruel as well as impolitic, she managed to keep her face in order and listened to him with an expression of mild interest.

Keovan again offered the necklace, as well as satins and laces and leather for fine clothing, and dreams of future riches.

Henrik was off chasing adventure and riches, perhaps not gold or silver, but experience, knowledge, new sights, and sounds. For a moment she visualized herself on the boat beside him as they sailed into the harbor of a strange and grand city unlike anything she'd ever seen before.

Even Walter, the blacksmith's apprentice, came to her one day while she was out in back of the house, digging in the garden. The big, hulking, awkward young man took the shovel from her and made short work of turning the dirt. She brought him water and food in thanks. He smiled, but when it came time to make his pitch, he was too abashed to say even a word. Instead he took her hand and sat, looking at her with large, pleading eyes. He finally stood up and moved to leave, clearly frustrated and unhappy with himself. She stopped him and thanked him. Her smile and kind words turned his attitude around, and he left, humming softly to himself.

Of the four choices, Fianna felt Walter might be the best. Though he was slow of thought and speech, his heart was good. He wouldn't repulse her. She might manage to live with the rest.

She wished there were more choices. Never before had she thought of the town as too small, too constricting, but now she felt its collective will wrapping around her and squeezing.

More and more she thought about Henrik and longed to be with him, whether here or off sailing the world.

But she was a healer, with important work to do. The town needed her.

The town would exile her did she not choose to settle down with some young man. The town valued its peace above her talent for treating the sick and injured. Perhaps she might as well have chosen to go off with Henrik on his adventuring. If he would have allowed it.

Too late to think on such now, though. He'd surely have already set off.

Time moved too slowly most of the time, as the empty minutes and hours dragged. Yet it sped all too quickly to a day when she'd have to make a decision and face the consequences of her choice.

It arrived before she was prepared to face it. Though she knew what her choice would be, Fianna still felt no joy or enthusiasm for the prospect of embracing it and committing to it.

On that final day, while others made excited preparation for the May Day celebrations on the morrow, Fianna kept to herself, working in the garden and organizing her herbs.

Artur, Jerrod, and Keovan each sought her out to make one last attempt to woo her and discover whether he was her choice. She gave none of them any encouragement, nor did she discourage them. She listened to their speeches, nodded, smiled for them, but told them nothing. When Artur tried to steal a kiss, she kept herself still and unmoving until he realized she would not be cajoled in that way.

Night fell at last, and a bonfire was lit in the town center. Musicians warmed up their instruments and fell to playing happy, dancing melodies. Food and wine were passed around. Fianna stood at the side of the town square, away from the bulk of the crowd, and watched, unable to join in the revels.

After a while Alfred and a group of the town's most influential people stepped up to the dais where the musicians played. When Alfred raised his hand, the music stopped. Drawn by the sudden cessation, people turned to see what was happening. Laughter and conversation died out. A hush spread over the gathered group. Fianna's heart began to pound faster and harder.

"We have an important piece of business to take care of this evening before we can return to the celebration," Alfred announced to the crowd. "Some weeks ago, a young woman of this town was made aware that she was causing a disruption to our peace and unity. She was told that on this night she would have to make a decision, in order to keep the harmony of our town."

He waited a moment, clearly enjoying being the center of attention. "Fianna, daughter of Eislinn, come forward."

She drew a deep breath and moved toward the dais. Her legs felt rubbery, and she wondered that they held her up. She passed Marla. The woman gave her a nod of support.

As she walked into the space in front of the dais that had been cleared for her, she noticed that the candidates for her hand were pressing forward as well. Artur, Jerrod, and Keovan pushed through the group to be near the front. Walter stood nearby, watching patiently.

Alfred raised his voice again. "Fianna, have you made a choice?"

She had to clear her throat to get rid of the lump in it before she could answer. "I have."

Chapter Thirteen

Another group of men was also making their way through the crowd toward her. Tall, fair, two of them very blond. Norsemen. One of them looked like... Was it possible? Her breath caught again when she recognized Henrik, accompanied by a recovered Ranulf and the two other companions who'd been with him at the previous bonfire. Surely Henrik should have left by then. Why was he here?

Alfred had waited for her to continue, but when she didn't, he prompted, "Who is your choice, then?"

A possible answer occurred to her, but it was so absurd, so truly ridiculous, she hardly dared even consider it. Still...

"May I have a moment to ask a question?" Fianna requested. "It will not take long."

Alfred considered, then nodded.

Fianna walked over to the group of Norsemen and stopped, facing Henrik. She had to restrain tears to be able to look into his beloved face, when she hadn't expected to see him again and still might be facing the loss. Though she fought it, a spark of hope dawned. He didn't smile at her, but there was something akin to sympathy in his eyes.

"I thought you would have left this land," she told him. "Why are you here?"

"My ships set sail at first light tomorrow." He stopped and drew a breath. "I could not leave until I knew you were settled. I...I needed to assure myself you would have all the choices you needed."

Her heart swelled with love for the man. How could she even consider choosing any other? It was all she could do to keep from throwing herself into his arms. Hope began to grow, though she dared not indulge it. The thought was daring, different, startling, unheard of. He might yet refuse her.

It took a moment to work up the nerve to ask her question. She drew a breath to calm herself. She clenched her hands into fists to still their shaking.

"Henrik, would you take me with you?" she asked.

Her request startled him. For long moments, he did naught but stand there, eyes widening into amazement as he considered all the implications.

"A ship is no good place for a woman," he answered carefully. "The conditions are rough, there is little privacy, much work to do, and few comforts."

"If I were with you, that would be all the comfort I needed. And I should very much prefer it to a lifetime of greater comfort here with someone who was not you."

"There are many dangers. It is no safe place to be."

"I do not want safety. I want to go adventuring with you. And someday, God willing, to return and settle down with you and our family."

His hands were clenched as well, his body so tense, a good push would knock him flat. "Fianna, are you certain you understand what you're asking? It will be a hard life, with constant peril."

"On our first night together, I made a promise to you to do all you would ask, without knowing what that might be. I would now make a promise to you to go into whatever danger you face along with you, trusting to your best efforts to keep us safe, knowing there's a risk that might not be enough. I will work as hard as any of the men, share whatever discomforts and perils might arise, and ask only that I be allowed to share some time with you as reward. Is that enough?"

A slow smile spread across his face. "If you are sure, nothing could make me happier than to have you come with me. Though I would not have asked it of you, if it is your will and your desire, I will rejoice in it."

She could barely hold back the tears as relief and a swelling joy filled her. "Come with me, if it please you," she said, taking his arm and drawing him toward the dais.

"This is my choice," she said to Alfred and all those watching. "Henrik, Hjallmar's son. We will leave this place for a while, but I hope to return with him some day. I would beg that I be allowed to return at that time."

Alfred looked as startled as everyone else gathered around. There was much murmuring and some consternation over her choice. After considering it for a while, Alfred answered, "We directed only that you should make a choice of one man or leave, under pain of death. No restrictions were placed on who you might consider. You have fulfilled the requirement to choose a protector. I deem it wise that you do go away for a while to let hard feelings fade, but you may return, if you so desire, settle here, and move freely among us."

"I thank you," she said.

Henrik's arms came around her and he kissed her thoroughly in the midst of the crowd. There was much laughter and some cheering as it went on and on. Finally he drew away.

"My ships sail at dawn, and we've much to do before then." As he led her through the crowd, back to Marla's house, he added, "We'll collect what you wish to take with you. There is little space on the ships, so choose carefully. I'll ask my father to perform the mating ceremony for us this night. They are having the Walpurgis celebration in our village with a bonfire and music and food. My father will rejoice to add this to it. We'll have to stay a while and be merry with my people, but eventually we'll get some time to ourselves. Perhaps just enough to launch us well-satisfied."

He stopped and kissed her again. "'Tis a small pity we'll get no sleep this night, but there will be time in the future to make up for it."

He kissed her some more. It made her heart swell and the heat rouse in her belly. She pressed herself against him as need for him clamored for fulfillment.

So lost were they in the feelings they had for each other, both jumped when Ranulf laid a hand on a shoulder of each of them.

"It is good," he said in halting, accented Anglish. "But go now."

Henrik laughed and slapped his brother on the shoulder. "It is good," he agreed. "And now I have a lifetime to enjoy it."

Chapter Fourteen

The Norse Walpurgis night celebration was in full roar as they rode up to the settlement. Fianna rode behind Henrik on his horse, holding onto him, though this time it was more from a desire to be close, to hold and to feel him than from fear of falling off.

In the open area in front of the semicircle of buildings, several bonfires blazed high. Around them the people of this town gathered in groups or walked in circuits. Children charged in small packs, yelling and screaming. It appeared everyone was making noise — not the music it would be in her town, but a cacophonous racket created by banging boards together, cracking whips, and ringing bells.

"What is all the noise for?" she asked Henrik, after they'd dismounted and were making their way through the crowd in search of his father. She had to yell to make herself heard over the melee.

"To drive away the witches and evil spirits, so they won't bother the crops soon to be planted," he shouted back.

They finally found his father with a group of elders of the settlement. A huge smile broke over the older man's face when he saw his sons returning with Fianna. Hjallmar opened his arms as she approached and drew her to him, folding her in a bear hug that surprised her with its strength. Henrik and his father held a long conversation in Norse. In the older man's face puzzlement was chased away by concern and then finally by delight. After a bit he nodded and began to chatter with some of the others gathered nearby. A considerable commotion ensued.

A group of excited, laughing women drew her away. Henrik nodded for Fianna to go with them. "They'll help you prepare," he assured her. "There isn't time to ready all the ceremonies and arrangements for a normal Wedding among us, but we'll do all we can."

An hour or so later, dressed in borrowed finery, wearing a crown of green vines with a few pale flowers woven in, she followed the same women back to the center of the town. They marched ahead of her single file, in procession, toward a group of men waiting for them. Henrik's expression as she approached him set her heart pounding harder and more rapidly.

She moved through most of the ceremony in something of a daze. Later she would remember that they exchanged rings placed on the hilts of a pair of swords. Ranulf provided a sword for her. Henrik explained that the bride traditionally brought a sword to give her husband in exchange for his, which she would keep to give to their son. They clasped hands on the hilt of the sword she presented to him. His father said a few words to them. Henrik proclaimed something in Norse, then prompted her to make her vows, letting her repeat each phrase after him. He didn't translate, however, so she had to assume she'd promised to be faithful, to love, and to honor him.

At the end Henrik's father extended his hands toward them, said a few words, and a cheer broke out from the crowd. People began scooting around again. Some gathered close around them, folding each of them in hugs and words of congratulation. Others ran to and from the longhouses, bringing out trestles to set up a table, setting out food on it, and fetching a pitcher of mead and cups.

She, Henrik, and Hjallmar were led to the three chairs that had been placed beside the table. Henrik seated her in the center again. Young women who'd obviously changed hastily into their best gowns brought more food, and pushed the pitcher of mead toward Fianna, along with two cups. Then they stood around and waited.

"You should pour some mead into a cup and help me drink from it," Henrik directed.

Fianna nodded, filled the cup, and held it to his lips. It took an effort to steady her hands. Being so close to him, watching the expressions on his face, the way his lips parted to sip from the cup, while his gaze stabbed into her, all combined to overwhelm her with love and gratitude. Desire for him rose again, as it always seemed to when he was near. The firelight that made the area so bright cast wicked, sparkling reflections in his eyes.

The feasting went on for a while. Having learned her lesson, Fianna was careful with the mead, drinking only enough to make her pleasantly relaxed. She ate even less. She didn't need food. She felt replete with the unexpected happiness and reached over to touch Henrik as often as she could manage. She needed the contact to convince her this whole evening was happening and wasn't just some dream of her longing imagination.

When the feast ended and the bonfires began to die down, Henrik stood up. Immediately a group of men surrounded him, while many of the women surrounded Fianna and began to chivy her off toward Henrik's house. Since he still stood with the men in the square, she looked at him for direction. He smiled and nodded for her to go with the women.

They took her into Henrik's house and off to the sleeping area. The borrowed finery was removed and replaced with a brand-new, white linen night rail. Though they took off the floral crown, they put it back on before they helped her into the bed and covered her with a sheet. Then they stood around and waited, sharing jokes and giggles. Fianna planned to learn the language as quickly as she could.

A few minutes later, they heard the men at the door. The group entered amidst loud gibes and boisterous joking. The women moved back against the walls to make room for the newcomers. Though she hated to take her eyes off Henrik, Fianna did notice a few of the young women eyeing the men.

With his entourage surrounding him, Henrik came and stood by the bed where she lay. His smile drove all other thoughts from her mind. She wanted him more than anything in the world. She'd never stop wanting him.

He knelt by the side of the bed and leaned over to kiss her. A cheer went up from the onlookers when he removed the floral crown from her head and set it aside. He kissed her again and stood up. The men helped him remove his vest and shirt, belt and boots, but when one of them reached for the laces on his leggings, Henrik stopped them. A sharp order from him raised eyebrows of most of the people in the room. Moments later they began to file out. Several threw a few jests or teasing comments behind as they went.

Finally, they were alone. Henrik went to the door to be sure all were gone. Fianna watched him return to her, admiring again his beautiful form, the way the torchlight created gold ripples in his hair, the supple grace of his movements.

He knelt by her again and began to roll the night rail up, kissing each stretch of skin along her legs, stomach, and breasts as he revealed them. Finally he dragged the cloth up and over her head. He explored her body with fingers and lips until she was moaning and writhing in a fiery heat of need for him. While he sucked on her nipples, she reached for the laces of his leggings, pulled them open, and dragged the leather off, releasing his rampant cock.

She reached for it and wrapped her fingers around it. A couple of pumps up and down had him gasping as well.

He reached down and stilled her hand. "Fianna, I need...I've waited too long. I cannot hold..."

She spread her legs and drew him toward her. "I need you, too. Touch me. Fill me. Please!"

He positioned himself and pushed in. Fianna wrapped her arms around him, kissing every bit of flesh she could reach, running her fingers into his hair. She couldn't get enough of him. She never would. Then he moved in and out. His balls pressed against her quim and she began to tense with the need.

His breathing was harsh and ragged as he fought for control and lost. "I cannot..." he gasped. "I cannot hold it."

"Don't." With her body she urged him deeper and faster. "Come to me," she begged him.

The rhythm quickly grew to frantic. They both gasped and moaned as the fire in their blood drove them toward completion. Fianna was nearly sobbing as he slammed into her.

It broke over her like a sudden sharp wave, convulsing her body, drawing a small shriek from her as the pleasure overwhelmed her. While she jolted and spasmed against him, he poised above her one last time, then rammed himself all the way in. He spurted his seed into her with a long gasping moan.

They held onto each other while their breathing slowly returned to normal. Lying under him, Fianna wished she would never have to move again. Heaven was right there, joined with him. She regretted it when he rolled off her and settled beside her, but he immediately drew her up against him, settling her head in the crook of his shoulder.

"I must have won the favor of the gods," Henrik said to her. "Though I know not how. Yet in a short time I've gained the opportunity I've waited for all my life and the lady I've waited for all my life to share it. I cannot think I've deserved so much, yet I'll not refuse it."

"You certainly won't," Fianna answered. "I am blessed as well. To have gained your love is a treasure I could never have hoped for. Tell me about your ships and where we sail to."

For the next hour or so, as they lay together, he described his ships, what they looked like, how they sailed, how they judged the winds, knew how to steer, and where they would plan to go. His enthusiasm for the adventure ignited her own interest. They discussed places they might go and sights they hoped to see.

After a while, though, he began to caress her breast, and the banked heat roused inside her.

"This time we go slow," he promised her, as he nuzzled at her throat. "Now that you are mine, I want to know every inch of you, and show you what it means to belong to me."

"As I would know every inch of my husband," she answered, marveling at that word and the reminder they were bound together.

He began a very slow exploration of her body, using both hands and lips, searching out every interesting curve, each fold of skin, every sensitive area, and all the little hidden places. His touches made her gasp and squeal. When she insisted on doing the same, he lay back and let her fingers roam over his flesh until he couldn't bear her caresses any longer.

He knelt and flipped her over onto her belly, then tugged her up to her knees. Fianna wondered what he was about. She felt oddly exposed and vulnerable in that position. At first, though, he merely continued his explorations, running his hands over her bottom, prying apart the cheeks to run first his finger and then his tongue up and down the crack. The sensation was unnerving and exciting at the same time.

"Which of those young men would you have chosen, had I not come along to offer you another choice?" Henrik asked her.

Puzzled by the question, she turned to look at him. A light of mischief danced in his eyes.

In the same playful spirit, she answered, "I am still not sure. They all offered me great gifts. Jerrod would have given me a grand home to live in."

He suddenly brought his hand down sharply in a loud spank on her bottom. "Jerrod is not for you," he said. He spanked again and she squealed at the burning pain. "I have a home. 'Tis simple, true, but solid, and will shelter us well when we return." Another smack on her bottom had her wiggling. He wrapped an arm around her waist to steady her.

The burning pain of spanks faded quickly but left a sizzling excitement behind. The moisture began to gather at her quim.

"Artur promised to pleasure me well and leave me satisfied," she continued.

He spanked her even harder. She wriggled, but the burning was such a sweetly intense agony, feeding the fires he was rousing, she wanted more rather than to escape.

"Artur is not for you. No man will ever satisfy you as I can," he proclaimed and followed the words with another series of spanks.

"Keovan offered me a gold chain necklace and other riches."

Smack. He spanked her twice more. "Keovan is not for you. Someday I'll put gold chains around your neck and your wrists and your ankles. Perhaps I'll even wrap one around your waist and down around here." He traced a line with his finger down the crack between her bottom cheeks, before he spanked her again. A series of sharp whacks covered her bottom with liquid, burning heat.

"And then there was Walter, the blacksmith's apprentice," she added. "He's a bit slow and offered me nothing but his good nature. It might have been enough."

Whap! He smacked even harder. "It would not have been enough, and well you know it," he said. "Walter is not for you." He rubbed her aching bottom and it helped transmute the remaining pain into sizzling desire. "You belong to me and only to me." A few more sharp, hard spanks, punctuated the words. "I'll love you and shelter you and pleasure you and care for you from this day forward."

One more hard spank made her cry out. He stopped and rubbed her bottom again, caressing it so sweetly she began to move against his hand. He reached forward and took one of her breasts in his hand to knead it. A finger of the other hand traveled down the crack and into the slit to find her engorged bud. The sensations were so delicious, she could barely stay in position.

He moved so that he was behind her as she remained on her hands and knees. His hard cock probed at her backside for a moment, then slid into her. He reached around her to hold and caress her breasts while he pumped into her. The angle was different and felt strange at first, but as she adjusted to it, he found again the sweet spot inside her that jolted her with lightning bolts of pleasure.

He squeezed and pinched her nipples, bringing her more of the sweet pleasure-pain that was driving her wild. He withdrew his cock, only to plunge in again, harder and deeper. With his body covering her, she could feel his tension mount along with hers. The pressure built within her until she knew not how she could contain any more, yet his fingers and his cock continued to push her higher and tighter.

One of his hands moved down to her slit and stroked over her bud, softly, then harder. She screamed as the pressure suddenly burst and huge spasms rocked her. It took her out of herself completely, into a universe of brilliant lights and thunderous explosions.

Henrik came as well, spurting into her with a roar of triumph. His climax seemed to roll on forever, joining the rocking jolts that continued to blast through her. They moved in tight rhythm, absorbing each other's spasms and feeding them back, keeping it rolling through them until exhaustion finally brought them to collapse.

Henrik fell over, taking her with him. They lay together on their sides, her back to him, their bodies aligned and touching from shoulders to feet.

"You're mine," Henrik proclaimed again. "Mine for the rest of our days. And I can scarce wait for all the days ahead of us. There's so much yet for us to do and to learn. So many more things to try. We'll make love in the ocean some day. And on the beach. In the ship, with the waves rocking us. Whatever makes you happy. I'll spend the rest of my days making you happy."

She turned in his arms and kissed him. "Someday we'll make love on the top of a great mountain. We'll be together in distant lands. We'll find wonders beyond imagining and see such sights as great tales are made from. Yet none will compare to what I've already seen. You are the greatest wonder of my life and such a treasure as I could never hope to find."

About the author:

KATHERINE KINGSTON welcomes mail from readers. You can write to her c/o Ellora's Cave Publishing at P.O. Box 787, Hudson, Ohio 44236-0787.

Also by KATHERINE KINGSTON:

- Binding Passion
- Daring Passion
- Ruling Passion

NIGHT OF FIRE

Vonna Harper

To everyone who shares my love of spring's energy and life.

Chapter One

A fine mist drifted around the silent maiden and her companions. Like her, the other five wore simple gray gowns that skimmed their youthful bodies. They were all barefoot, and their hair hung to their waists. Except for the deep charcoal color of her hair, the only thing that made this maiden different from the other virgins was a singular brightness to her deep-set green eyes. Someone who took the time to study her would conclude that either this one was higher-born or more intelligent than the others; they would have been right on both accounts.

"She comes," a slightly pudgy maiden with small hands and feet whispered. "All night I prayed to the spring-spirits and simmered dried lavender to give The Lady strength."

The green-eyed virgin said nothing. If Kilee needed to believe that the spirits would heed the plea of an untested girl, so be it. As for her, she would simply wait.

The woman who'd been chosen by her knowledge of all things mystical to approach the Church's angry, powerful priests, rode a white stallion with flowing mane and tail. The Lady's own hair was as long as the stallion's tail and nearly as pale. She'd draped it over her right shoulder, perhaps so she wouldn't risk sitting on it, perhaps because only that covered her nakedness.

At the sight of The Lady's unclothed state—proof that she'd failed at her mission—the virgins dropped to their knees on the wet, clover-coated earth. All sobbed except for the green-eyed one. She would have, too, except that her heart and head had already told her the priests would not listen to The Lady.

With each hoof beat, the green-eyed one felt, not the approaching horse, but an earth-drumbeat. The sound was as old as her grandmother's, grandmother's memory. Respect and submission called for her to drop her gaze from The Lady, but she continued to look up at the clan's most beautiful and revered woman.

Although she was still exquisite, the green-eyed one noted fine lines around The Lady's eyes and mouth and felt the sorrow and determination that permeated every inch of her being. When The Lady locked eyes with her, the green-eyed one returned her gaze.

"I do not wear the robes of my station," The Lady said. "Because my mission is incomplete."

"The priests—they have not decided?" someone asked hopefully.

"Oh, they have," The Lady said. "They hear only their own truth; it is beyond them to accept anything different." She shook her head. "I did not have to go into their cold, dark building to know what their words would be. Even now it is being written on parchment so their decision can be sent to each clan's leaders." She took a deep breath as if gathering the strength to continue. "Our ancient rites to insure the return of spring have been declared heathen, the work of devils. They have been banished from the land."

"That cannot be!"

"Winter will never end."

"Plants will not grow anew; there will be no crops."

"No fertility dances? No sacred night unions? Without that there will be no babies."

The green-eyed one listened to her companions' wails but didn't add her greatest concern, that if virgins didn't make love in the fields, the earth would not be made fertile. Instead she waited until the wailing had faded away before getting to her feet and walking over to the woman she considered her Queen.

"You say that your mission is incomplete, my Lady," she said softly. "Why did you come to us, to virgins, when the leaders of all the clans wait to offer their advice?"

The Lady looked down at her, seemingly oblivious to the rain dripping from her temple down the sides of her neck. Was that a smile? "What is your name, child?"

"My — my mother named me Heather."

"Heather." The Lady leaned over her horse to draw Heather's hair back from her face. "Green eyes," she said softly. "The color of the wood spirits."

"That — that is what my grandfather said when he first held me. I am the only one in my family with…"

"Tell me, child. Do you feel as if you are different from your brothers and sisters and from these, your companions?"

"I, ah, I am impatient. I want more than to plant gardens and tend sheep. I love to sit near the elders and listen to their wisdom. I…my grandfather taught me to read."

"Excellent. What do you think of our rites and ceremonies? Perhaps you believe the priests who came great distances to teach us their ways are right, that the setting of great fires by three times three men using wood from the sacred trees to celebrate the triumph of light over the dark half of the year is pagan. Perhaps you have read books that taught you it is foolish for the villagers to bring their animals to the highest place where the sacred fires burn so the animals can walk between them and thus be protected from disease and sterility."

"No, never!"

"Hm. Have you read the great black books the priests brought with them? Perhaps you have gone to Church to listen to them preach."

"I have gone," she admitted because the women in her family had taught her to never apologize for her thirst for knowledge and because she believed it was important to understand the newcomers' religion. "But I do not believe what they say."

"Why not?"

"Because my heart and soul believe that the way of my ancestors is the true one," she said, her voice strong. "The earth and sun which are our mother and father must be revered, not the Church's god who I have never seen or heard."

The Lady slid weightlessly to the ground. One breast poked through the curtain of long hair. She held a strange silver, long-bladed dagger, but Heather had no fear of it. Instead, her own hand burned with the need to feel its weight.

"The spirits told me I would find you this morning," The Lady said.

"Me?" Her wet clothes should have had her shaking with cold, shouldn't they? Instead, she felt hot.

"Maia, it is not for us to question or fully understand the earth-born forces that rule us. Our duty is to believe."

Maia?

"I do believe," she whispered. "From the time I was old enough to know what it meant to be a girl, I knew it was my duty to surrender my virginity on Bel-fire night so the seed spilled will nourish the land."

"And nourish you, Maia. Fill you with a child."

"If it is so willed."

"You are right. Not all girls and women become pregnant on Bel-fire night. Only those whose fruit is ripe."

Heather—or should she now call herself Maia?—felt no hesitancy in talking about her fertility. How could she when her entire life had been about that one thing—or it would have been if the dour priests and their soldiers who'd arrived in deepest winter hadn't forbidden that most holy of celebrations.

"What do you want of me, My Lady?" she asked.

Another soft smile touched The Lady's lips. "Good. I did not have to tell you why we are speaking; you knew."

"Am I now Maia?"

"You are. The first Maia was once a mountain nymph, but she became a goddess."

Maia had to struggle against the impulse to admit she had no desire to become a goddess. "Some say the first Maia was wife of Zeus," she said. "Mother of Hermes who is the god of magic, and that her parents were Atlas and the sea nymph Pleione."

"You are well-read."

"I am only a simple village maiden."

"Are you?" The Lady extended the dagger toward her and turned it so she could see a red jewel imbedded in the hilt just above where the blade began. "What is in there?" The Lady asked.

Maia wiped off the rain clinging to the irregular, polished red stone. Doing so heated her fingers, but she wasn't afraid. The dagger and predominant jewel were beautiful, a combination of deadly strength and mystery. Although she knew the other virgins had gotten to their feet and were crowding around, she paid them no mind.

The more she concentrated on the exquisite jewel, the more she became aware of a heat between her legs, in the place where a man would place his seed-bearer.

"Fire," she whispered. She blinked and leaned closer. "I see fire. And people dancing. I hear drums. Drums that seem to come from the roots of the deepest tree, perhaps deeper. There is...a hill with a strange unfinished structure, and a woman who..."

"What about the woman?" The Lady pressed.

"She looks like you, only she wears a garment of many colors that flutters about her like butterflies. Flowers hang from her hair and clothes; they are everywhere on her. She is not alone."

"What?" one of the other virgins asked. "I see nothing. What a strange dagger. The workmanship is the finest I have ever seen."

Ignoring them, The Lady wrapped her arm around Maia and drew her to her side. Maia felt her warm nakedness. "Who is with her?" The Lady asked.

"Handmaidens. They are all dressed in white, and there is a man in green and other men who are red even on their faces."

"Do you know where this place is?"

The Lady's somber tone caught her attention, and she looked up at her. "No. My Queen, it does not seem to be of our time."

"No, it is not." The Lady squeezed Maia's shoulder. "Look. Tell me everything."

For the first time since The Lady approached, Maia felt fear. Still, she did as she was ordered. "There is great activity and movement. So much drumming that I can hear nothing else. Now—now I am no longer looking at the flower woman. Many, many people are standing and watching. I see..."

"What do you see, Maia?"

Maia shivered, and yet she felt even hotter. She couldn't get enough air into her lungs, and the fire between her legs threatened to overwhelm her.

"A man."

"Only one?"

Determined to answer her Queen as fully as possible, Maia brought her face even closer to the stone and waited for the fine mist to clear. There were many, many men, women, even children standing near the top of the hill where the dancers and fires were, but although she'd never seen clothes like they were wearing, it didn't matter. Only that one man did.

"He is dark," she said. "Large. He stands alone."

"Dark?"

Maia's breasts felt heavy, and it was all she could do not to press her hands between her legs to try to silence the energy there.

"Black hair. Eyes of the same color. He watches what is happening. Sometimes..."

"Go on."

"Sometimes I see him, the man. Sometimes he is a bull."

"It is *him*."

Alerted by the awe in The Lady's voice, Maia continued to stare. "Who is he?"

"The man who must come to us. Taurus."

Maia didn't know whether to turn and run or try to climb into the scene the jewel had revealed. If it wasn't for The Lady's body next to hers, she might not have been strong enough to stand.

"The bull Taurus," The Lady whispered. She stepped away from Maia and extended the dagger toward her. "Take this gift. It came to me, for me to pass onto you. Go home. Tell your family that you must leave. You do not know when you will return."

Without hesitation, Maia closed her fingers around the dagger. It felt heavy, warm, alive. "Where am I going?"

"To where the red stone has shown. To reach Taurus. Trust, Maia. Believe. Be true to who and what you are."

Chapter Two

Taron Stanten woke as he always did, fully alert and with a hard-on. Even before he opened his eyes, he'd assessed his surroundings and knew he wasn't in his San Francisco penthouse. That didn't surprise him since business kept him out-of-town more than not, particularly now. He became aware of a not unpleasant smell, something earthy. Going by the cool air on his cheeks, he guessed that the window in whatever bedroom he was in was open.

Sitting up, he swung his feet over to the side of the unfamiliar bed and stared down at his naked body. Yep, his cock was still in perfect operating condition, a little surprising given the stress of the last few months. The window was open, and through it he could hear a faint, not unpleasant sound—drumming, unless he was hung over.

He was never hung over. Even on those rare occasions when he drank with abandon, he'd been blessed with a cast-iron stomach. As a result, when the business associates he wined and dined might wish they'd been shot and put out of their misery, he kicked any residual lethargy out of his system by going for a run.

When he walked over to the window and spotted the nearby hill with the unfinished Athenian acropolis at the top, the pieces fell together. He was in Edinburgh, Scotland and that was Calton Hill. He was here because his college roommate Paul Livingston now lived in Edinburgh and had invited him to stay for a couple of days before going on to London for a series of high-powered and high-stress meetings that would decide the future of the company he'd created.

"Good idea, Paul," Taron muttered. "Nothing like going on vacation—the first vacation I've had in years—before turning back into the stubborn, bull-nosed bastard those bastards think I am."

He was, damn it! Wasn't his company's enviable position on the stock exchange and countless glowing articles in financial magazines proof of that? Unfortunately, his success had bred greed on the part of the competition, which had led to the hostile takeover bid that now consumed him. Even with that weighing on him, he had to admit that for a bounced-around foster kid, he hadn't turned out half bad — rich enough to be considered a multi-millionaire. His business was on the cutting edge of electronic technology. Hell, he'd even been an honored guest at the White House, twice.

Only from the looks of the goat staring back at him, oblivious to his straining cock, not everyone was impressed.

* * * * *

The goat, Paul had told him that evening as the two men shared a beer, was part of some local spring festival that would be getting underway in a few minutes.

"The city fathers would just as soon keep animals out of the Beltane celebration," Paul explained. He lit a cigarette before continuing. "But local farmers are always dragging them in. That's why I'm glad you could make it for this. My friend, Beltane is like nothing you've ever seen."

Taron groaned. "I thought we were going to relax."

"You don't know the meaning of the word."

He couldn't argue with that. At the same time, he didn't feel up to telling Paul that the energy that had gotten his business to where it was, had changed focus from intellect and creativity, to finance and survival; if he did, the conversation might turn to the strategic meetings he'd set up, how vital they were, how high the risks. These days, just thinking of what was at stake drained him. Yes, he could still run rings around most people and had enough ideas to keep the company on the

Vonna Harper

cutting edge for the rest of his life, and he'd sure as hell never disappointed a woman between the sheets, but...

"You'll see," Paul went on. "As soon as the music starts, you'll be off your ass. Besides, that's what Beltane's about—humping any girl you can get to drop her shorts for you."

"What the hell are you talking about?"

Paul scratched his head with the hand holding the cigarette. Then he ran his hand through his hair to make sure he hadn't left any ashes there. "Damn, I've got to kick that filthy habit."

"Then do it."

"Don't push me. I've—" A coughing spasm bent Paul over. Finally he gasped and straightened.

Taron held out his hand. "Give me the damn lighter," he ordered. "Until you get a new one, you aren't smoking. You want to die before your time?"

"You're a hell of a one to talk. At the rate you're going, your ticker will give out before you reach forty."

"Give me the damn lighter," Taron interrupted.

Paul stared at him, then shrugged. "What the hell." He dug into his pocket and handed Taron the expensive silver lighter. "Maybe it'll work."

Taron had his doubts but tucked the lighter in his pocket anyway. "So tell me about this festival."

"Shit. Look, all I know is that Beltane takes place on April 30—something to do with celebrating spring. There's dancing and drumming until you think the top of your head's going to come off, but you don't care. There's some kind of play or something with people dressed in costumes. They paint their skin different colors and jump through fire. That's where the animals come in."

"They're roasted?" Taron didn't like the idea of that cute little goat winding up on someone's dinner plate.

124

"Hell no. Like I said, farmers and anyone who feels like it brings their livestock near the smoke. Some kind of purification thing, I guess."

"Sounds like chaos. And you think I'd give a damn? Why?"

Paul laughed and punched Taron on the shoulder. "Because it's *the* night to get laid. It's like the whole place turns into a huge orgy. People jump the nearest bones. I know; I know. You don't have to look for excuses to have the broads fighting each other over the chance to rock and roll with you, but you've got to admit, it sounds like a hell of a lot more fun than picking up some broad at a bar."

* * * * *

Movement, noise, light and dark. Flames from the fire at the top of the hill seemed to dance with the night sky. What had to be thousands of people packed Carlton Hill, and so many musical groups were doing their thing that Taron felt as if his head might explode.

Despite his better judgment, he'd agreed to accompany Paul in trekking up the steep staircase once it got dark. What he hadn't counted on was the sheer mass of bodies he'd encounter. One moment Paul had yelled at him to look back down for a panoramic view of the city. The next, he'd lost his friend.

He'd briefly thought about going back to Paul's place, but that would mean fighting the tide of humanity surging upward. Besides, there was something about the music — especially the drums. The longer the frantic-sounding beats went on, the more his body seemed to absorb them.

He *had* to get closer to the action.

Using his size and strength, he pushed past knots of laughing, yelling merrymakers until he caught a glimpse of a group of brightly costumed people who were obviously the center of attention. Most noticeable was a tall woman dressed in veils of every color in the rainbow. In addition, she was weighed down by flowers and assorted greenery. She was surrounded by a number of women dressed entirely in white who looked for all the world as if they were protecting the rainbow woman. A man who was green from head to foot hung near Rainbow Woman. In contrast to the others' exuberant dancing, he trudged along like an old man.

"Hell if I know what that's about," Taron muttered.

The group had been whirling to and fro in one spot, but now a number of Blue Men — Taron couldn't think of anything else to call them — presented themselves to Rainbow Lady and her attendants.

Suddenly the drumming kicked up a notch. Now the earth itself seemed responsible for the driving rhythm; it was almost as if lava was trying to break free. Barely aware of what he was doing, he swayed with the reverberation. Extending his arms, he stomped and whirled, grunted in time. His vision blurred; he no longer cared about the celebration, about tomorrow's agenda, or the rest of his life.

He was — simply *was* part of the force and power.

Wild, free, totally in the moment, he looked up. The night was clear, making it possible to see the stars. Stars? How long had it been since he'd studied the sky? Danced? Existed only in this single moment?

No one seemed to notice his pounding, driving legs; no one cared that this sophisticated and wealthy businessman could barely catch his breath and had broken out in sweat. How could they when many of his fellow celebrants were under the same spell?

A kink in his neck forced him to look down. The crowd had shifted, blocking his view of the performers. He started to look for a way to get closer and then...

She was all in white, a single, nearly transparent layer of lace that shimmered over her ripe body. The gown, if it could be called that, was caught by a thin gold belt made from what looked like rope. Unless he was wrong, there was a knife or dagger attached to the belt.

She stood apart from the others, a small island of stillness in a surging tide of humanity. Her hair was black and long and loose, trailing down her back. She was barefoot. Young.

She smiled at him.

Holy shit. If I'm going to die tonight, what a way to go.

It didn't seem possible, and yet she made her way to him without having to dodge bodies. It was almost as if she was a creek flowing effortlessly around all obstacles.

When she stood a couple of feet from him, he took a deep breath, hoping to calm himself. She had large green eyes and smelled of lavender, and no two ways about it, that near cheesecloth she was wearing didn't hide a thing. Her breasts weren't particularly large but high and full and firm and luscious. She didn't have much of a muff; what there was of it appeared as dark as her hair. Just like that, his cock stood at attention.

She looked down at him as if appraising his equipment. "It is ready?" she asked in a smooth, lilting tone.

He'd seen some easy lays in his life, but this was ridiculous. "You don't mince words, do you?"

"Mince words? I do not understand."

Now that he'd gotten over his initial surprise at being approached by a goddess, he took note of her formal-sounding speech. Besides, much as he wanted to, there was no ignoring the dagger. Whatever he did, he wasn't going to piss the lady off.

"Maybe we'd better back up here a bit," he said. "If this is a come on, I'm interested, but I believe in laying things out on the table with an armed woman."

"Back up? What table?"

What was she, slow-witted? Drunk or on something? Ripe as she might be for the plucking, he'd never taken advantage of a woman. Despite the argument he was getting from his cock, he wasn't going to change now.

"Did you think I was someone else?" He had to nearly yell in order to make himself heard.

"No, I know who you are."

Yeah, right. The only person he knew in Edinburgh was Paul. "Do you?"

A large woman jostled the black haired beauty, causing her to stumble. "You are Taurus," she said as she righted herself.

"Taurus? From the zodiac? You've got to be kid—what makes you think that?"

"The Lady told me."

What lady? As Alice would say, things were getting curiouser and curiouser. However, unlike Alice, he wasn't particularly interested in an explanation. Despite his all but legendary success with women, the truth was that his world didn't revolve around the opposite sex. Like he'd told a few of his envious male acquaintances—except for Paul who'd grown up in foster homes himself, he didn't really have what he could call friends—once you've humped a hundred women, it gets to be pretty much the same thing. Those acquaintances hadn't agreed with him, but that's how he felt.

Until tonight.

"I appreciate the compliment but—"

She leaned forward and cocked her head. "I cannot hear you."

That he could remedy. Doing what he'd wanted to since he'd first spotted her, he draped his arm over her slender shoulder and drew her to his side. He'd expected her to be more substantial. Instead, she felt almost childlike. *Shit! How old was she?*

"I said—" He spoke into her ear, fought the desire to take her hair between his teeth and nibble it, to trail his hand down to her breast and tease her nub into hardness. "No man objects to being compared to a bull, but if you're looking for someone named Taurus, you've got the wrong man."

Either she hadn't heard him, or she didn't give a damn about his explanation. Because his wardrobe was sadly lacking in casual wear, he'd put on a pair of dress slacks today, expertly tailored to minimize his more than average size cock since that was hardly what he wanted on display as part of his career. At least the camouflage worked when he didn't have a hard-on.

"I am not wrong," she said. Now, despite the noise, he had no trouble hearing her. "I know who you are." She turned so she was facing him. "You are ready for mating?"

"What?"

Before he could even guess that it was going to happen, she closed her small, warm hand over his straining cock. "Your seed-organ is ready."

"My..." How the hell was he supposed to think with her holding him like that?

"We cannot do the joining here."

No argument there. They'd be crushed under the humanity. "You want to have sex? Just like that?"

"Sex? Ah, yes, I must remember what you would call it."

Eventually, maybe, he'd sort all this out. Right now, however, he had a dagger-armed, nearly naked, cock grabbing broad to deal with. "One question before we take this any further." *Shit, did she have to handle his cock as if it was a slab of meat she was contemplating buying?* "How old are you?"

"Of age."

Whatever that meant. "In other words, I'm not going to get busted if we get it on?" *What did he mean, if?*

"Busted? Get it on?"

Unable to take any more of her enthusiastic and yet analytical groping, he grabbed her wrist and pulled her off him. "Sorry, lady. Much more of that and we'd have a spontaneous eruption right here and now."

"Spontaneous? I do not—"

"Why did I know you were going to say that? Look..." He gathered himself to go on yelling, then decided not to risk a lacerated vocal cord after all. "We've got to get out of here."

Chapter Three

Here turned out to be the backside of Calton Hill. He could still hear the drums, still feel them vibrating in the night, but at least they were away from most of the crowd. Between the moon and firelight and occasional flashlights, he was able to spot a fair number of couples doing what came naturally in and about the volcanic rockbase and low shrubs. No doubt about it, Paul had been right about Beltane being *the* night to get laid.

The girl-woman hadn't objected to coming here, and with her hip brushing against his with every step—he'd kept his arm around her so they wouldn't get separated—he was close to not giving a damn how old she was, where she came from, or whether she'd escaped from some mental ward. What had she told him, that she was *of age?* Hers was indeed a woman's body. Ripe. Ready. And with the wind blowing her not-quite-a-dress against her breasts and hips, he easily placed her in the top one percent of her sex in the bod department. Sure as hell he'd never had his hand on someone like her, half sprite, half human.

"Well, here we are," he not too brilliantly announced when he'd found a relatively smooth spot behind a boulder.

"This is a good place." She ran her bare toes over some low-growing flowers. "The earth is fertile."

What's that got to do with anything? "Speaking of fertile, I hope you're on the pill."

"Pill?"

Shit. Here we go again. "Protection. I don't need a paternity suit."

She was looking up at him, obviously content with their close proximity. He noted her long, slender neck, lips just begging to be crushed under his, slender arms and flaring hips. He also noted that she didn't wear a speck of makeup. What modern woman on the prowl didn't slather on war paint? But then who said she was modern? The thought made him a little uneasy.

"Taurus, I have been sent to your time to find you, only you," she said. "To take your seed into my body."

You're not going to get any objections from me. "I'm—I'm glad to hear that. But I'm serious. I don't want you getting pregnant."

He could swear her features became darker, older even, but that was probably just because it was night. For a moment she was absolutely still as if listening to someone he couldn't see. Then she relaxed.

"What happens tonight, I take full responsibility for. All I want from you is this."

He'd known she was going to take hold of his cock again. He could have backpedaled, but he didn't. Instead, he simply stood there as still as she'd been earlier while she trailed her fingers over, around, and under his bulge. The weird thing was, there was nothing crude about what she was doing. Rather, she handled his cock as if he was a prime piece of horseflesh she'd just bid on.

"Lady, I don't know what game you're playing," was the only damn thing in the world he could think to say.

"I do not play games." She'd taken hold of the tab on his zipper but didn't seem to know what to do with it. "This night is destiny. You and I, we must mate."

Who could he tell about this? No one would believe him, and yet he couldn't keep it to himself. "You aren't part of this play or whatever it is, are you? Am I on *Candid Camera*?"

"What is this?" She ran her nails over the zipper; he felt the vibration throughout his groin.

"You don't know—? Who the hell are you?"

"Maia. Your mate," she said. Then she rose up on tiptoe, pressed her mouth, her body, against his, and he forgot how to talk. Needing more of her, he cupped his hands over her buttocks and pulled her hard and tight against him. Having his cock mashed inside his slacks was driving him crazy, and yet she felt so damn good. Ripe and lush and—oh hell, like something out of an adolescent fantasy.

She wrapped her arms around his neck and gently slid her body up and down his, rubbing her hard, young breasts against his chest. With every move, his chest and belly and groin became more heated. He grabbed a handful of whatever it was she wore, fascinated by the way it glided like water over her butt. She'd tipped her pelvis toward him.

Now—hell, now she was massaging his arms, sides, hips. She was everywhere on him, her fingers both cool and warm, pressing into the small of his back before riding low on his hips, under his buttocks.

Unable to take any more of that torture, he shoved her away just long enough to unfasten his slacks and free his cock. As soon as he exposed himself, she was all over him again. This time she came at his side. First she pulled down on his slacks until they were bunched around his ankles. Then she reached between his legs both fore and aft. Without so much as a *by your leave*, which of course he would have granted because he was no longer thinking, she probed until her fingers came together in his crotch. His snug briefs were in the way. He felt her fingers through the single layer, teasing his balls, moving them first one way and then the other. Over and over again she massaged and manipulated while he stood dumb and straddle-legged with one hand half around her neck.

Shit! He was going to go off just like that.

"Maia—that's it, right? Maia? Do you know what the hell you're doing?"

"Y-es."

What did it matter? A heartbeat later, he'd answered his own question. It mattered a lot.

"Wait." He sounded every bit as confident as he had the first time he'd stood at the top of a steep ski slope. "Wait. Not like this."

She took his testicles in one hand. The other was spread over the length of his cock. "You do not want...?"

"I'd have to be six feet under not to want. But haven't you heard of letting the man be the aggressor?"

"You think I am aggressive? No, I am a maiden."

What you are is a nut case. "Look." Despite the cost to his electrified nervous system, he hauled her off him and held her at arms' length. God, but she was incredible! Nowhere close to civilized. "We've got all night. We don't have to go at this as if we're in rut."

She stared at her captured wrists but didn't try to break free. "Rut is sheep, cattle."

"And sometimes, humans. At least that's the way we're going at it. Tell me something. Are you from this planet?"

"From this place, yet. But not of this time."

The man who The Lady said would call himself Taron stared at her for so long that Maia was afraid she'd said the wrong thing, but The Lady had told her to be honest when she approached Taurus. The Lady had also warned her that this man, her spirit-chosen mate, wouldn't understand his role at first and might need guidance.

But I have never been with a man, she had said. *I cannot guide if I have never been there before.*

Trust, The Lady had said. *Trust your body.*

She wanted to do that; she needed to. But all she knew was that when animals were ready to mate, they did so. She'd seen and heard her parents having sex but didn't know what they did or said before her father shoved his seed-bearer into her mother's baby-making place. They'd promised to tell her those things once she'd been spoken for, but then the priests and their armed soldiers had taken over the village and nothing else had mattered.

With a mental shake of the head, Maia brought herself back to the here and now. The earth seemed to be rumbling. She knew what *djembes, surdus, dharbukas,* and *shakers* sounded like when they were played, but this soul-touching rhythm was different.

Maybe Taurus was responsible.

When she relaxed her fingers, he released her wrists but didn't stop staring at her. His eyes heated her in a way that reminded her of the heat she'd felt between her legs when The Lady first told her about him. She hadn't felt more than a twinge of shyness when The Lady had told her to disrobe and then put on this filmy gown, but Taurus was looking, not at but through it. Seeing her body.

"What do you want?" she asked when his stare began to harden her nipples.

"Maybe a keeper for you. No, not really. One last time. You really want to do this?"

Of course she did; fertilizing the earth with their sex fluids was why she'd been sent here. And yet, she couldn't quite silence the part of her that wanted to remain a child. "You do not?"

"If you have to ask that, you don't understand men. Honey, we'll take it any time, any way we can get it."

Not quite sure what he meant, she nevertheless smiled at him. She didn't feel comfortable taking off her belt and dagger, but most times people didn't have sex with clothes on. The shadows didn't completely hide the other couples, but none of them would care what she and Taurus did.

He watched, still and alert, as she untied the gold-dyed hemp belt and lowered it and the sacred dagger to the ground. Then she lifted the gown over her head, folded it, and placed it beside the dagger.

"I am ready," she said.

"Shit." Shaking his head in time with the drumming, he kicked off his shoes and stepped out of the garment she hadn't known how to unfasten. His top was held together with small stones that effortlessly gave way under his experienced fingers.

She thought about asking him why he dressed that way. Then she looked down at his seed-bearer and forgot the question.

Male horse and cow sex organs were much bigger than humans, but she'd never quite gotten used to the difference between how a man looked when he was going about his work and when his seed was ready to be spilled. Taurus' organ looked larger than any man's she'd seen, maybe because he was part bull. She didn't see how it could possibly fit inside her.

And yet the thought of feeling him in there caused her breath to catch and the place between her legs to swell slightly.

He was naked. Seeing him standing there, his hands extending toward her, waiting for her, flooded her body with heat. Her lips, breasts, belly, and baby-place buzzed. She couldn't move.

"What is it?" he asked.

He is your destiny.

"I—nothing."

"I don't think so," he said. Then he fastened his hands around her elbows and drew her to him. Light from the fire she could no longer see painted the sky. Her bones, skin, muscles felt the everything-music, but maybe he was responsible for her strange new and wonderful reaction.

He bent his head toward her, and she found the courage to meet her mate. At first, all she could think about was how soft his lips were. Then he parted them, and she opened hers in response; his tongue entered her mouth. She hadn't known that would happen; her initial impulse was to bite him.

His seed-bearer ground into her belly, hard and huge and demanding. She felt her legs weaken. Something was growing up inside her, some part of her she'd never suspected existed making itself known. Sensitive. As demanding as his organ.

She wouldn't bite his tongue after all. Instead, she'd let him do what he wanted with her mouth. And because they wanted to, she wrapped her arms around him and held him close.

His tongue probed and challenged, filling her and lighting even more of a blaze between her legs. Her parents had grunted and groaned, sometimes even screamed when they were joining, but she didn't think they'd been in pain or they wouldn't have done it so often. Now she began to understand.

By forcing her thoughts, at least a little, off what was happening inside her mouth, she concentrated on her fingers. A bull was all muscle and hair, but the man Taurus' skin was nearly as soft as a child's — at least the flesh over his buttocks was. Starting with the lightest of touches, she grew increasingly bolder, exploring everything she could reach.

He must be ticklish because he kept shivering. When she sucked her belly and hips away from him so she could explore what of him existed between his pelvic bones, he withdrew his tongue and stood, still shivering, as if thinking of nothing except what she was doing.

She'd touched his seed-bearer before; it should be easy to do so again. But the first time she hadn't felt so alive and hungry up inside herself. Still, because he'd soon place it in her, she needed to be certain about its length and breadth. At least that's what she told herself.

It was amazing that something capable of growing so large could feel like silk and stone at the same time. It was ribbed with what surely must be blood-filled veins; on top, she found nothing except an intriguing knob and warm moisture.

Moisture? Had he already spilled himself? No, that couldn't be, she concluded as she continued her exploration because — because it made her feel soft and full and alive inside to do so. There was so little fluid; surely much more was needed to hold the precious things that would become a new life. How would she get him to release more? Was there something she should be doing that she wasn't?

"You're making me crazy."

His voice was a growl and came from deep inside him. His skin was becoming sweat-soaked, and he kept rocking from side to side. When her father was inside her mother, his buttocks pumped back and forth, back and forth almost like a drummer's hand.

"I do not mean to make you do that thing—crazy," she said. "What do you want me to do?"

"You have to ask? Ah, how important is foreplay to you?"

She'd never heard the word. "It does not matter."

"Get right to the main course. Is that what you mean?"

Not at all sure, she tried to think what he wanted. Her father always seemed pleased and tired after he'd had joining. Surely Taurus wanted to feel the same way. Besides, she wanted to get the first time over so she wouldn't feel so uncertain.

"The main course, yes," she told him. She hoped she'd said the right thing.

"Lady, you're incredible."

She wasn't a lady; she was a maiden. Now that she was no longer exploring his seed-bearer, he'd stopped moving in that jerky way. She'd focus on getting him going again. That way, hopefully, he would take over.

He was enough taller that she didn't see how they could come together while standing up. Besides, usually her parents joined in bed although sometimes her father took her mother from behind or her mother would fasten herself to his hips. Thoroughly confused, she looked down. If she lay on her back—

"Wait," Taurus said. "We'll use our clothes."

Chapter Four

His shirt protected her back from brush and rocks while his slacks provided a cushion for her buttocks. As soon as he'd spread out his clothes, she'd lain down and spread her legs because that's what she'd seen maidens do at Bel-fire. She wasn't sure whether he approved because he'd again shaken his head and muttered *incredible* several times, but then he'd lowered himself between her legs, his knees pressing against her inner thighs.

For a moment she'd felt trapped, but then he'd leaned over her and kissed her breasts.

He was still kissing them—occasionally taking one and then the other nipple into his mouth and washing them with his tongue. Why he'd want to do that was beyond her comprehension unless he didn't think she was clean enough, but it felt so good! Her skin where he bathed her tingled in a way she felt all the way to her woman-place. Again she tried to comprehend how he was going to get his organ inside her and whether she needed to do anything to help him insert it, but she felt so alive that it was nearly impossible to think. Soft and hot at the same time.

When her woman's moon-cycle had begun, her mother had shown her how to use cloth and leaves to absorb the blood and had given her an herb tea to take away her belly cramps. She'd complained that she didn't like this part of being a woman, and her mother had laughed and told her it was worth it. Back then she'd wondered if her mother was making fun of her.

She no longer did. Becoming a woman meant feeling alive in ways the child she'd once been couldn't have comprehended. Yes, she was here because her clan needed Taurus, but so did she.

Somewhere beyond her sight, people were singing and clapping, and the drums seemed to be getting even louder and more urgent, but she didn't care. In fact, the noise added to her pleasure. Taurus had an amazing amount of her breast in his mouth and now his hand — his hand was between her legs.

The moment he touched her in that fascinating place, she felt something ooze out of her, but she didn't think it was blood. This felt nothing like her moon-cycle, more as if her baby-place was readying itself for him.

She wanted — needed him inside her.

When he used his fingers to push apart the two flaps of flesh there, she stopped existing anywhere else. She couldn't remember how to breathe, and her hips didn't want to remain on the ground. Instead, they lifted toward him, and her legs spread even wider without her telling them to — at least she didn't think she had.

His finger pushed deeper inside her to the most sensitive place on her body, the place that so often fascinated her. It was all she could do not to clamp her pelvic muscles around that finger so he'd keep it there forever. Putting her own fingers up in her had been pleasurable but nothing like this. She didn't think a man's hand had anything to do with making a baby or spilling seed, but that was all right. More than all right!

He released her breast. "You're tight in there," he said.

"I am sorry." Had she disappointed him? If only he'd tell her what to do!

"Sorry? Lady, a snug fit is what all men dream of."

That was good, wasn't it? Eager to increase his pleasure, she again tilted her pelvis toward him and bent her knees outward. She wished she could see what he was doing. Much as she'd loved having him play at nursing her, she was more interested in having her opening explored.

"Damn. You're amazing."

He was still up inside her, but his finger jerked and slid here and there; she felt his legs brush against her right thigh.

After blinking several times, she managed to get her vision to clear and saw that he'd repositioned himself so he was now stretched beside her, propped up on an elbow, staring at what she'd offered him.

"Amazing?" she asked. "What do you mean?"

"You don't have a single, solitary hang-up, do you? What are you, some leftover flower child?"

Did they speak the same language? So much of what he said made no sense. "Flowers, yes. Without them there can be no Bel-fire."

"Yeah, right. Whatever."

She was afraid he'd say something else she didn't understand and she'd have to pull her mind off the sensations he'd ignited inside her, but he scooted down a little, probably so he could have a clearer look at her opening. His finger continued dancing inside her.

No, not dancing — something more.

Although she'd explored up inside herself and found the experience so enjoyable that she had no intention of quitting, it had never felt like this. Instead of checking to see if her cave was large enough to nurture a baby as she'd done, he seemed more interested in touching her here, there, everywhere. Some part of her seemed to be trying to push out. It was getting larger, more sensitive; she was positive of that. And when he touched it—

"Ah! Oh..."

"Like that, do you?"

"Yes! Yes!"

"I mean to please."

What was he doing now? Although her head roared, she struggled to comprehend. All those nooks, crannies, and pieces inside her felt as if they were on fire and would blaze until she lost consciousness. In contrast, her arms and legs felt as if they'd been weighed down with rocks. It couldn't be; yet, she wouldn't be surprised to find a burning brand resting on her belly.

Her cave was now full, crammed with him. Not one finger but two. Maybe — maybe more?

He kept touching, what?

"I...I cannot breathe!"

"Don't worry about it," he muttered. "No one's ever died from being finger-fucked." She thought he said something else, but she couldn't concentrate. Now he scooted into a sitting position and placed a hand over her mouth. The other — thank goodness — continued to plug her. Continued to dance, run, tiptoe, maybe gallop.

"Ah —"

"Hush. Hush. Let it go. Just don't telegraph it to the world."

Tiny volcanic eruptions spread over and up and through her cave. They raced to her belly, lightly hammered her breasts. She felt herself begin to fly off in all directions; half terrified, she tried to sit up.

Before she could, he pulled out of her. Then he gripped her inner thighs and splayed her legs. He was there — his seed-bearer probing her opening.

Pushing into her.

Shoving.

Hard!

The pleasure she'd been experiencing evaporated to be replaced by a sharp pain. She gasped.

"Shit! No."

He was starting to withdraw, leaving her. No, that couldn't be! He hadn't spilled his seed inside her. The earth, and she, hadn't been fertilized!

Panicked, she clamped her legs as best she could around him and held him where she needed him. At the same time, she grabbed his shoulders with all her strength. Already the pain was fading.

"No! Please! Feed me."

His seed-bearer was still in her, filling her, it seemed, clear up to her navel. He couldn't have felt more tense if he'd been a bow string. "You're a virgin," he whispered.

"Yes."

"Damn. Why didn't you…?"

She felt him start to draw back again and increased her hold on him. "Please," she begged. "Please do this. Tonight. Now."

"Holy shit. What is this? You're looking for a stud to take your cherry?"

She knew what a stud was, and although there weren't any cherry trees near where her people lived, they'd traded for the delicious dried fruit. "Yes," she said, hoping that's what he wanted to hear.

"Shit."

"I—I have come so far," she managed. "What I ask is not so much, is it? Surely it is not so hard for you to do." If she kept him inside her, would a little of his seed dribble into her? Would it be enough?

"Lady, this is hardly a hardship on me. But damn it, a virgin."

"I thought you would want—"

"I want. Believe me, I want." He took a ragged breath. "Shit, I'm going to burn in hell for this."

"No, you will not burn," she said although she didn't know what he was talking about.

"I hope to hell you're right. What a—you're sure about this?"

"Yes." *Yes!*

Apparently that was the answer he wanted to hear because he stopped trying to draw away and pushed himself deep into her again. While they'd been talking—and even before that when she'd felt the pain—she'd lost touch with at least some of her inner volcano. But its strength hadn't been spent. It waited for her, ready to grow and heat again.

How could a man be so strong? She understood the kind of muscles needed to hunt, farm, even fight, but this? He pushed and pushed at her, jolting both of them so she wasn't sure she was still on the ground. Maybe he'd speared her and was carrying her along.

Along where?

Her cheeks were so very hot, as were her arms and breasts and stomach. Most of the fever, however, was centered in her baby-cave. She felt enough discomfort to know she'd be sore once their mating was over, not that it mattered.

"Virgin. Virgin. Damn."

She wanted to tell him — tell him something. But he had become part of her. Her cave felt as if it was trying to empty itself and suck all of him into her at the same time. His thrusts increased in intensity; he grunted with each breath. Suddenly something warm and wet flooded her cave, and he rammed into her like a stallion mounting a mare. She rode the wave, sensed it rise up around her, cover her. Drown her.

"Ah — ah!"

Chapter Five

"Why didn't you tell me you were a virgin?" Taron demanded when, finally, he could talk again. Maia—that was her name, wasn't it—was lying beside him, looking for all the world as if she'd been pole-axed. He wasn't all the way back to the here and now himself, but enough progress had been made that he at least had a toehold on reality.

"Would you not have mated with me if you had known?"

Like him, she was drenched in sweat. He didn't need to ask to know he wasn't the only one who'd come. Shit, she'd had a climax during her first sex act. Either he was stud of the year or this was one sexy broad.

"Mated? All right, if that's what you want to call it, who am I to argue? And no, I wouldn't have gone at it the way I did if I'd known, that's for sure," he admitted. "I'm sorry. I didn't mean to hurt you."

"You did not. Not really."

Noting that she was trembling, he pulled her onto her side and into his embrace. It was cool enough that they wouldn't be able to lay here in the buff much longer, but he'd take all he could get. Hell, the last thing he wanted to do tonight—or for the foreseeable future—was let go of her.

"Look, let's don't play games, all right?" he said. "The way you came onto me—hell, I figured you had more experience than I did, and that's saying a lot."

When she didn't ask for an accounting of his experiences and tentatively—at least it seemed tentative—curled down enough that she could kiss his nipple, he went on. "I've only had one other virgin. And since I was in a like condition, it was pretty awkward all the way around. You're so uninhibited, prancing around the next thing to naked—what gives?"

"Gives?"

Guessing this was going to be another of those conversations that went nowhere, he tried to rub away the goosebumps on her shoulder. Before long, his effort progressed to what he could reach of her flattened breast with their bodies sealed together the way they were.

"Look, I'd like to know one thing," he managed despite the stirring of a certain part of his anatomy. "I need to know. Are you on the pill? Maybe you're wearing a patch. IUD?"

"Yes," she whispered after a too-long silence.

If he'd been set up—"I'm holding you to that," he said firmly. "Believe me, lady, you better not be lying to me." She didn't say anything, which made him feel more than a little uncomfortable. "You don't sound as if you're from around here," he said in an attempt to pull more out of her. "Where do you live?"

Instead of answering, she arched her back, giving him greater access to her breasts. Despite her somewhat roughened fingers and the calluses on her heels that told him she spent most of her time barefoot, the rest of her lush and freely-offered body was silken. Maybe that's what came from clean living, not that he knew what she did for a living, where she came from, who the hell she was, whether she was wearing a wire and had been hired by the competition, unimportant things like that.

Her nipples had turned into not too small pebbles, and seemed several degrees warmer than the rest of her breasts. If someone put a gun to his head, he couldn't say how many breasts he'd been invited to explore, and after awhile he'd come to the conclusion that they were all pretty much the same. Yes, there were differences in size, color, position, sensitivity, but since they all existed to serve the same basic purpose, there wasn't all that much to be said about them.

Something, however, was different with Maia's. He just didn't know what it was—only knew he hadn't come close to being done with them.

Or with her.

He repositioned her so they were sitting up and her back was now against his chest, and he'd cradled — strange that he'd think of it like that — her legs between his. He'd managed to prop his ass and lower back against a clump of grass, and although it was far from the most comfortable back rest he'd ever had, he didn't care. Strangely, he cared only a little that his once again alert cock was being smashed by her ass.

Her head rested against his left shoulder. Her hands lay unmoving on his thighs. The message in her open-to-him body was about as basic as it could get. No fool he, he alternately played with her breasts, stomach, hip bones, even curled himself around her so he could gain access to her muff and the lush cunt underneath.

The first time he cupped her pussy and pressed down, she responded by grinding the back of her head into his collarbone. She was leaving fingertip sized divots in his thighs. It had been an experiment — at least that's what he told himself — a test to see whether he'd made her so sore that her pussy was incapable of registering pressure. Obviously it wasn't.

Encouraged, or maybe the truth was he had no control over what he was doing, he spread his fingers to increase his control over her cunt. His middle finger was positioned at the entrance to her hole. He entered, wiggling his finger just a little to make sure he'd found ground zero.

Her breathing picked up, and so did his. Just like that, he felt pressure in his groin; the message in his cock came through loud and clear. There was only one place it wanted to be.

Amazing. Contrary to what the men's magazines said about the early thirties still being prime-time sexually for men, he hadn't gone for two jerk-offs in one night since his early twenties. Sure, he was capable — he thought — but like drinking too much, blowing a whole night with sex was no way to run a business.

Screw his company, his career.

The nymph to end all nymphs was here, between his legs, offering herself to him like a Christmas morning gift.

Unfortunately, there was a limit to how wide he could spread his legs, which meant she too was under the same constraints. In addition, leaning forward like this so he could play in her playground was going to kill his back. However, until the death knell had been sounded —

Maybe there'd been a change in the drumming; maybe he'd simply become aware of it again. Whatever it was, he matched his hand's rhythm to the beat that seemed to have permeated both earth and air.

She'd stopped digging into his legs. Now she painted and caressed them, touching the same area over and over again. It was always new, always traveling from thigh muscle straight to his cock.

When he slid his hand further over her sex and buried his middle finger up to the base in her, her hands stopped moving. Now they lay nearly still on him, trembling just a little.

"You're cold?" he asked.

"No. I…"

"You what?" He straightened his finger so the back of it rubbed against her pussy wall. Her next breath came out a sob.

"I did not expect…"

"What? That you'd climax the first time?" Could he take credit for that?

"Climax?"

What planet was she from? And did it matter? "Come? Get off on me? Whatever you want to call it?" Her juices were drenching his finger and some had already leaked out to dampen his palm. He wondered how much of his sperm was mixed in with her sap. Curious about how close she was to the brink, he curled his finger so it now brushed the back of her pussy. Her cunt muscles clamped around him.

Hmmm. Time to bring in the reinforcements.

Ignoring the increased discomfort in his back, he leaned even further forward so he no longer had to brace himself. Now that his other hand was free, he put it to good use. Stroking her pubic hair and finger fucking her at the same time took both dexterity and concentration. He sure as hell didn't mind, and from her little grunts and groans, he had no doubt about how she felt.

Calling on his inventive nature, he pulled her tight against his hard-as-nails cock and caught a pussy lip between the thumb and forefinger of his left hand. Now that that silken piece of flesh was out of the way, he had no trouble working a second finger inside her. Sweat broke out on her. She shoved her ass against him, grinding her buttocks into his cock.

Shit!

"That's what I'm talking about," he whispered into her ear. His voice sounded as if he hadn't used it in a month. "Lady, you're randy."

"I—it feels so good."

"Makes you sorry you put it off so long, does it?" *Shit. Did he want to go there?* "How—how old are you?"

"I am a woman."

You are now. "I won't argue that, but—" Despite her pussy-grip on him, he straightened his fingers. Her G-spot was around there somewhere. If he connected… "I don't understand you, not even a little bit." *About as much as I understand what the hell I'm doing with you.*

"And you want to?"

"Damn right." *I also want to screw you until I can't see straight, but that's another story.*

"I—I want to tell you about me," she said in a small, uncertain voice. "About my people. Our fears."

"Fears?"

Whatever he'd just touched, her cunt spasmed as if an electrical probe had been applied to it. Never one to deny a lady, he stroked again. Just like that, a small stream of hot fluid drenched his hand. He held it against her, no easy task given the way she was jerking.

Climaxing. Right here, right now, without him having to do more than a little freelance finger-play.

"Come on, Maia," he encouraged. "Let it happen; just let it happen."

She bucked against him with such force that he was knocked backward. He felt himself start to slide off his clump of grass and tried to straighten. However, with his hands otherwise occupied, he had nothing for leverage.

He landed on his back with her on top. She lay there a moment, sweating and shaking, making tiny, continuous mewling sounds. Then, just like that, she went limp. Her breath came out in a long, loud sigh.

Climax number two.

Despite whatever was poking into his back, he was in no hurry to have her get off him. Although his hands were sticky with her come, he felt compelled to cover her breasts. After all, he didn't want her getting cold. The moment he spread his fingers over them, however, compassion and consideration changed into something else.

Splayed out by gravity, her breasts were nevertheless incredible organs. They were hers; he could touch them only when she gave him the right, but he'd taken her virginity. He'd showed her the meaning of climax—a damn simple task—and now she wanted to tell him about her people and their fears, whatever that meant. She knew what his cock felt like inside her cunt and in her hand.

That made them, what? The word *soulmates* flitted through his mind, but that was way too heavy. Too dangerous.

In the space of what couldn't be more than a heartbeat, she went from out cold to sitting up. Alarmed, he reached for her, but she was already on her hands and knees, not because she was leaving him but because...

Although she was still putting her mind back together, Maia had been aware of what was happening on the other side of the hill. There'd just been a great whooshing sound, almost an explosion, and now the night sky was becoming brighter, redder. The fire-arch The Lady had told her about had been lit. Soon it would be time for her and Taurus to step under it, but they still had a few minutes—maybe enough time for her to make him hers, at least a little bit.

She turned around. He was on his back, staring up at her, his arms reaching for her. His seed-bearer put her in mind of a shaft stuck into the ground, only it was coming from him, not the earth.

Positioning herself so her legs were outside his, she rocked over his organ until her baby-place was directly over it. She'd felt him inside her before; it shouldn't be such a soul-changing prospect to have it happen again, and yet she couldn't get enough air into her lungs.

Down, down, down she came. She moved as slowly as she could because she wanted to draw out the experience for both of them. The tip of his organ pressed against her opening and seemed to hang up there. Although she'd never done it before, she used her hand to move her flesh out of the way. He slid in.

"Good grief, woman."

Grief was something no one wanted, but Taurus didn't appear to be in pain. In fact, he seemed interested in nothing except pushing even more of himself into her. She accommodated him by widening her stance, lowering herself onto him, and sucking him into her. The two bags of flesh where she'd been told a man's seed was stored pressed against her bottom. It felt wonderful.

He couldn't pump into her the way he'd done before because he wasn't in the right position. However, she was.

Rather pleased with herself for having figured that out, she lifted her head so she could study the red-tinted sky. She rested her hands on his ribs for leverage and began moving her hips up and down. His hands settled over her thighs, not in a punishing way but not gentle either. Down against him she went. When she'd gone as far as she could and his seed sacs pressed harder against her, she stayed there for several heartbeats. He felt so big inside her.

When she straightened and drew away, she brought his organ with her. Keeping him inside her called for concentration, no easy thing since his skin gliding against hers had become like small, continuous lightning strikes.

She'd been sent to this time and place to claim Taurus and take him back with her. But tonight, right now, was all she could think about.

Tiny lightning strikes were good. Delicious. Like the finest food only countless times better. Her skin, not just where his seed-bearer was touching, became hotter and hotter and was so sensitive she might have felt the weight of a single grain of sand.

She forgot who she was, couldn't remember what it felt like to be separate from him. His seed-bearer was amazing. Like a predator after prey, it effortlessly trapped her. But she had no desire to break free.

Sensing that he was approaching the moment of release, she increased her own efforts. They quivered as one, created their own music, beat a single drum. As before, he pounded into her, each thrust squirting his fluids into her. She caught fire, exploded.

Chapter Six

Maia had collapsed on top of Taurus—his softened organ still partly inside her. Although she'd become aware of her now cold back, she couldn't make herself move until he started to lift her off him. She rolled to her side next to him and propped herself up on one arm. He was looking at her with the strangest expression—something akin to the look on her youngest brother's face the first time he'd seen an eclipse of the moon.

"I may have died and gone to heaven," he muttered.

"No." She gasped, alarmed. "You are very much alive."

"Figure of speech. Besides, you're absolutely right. I couldn't possibly feel more alive. Lady, I don't know who the hell you are or what we're doing together, but thank you—thank you very much."

What we are doing together? The question reverberated in Maia and reminded her that she hadn't just been sent here to mate with Taurus, but to bring him back with her.

Afraid too much time had passed, she scrambled to her feet and slipped on her gown. She fastened the dagger around her waist, then grabbed Taurus' hand and tried to pull him up.

"Wait a minute," he protested. He tried to pull her back down, something she was tempted to let him do. "What are you in a hurry about? Look..." His amused expression turned to one of concern. "You're not leaving, are you?"

"Yes. I must."

She pulled again, this time succeeding in getting him to stand. He reached for her, but she ducked out of his way, leaned down and handed him his clothes. He took them and stepped into his briefs.

"Where are you going?" His tone matched his somber gaze.

"You—you would not know its name."

"No argument there. There's practically nothing I know about you. Look, Maia, isn't there some way I can get you to stay? Ah, how would you like to go to London tomorrow?"

London? What was that? "I cannot. Please, hurry. We must not be late."

"*We?* I'm going with you?"

"Yes, of course."

That seemed to reassure him, and although he didn't take his eyes off her, he wasted no time getting dressed. He put on his foot-coverings and then indicated her bare feet.

"I don't know how you do that. This is volcanic rock, sharp as hell in places."

She had to admit that the ground was harder than she was used to, but she had no trouble walking on it. "The fire arch." She pointed in the direction the glow was coming from. "We must hurry." To give her words emphasis, she grabbed his wrist.

"I'm coming," he reassured her. He started to wrap his arm around her waist, then touched the dagger. "That's no toy, is it? If need be, it could get deadly?"

Although she didn't quite understand what he meant, she reassured him that one of its functions was for protection. As for the other—it wasn't time for him to know that.

Much as she wanted to run, it was too dark to safely do that. Besides, the closer they got to the top of the hill where the fire arch had been lit, the more crowded it became. People, particularly men, stared at her. Maybe they could look at her and know she'd just mated. She supposed her gown, so simple compared to what most people wore, was too much of a contrast to be ignored. When an older woman shook her head in disapproval, it dawned on Maia that her veil-dress exposed a great deal of her body. Interesting. People from Taurus' time covered themselves; she just didn't understand why.

As soon as they reached the top of the hill, Taurus ran interference by shouldering their way through groups of onlookers. She clung to his side, feeling both protected and on the brink of asking him if he wanted to mate again. Given how sore she was between her legs, that wasn't wise, but it would be worth the discomfort. They would mate again as soon as they'd returned to her time, she reassured herself. The thought of mating on a down and feather covering prompted her to slide her hand down his hip.

"What?" Taurus caught her hand. "Don't tell me you're getting raunchy all over again. You're going to be the death of me."

"No. You will not die. You must not!"

"Calm down, will you. It's just a figure of speech. I swear, you are the most confusing—"

Much as she loved the sound of his voice, particularly the way it seemed as if she could feel it in her spine, there wasn't time to talk. Grabbing his wrist again, she plunged ahead.

The arch fire had been constructed out of tree branches and limbs fastened to a frame nearly twice as tall as Taurus. Although she knew what they had to do, the sight of all those dancers and other performers stopped her.

"I do not understand," she said. "The women in white, men who have painted themselves the color of fire or summer grasses. Why do they do those things?"

"I'm not the one to ask. My friend explained some stuff about the festival, but all I can give you is the short course. It's all supposed to symbolize the seasons, concentrating on spring of course."

"The fire arch. Have the color-people already gone through it?"

"I think so. According to Paul, that's the first thing they do. Then the May Queen—she's the one wearing all those colors—makes a circuit of the hill with her companions. From what I understand, they visit sites that represent Air, Earth, Water and Fire. They must have already done that because—yeah, see those Red Men?"

The Red Men were running around the Rainbow Woman and the others with her. At first Maia was afraid the Red Men would attack and kill someone, but no one acted afraid, and no one had pulled out a weapon. Instead, everyone ran here and there, yelling, laughing. So many colors and bodies were in motion that she was getting dizzy watching them. None of it made sense.

"Do you want to try to get closer?" Taurus asked. "I take it you haven't seen this before. Neither have I so if that's what you want to do before we— Well, you don't need me to spell that out, do you?"

His hip grinding into hers left no doubt of what he had in mind, and if this was any other time, she'd take hold of his seed-bearer and find a way to put it inside her again.

But this was tonight. Her mission had to be completed before morning.

Turning her back on the barbaric spectacle, she propelled Taurus toward the burning arch. A few people stood within a few feet of it, but everyone's attention was on the heathen dancers who knew nothing of the magic of Bel-fire. She felt the heat on her face, breasts, arms. The flames were so intense that she couldn't keep her gaze on it, and the way it crackled and snapped gave her pause. Just the same, she didn't stop walking.

"What are you doing?" Taurus demanded when they were only a few steps from it. "What if it collapses?"

He was right. All the wood was ablaze and much of it had already been destroyed. From what she could tell, the branches had been fastened in place with rope and when that burned through—

"We must hurry."

"Wait a minute." Taurus grabbed her around the waist and pulled her against him. His seed-bearer poked her backside. "I've gone along with everything you've wanted so far, but I don't have a death wish."

Neither did she, she wanted her people to live and flourish and celebrate as they had since the beginning of time.

"We must run through it."

"No, we don't! This is crazy."

"Taurus, please! I will not let anything happen to you, I promise."

"That's not a promise you can keep, so don't throw that at me. Look, lady, sometimes you flat out scare me."

How could that possibly be? He weighed nearly twice what she did, and she'd have to stand on tiptoe to kiss him. Alarmed by how much time was passing and how unsteady the arch looked, she turned in his arms and did the only thing she could think of; she grabbed his seed-bearer in both hands.

"Ow! What the hell—"

Concerned that she was hurting him, she let up a little but didn't release him.

"Careful there." His hands hovered over hers as if afraid to disturb her. "Those are the family jewels. Geez, you don't mess around, do you?"

"Now, please. We will run. It will take only a few heartbeats."

"If you keep on holding me like that, I'm not going to be doing any running."

Why was she wasting time listening to his arguments? Calling on the only thing she could think of to reach him, she leaned into him. "I was a virgin before I took you into me." The fire made so much noise that she wasn't sure he could hear her. The wind pushed smoke around them and the glow—the glow was like the sun. "That was what I did for you; let you change me from a girl to a woman."

He sucked in his breath. "No argument there," he said softly, almost reverently.

"That was my gift. Now..."

"I know." He glanced over her shoulder at the burning arch. "You want me to risk frying every hair on my head." He shuddered. "Promise me something. This is the last crackpot thing you'll ask me to do."

"Crackpot? I do not have a pot with me."

"Forget I said anything. Look, will you please let go?"

"You will take my hand, and we will walk under the fire together?"

"Walk, no. Run, yes."

Relief surged through her. Releasing his seed-bearer, she held out her hand.

"I should be locked up," he muttered, taking her hand.

The arch crackled; the sound was followed by something that resembled a scream. Taurus muttered, "Damn." She couldn't get out a word.

Though he tried to hold back, she led the way to the base of the arch. The people nearby either stared or loudly warned them not to do anything stupid. In truth, her heart was pounding so that she felt light-headed, but she'd already spent a long time where she didn't belong and was desperate to return to her world—with Taurus. In her mind's eye, she saw her parents, siblings, and other relatives. Most of all, she thought about The Lady and the Bel-fire ceremonies that had marked all the seasons of her life.

How could her child grow without Bel-fire?

"Now!" Clutching Taurus' hand with all her strength, she lowered her head and ran. Instead of trying to hold her back, he matched her stride. She felt heat and smelled smoke, heard people scream.

Then there was nothing.

Chapter Seven

Even before he became fully conscious, Taron concluded that he'd just had the best sleep of his adult life. The first thing to counter that impression was the realization that he was on his feet and not in bed. Then he felt a small, warm hand in his, and it all came back.

He reluctantly opened his eyes. If he'd burned himself— No. Somehow he'd come through the fire unharmed.

But where the hell was he?

As his vision cleared, he took in more and more impressions, not that they made any sense. At first blush it appeared that he was still at the top of Carlton Hill with the town of Edinburgh below, but this wasn't the hill he'd been at last night—if it had indeed been last night.

For one, the unfinished but impressive Athenian acropolis wasn't there, and there was no sign of the steep staircase he'd trudged up. Someone had taken away the trash cans, temporary restrooms, sound equipment, stage sets, and other equipment. Even the parking lot and cars were no longer in evidence.

Holding Maia's hand tighter than he wanted to admit, he looked down at the town—or rather what little there was of it. Because it was dusk, he couldn't tell much except that there were no streetlights. Hell, there weren't even any streets—or houses or commercial district or roads in or out. Except for a collection of what looked like huts and a larger stone structure nearly hidden in the shadows, the valley was empty.

His throat dried.

"Where are we?" he demanded.

"Home," Maia said.

Not my home. But even as he thought that, a sense of peace trickled over him. No two ways about it, there was a lot to be said for a place empty of the sound of automobiles and bright lights.

Dusk? Wait a minute. Hadn't it been night the last he knew? So, along with everything else, he was in a time warp of some kind. *Time warp? No, it was more than that. He'd gone back, back in time.*

"What year is it?" he demanded. For the first time in hours, he thought about his schedule and what was at stake.

"Year? I do not know what you mean."

About to point out that that wasn't the only thing she hadn't been able to supply, it occurred to him that he, not she, was the one who was out of step now. Out of his element, his world.

"You do not have to hold on so tight," she said wiggling her fingers. "I will not leave you."

He let up on his grip but didn't free her because she was the only thing that connected him to reality — or was she?

Bombarded by questions that might never have answers, he again turned his attention to his surroundings. Modern trappings still hadn't miraculously appeared, but his initial impression that the hill was deserted had been wrong. They weren't alone.

The knot of people was far enough away and in enough shadow that he had difficulty making them out, but Maia seemed eager to join them. He went with her, not because he gave a damn who these folks were, but, well, hell, because for reasons that went beyond his cock, he wanted to stay near her.

There was a small fire inside a stone circle, and that provided enough illumination that he realized that the group was made up of men, women, and children, all dressed in what looked like peasant costumes — only maybe they weren't costumes. A trio of old men with long beards wore light gray, almost white capes, and the way the others looked at them brought him to the conclusion that they were some kind of leaders.

Then he spotted a tall, stately woman with long, white hair. She had on a ground-length red cape made of gauzy material that left no doubt that she was naked under it—like Maia. He guessed her age at around fifty. She carried herself as if she was royalty. Behind her stood a huge, snow-white horse. It took a conscious effort not to bow.

Maia released his hand and bent her head before the queen-like woman.

"My Lady, I return," Maia said.

"It is good to see you, Maia," the older woman replied. "You have done well. Taurus is here. You have mated with him?"

"I have. Twice."

So much for privacy.

"Good. He willingly walked through the fire passage with you?" the woman asked.

"He did what I needed him to do," Maia explained. "But he has no knowledge."

You can say that again. Although it irritated him to be talked about as if he was deaf and mute, there was no denying that there wasn't a whole lot he could add to the conversation.

"He belongs to you?"

"I do not know. Everything between us is new."

Everything's new — and I'd give anything to know what the hell this is about.

"He needs to be tested," one of the old men said. "Until he has proven himself, we cannot trust him."

Before Taron could point out that he could hardly hang around forever, the old man loudly clapped his hands. Maia stiffened. Then the knot of onlookers parted, distracting him.

A half dozen young women—or teenagers maybe—were walking toward him. Like Maia, they all wore see-through veil-dresses. Their bodies were—hell, they were ripe.

"They are yours," the old man told him. "All virgins and ready for sex."

Maia had called it mating; was there a difference between that and sex? *And more importantly, what the hell was going on?*

"You want..." He swallowed and tried again. "You want me to have sex with them?"

"The decision is yours."

What red-blooded man wouldn't die happy after that kind of offer? Distracted from the question he'd just asked himself, he studied the young women. A couple were taller than Maia. One was overweight with amazing breasts that stuck up and out as only breasts that hadn't been attacked by gravity for long can. There wasn't a thing physically wrong with any of them, and although they giggled and stared openly at him as if he was about to be auctioned off, he figured he'd be able to carry on some kind of conversation with them, if given time and inclination.

"Perhaps your first choice would be a girl with wide hips made for childbearing and fun," another of the old men offered. "Kina, let him see."

Without so much as a blush—at least he didn't think she was embarrassed, a girl with wavy hair and a small, upturned nose unceremoniously hiked up her gown until it was around her waist. She stepped close and turned in a slow circle, looking over her shoulder at him all the time. She was smiling. No two ways about it, Kina had a richly rounded ass.

He felt nothing.

"You mated twice with Maia," the second old man continued. "Perhaps your seed-bearer is worn out. We can bring you sweetbread and fruit, and your strength will return."

What was he to them, a breeding bull? Maybe so since, like Maia, they called him Taurus. Strange, he didn't remember falling down a rabbit hole to Wonderland.

"Look," he said, suddenly angry. "I don't know what this is about. I'm not sure I ever will. But I'm more than just a cock. I also have a brain." *One that's on overload right now.*

"You took one virgin. You are not interested in another?"

Maia wasn't just a virgin. She was — what?

"That's not the way most men do things where I come from," he protested. "Usually — usually people have sex because they care about each other, not because someone dangles a cherry in front of them."

"Cherry?"

When was he going to learn to watch what he said around Maia and her people? "Never mind. It's just an expression."

Because he didn't want to offend the still giggling girl-women, he studied each of them in turn, nodding approval. Then he dismissed them. He hadn't intended to connect with Maia, but his gaze settled on her. Even with that dagger around her waist, she reminded him of Tinkerbelle.

"Look," he said. "I don't know who or what you people think I am. Hell, I don't know who *you* are. But I'm not some stud you can put in a pasture full of mares in heat."

That garnered nods he took to be understanding. Heartened because he was with people who understood livestock if nothing else, he continued. "I don't know if you know this, but some animals, like wolves, mate for life. I'm not saying that's what's happened between Maia and me. We've just met." *Met and fucked.* "But I don't sleep around." Hoping to give emphasis to his words, he covered her all but naked breast with his hand. She didn't try to remove it so he left it there.

"What do you want of me?" he demanded. "Why am I here? And — and there's something I need to make perfectly clear. I can't stay. I have...I have important things to do."

The woman Maia called The Lady clasped her hands over her breasts. "We are earth-people. From the time of our first ancestors, we understood that our existence depends on the sun. In spring, the sun is born anew and provides the light and warmth the crops need to grow. During summer, Sun is a mother who nourishes her children from her body, but at length she grows weary and needs to rest. The plants and trees, even the animals know that. They rest with her."

Maia nodded in time with the others. Covering his hand, she held it to her breast.

"But Mother Sun will not awaken from her sleep unless we, her children, honor her as we have since the beginning of time," The Lady finished.

The reverence in her voice, reinforced by the others' agreement and the way Maia held onto him left no doubt of how deeply they believed this; he couldn't begin to make fun of them.

"If that's your belief," he said, "I'm not going to argue with you."

"Then you believe?" Maia asked.

He hadn't heard her voice for too long; at least his cock must feel that way because he was now thinking about putting it where it had already been twice recently. "Honey, all this is too new to me for me to say yes or no about anything," he told her.

"The priests are not like that," the first old man said. "They do not understand; they do not try to understand. All they do is forbid."

"What priests?" *No two ways about it;* Alice in Wonderland *had nothing on him.*

"There." The old man pointed down the hill to where Taron had spotted the stone structure. "They and the soldiers they brought with them say that Bel-fire is the work of the devil."

He wasn't about to get into a religious argument, especially when he didn't understand where either these people or the priests were coming from. However, he felt aligned with those who were part of Maia's world. Maybe she knew what he was thinking because she all but wrapped herself around him. She obviously had no hesitancy about pushing her pelvis against his.

"What do you want from me?" he asked the old men and The Lady. *Where the hell had that question come from? I should be asking how I go about getting off this merry-go-round for the insane.*

"Use your power to make the priests leave us in peace."

No problem. I've got a machine gun in my back pocket. How about I pick up a phone and call the National Guard?

"Powers?" he said instead. "I'm afraid you've got me confused with someone else. Superman maybe?"

"You are Taurus," The Lady stated.

"Not you, too?" He groaned. "Look, that's what Maia calls me, but my name is Taron. I'm a twenty-first century businessman, end of discussion."

"Taurus the bull is potent. No creature is more powerful than he."

Given the way he'd performed so far tonight, he was hesitant to argue with that. "Interesting," he said. Maia's hand was now only inches from his cock. Not at all concerned with anything else that was going on, his cock responded.

"Taurus' blood upon the land fertilizes it."

"Blood? Wait a minute. Sperm, yes. I've got no argument with that, but I'm not interested in spilling any blood, especially mine."

"Sperm?" That came from Maia who seemed to be taking great pleasure in seeing what she could get his cock to do without touching it. "What is that?"

"Semen. You know, cum." He indicated her hand. "I hope you know what you're doing," he whispered.

"Where will you come?" she asked.

In my briefs if you aren't careful. "Shit. Never mind. I'm talking about my—my seed-bearer and what comes out of it when we have sex."

"Ah. Yes. Life's juice."

The first old man had spoken, and now everyone was nodding. The Lady stared at the bulge in his slacks and smiled with what he took to be approval. This place might be a close kin to Oz, but he had no objection to what appeared to be their open and enthusiastic view of sexuality. A man could get used to this.

"Ah..." He cleared his throat. "Let me get something straight. Are you being literal? I was brought here because — because you people want to indulge in a little blood letting?"

No one answered, leaving him to study the wise old men, The Lady, and other people who obviously believed they were part of this discussion. A few of the younger men looked strong enough to make good on their threat to turn him into a blood donor, if that's what it was. If he grabbed Maia and used her as a hostage —

"Taurus, your blood will not be spilled," she said softly.

Despite his efforts, a sigh escaped him. "I hope I can believe you."

"Not your blood," she continued. "Your life juice." With that, she closed her fingers around his standing-at-attention cock and tugged on it.

Geez Louise! "Maia," he warned as self-control faded. "I hope to hell you know what you're doing. Much — much more of that, and I'm going to explode."

"Explode?" Still holding his cock as if she had claimed ownership of it, she frowned.

"Jack-off. Is that what you want, for me to shoot my wad in your hands?" *Shit!*

"Shoot? Wad?"

Right there in front of everyone, she unzipped his slacks, found the opening to his briefs, and pulled out his cock.

"Never-never mind," was the sum and substance of what he could think to say.

To his shock, The Lady stepped close and leaned over. She was still taking her measure of his cock when the trio of old men shuffled up and did the same thing. He heard mutters of what he took to be approval. Several women giggled.

Shit. He might as well be a breeding bull.

"He is big," the only old man not to have spoken yet said. "Maia, he did not cause you pain?"

"A little the first time." She ran her forefinger over the tip of his cock. As he could have predicted, a little pre-cum oozed out. "But that did not last long."

"Was it enjoyable?" The Lady asked.

"Very. I did not know I would like it so much."

"Ah, look," Taron interrupted. Although it was obviously way too late for that, he regretted drawing attention to himself. "I know you people think you're giving me a compliment. But..." He pointed at his naked and ready-to-service cock. "Where I come from, this is hardly the way a girl acts when she takes a boy home to meet her family."

No one laughed, poking a major hole in his attempt to turn the most embarrassing experience of his life, bar none, into something humorous. Shit, he'd endured several detailed physical exams in order to qualify for a multi-million dollar life insurance policy and had managed to get through them without getting a hard-on. However, this time Maia and not some doctor had hold of him.

"Maia, what is this about?" he ground out.

"We are sorry," The Lady responded. "You are not from our time. We should have known you could not simply come here and understand our ways. But you will."

It'll take awhile. "Would-would you like to start?" *I'm just not sure I can concentrate because, strange as it may seem to you, this is the first time I've had the family jewels on public display.*

"Understanding will come," The Lady said. "But not now, later."

Chapter Eight

"You want me to what?"

Maia had been lost in the comforting notes of the spring-song her clans-people had been singing and thus was slow to realize that Taurus didn't feel the same way. After his seed-bearer had met everyone's approval, she'd covered it with his clothing, and the two of them stood in the place of honor as the Bel-fires were lit.

Because it had rained recently, it had taken awhile for the fires on all the surroundings hills to catch fire, but now, in defiance of the priests' orders, flames leaped into the sky and turned the night from black to deep red.

Taurus had been content to stay with her through Bel-fire's opening ceremony, and the longer they sat with their thighs touching, the more eager she'd been to spread her legs for him. In truth, it had been hard to think of anything else, and her breasts ached to feel his hands and mouth on them.

Wondering if her flushed cheeks gave away her thoughts, she looked up at Father Kaylen. As the oldest of the old men, he carried great wisdom from the ancients, and she'd spent much of her childhood listening to him talk about the beginning of their people.

"It is time," Father Kaylen said. "For Taurus to prepare for his journey by leaping backward through the fire three times followed by three forward jumps."

Excitement propelled her to her feet. When Taurus remained where he was, she reached down for him. Reluctantly, it seemed, he stood. He continued to hold her hand.

"Look," he said. "I ran under that damn burning arch when Maia told me to, and granted, I came through that unscathed, but if it's all the same to you, I'd just as soon not tempt fate."

Hopefully the day would come when she understood her mate's words. Until then, however, she'd have to be content with the act of mating itself — which she was.

"You must do as our father says," she explained. "Otherwise, you will not be prepared for your journey."

"What journey? Look, the only one on my agenda is related to my business. There's so much at stake there that—"

"Your journey can be a dangerous one," Father Kaylen interjected. "You will need a great deal of luck."

"Danger? I don't need to be told that. Besides, I'm going to need more than luck to keep from burning myself."

Taurus' continued reluctance bothered her, but she didn't know how to get him to explain why he felt that way. Hoping to remind him of what they were to each other, she drew his hand closer to her woman-place.

"Now wait a minute," he said and pulled free. "Maia, you know how to get to me; I'll give you that. But this isn't a game, all right. Why in the hell should I jump backward over a pile of burning wood? It makes no fucking sense."

On the brink of trying to reassure him, she became aware of heat at her side. At first she thought her body was responding to his, but then she realized the warmth came from her dagger. Releasing his hand, she pulled the dagger out of its sheath and held it close.

In the red jewel she saw a great, all-encompassing shadow. There seemed to be a small point of light in the middle of it, but she didn't let that distract her from the truth she knew would emerge.

"What is it?" Taurus asked. "What are you looking at?"

"My future."

"Your…"

"When I looked in it before, I saw you but nothing more. Now something else is coming."

Maybe Taurus understood her need to concentrate and maybe she'd gone past the point of being able to think about anything except the jewel's message. The Lady had said she didn't know where the dagger had come from; she'd prayed for guidance in protecting her people's future, and it had been there when she opened her eyes. The thought that it might have always existed and would continue to long after she was dead, caused Maia to regard it with awe. Most unsettling was the conviction that her tomorrows would soon be revealed.

"Maia, you're shaking," Taurus whispered.

"I cannot help it."

He slid his arm around her, and she took comfort from his strength, but even that didn't distract her from what she had to do. He too peered into the burnished depths. "I'm sorry," he said. "I don't see anything."

She did. Slowly, like a plant when it first breaks through the earth, she made out a female figure draped in white. Because she couldn't see the woman's face, she couldn't be sure it was her. Then even more of the shadow lifted, and the gown was no longer the purest of white. There, at the side, was that blood?

"What is it?" Taurus pressed. "Honey, something's scaring you?"

"Hold me," she whispered.

He did, his fingers on the side of her breast, reminding her of the heat and small volcanic eruptions she'd felt in her woman-place when he massaged her breasts before. With less of her mind on what was in the jewel, now that he'd captured part of her attention, she studied the image with a measure of detachment. The woman in the white, blood-stained dress was young. She was having difficulty standing and appeared to be alone.

Maia touched the jewel. She'd no sooner made contact when she felt on the brink of tears—the ones the white-woman was shedding.

Why are you crying? she asked. *Is it from sorrow or pain? Maybe, maybe you have been wounded by what you know of my people's future.*

No! She couldn't allow herself to think like that! Her people *couldn't* become like those from Taurus' time, children playing silly games instead of performing enduring and vital ceremonies.

"I cannot do this!" Not giving herself time to think, she slid the dagger back into its sheath and locked her arms around Taurus' waist. His seed-bearer, swollen with fluid and blood, tried to push itself between her legs. It took all her strength not to lift her gown. "Taurus, please. I will jump with you."

"Maia, what are you saying?" Father Kaylen demanded. "What did you see in the sacred jewel?"

"Taurus, please."

"All right, all right," he said, sounding the way her father had when something with long teeth and fangs crept into her dreams and he'd comforted her. "We'll do it together."

"Maia," Father Kaylen warned. "The act of leaping is for those who face a dangerous journey. Your time will come when—"

"My time is now, Father. Do not deny me this."

* * * * *

No matter how much she tried to will it to be otherwise, Maia's legs lacked their usual strength as she and Taurus walked up to the mother-fire from which all the others had been lit. By now, the stars and moon were out, and the young children had been put to bed. Already some of the girls who'd been her fellow virgins had linked their arms with young men and wandered off into the night. Just thinking about their taking off their clothes and spreading their legs so seed-bearers could enter their woman-places made her hungry to feel the same thing. But first she and Taurus had to—

"I'm still not sure of this," he muttered. "Sane people don't do this, at least none of the sane ones I've ever known."

"We will go together. It will be all right." *And, please, my journey will be made safe.*

He pressed his fist into the small of her back; she felt the contact deep inside the place that began between her legs. "I wouldn't do it for anyone else," he said. "I want you to know that. I just wish to hell I understood what this was about."

She couldn't tell him that yet, not until the elders had assured her that he would remain beside her, her companion and mate, but soon, soon he would understand his place among her clan.

Buoyed by what was surely the truth, she reluctantly pulled his hand off her. Then, aware of the many eyes on them and what they had to accomplish, she laced her fingers through his. Together, they turned their backs on the burning pile that was now no taller than his waist.

"This is insane," he grumbled. "You know it is."

Now, before the fire burned down to coals and she finished her role by jumping over it alone, she'd do this with the man the spirits had chosen for her.

Like her, Taurus glanced behind him before readying his muscles. "Insane!"

Propelled by his shout, she sprang backward. He left the ground at the same instant so they leaped as one. She felt heat on the soles of her feet and legs, then the sharp sting of the rocks she landed on. She might have lost her balance if his strong arm hadn't been there.

"That was fun, not!" He gasped. He stared at the fire, then over at her. "We really have to do this again?"

"Quickly. All of one movement."

"Nothing to it. Nothing!"

Going forward was easier, and she took pride in how high and far she went. They'd just completed one circuit when the old men stomped the ground.

"I take it that's their way of telling us we've just gotten started," Taurus muttered. "Maybe you should hold up your dress. It might catch fire."

"No, that will not happen."

"Because some half-demented old farts have convinced you that you're invulnerable? Not bloody likely."

This wasn't the time for convincing Taurus that the ways of her people should never be questioned. She ran her fingers up his forearm to get his attention.

"Now," she ordered. "While we are strong."

"Shit. *Shit!*"

She didn't lose her balance when she sprang backward the second time and somehow her feet found only smooth earth. Beside her, Taurus' footwear made a muffled thunk. He squeezed her hand.

"Ready?" he asked.

"Ready."

As she sprang forward, she looked down. Taurus was right. Her hem dragged through the flames, but it didn't catch fire. He no sooner landed when he grabbed her skirt. "I'll be damned," he muttered. "What's this thing made out of, some kind of fire-retardant material?"

Before she could think how to answer the question she only half comprehended, the old men started clapping. Taurus grumbled but took her hand again and propelled them backward over the fire once more. When they jumped forward the last time, he kept his gaze on her flowing dress.

"I'll be damned," he repeated once they were done. "So, is that all we have to do?"

Suddenly, joyously, she wanted to laugh. "Now it is our time," she told him.

"For what I'm thinking of?"

"Yes. Yes!"

* * * * *

"Wood is taken from many trees so that the fires celebrate apple, alder, elm, oak, rowan, gorse, even thorn. But most important is hawthorn."

"Why is that?"

She and Taurus were sitting across from each other, naked and alone. She doubted that he cared about what she was telling him, but he needed to know this and many other things. Also, talking about sacred trees was easier than asking him what he wanted her to do to please him.

"On the morning after Bel-fire," she continued, "when men and women return from the Greenwood, they bring with them great budding boughs of hawthorn, the spring-tree, and other spring flowers. Some of those flowers they use to dress themselves. The rest is left at every doorstep they pass along the way."

Taurus cocked his head. Although they were so close that their bent knees touched, he kept his arms by his side. "They dress themselves in flowers and hawthorn boughs?" he asked. "That's all they wear?"

"Most. They have spent the night mating and nourishing the ground. They want their families and neighbors to know what they have been doing."

He whistled. "No getting around it, your people are uninhibited. No hang-ups?"

"Hang-ups?"

"Never mind. I'm not interested in an English lesson, and unless I miss my guess, neither are you. So, now that we're down and naked, what next?"

"We mate."

"Just like that." He rubbed his hand over his eyes, then looked down at his limp seed-bearer. "Hm. We have a problem here. Nothing that can't be remedied, but I'd like to make it more than fitting tab A into slot A if you don't mind."

She frowned.

"All right." He sighed, and she wondered if he was embarrassed. "Look, I just said I didn't want to get sidetracked by the differences in how we express ourselves, but that might be just as good a way to start as any."

This time she nodded. If she put her hands on his seed-bearer, it should spring to life, but she didn't think that was what he was talking about.

He pointed at himself. "What do you call it, a seed-bearer?"

"Yes."

"Why?"

"Because that is what it is, what it does."

"Hmm. No argument there." He indicated the space between her legs. "And your sex organ, what label does it go by?"

Label? "That is my woman-place."

"That it is, all right. However, where I come from, the woman-place is called other things. Would you like to learn them?"

"Yes." Strange how having him point at the dark hairs and what they partly hid made her feel as if her woman-place was being walked on by tiny, soft-footed creatures.

"Good enough. All right, I guess I can be just as uninhibited as you've been. Lean back and spread your legs. It's Sex 101 time."

After a momentary hesitancy, she placed her arms behind her and braced her weight on them. Then she unfolded her legs. He crawled close and squatted between her legs.

"Hmmm." He leaned so near that she felt his breath on the sheltering hairs. The sensation of warm moisture on warm skin made her squirm. "All right," he continued. "We'll start conservatively. These—" He took the protective pieces of skin over her opening between his thumb and forefinger. "These go by a number of names, some pretty crude, but a gynecologist is going to call them labial lips."

"Labia..." Why was it hard to talk?

He chuckled and ran a nail over the inside of the loose skin. "Close enough. And while we're at it, that's your pubic hair. Can you say pubic hair?"

"Pu-bic."

"Close enough, young lady, close enough."

Still holding onto what he said were her lips, he ran his other hand through the curly hair he'd been talking about. She squirmed again, and it was all she could do not to close her legs so he'd stop tickling her—only it didn't really feel like tickling.

"Having trouble concentrating already, are you?" he asked. "Would you like to conclude the lesson and get onto recess?"

How could they speak the same language and yet not? "What—what is recess?"

"Oh, you'll like that; believe me, you will. However, I'd be remiss as a teacher—probably get myself fired—if we quit so soon." Once again he ran his nail over flesh so sensitive she thought she'd cry out with the wonder of it. "You're concentrating, aren't you?"

"I..." She didn't want to look down at herself; that would make it worse. But was meeting his laughing eyes any easier? "I want—to learn."

"I bet you do. And so do I." Tipping his head to one side, he continued his study of her woman-place. "Good thing the moon's out tonight," he observed. "Otherwise, I'd really be hunting in the dark, not that I'd mind."

"Pubic hairs," she whispered, proud of herself.

"Yep, you've got that right." He blew on her woman-place. "There," he said as her hips of their own will bucked off the ground. "That was your reward. At least your first one. Would you like another?"

She wanted anything he chose to give her and told him so by scooting forward so she was even more exposed.

"Boy, do I love you and your people's uninhibited ways." He sounded a little breathless. "All right, where were we? Oh, that's right. Labial lips. But that's just the teaser, at least as far as a cock is concerned."

"Cock?"

"That's right; you don't know. Where I come from, seed-bearers are called cocks. Sometimes penis. It depends on who's doing the talking and in what context."

"What—what do you want me to call it?"

He blew on her tender place again. When, once more, her hips refused to stay on the ground, he released what he called her labial lips and cupped his hand over her opening, pressing. She started to back away.

"No, no," he warned. "You don't want to do that. Believe me, you don't."

Beyond concentrating on anything but her body, she willed herself to stay where she was. The more he pressed on her there, the hotter and hungrier she felt up inside.

"Remember that gynecologist I told you about?" he asked.

She didn't but muttered, "Yes."

"Good." He began running a fingertip up and down, up and down against the opening to her woman-place. Her mouth parted, and she breathed through it.

"Good," he repeated. "Now pay attention. You are paying attention, aren't you? At least you're zeroed in on your body. This place I've got my hand on, not just my forefinger—is sometimes called the female genitalia."

"Gen…"

"Tsk, tsk. You really have to pay attention, Maia. You do want recess, don't you?"

"Yes. Genitalia."

"That's my girl."

His finger had stopped moving. Maybe he'd noticed that she was becoming swollen there—at least it felt like that—and didn't like it. Before she could think how to ask him, he found her opening and slipped into her. It was just one finger, a small thing compared to his—his cock. But that finger had to be responsible for the moisture filling her. It felt incredible.

"Good, good," he muttered. "You're a fast learner. No doubt about it, you're going to the head of the class. Moving along, that wetness—you know you're getting wet, don't you?"

If she reached for him, would he ram his cock into her? Maybe she'd have to ask him to.

"There's a name for what's happening to you," he continued. "Well, more like a phrase. You're turned on."

"Turn?" The word came out a squeak. "You want me on my stomach?"

He laughed. "Another time, you bet. But I'm not going to press my luck by trying to take you too far too fast. Pay attention. It shouldn't take you long to figure this out—and get off on it." He pushed his finger further inside her and wiggled it.

"Oh. " She moaned. "Oh."

"That's turned on," he whispered, his tone now serious. "When that happens to a woman, juices—her pussy starts to flow."

"Oh," she said even though she wasn't really concentrating. She wished she could lay down and put her legs on his shoulders so he could get at her—her pussy—with less effort. At the same time, she was content to remain where she was, learning everything her pussy was capable of.

"Taurus?" she managed as something that felt like winged creatures beat at her pussy walls.

"I'm not Tau—what?"

"Is—is it the same for a man?"

"Is what the same?"

"The way mating feels?"

"We aren't mating yet. This is foreplay, getting you turned on."

She opened her mouth to ask for an explanation, but he stopped her by placing his free hand over her breast. She felt the tip called her milk-giver harden.

"It works, doesn't it," he said in that low voice she could swear she heard clear through her. "It doesn't take much to arouse you."

"Is — it that a good thing?"

"You'd better believe it. Maia, you may be the most sexually liberated woman I've ever known, certainly the most sexual virgin."

She should tell him that she was no longer a virgin, but the buzzing that had started in her pussy — what a funny word — was spreading throughout her. She couldn't make her eyes focus, and it took all her strength to remain where she was. His finger was a traveler, an explorer capable of finding places in her she hadn't known existed. It shouldn't be like that; how could he have more wisdom about that hidden place than she, its owner, did?

It didn't matter. At least it didn't right now.

Her cheeks felt so hot, but that was nothing compared to her heated pussy-place.

"Why — why are you doing this?" she managed.

"You like it, don't you?"

"Yes! Yes." She tried to close her legs so she could trap his hand there, but he stopped her by bracing his elbow against the inside of her thigh.

"Sorry, Maia, but I'm not going to let you get off this easily. I'd be remiss in my responsibilities as your teacher if I did. It feels pretty damn good, doesn't it? Somewhere between pleasure and pain."

Some part of her pussy was trying to escape. She felt it throb and swell, and each time Taurus' finger touched it, it took all her will not to cry out. Sobbing low in her throat, she leaned forward and pressed her breast against his hand.

"I take it that's an answer in the affirmative." As if rewarding her, he began working another finger inside her. It filled her, pushed her apart. She wondered if she could swallow all of him this way.

"Your seed-bearer..." After a half breath, she tried again. "Your cock. When will you put it in me?"

"Soon, very soon. My god, I can't believe I'm—do you feel that?" He flicked his finger over the part of her pussy that was trying to escape.

"Yes!" Even with her eyes closed, her world was turning red.

"That's your clit."

"Cl-it?" What was happening to her? She felt out of control, rushing off somewhere she couldn't fathom.

"Whoever designed us wisely decided that women deserved as much pleasure as men get. It works, doesn't it?"

In a befuddled way, she knew he had asked a question, but she no longer knew where they were or where the world had gone. Something was scraping her skin and making it more and more sensitive. Everything centered around his fingers and his hand enveloping her hungry breast. Her pussy danced, jumped, jerked.

"There, there," he said. "Let it come. It's your cunt, Maia. Celebrate what it's capable of."

"Cunt?"

"Pussy."

"I, ah—"

"Shh. Don't try to talk. Let me do this for you."

He hadn't told her what *this* was, but she didn't need him to. The strength went out of her arms, and she fell back onto the ground. She heard herself pant. Her pussy—cunt—had become like a small storm, making her slow to realize that he'd withdrawn his fingers. How could he leave her like—?

No, he was still there.

Limp as a newborn, she felt him grab her legs and place them around his waist. Then he scooted closer, and under his guidance, she lifted her buttocks.

His cock pushed against her pussy-cunt, but her labial lips were in his way. Rocking up, she used her fingers to push them aside.

Then he was in her, his cock swollen and possessive.

He began pushing as if determined to drive his cock all the way through her, and yet she couldn't get enough of him. Reaching out, she found his thighs and dug her nails into them, urging him on. He bracketed her legs higher on his hips and drew her closer. With her body from the waist down off the ground, her movement was down to almost nothing, but he provided enough for both of them.

"Sex," Taurus spit out. "Where I come from—" He plunged into her, hung there a heartbeat, retreated a little, then plunged again. "This is called sex. Fucking."

"I—I like fucking."

"Just *like?*"

The two sacs behind his cock slapped against her bottom. She'd never heard that sound of flesh against flesh before. If someone had told her this would happen during mating— fucking—she would have wrinkled her nose in disgust, but now that it was happening—now that his cock filled her cunt, and her head felt like a drum being beaten, and she was on fire—

"I love fucking! Love it!"

He grunted something she didn't catch. She didn't ask him to repeat himself because she wouldn't have been able to concentrate anyway.

She was running, her feet not touching the ground but skimming over it like a bird. Ahead of her, she spotted, felt, tasted even, a great ocean wave.

The wave slammed into her. Instead of cold seawater, she felt heat. Fire.

Fire!

Chapter Nine

Taron couldn't be sure, but even bets were that he'd died and gone to heaven. He couldn't remember how many times he and Maia had had sex since she'd first come on to him. He felt as if he'd been ridden hard and put away wet — in more ways than one — and yet if she opened her legs again, he'd do his damnedest to service her.

"Just call me stud studly," he muttered. "Old and wrung out but still willing to give it another shot."

Maia didn't say anything. Maybe she was asleep, but he didn't think so because with her head on his outstretched arm, and her naked body spooned against his, he was a pretty good judge of her condition. They'd both sweated like pigs during their mutual climax, but that had dried in the night air. Maybe she was starting to shiver.

No, not shiver.

"Maia, what is it?" he asked when she suddenly sat up.

"They come."

Instead of asking who she was talking about, he forced himself into an upright position. Now that she'd drawn his attention to it, he could hear approaching footsteps, or more precisely, boots.

She scrambled to her feet and slipped her gauzy garment over her head. She was already fastening the dagger in place by the time he reached for his own clothes.

"We cannot stay here," she said. "We must join the others."

* * * * *

By *others* she'd meant the wise old men and others who'd been hanging around them earlier. The Lady was there too, as well as the other young women who he'd determined had been Maia's fellow virgins although from their disheveled looks, he concluded that they'd all lost that distinction. Everyone was watching an approaching procession consisting of three men in long, dark robes followed by at least a dozen heavily armed soldiers. Granted, their weapons consisted of swords, knives, even a couple of axes, but next to the unarmed villagers, they looked formidable. Drums had beaten while he and Maia were having sex, but now they were silent.

"They're the priests?" he asked Maia. "They don't look happy."

She indicated the nearby hills, each with its own fire. "They tried to forbid us to celebrate Bel-fire."

"Pushy, aren't they. What are they going to do?"

"I do not know."

The fear in her voice put him on edge. Reacting instinctively, he reached into his pockets, but a wallet full of credit cards wouldn't cut any ice here. The only other thing he found was the cigarette lighter he'd taken from Paul.

He was taller than most of the villagers and in darn good physical condition, if he did say so himself. Besides, his short hair, button down shirt and slacks set him apart. He positioned himself near the old men and The Lady, uneasy because Maia was with him when he wanted her somewhere safe.

"Godless heathens!" the priests announced in unison the moment they reached the top of the hill. They all had walking sticks or staffs or whatever they wanted to call them and used them to point at the fire that was now little more than ashes. "This is the devil's work!"

"Excuse me," Taron said in his chairman-of-the-board voice. "What gives you the right to try to order these people around? In case you haven't noticed, you're in the minority here."

One of the soldiers, a man who wore a metal helmet in addition to the breastplates the others had on, stepped closer. He aimed a spear with a sharp point at Taron.

"Silence, infidel!" he ordered. "You will not defy men of the cloth."

"Who died and made you king?"

The soldier blinked and frowned. "The king is not above the priests," he said. "Priests speak the word of truth and subservience. No one will defy them."

"We do not defy. All we want is to celebrate spring as our people have done since the beginning of time."

Taron had to hand it to The Lady. She didn't sound at all intimidated.

"Silence!" one of the priests ordered. "No woman shall treat a man of the cloth with disrespect. You heathens do not understand. You are too simple. You must be taught—"

"Watch it," Taron interrupted. "These aren't dumb animals you're talking to. Just because they don't buy your nonsense doesn't mean they're wrong. Did it ever occur to you that you're the ones barking up the wrong tree?"

This time all of the newcomers gaped at him as if he was speaking a foreign language. At least they weren't telling him to take a hike—yet.

"Look," he continued. "I just got here myself so I'm no expert, but Bel-fire means a great deal to these people. They're not going to scrap it just because you and your thugs say they should."

"Silence! Yours is the voice of the devil."

Not interested in debating that, Taron indicated the fire. "Why didn't you get here earlier? It's almost out. Any chance you didn't want to push your luck?"

"Silence!" the shortest priest ordered. "Our prayers came first. Only when we had received the word of the ruler of the universe could we turn his preaching into action."

"Yeah, right." Maia was tugging at his arm, but he didn't let that distract him. "Why don't you and your hired guns blow town? No one needs you telling them what to do."

The helmeted soldier jabbed his spear at The Lady. The tip was only inches from her middle.

"Silence, heathens!" the short priest repeated. "Our weapons are the weapons of our lord and master. They will shed the blood of unbelievers and bring glory to our master."

On the verge of telling the priests they were insane, Taron decided he was wasting his breath. There was no reaching people whose beliefs were so deeply entrenched that they wanted to kill anyone who didn't agree with them. Besides, he hadn't seen a single weapon among the Bel-fire celebrants. What were they, pacifists? If he'd been like that, his company would already be in enemy hands.

"The bonfire is almost burned down," he said, his attention locked on the sharp tip now pressed against The Lady. He spoke to the villagers. "It's going to be morning soon. Maybe — maybe we should just put it out, for now. Once we have these jokers —" He indicated the priests and soldiers. "Off our backs, we can strategize. It's not worth anyone getting killed."

Out of the corner of his eye, he saw the old men exchange glances. Then they went back to studying the soldiers. The Lady stood there calm as could be. He could hear Maia's uneasy breaths.

"Look." He addressed the priests. "In my book, you're bullies. You think you've got some divine right to march in and throw away generations of tradition and belief. What the hell good is it going to do to solve this with bloodshed? We, everyone who gives a damn, needs to sit down and present their views. Then we'll reach a compromise, develop a strategy. That's the way I run my business; it can be done."

"The ruler's ways must become law."

The gibberish that had just come from the short priest's mouth nearly set Taron off, but he knew nothing was going to be accomplished here until tempers had calmed down.

He turned to the onlookers, his gaze taking in The Lady and old men. "It's a strategic move," he told them. "We're not giving in. We're not even compromising, but damn it, if there's a battle right now, we're not going to win. Extinguish those embers."

"No!"

The last person he'd expected to disagree was Maia but there she was, standing toe-to-toe with him.

"No," she repeated. "That *cannot* happen!"

"Why the hell not? Maia, we're talking about saving lives here."

"Embers must be scattered among our crops to protect them. More must be taken by each household to light their hearth. And I—I must jump over them to ensure that I will have an easy birth."

Every clan member within earshot was now nodding vigorously, but he couldn't concentrate on that. "Easy birth," he managed. "What are you saying?"

"I am with child. Your child."

Just like that, he felt his world tilt. "You can't know—we just—wait a minute!" Ignoring the onlookers, he hauled her so close that her features blurred. "What the hell is going on here? You told me—you said you were using protection. You tricked me." *Why the hell was he saying that?*

"I did what My Lady said I must."

She sounded so calm and confident that a little of his shock and outrage—if that's what it was—dissipated. "You got me to fuck you so you could get knocked up, didn't you? You lied—hell, even if you didn't lie, you weren't honest."

She glanced at her flat stomach. "This is a child of Bel-fire. Conceived of you so even those who do not believe in our ways

will understand that we are more than what they say we are—
infidels. Our beliefs are strong. Right." Still in his grasp, she
stared at the priests. "This Bel-fire baby was conceived by a man
from a time far in the future. By Taurus the bull."

Shit. What is she saying?

"A heathen bastard!" the short priest insisted. "It cannot be.
It must not!"

Although he was still reeling from what Maia had just said,
Taron didn't need to be hit over the head to realize things were
getting out of control. The short priest was actually foaming at
the mouth and shaking with fury.

"She can't be sure," he heard himself say. "Hell, she was a
virgin the first time we had sex earlier tonight." *Or whenever all
this started.* "And I'm not Taurus. I'm a man some woman has
tricked—"

"Not a trick, Taurus!" Maia interrupted. "If you do not
want this child, I do not want you as its father. Go!" She yanked
free. "We had sex. We fucked," she told him. "And now it is
done. Go!"

"Kill the bastard child!"

Taron whirled. To a man the soldiers stared at the short
priest.

"Do not defy me!" the priest yelled. "Do the work of your
lord and master. Rip the bastard from her belly."

Not fully comprehending what he was doing, Taron
positioned himself between Maia and the soldiers. Most
continued to look uncertain, but two who put him in mind of TV
wrestlers drew their knives. He quickly assessed his chances of
knocking the weapons out of the soldiers' hands and grabbing
them himself; not good. Nevertheless, they'd have to go through
him to get to her.

"Leave," Maia hissed. "This is not your battle."

Too late for that. "You can't be serious," he told the priests,
but he was only stalling for time. "This is murder."

"Who are you?"

About to give them everything including his social security number, it hit him that that wouldn't get him anywhere. However—

"Taurus, the bull," he announced. "Brought here because The Lady and clan elders were afraid something like this was going to happen. They needed a fighter, a *bull*."

"Brought from where?"

Well, that's a little hard to explain. "The future," he said, not taking his eyes off the two wrestlers.

"Liar! Infidel!"

Now what, smart ass? he asked himself as the wrestlers separated and stalked closer. Not thinking, he rammed his hands in his pockets. His fingers closed around Paul's lighter, and he withdrew it.

"Do you see this?" he demanded as he held it up. "This is my proof."

One of the soldiers laughed. The priests didn't look impressed.

"Like me, it is from the future," he insisted. "Magic. Powerful magic."

"Kill him, too," one of the priests said.

"No!" Maia slid around him. "This is not his concern. He does not care—"

No time like the present, he thought and flicked the lighter. Nothing happened. He flicked it again. A white-red flame shot up nearly four inches. *Thank you, Paul. You always had to have the biggest, baddest toy on the block, didn't you?*

For a few seconds no one spoke. Hell, no one so much as moved. And no two ways about it, he was the center of attention. He felt stronger than he had in his entire life.

"See this." He held the lighter high enough for everyone to see and then let it go out. "In my time, everyone carries fire in their hands. They can make it go to sleep the way I've just done.

But because they are all powerful, because they believe in Belfire, it is nothing to bring fire to life." He flicked, and to his relief, the flame ignited again. This time he kept it going.

"What do you think of that?" he demanded of the priests. "Nothing like a little magical flame to make your babble about infidels and the master of the universe sound like crap."

He wasn't sure what kind of response that would elicit. Hell, he hadn't thought past doing whatever it took to keep those knives away from Maia and the baby—his baby. He should have.

Something that might be a prayer spewed out of the short priest's mouth. Gripping the cross he wore, he stalked toward Maia. As he did, the wrestler/soldiers backed up. Obviously Paul's lighter intimidated them. So much for a well-trained army.

"I am the voice of the lord and master," the priest insisted. "I speak the truth, only me. And I say the devil *must* be destroyed." He whirled on the soldiers. "Obey me! Obey! Kill the devil's spawn."

Deciding that the armed soldiers constituted more of a threat than the crazy man in dirty, flowing robes, Taron kept the still-burning lighter aimed at the military force. Still feeling all-potent, he took his gaze off the priest for only a second.

Screaming, the man launched himself at Maia. An elbow caught her under her chin and knocked her backward. She staggered but didn't fall. The priest's thick-knuckled fingers closed around her dagger.

"Maia!"

From what he could tell, the blow had stunned Maia. She tried to pull the priest's hands off her, but she wasn't having much success. The priest leaned back and punched her, hard, in the stomach.

Taron's world turned red; fury and fear filled him. "Damn you!" he bellowed.

The soldiers were again focusing on their weapons. Any moment now they might lose their awe of the lighter and attack in mass. For maybe a second, the priest looked indecisive. Then he yanked the dagger out of its sheath.

"No!" Taron bellowed. He started forward.

Quicker than Taron could believe, the priest lifted the dagger so that the gentle firelight glinted off the red jewel. Then he plunged it into Maia's side.

"No!" Taron yelled; he felt sick.

Struggling not to be undone by the blood already soaking Maia's garment, Taron closed the remaining space between himself and the loudly chanting priest and shoved the lighter against the bastard.

The man's robe instantly burst into flames. He gaped at Taron, then began beating frantically at himself. The flames grew, and screaming, he ran at the soldiers.

"Save me! Save me!" he begged.

Taking advantage of the confusion, Taron scooped Maia up in his arms and ran.

Chapter Ten

Being stabbed did strange things to her body. No matter how hard she tried to make sense of what damage the dagger had inflicted, Maia's mind refused to focus. Some of it, she knew, came from loss of blood, but she kept thinking about how wonderful it felt to be in Taurus' strong, protective arms and that stopped her from concentrating on anything else.

He was breathing like a horse at the end of a race, and his body, like hers, was drenched in sweat. His heartbeat felt quick and desperate. He hadn't run all that long, but neither did he show any sign that he was ready to stop.

That was fine with her, wonderful in fact. Why she felt like that didn't matter.

She closed her eyes, but opened them again when that conjured up an image of the priest with his robe ablaze. The man had stabbed her and tried to kill Taurus' child; she could hate him, couldn't she?

Taurus hadn't wanted the baby, had called her a liar...

He staggered and nearly dropped her. Jarred out of her semi-conscious state, she lifted her head off his chest.

"Taurus, put me down."

"Thank god! You're—I thought—are you all right?"

She wasn't, but as her memories of the horrible things he'd said to her became clearer, she couldn't think about that.

"Put me down," she repeated, more forcefully this time.

He did so, reluctantly it seemed. She tried to stand, but her legs wouldn't hold her. If he hadn't eased her to the ground, she would have collapsed.

"You've lost so much blood," he whispered. Although she tried to brush his hand away, she soon gave up and let him pull up on her gown and look at her side.

"Damn," he cursed. "That crazy old fool—look, I've got to get you into the present right now. What do we have to do, run under a fire arch?"

"The present?" She couldn't make him come into focus.

"My time. I *have* to get you to a doctor." He sounded on the brink of panic.

"No." Her side burned, but the pain wasn't anything she couldn't handle. "My belly? The dagger did not penetrate it?"

"No."

Relief flooded her. "My baby is safe. That is all that matters."

He didn't say anything. "The dagger is blessed, its origins and future beyond comprehension," she told him. "It is given to those who need it. Such a gift would not destroy life."

"It's going to kill you unless I get you some help." He'd been kneeling beside her, his hand on her shoulder. Now he ran the back of his hand over her cheek. "Maia, it's just a knife; that's all it is."

"No."

"Yes. Damn you, I know where your thinking is going. You're content to stay here and wait—for something. Black magic or some damn thing." He slipped his hand between her legs. "We had something—something mind-blowing going between us. I'm not going to let it end."

She felt his hand on her pussy, and yet she didn't. Her mind held remnants of climaxes so intense that the drums of Bel-fire paled in comparison, but those body-eruptions lasted only a little while. What would be part of her for as long as she lived was her role in the clan—and the role her child would play in Bel-fire's future.

"It is over," she whispered. "You and I do not matter. Only this place and time, my people do."

"No! Damn it, Maia, you didn't need to risk your life just as you didn't have to seduce me the way—"

"Go!" She weakly swatted at his hand and tried to pull her legs together. "I do not need you any more. Your job is finished."

He didn't say anything, and in the silence she wondered if she was dying—not from the wound although that was possible—but because of what she'd just told him. His fingers continued to rest against her labial lips, causing her to heat and moisten inside, but that wasn't enough. He'd provided the seed-bearer that her baby-place had needed. Now he could go, return to his place, be safe.

"I do not want you," she whispered. "You had my virginity. Is that not enough?"

"You don't want me?"

I don't know; I can't think. And I'm afraid for you. "Go to The Lady. She will show you how to return to your time."

"I'm going only if I can take you with me."

"No!" she exclaimed and tried to sit up. "No! I do not want..." *I cannot leave those who need me.* She needed to tell him that, didn't she? Desperate to find the answer, she blinked repeatedly, but his features remained blurred. She felt herself being sucked into a deep hole. The last thing she knew was his fingers caressing her pussy.

* * * * *

Taron had tied his shirt around Maia's wound with shaking fingers and was trying to take her pulse when he heard approaching footsteps. He jumped to his feet, positioning himself between her and the unknown intruders. If only he really was a bull, anything except a shirt and tie helpless-as-hell businessman. He still had Paul's cigarette lighter but wasn't sure he could chase off anyone with it. A branch-turned-spear or handful of rocks might delay the inevitable.

"Maia, Taurus, it is us."

The voice of The Lady was a relief. At the same time, he was leery of her reasons for wanting to find Maia. Not only that, she wasn't alone. Silent, he waited for the newcomers to come into view. The Lady, naked as the day she was born but with her long, flowing hair covering her breasts, was on horseback as were the three old men.

They stopped as one when they spotted him and Maia. After giving him a cursory glance, they focused on Maia. Finally The Lady dismounted and approached. He had to hand it to her. For a woman who looked to be in her fifties, she was a fine figure indeed, lean muscle under the slightly sagging skin, and pride in the way she carried herself. He wondered if Maia would have that same bearing and self-confidence when she was that age — if she lived that long.

"She is alive," The Lady said. It wasn't a question. "Taurus, thank you."

No longer concerned with correcting anyone about his name, he nodded. "She's lost a lot of blood," he said. "What about those damn priests and their puppet soldiers? Where are they? What about the one I torched?"

One of the old men grunted. "The priest tore off his robe; all could see his reddened shoulders and arms. His hair is burned; it stinks. The last we saw, he was standing naked with his white belly hanging down over his man-thing."

It struck Taron that the old man hadn't said *seed-bearer*, maybe because the priest had no value in that department. The Lady dropped to her knees beside Maia and placed the back of her hand over Maia's nose. "Yes, she breathes," she said softly. "Taurus, again we thank you."

"Someone had to do something," he snapped. "Everyone else was standing around with their hands in their pockets."

No one said anything.

"I don't want some witch doctor or whatever you people have caring for her. I've got to get her to a full service hospital, pronto."

"Hospital?"

Shit. They weren't going to waste time playing word games, not with Maia's life at stake.

"Look." He grabbed The Lady's shoulders and hauled her to her feet. Too late he realized that put him face to face with a buck-naked woman. His cock paid no mind. "Maia said you know how this time-travel stuff works. Whatever you have to do, do it! I'm getting her to an emergency room, damn it!"

"That place is not what she needs."

"What are you, a trauma specialist? Never mind; we both know the answer to that. What's the mortality rate around here? I can guarantee it's a hell of a lot higher than where I intend to take her." *If I can figure out how to get there.* "You want her to live, don't you?"

"She will."

The Lady's calm and certain tone distracted him; he almost believed her. He sure as hell wanted to, but when he heard approaching footsteps, he dug into his pocket for the lighter. Why didn't any of these people carry weapons?

"Do not be afraid," The Lady told him. "Her family knows what must be done."

"What? Leeches? Don't get anywhere near her with something like that. You so much as try and I swear..." *What, you idiot? Run off the whole village with a Bic?*

He didn't know what to make of the ragtag bunch coming their way. It was light enough now that he saw everything from a baby in arms to a woman who had at least one foot in the grave. There were maybe twenty of them. Except for the young woman carrying the baby, they all had an armload of firewood. To his dismay, they piled the wood around Maia. He would have stopped them except—except what?

"Where is your fire-maker?" The Lady asked. "Light the one closest to her head."

"The hell I will!" *Shit, where was Rambo when he needed him?* "Don't you get it? She's — she might be dying."

"She is," The Lady said, causing his heart to skip. "But spring's flames will save her and the child."

He opened his mouth, but nothing came out. There wasn't anything remotely frightening about these people. Quite the contrary, their expressions were universally gentle — almost as if they felt sorry for him. There was something about their presence that gave him a sense of peace; when had he last felt that?

"What are you doing?" he asked.

"There is not time to explain it all, Taurus," The Lady told him. "This is Bel-fire, the time to celebrate the land and the life which springs from it. During the moons of winter, seeds have lain dormant. No newborn animals suckle at their mothers' breasts. It is as it must be; the world rests. But with our celebration, we awaken the souls of those seeds. They know that our need for them is great. The souls of all living things come together in the flames of Bel-fire. They will see Maia and give her their energy, their life."

Any other time, he would have retorted that that was the biggest bunch of bull he'd ever heard, but he didn't. For the life of him he couldn't say why. Maybe it was nothing more than the older woman's soft, sincere tone. Maybe the way everyone nodded agreement had something to do with it.

Possibly — probably — the utter and complete faith in everyone's eyes had seduced him. Feeling as if he'd lost all control when he was accustomed to exactly the opposite, he walked over to the pile of brush closest to Maia's head and lit it. Once the flames took hold, The Lady pulled out a burning branch and used it to light the other piles. It was now dawn, and yet the flames provided enough of a contrast that they painted her naked flesh in bright red. When he looked at the others, he saw that the same thing had happened to them.

Then he looked down at Maia and forgot everything else. Her features were paler than the villagers, almost white. Weak, he dropped to his knees and used his thighs as a pillow for her head. His cock stirred.

I don't know where you are, he told her. *Or whether you can hear me. I want you to know I'd do anything to get you to a hospital, but I can't find the way. If you're aware of what's happening here, I need you to come back so you can explain.*

That sounded selfish, a piss-poor reason for her to fight for life.

There's a lot that's unsettled between us, he continued. *We had something — something mind-blowing going. Do you know that? Look, I don't have the statistics; there probably aren't any. But almost no virgins climax the first time; I'm sure of that.*

"Sure you are," he muttered. "What'd you do, take a survey?"

You came, he told her. *That's proof that you're one sexy broad, and I'm one hell of a stud. Can you imagine what would happen if we were given half a chance? We'd never get out of bed. We'd probably kill ourselves, but what a way to go.*

That was all wrong! He shouldn't be begging Maia to live so he could fuck her senseless. No matter how appealing that sounded, there was still the matter of the crazy priests and their mindless soldiers. But first — first Maia had to live.

Unable to think beyond that, he cupped his hands around her breasts and began fingering them. Her nipples hardened, but she gave no other sign that she was aware of his presence — his touch.

All around him the flames danced with the rising sun. Drums began playing.

Chapter Eleven

Taron figured he must have dozed off because suddenly The Lady was beside him. Instead of explaining what she was doing, she slipped something into Maia's hand, kissed her on the forehead, and then walked away. When he blinked and looked around, he saw that the villagers were leaving. The fires would soon be down to coals.

A soft, unexpected sound made him start, but when he realized it was coming from Maia, he relaxed. The priests and their henchmen couldn't hurt her — at least not right now.

"What is it?" he whispered. "Are you in pain?"

She opened her eyes but seemed to be having trouble focusing. Finally, her attention locked on him.

"Why are you here?" she asked. She sounded strangled.

He didn't answer because the truth was, he didn't know — either that or he wasn't ready to confess all. As the survivor of more one-night stands than he cared to remember, he knew how to end things with a kiss and a closed door. When her stare intensified, he drew her attention to the dagger The Lady had returned to her.

"I don't know how they recovered it," he told her. "Probably the priest dropped it, and someone found it."

She held it up so she could study it. Her movement was a simple one, nothing nearly every human being on the planet couldn't do without thinking about it, but it thrilled him. Maybe the worst was over, and she was going to live. Did the fires and drumming and songs have anything to do with it? Maybe his insistent finger-play while she'd been unconscious had turned the tide.

"Do you remember what happened?" he asked because he didn't feel strong enough to face the questions he'd just asked himself. "That priest—"

"My blood is no longer on the blade."

She did remember. "No, it isn't. Someone must have cleaned it off. Are—are you sure you want it around? It's going to remind you—"

"Why are you still here?"

She was lying near him, her blood-stained gown just barely covering her crotch, but if she was aware of that, she didn't let it show. She might not have the strength to sit up, but there was no ignoring the fire in her eyes.

"What did you want me to do?" he retorted, furious without knowing why. "Walk away?"

"You wanted to return to your time. You did not want to stay."

"So I could get you to a hospital."

"I have what I need here. Bel-fire's magic is healing me. My child will live."

"*Your* child! In case you've forgotten, I had something to do with it—if indeed there is a child."

"You do not want one?"

"Don't do that! Don't! You knew what you were doing when you seduced me, didn't you? The thing is, you didn't clue me in. That was devious." The moment the words were out, he wanted them back—or did he? Damn it, she needed to know that he felt manipulated. Changed in ways he didn't understand and that scared him. "Being seen as nothing except a sperm donor isn't as much of a compliment as you obviously think it is. I believe I deserve to have a say in…"

She was no longer looking at him, and he had the sneaking suspicion she wasn't listening to him either so why the hell should he bother? What he didn't understand was why he was angry at her when not that long ago he'd been terrified that she was dying.

"This —" She indicated the dagger. "This sent me to you."

"What are you talking about?"

Instead of answering, she rolled over onto her good side and tried to sit up. She might have been able to make it without help, but he didn't give her the opportunity to find out. She crossed her legs slightly and leaned forward, apparently oblivious to the fact that her pussy was now fully exposed. It took everything in him not to stare at her there, and he wondered when, not if, she'd notice that once again he had an erection. Given the size of it, it was pretty damn obvious.

One thing about the lady; she knew how to get him hot and bothered.

"This." She indicated the dagger which she held as lovingly as if it was a child and not the weapon that had nearly killed her. "This is a gift. It comes to those who need it."

Maybe he should be used to the way she switched from being a practical and grounded woman to a sprite not at all in touch with reality. But the truth was, he was no longer so sure what constituted reality.

"It is not for me or anyone to know what magic rules this." She ran her finger over the side of the blade. "It is enough that I am blessed."

"You nearly died because of it."

"No," she whispered. "I did not."

Instead of trying to amass arguments against that, he simply watched as she stroked the ruby-like jewel. Even unconscious, her breasts had responded to his touch. What would happen if he ran his hand over her belly and between her legs? Was she healed enough that she'd want sex — one last time?

"The first time I looked into the jewel," she said softly. "I saw my journey to you. I saw us together, mating. I knew what my task was."

"Did you?"

"I knew I would find you on the night of Bel-fire, that I would love mating with you, and that you would guide me to becoming a woman."

His cock strained against his wrinkled and dirty slacks.

"I did not know that we would ma—that we would have sex more than that one time."

Much more of this trip down memory lane and I'm going to be adding a new chapter. "Ah, did you know about that?" He pointed a less than steady finger at her still sore-looking side.

"No."

That surprised him enough that a margin of sanity returned—a very small margin. "That's all you learned from that crystal ball then?" he asked. "That you and I would get it on? Mate," he amended when she gave him a confused look.

"Then." She was still whispering. "Now I know the rest."

Just like that, his heated blood cooled. His erection was still undiminished, but it no longer commanded his attention. Instead, he struggled not to be undone by her somber tone.

He slid closer so their thighs were touching, but although he wanted to take her hand—such a simple thing, taking a woman's hand—he tried to see what held her attention about the stone.

"What's in there?" he asked.

For the first time since regaining consciousness, she looked down at her crotch. With her free hand, she touched her pussy lips. "I was like a child there," she said. "My—my cunt was something I barely understood. You changed that."

Although—damn it—he'd love to help her expand her knowledge of herself, now wasn't the time. If he could just get the message to his cock.

"Maia, I asked you something. What do you see in the stone?"

She withdrew her hand from her pussy. "You do not want to know."

Go with that, all right. Don't push. There's nothing wrong with ignorance. Even as he tried to convince himself of that, he knew he couldn't hide from the truth.

"You're probably right," he said. "But I need to."

She didn't say anything, prompting him to take her wrist and turn it so he could look at the stone. At first all he saw was the flawless if simply finished jewel, but as he continued to stare, the ruby-like interior changed. There was a mist in there, and something he recognized as a figure began walking out of the mist. Even before he saw the long, glossy black hair, he knew it was Maia. How could there be any confusion when he'd already memorized her curves and angles?

Instead of the gauzy gown, she was naked, and her breasts were larger, harder looking than now, the nipples darker. For as long as he focused on her breasts, he couldn't pay attention to anything else, but eventually he forced himself to study the rest of her. Her arms and legs were as long and smoothly-muscled as they were now, her neck slender, her features small.

What had changed the most was her belly. She wasn't due to deliver yet, but it was definitely distended.

His child. His financial responsibility. His tax deduction.

Disgusted with himself, he shook off the materialistic thoughts and continued to study the jewel. He couldn't see enough of what was around the small Maia-figure to know where she was, but there didn't seem to be anyone near her. She walked slowly as if her thoughts were elsewhere. Her shoulders were slightly slumped, and she wasn't smiling.

Maia—the real Maia—sighed.

"What is it? Are you in pain?"

She shook her head. "I knew it would be like this."

That I would be alone. Numb, he couldn't do anything except watch as the Maia-figure plodded along what had now revealed itself as a narrow path. The land around the path came into focus, and he could tell that wherever she was, it was summer. The bushes on either side of the path were alive with bright leaves and flowers that covered the full spectrum of colors. He swore he could smell grass.

"Where are you going?" he asked. "Do you know?"

"To be with my people."

Your people, not with me. "Is it safe to be there? What about the soldiers?"

"I do not know," she said after a moment. "That part of the future has not revealed itself."

But your being alone has.

"What about the child?" he managed. "Is it all right?"

"Taurus, my child belongs to my people. Look."

Although that might be the last thing he wanted to do, he had no choice. The Maia-figure had reached a collection of huts, and a number of people were coming out of them and enthusiastically greeting her. An older woman who he didn't think was The Lady placed a cape around Maia's shoulders and then dropped to her knees, widened Maia's stance, and began what he had no doubt was a gynecological examination although Maia continued to stand.

"Who is she?"

"My grandmother. She will guide me during birth, and when my child is born, she will wrap it in furs and take it to our spirit-leaders to be blessed."

Your child? What about me? Shit, that's right. I have a business to try to save. "What then, Maia?" he challenged. He tried to focus on his company and the pride, effort, and determination behind it, but he couldn't. "Just because I caught that priest's robe on fire doesn't mean the threat to your way of life is going to go away. Your people don't know how to fight for their rights. You can't guarantee that *our* child will be safe."

"The child is my people's hope, our future. He will carry the clan's soul and spirit, and yet he will be more. His blood will be that of Taurus the bull. He will have great courage and that courage will protect our way of life."

Taron had never seen himself as a parent. To his way of thinking, a child needed a full-time father, and his company claimed so much of him that he wouldn't be able to give his children the love and attention he'd never gotten. His son — *son!* — was nothing more than a collection of cells right now, and yet...

His hand was less than steady as he focused on the dagger. He wasn't sure what he wanted to have happen; the last thing he expected was to have her image fade and be replaced by one of him.

He was standing in a massive, expensively decorated living room, something that would grace the pages of an upscale architectural magazine. The ceiling was ridiculously high, the white leather couch, so large he wondered how they'd gotten it through the door. A large-screen TV and entertainment center dominated one wall. The carpet felt lush under his feet. No doubt about it, the place belonged to someone who'd *made* it.

"Where are you?" Maia asked.

In the home I promised myself I'd buy if I defeated the take-over attempt, he nearly told her but couldn't spit out the words. "That's what houses — huts — look like where I come from," he said instead. "At least some do."

"Where are the others?"

"Others?"

"Who lives there with you? Surely it is too big for one person."

Surely.

He didn't think he was capable of manipulating an image, but by concentrating, he propelled *himself* through opulent rooms until *he* opened a pair of double doors and found *himself* in a bedroom nearly large enough to play football in. The king-sized bed was masculine with a dark, wood headboard and a royal blue bedspread.

"What is that?" Maia asked.

"Where I'll sleep."

"Who—who sleeps there with you?"

"I'm not sure." *Maybe no one.*

"It is so big. Perhaps many people—?"

"No." He rested his hand on her thigh. "That's not the way it's done in my time. The only one who'd share that with me would be a woman."

She didn't say anything, but he could hear her quickened breathing.

"What?" he asked. He started working his fingers toward her cunt. "How do you feel about that?"

"About—what you are doing to me?"

"That too. I was talking about my bringing a woman to my bed."

Not looking at him, Maia drew the dagger out of his grasp and laid it on the ground, stone down. So much had happened since she'd first approached Taurus, but this morning none of that mattered. Without checking it, she knew that her wound had nearly healed, just as her body told her she was carrying Taurus' son. When The Lady had chosen her to mate with the bull from the future, she'd willingly accepted her role, but that's all it had been back when she was still a virgin—her responsibility.

Since then everything had changed.

"When will you leave and go live in your house?" she made herself ask.

"I don't know."

"It must be soon. Your time waits for you. You said you had important things to do."

"I guess."

She couldn't think of anything else to say; just the thought of his walking out of her world brought her to the brink of tears.

She should stand, pick up the dagger and return to her people so The Lady and elders could tell her what she must do next—and learn what the priests and soldiers were doing. But how could she, with Taurus' hand on her?

Barely believing what she was doing, she took hold of his wrist and guided him closer to her baby-place, her pussy.

"Are you sure?" he asked.

She wasn't sure of anything, least of all herself. Right now the only thing that mattered was finding escape from the image of each of them walking alone. And only one thing would bring that escape.

"There—there was no one in your bed," she managed. His fingertips brushed the hair around her pussy, but already she was losing touch with her surroundings.

"No, there wasn't."

"If—if you could bring a woman there," she managed, "a woman who has come for sex, what would you have her do?"

"That's a hell of a question."

"You have not thought of such a thing?"

"I'm a red-blooded man. Of course I have, practically full-time, back when I was a teenager."

He started rolling some of her pubic hair back and forth. Because he was doing so gently, it didn't hurt, but it wouldn't take much to turn pleasure into pain. Despite that, she trusted him.

Trust this man who the stone said would live alone in a great house?

"What about you?" he asked. "Back when you were a virgin, didn't you have thoughts—needs? Don't tell me you never touched yourself here?"

He began a slow circuit of her pussy, not touching her hungry labial lips but their outsides. Just like that, she felt as if he'd touched her with a burning branch. She braced her arms behind her and leaned back so he could have easier access.

"You're incredible, Maia. Your pussy's a playground to you, isn't it? No hang-ups."

He'd said that word before. She wasn't sure what it meant except that to have a hang-up meant she wouldn't want him to touch her pussy, her cunt.

"No," she told him and slid closer to him.

"Whew. You've got that right."

He'd completed one journey and had started another. This time his fingers tiptoed closer to her cunt lips. The blaze he'd started burned hotter. She wanted him to put his fingers deep inside her so she could close her muscles down around him and keep him there. If she didn't, when this last mating was over, he'd go back to his world and the things that were important to him, and she'd...

With a start, she realized he'd completed his second journey around her sex-place. Her breasts felt hot and heavy as she waited for him to start again. He didn't.

"I don't want this to be fast, Maia," he said. "I want it to last."

"So — do I."

He sighed, the sound long and slow. "Shit, I don't want to think. That's the hell of it, I don't want to think."

They could do that, couldn't they? Just be?

Chapter Twelve

Taurus hadn't told her what he wanted her to do, but when he took hold of her blood-stained gown, she lifted her arms so he could pull it off. Then she said she wanted him naked and he complied. Maybe he'd wanted her to disrobe him, but she didn't trust her strength. Besides, she loved watching him unfasten his strange clothes and push what he called his slacks down his well-muscled legs. Even before he removed his briefs, she saw enough of his cock to know it was large and hard enough to completely fill her.

And not just her pussy.

"There is a thing husbands and wives sometimes do," she said when he stood naked over her. "Not always does a man put his cock in a woman's pussy."

"Is that a fact?" He was looking at the space between her legs. "And how do you know about that?"

"You know my people do not sleep each to their own house. That way, together, we can share what we have."

"Maybe it's better that way," he muttered. "So you've watched more than just your parents going at each other? Having sex, I mean."

"Yes." She bent her legs a little to make it easier for him to see her pussy. Although he was no longer touching her, the fire he'd started hadn't gone out, and she felt warm fluid building inside her. "Sometimes the women take their husbands' cocks into their mouths. Do you like that?"

"You're assuming I've, ah, had the pleasure of that experience?"

"Have you not?"

"Guilty as charged, but don't ask for details because you're not getting them." He lowered himself to his knees and was so close that she could easily stretch out her toes and rub them against him. She'd have to change positions to reach his cock however.

"You might have been a virgin," he said. "But you're pretty earthy. I think—maybe that's what I sensed when you walked up to me that first time."

She wondered if he had any idea how nervous she'd been. More than that, she wanted to ask if he too had to guard against thoughts of what would happen when this mating was over.

Determined to put that off, she slid closer and spread her legs so he was now between them. He wasn't smiling, and his eyes seemed to have sunk deep in his skull. "What are you thinking?" she made herself ask.

"Nothing."

"Nothing?"

"That's right, Maia. My thoughts don't go beyond this moment. I won't let them."

She reached out and grazed a fingertip over the underside of his cock. As she did, the sacs where his seed were stored, tightened. Curious about what else she could make them do, she cradled them in her palm and then folded her fingers over them.

"I think—" He kept his eye on what she was doing. "That might be what they mean by having a man right where you want him, or maybe it's having my balls in the palm of your hand."

"This." She lightly jiggled his balls. "This is an amazing thing. So soft."

"So vulnerable."

So am I, she nearly told him. Because she didn't dare, she released his balls and slid her fingers over his cock. Although his skin here was just as soft as the flesh over his balls, beneath that he was all hardness, all strength. "How were you injured?" she asked.

"Injured?"

She indicated the knob at the top. "The flesh which covers a man's cock is missing. You cannot have been born like this. Who hurt you?"

He shrugged. "Probably the pediatrician. I was circumcised at birth so my memory's pretty sketchy."

"Cir-cum-cised? What is that?"

"That—that flesh you're talking about is called foreskin. For reasons I'm not going to go into, the majority of American boys have that removed."

"How cruel!" Did he want her to kiss him there? Maybe he didn't want to be reminded of the pain. "I would hate to live where such things are done."

"It's all right. I have no memory—"

"But why?"

"Maia, I'll never be able to explain everything about my time and people."

And it doesn't matter because when you return to it that will be the end of us.

Although the ground wasn't free of twigs and other sharp things, she didn't hesitate to position herself on her side so she could get her mouth close to Taurus' cock. It was larger than she'd expected, at least it felt that way against her lips. Despite her initial shock, she opened her mouth and licked the tip. The tiny bit of moisture there tasted salty.

She didn't expect this to happen, but her pussy moisture increased, and she involuntarily squeezed her thighs together. He must have seen because he leaned over and ran his hand over her hip. Just like that, her pussy-fire increased. Much as she wanted to spread her legs again so he could play there, she didn't. Soon, yes, but now was for him.

She thought he'd warn her to be careful not to bite him, but he didn't. Every man acted as if his cock was precious, and she wanted Taurus to know she understood. After licking him again and hearing him gasp, she opened her mouth as far as it would go and settled it around him. She wanted to feel him deep in her throat and give him shelter there, but she might gag if she went any further. If they had more time, more days and nights together, she'd learn—

No! She refused to take her thoughts beyond now.

Her cunt was deep and large enough to swallow all of him; it seemed cruel that her mouth wasn't made the same way. Just the same, she managed to draw her tongue out of the way while he was going in. Now she touched, licked, and caressed every bit of his cock that she could reach. His hold on her hipbone tightened. Closing down with her lips, she alternated between pushing and pulling motions.

He must have liked that, because he took hold of the sides of her head and helped with the rhythm. Having his cock in her mouth, close to her teeth, gave her an unexpected sense of power. Was it possible, did men sometimes release their seed inside a woman's mouth? If so, what did the women do with it? Those questions kept her from concentrating fully on what she was doing.

Although she hated to, at length there was no denying that her jaw muscles were getting tired, and she reluctantly pushed him out of her. Instead of leaving him completely, she cradled his tip between her lips, softness against softness, moisture mating with moisture.

"That was mind-blowing," he whispered. "Are you trying to make me your slave?"

"My people do not have slaves!" she gasped, appalled. "Only barbarians do."

"That's a figurative slave, not literal," he told her. "And I'm glad to know that. Now, because I seem to have broken your concentration, it's my turn."

She had no idea what he was talking about until he positioned her so she was on her back, her legs bent and widespread. A momentary embarrassment because she couldn't remember when she'd last bathed herself turned into hot anticipation as he lowered himself before her exposed cunt. For a moment he remained still and silent; she ached to know what he was thinking but didn't dare ask.

"I can't remember my past," he muttered. "Anything about it. You've stolen it from me."

"I do not steal."

"Don't you? Never mind, right now neither of us wants to go there."

She hoped he would explain himself, but he didn't say a word. Looking up at the sky the way she was, she couldn't see what he was going to do, but she trusted him. Besides, she now lacked the strength to move.

Something warm and soft and moist touched her inner thigh, sending a fiery shudder through her. Halfway through trying to determine what he was doing, she decided to simply let it happen—or maybe *decide* wasn't it at all.

He stayed there, painting her sensitive flesh, covering her in dampness. Somewhere in the middle of feeling—just feeling— she realized he was bathing her with his tongue. He periodically deserted her hungry skin, but he always returned, and when he did, he was newly wet. When he moved from her thigh to the fold between leg and pussy, she started to shake—just a little but it was impossible to control. She thought she heard him chuckle, but her head was roaring now, and she couldn't be sure.

He stayed there for what seemed a long time, teasing her entrance. Her hunger for him grew until she felt starved, and her woman's moisture increased. Inside her cunt something was swelling, becoming hot and hard—desperate to escape.

Using his hands, he separated her burning pussy lips. Then, while she helped by lifting her so-heavy hips and widening her stance, he licked at the entrance to her pussy. Her nerves there hummed, the tempo increasing. Now she felt hot everywhere, even the top of her head. She'd broken out in a sweat.

He licked again, deeper this time, the tip of his tongue intruding. She began whipping her head from side to side but was only barely aware of what she was doing. She moaned, then her breath whistled.

Deeper now, tongue pushing in, seeming to laugh inside her, light and strong all at the same time. She couldn't keep her hips on the ground and dismissed the strain in her lower back as she struggled to make herself even more accessible.

His tongue—his tongue on that hard, swollen piece of her he called her clit— challenged and caressed it all at the same time. She couldn't think how to breathe and had ceased to exist except where he'd laid his claim.

Her engorged organ was filling her, taking up every bit of space, maybe forcing his tongue out. Still he pressed against it and seemed to be trying to cleanse every part of it. Would it explode?

Would she?

She tried to sit up so she could watch the explosion, but she felt weaker than she'd been right after the priest stabbed her. Fear lapped at her consciousness because he shouldn't be capable of doing that to her. Then the fear slid into something else.

There! There it was! Everything wrapped up in his experienced and demanding tongue, his fingers spreading her as if her cunt had been ripped open, ruling, controlling. Helpless, she writhed to his rhythm—to her own rhythm.

It was happening again! No longer herself, she became some primitive creature instead, an animal perched at the edge of a mountain cliff. Not seeking safety but leaping off into space, fire and something beyond her comprehension leaping with her.

Sobbing. Screaming.

* * * * *

She'd landed. She didn't know where she was or how long she'd been there. Her muscles had a little strength now, not enough, but better than total helplessness.

214

Taurus was still between her legs. His tongue was no longer inside her, maybe because she'd bucked him out of her. But he wasn't done with her, and gradually she realized that he had hold of her pussy lips and was lightly massaging them.

"You come easily. From virgin to a woman of experience didn't take long," he said.

"You," she whispered. "You have done this thing to me."

His touch was so gentle, a caress. "Maybe I have," he said. "If that's true, it scares the hell out of me."

"Why?" she asked and tried to sit up. He pushed her back down.

"Because this has gone way beyond a one-night stand."

His somber tone penetrated her fog, and this time she managed to work herself into a reclining position. He lay on his side, one arm propping him up much as she'd done when she had his cock in her mouth. His fingers were still between her legs, close—so close—to her pussy.

"Your clit is unbelievably responsive," he said, and yet she had the feeling he wasn't thinking about that.

"Yes," she admitted. "It is. Taurus, you have not yet come. I want to give you that."

"Before I take a hike, is that what you mean?"

Now that her vision had cleared, she saw the sorrow and bewilderment in his eyes. She felt the same way. Knowing he was going to return to his world where he had important things to do made her heart ache. If only The Lady or dagger-stone had told her it would turn out this way!

She couldn't keep him here. Silence was safe. Silence and action.

Repositioning herself so she too was propped up on one arm with his sex organ within easy reach, she picked a few blades of grass and used them to lightly paint his cock. Around and around she went, dragging the soft, sweet blades over every part of it. His erection had already been huge, but it seemed as if her caresses were making him even more so. Scooting down, she leaned toward the fascinating space between his legs and breathed on the glistening tip.

He gasped and fisted his fingers in her hair. She looked up at him. Then, because the clouds in his eyes scared her, she turned her attention back to what she was doing.

"From earliest childhood," she told him because she didn't want silence after all, "I have seen men's seed-bearers. Like women's breasts, each is different." Putting down the grass, she cupped her hand under his balls and lifted them. Knowing she might never do this again brought her to the brink of tears, and she kept her head angled so he couldn't see. "Being naked is nothing to us. Neither is hearing and seeing people having sex."

"It—it's not like that where I come from."

Where you come from and where you will return. "Is your way better?" Cradling his balls to keep them warm, she blew on them. He shuddered.

"Better?" His voice had a strangled quality. "Hell, no."

"What is good about it then?"

"Don't go there, Maia. I don't want to talk about it."

Maybe he wanted her to leave now, stand and walk away without saying a word. No, his cock was telling her that he wanted her. Besides, she'd made him a promise. Releasing his balls, she picked up the grass again. This time she draped the slender blades over his tip; his moisture kept them in place.

"Bel-fire is a time of celebration," she told him. "We pick flowers and other living things and decorate our homes. Today I decorate you."

"Today you're driving me crazy."

"You do not like that?"

"You know the answer to that, damn it."

She wanted to laugh, but the sound caught in her throat. No matter what she did, she couldn't turn her back on the sorrow waiting deep in her mind. Determined to hold it at bay

Night of Fire

for as long as possible, she searched the ground until she found some clover. She picked that and brushed his balls with the small rounded leaves. His breathing had no rhythm, and she could smell his sweat.

You will not easily forget me, she thought. *No matter what you do, who you fuck, I will remain in your memory.*

After placing the now-sticky clover on his hip, she dug around the ground cover until she'd loosened some dirt and sprinkled that over his cock.

"What are you doing?" he asked.

"Life comes from the earth, Taurus. You may not want it on your body, on what you used to place your seed inside me, but it is my gift to you." She positioned her palm along the underside of his cock. "This is a simple piece of flesh, no good for fighting or hunting. It is vulnerable, sensitive."

"Right now...it sure as hell is."

"It controls a man. Perhaps he should hate it, but nothing is more important to him." After running her fingers over his now dirt-touched cock, she collected more earth and sprinkled that over him. "I give you what is most important to me—the earth where my ancestors walked and where someday my grandchildren will do the same."

A lump caught in her throat. This time when the tears came, she was helpless to stop them. When he placed his hand under her chin and lifted her head, she saw him through blurred vision.

"That's why you brought me here, isn't it?" he whispered. "Not just to get you pregnant, but so I, a man from the future, would understand what's special about this place."

"I did only what I was told to. But you are right; this land is magic to us." It hurt to speak. "The priests want to take away that magic, but they will fail. I know they will."

He wiped at a tear, then put his finger against her lips so she could taste her salt. "I hope you're right."

"Taurus, when I was in your time, it was Bel-fire. No one has destroyed that."

"Destroyed, no. But it has changed a great deal; you said so yourself. Most people have no idea of the celebration's roots. I want…"

"What do you want?"

He shook his head and touched his cock. "What you promised."

She could do that. As thoughts of how wonderful it would feel to have him inside her took over, she shoved everything else aside.

A gentle brushing with the grass and clover removed the dirt from his cock. Once he was clean, she pressed on his hips to let him know she wanted him to lie down. Then she positioned herself over him, her cunt dripping. Before she could settle herself over him, he slid his hand between the two of them and ran his fingers over her heated lips. Then he licked one of his juice-dampened fingers and offered another to her. The act of sharing her sex fluid felt like a kind of marriage.

Again tears threatened. She fought them by manually spreading her lips and positioning her pussy over his cock. As soon as she felt him inside her, part of her, she lost touch with everything except the fire flowing through her veins.

He gripped her pelvis and set the pace. Under his guidance, she began with a series of slow thrusts and retreats. Every time she pressed down, she felt as if they were becoming one. Maybe she could swallow all of him.

Then he pushed up and she lifted off him, nearly losing him. She hated the loss, yet she knew he'd soon fill her again. She could celebrate every step of the journey, play with him and have him play with her. In. Out. Up. Down. Wet pussy being rubbed and heated, tested and tasted.

Then with the strength in his fingers, he directed her to pick up the pace. Her thigh muscles began to burn and thrusting up and down as rapidly as she could caused her to break out in a fresh sweat. His cock jerked out of rhythm with her movements, adding to the friction.

Everything else faded into nothing. There was only her pussy and his cock, trying to breathe, settling down and lifting, faster, faster, her cheeks on fire and sweat sealing her hair to her forehead, throat, and neck.

She took the initiative by leaning forward and bracing her hands on his hips. She felt his gaze bore into her. His mouth, like hers, hung open. His cheeks had turned red, and the tendons along the sides of his neck were taut.

He stared at her. She stared at him. And she drove down, down until she'd flattened his balls. Then she clamped her pussy muscles around his cock and drew both of them up.

He grunted, lifted his ass off the ground, and drove into her, slamming his cock against her pussy walls. She released her grip, spread her cunt and felt herself soften inside, ready to accept his liquid seed.

He came, and came, and came. His cock jerked, jerked again. She felt everything about his ejaculation. Then fire-fingers took hold of her cunt and seared it. She was losing — losing…

Lost.

In whatever space he was in.

Chapter Thirteen

Maia had collapsed on top of him, but although Taurus' right arm had gone numb, he didn't try to ease her off him. He was acutely aware of her earthy smell blending with his own drying sweat and cum. He also noticed the scents brought by the wind.

Although he couldn't name the various trees and flowers, he couldn't imagine anything more perfect. More than perfect, he amended because the wind had brought him a soul-deep sense of peace. It could just be the result of having spent himself sexually, but always in the past, as soon as he'd gotten his rocks off, he'd start to think about the responsibilities and decisions ahead of him. This morning his mind refused to go beyond this moment.

He was so intent on monitoring what his nostrils were telling him that he was slow to notice anything else. Maia, however, went from what felt like unconsciousness to alert so quickly that she put him in mind of a wild animal conditioned for survival. Like the proverbial cat, she sprang to her feet and pulled on her gown—not that it hid her nakedness.

"What is it?" he asked as he reached for his briefs.

"Someone comes."

Where the hell was his lighter? If those idiot priests—no, not the priests, he amended. Drums echoed on the air, seeming to drift toward them. He watched her relax.

"Your people," he said.

She nodded. "They come for...for me."

Had she been about to say *us?* Because he wasn't ready to go there, he concentrated on dressing, not that putting back on his rumpled, grass-stained slacks did anything for the image of a successful company president. Out of the corner of his eye, he saw Maia pick up the dagger; she didn't look at the jewel.

"What do they want you for?" He forced the question.

"It does not concern you."

The hell it doesn't. But maybe she was right, because he belonged in another world, another place, other responsibilities.

What felt like a thousand thoughts, all of them conflicting, bombarded him. He was grateful when a group of perhaps twenty villagers, including The Lady and the old men came into view. Two boys who looked to be nine or ten years old walked at the front and were responsible for the drumming. When the boys slapped their cupped hands against the thin, stretched leather, at first there was no sound. Then, maybe a second later, something deep and guttural reverberated. It felt like it came from the earth and trees.

"Incredible," he whispered.

"It is our world's heart beating," Maia said.

He didn't know he was going to wrap his arm around her and pull her against him, but he did. Her hip rubbed against his, sensual and familiar, precious. He slid his hand down over her stomach until his outstretched fingers touched her pubic hair through the disheveled and nearly nonexistent dress.

The group stopped when they were about fifteen feet away. The drumming continued. He was starting to feel uneasy when The Lady stepped forward. Now she was dressed in a gown the color of new grass and carried a couple of flower and vine arrangements in a circular design. Maia lowered her head so The Lady could place one on her. Then when The Lady turned to him, he did the same. The headdress—he couldn't think what else to call it—was feather-light and smelled of roses and lavender.

"What is this?" he asked.

The Lady smiled. "Our gift to you for what you have done."

"What have I done?"

"Stopped the priests."

"For now. It isn't over; you know that. What about the one I caught on fire? Is he dead?"

"Not yet."

Not yet. "But you think he's going to?"

The Lady shrugged. "His companions will not let me near him. If I was, I could save him."

"How can you be sure?" Maia's warmth under his fingers was distracting him, and was he only imagining it, or was she pressing her hip against his?

"The priests brought their own medicine here, that and prayers. But they do not help because those medicines are not from the land."

Who was he to argue when she'd been right about everything else? He nodded, hoping she'd continue. At the same time, he acknowledged that he was getting yet another erection. Everything felt intense, clear.

"The earth provides," The Lady continued. "It blesses us with countless growing things. Some of them heal."

Recalling Maia's miraculous recovery, he nodded. "What do you care what happens to that priest?" he asked.

"It is not our way to fight," The Lady whispered. "We celebrate the seasons; spring with its renewal is most important. That is what the priests and soldiers do not understand."

"And they call you heathens? They don't care what you celebrate, or why. All that matters to them is that you bend to their will."

"You understand then."

Did he? The answer was more than important. He sensed it had everything to do with these people's future. "I'm trying to."

"Why?"

Why indeed? His head pounded, distracting him from his erection. Maia turned into him, increasing his access to her pussy. She was taking advantage of his lust for her, but instead of being angry, he wrapped his arm around her hip. He wanted to cup her pussy, but even more he needed to keep his thoughts clear.

"I care," he said. "About all of you. Maybe more than I've ever cared for anything in my life." The words slammed into him, spread over him.

"Why?" The Lady asked.

"I don't know," he admitted. "That's the hell of it, I don't know."

"I believe you do, Taurus."

Before he could remind her that that wasn't his name—if he was going to—the drumming increased in volume and tempo. The sky was crystal-blue, but he swore he heard thunder. When he looked over at the villagers, he saw everyone stomping their feet in time with the drum beats. A trio of preschool-age girls stepped in front of the drummers and began dancing enthusiastically, their arms over their heads, swaying. The look on their faces—like children on Christmas morning. The old men smiled and nodded and kept on stomping.

Maia began to move, at first only a faint swaying but then more and more vigorously. Although he didn't want to, he had no choice but to release her. The moment she was free, she hurried over to the girls, stretched her arms toward the sky, and threw back her head. Then she closed her eyes and started a dance that looked for all the world like grass blowing in the wind.

She still held the dagger. He saw, not her limp and wrinkled gown, but her naked body beneath it. Her breasts, free of modern restraints, danced with the rest of her. Her nipples were hard, dark points. He rubbed his hand over his swollen cock, unsuccessfully trying to ease his discomfort.

"She will return to you for as long as you remain here," The Lady said. "She wants to breed as much as you do. But now she belongs to Bel-fire."

Only then did he realize that some men had been building a pile out of dead branches. One took a burning brand from an onlooker and caught the pile on fire.

Flames leaped upward like exuberant children. The drumming became even quicker-paced; the dancers whirled and reached for the sky. Maia, looking as if she was in a trance, was part and parcel of the frenzied movement. She seemed to weigh nothing, to be more fairy-spirit than woman. He lost himself in her curves and long arms and legs, the small feet kissing the ground, slender fingers stretched to grasp the heavens. Her dark hair trailed down her back and caressed it. Damn but she was beautiful, part earth-woman, part sex-goddess.

Mother of his child.

On legs that seemed to move without direction, he walked over to her. He placed his hands lightly on her waist so as not to restrict her movement. Her eyes remained closed and the look on her face — peace and promise rolled into one — snagged his heart.

Together they danced, not a dance really, but fucking standing up without his cock in her cunt. She dictated their movements. He had no trouble following her, heard the drums, pounding feet, and thunder, not as he'd always heard sound before but through his pores, running in his veins, heat spreading through him. Taking over.

He glided with her, hummed deep in his throat when she did. His feet kissed the earth, too. He smelled sweet smoke, roses, lavender, her. Them.

Her movements changed. She no longer swayed from side to side but now thrust her pelvis toward him. He met her in that as well, inhaled her sexual excitement and his sweat. He pumped, pumped, pumped, unaware of anything except fucking her through their clothing.

He came fast and hard. She too climaxed, the truth evident in her sharp, low cries. Still moaning, she began swaying from side to side again, arms high over her head.

Holding her against him with one hand, he lifted the other and gently drew the dagger out of her fingers, leaving her holding the sheath. Only then did she stop and become still and quiet. Like him, she stared at the dagger. The drumming had taken over everything, touching his skin. He heard the fire crackle. Bel-fire.

She placed her hand over his and turned the dagger so they both saw into the jewel.

Two figures stood face-to-face. Maia's belly was rounded, her breasts heavy with impending motherhood. Taurus covered her belly with his hands.

Epilogue

Maia found it hard to believe that she, Taurus, and The Lady were in the stone structure where the priests lived and prayed, but although she'd been afraid to enter, she'd taken courage from Taurus and The Lady.

When they'd walked down the hill and approached the priests, the soldiers had drawn their swords. Looking determined and brave, Taurus had held up his fire-maker and they'd shrunk away. Now The Lady was spreading her herbal salve over the burned priest, and his moans had already given way to sighs of relief.

"What if the soldiers come after us?" she asked. Even with Taurus by her side and his seed inside her, she couldn't quite grasp his power over those who threatened to destroy her people's way of life.

"They won't, at least not unless the priests tell them to, and that won't happen today."

"How do you know?"

Taurus nodded at the burned priest and the others who hovered around him. "Whatever they were using on that poor soul didn't work. The Lady's medicine did."

That was true. However, she still feared tomorrow. "Taurus, the stone—in it we were together."

"Yes."

She hated being in this small, dark place with rock walls and a heavy wooden roof. How could people live like that? "Do you believe in it?"

Instead of answering, he led her outside. The moment the sun touched her skin, she relaxed a little. She should be exhausted from fucking and dancing, but she wasn't. In truth, she could hardly wait for his cock to be inside her again. The dagger-stone had shown that to be their future, but if Taurus didn't believe—

"I have to go back," he said. "To my time."

She swayed and might have fallen if he hadn't wrapped his arms around her. "I didn't say that right," he muttered. "I'm sorry. I want to tell some people that they're welcome to my company because I've decided to fight for something more important. And I need to bring certain things back."

Back? He was going to return? "What things?" was the only thing she could think to ask.

"Whatever it takes to convince the priests to back off. I'm thinking—photographs and a video camera might do the trick. Something to convince them that nothing they try will end Bel-fire, so they might as well save themselves the trouble."

"Photographs? Video camera?"

"You'll see. I need to present them with proof that Bel-fire continues up to my time. And if that approach doesn't work, I have a pistol."

"Your time?" Her heart hurt.

He looked down at her and began massaging her upper arms. "Your time. My time. It worked, Maia. Whatever you and your people did to me, it worked."

"I—I do not understand."

His sigh seemed to seep into her, and his eyes closed to slits. "Neither do I, but I'm getting there." He cupped her chin and lifted her head. Their mouths joined; she felt the contact all the way to her pussy.

"Maia," he said when they were finished. "When you first called me Taurus, I thought you were crazy, but now it feels right." He looked around. "This place feels right—like home."

"Home?"

"I've never felt I belonged anywhere before," he went on. She was aware of the nearby soldiers, and in the distance several villagers were watching them as well. None of that mattered.

"It—it is different now?" she asked.

"Because of you. Of what we've started."

"The baby?"

"That's part of it. I'm needed here. I'm not where I came from, not in the same way."

"I—I am so sorry."

"Don't be. It doesn't matter—not any more. Honey, when I go back, I'd like you to come with me. I don't want us to be apart."

"I do not either," she told him. "We have mated. That changed us."

"Yes, it has."

She might have said more, but he was kissing her again, and her pussy felt hot and damp.

Her hand trailed to her waist and the dagger so they could see the two of them together again. But it was missing.

Its job here was over.

About the author:

VONNA HARPER welcomes mail from readers. You can write to her c/o Ellora's Cave Publishing at P.O. Box 787, Hudson, Ohio 44236-0787.

Also by VONNA HARPER:

- Forced
- Hard Bodies
- Her Passionate Need
- Thunder

HANDLE WITH CARE

Annie Windsor

Chapter One

Earth, 3012

SETI-WHO Main Research Compound

Isis, Arizona

Tia Belmont groaned as she massaged her aching clit with a tiny egg vibrator.

"Come on, baby," she murmured. "Come on."

The pink machine purred against her damp folds as she pressed and released, pushing herself closer and closer to orgasm.

Around her, in the deserted SEARCH lab's shiny surfaces, she could see herself reared back on the stainless steel counter. Bright lights illuminated her 5'8" full-figured frame, her large breasts hanging from her unbuttoned white blouse, her hiked white skirt, and the silky purple thong she had pushed aside for better access to her vagina.

The thong was actually a moisture-activated sex toy, too — but for the next few minutes, it wouldn't trigger. Tia had tugged the waistband to engage the time delay while she enjoyed the egg's more direct stimulation.

Sweet goddess. Please don't let the night janitor come in, unless it's a horny guy with a huge cock. As if that could ever happen.

Her red hair fell across her shoulders and teased her nipples as she moaned and arched her hips. Even darker red down tickled her hand as she worked between her legs. The egg rumbled against her slippery clit, twirling flesh like a skilled tongue. Tia was so close to the edge she wanted to scream. Once more, she stole a glance at herself as she spread her legs farther and hunched against humming plastic. Her arousal scented the pristine laboratory air with musk.

How wonderful it would be if a man appeared between her thighs to bang her silly.

"Yes. Yes!" Tia stared at her reflection and imagined her fantasy man's powerful pecs and thick cock. She could see him, muscled arms braced on the countertop as he drilled her throbbing slit.

Would he fuck her too hard?

Could he fuck her too hard?

Black hair would be nice, shoulder-length—so she could pull it as she came.

The phantom image was just enough to do the trick. Pressing the egg full-force against her clit, Tia shook with her orgasm. Her body bucked on the counter three times, four—and then it was over, quick as that.

"Ah, well. That's mechanical satisfaction. Love it or do it yourself." She laughed as she slipped off the countertop and stood on shaky legs. Even a thousand years after women's sexual liberation on Earth, there was still something naughty about masturbating at work.

"Colleen would shit a brick if she caught me." Tia allowed herself a wicked grin, thinking about her willowy blonde second-in-charge. Colleen was so…proper. So starched and self-righteous. And so enamored by the thought of Tia's job.

Yep. If Colleen had walked through the door, she'd have fallen right over. Then hopped right up, run to the digimail, and fired posts to every higher-up in SETI and WHO. *Tia's gone crazy! The fat bitch is masturbating on the lab counters! Give me her job. I need her job…*

Tia shook her head. If ever a woman needed a good fuck and some solvent to get unstuck on herself, Colleen did.

Well, Tia needed a good fuck, too. She had a sudden image of Colleen's snide remark on the subject, just last week. *Honey, those hips are getting out of hand. Better get to work on yourself. If we actually find a planet full of men, they won't want* you.

Whatever.

Colleen's lame opinions didn't stop Tia's fantasies, one of which involved an incredible fuck at work. Unfortunately, that was about as likely as getting struck by lightning sixteen times in one month. Tia knew she was consigned to her own fingers or the myriad of available toys—and occasionally, one of the willing lab techs who wielded a mean dildo.

If only dildos could give real, lasting pleasure.

Even the *BigMan 3013*, the latest in a long line of android pleasure protocols, couldn't approximate the real thing, according to women who'd actually *had* the real thing.

Tia wasn't one of those women. At thirty, she had yet to experience flesh-and-blood sex—a situation unlikely to change. Earth's males had become an endangered species, thanks to a y-linked genetovirus loosed in 2800. Women now outnumbered men by roughly 1413:1, and male births had slacked to zero in the last three years.

"Not good for the survival of the species," Tia noted as she repositioned her thong. After a few seconds, the time-delay ended. Silken fabric hummed across her pussy, more a comfort than a relief at this point. She didn't tug the waistband to shut it off.

For the millionth time, Tia wondered how a man's hand would feel, rubbing her sensitive labia. Drawing out her pleasure after long hours of body-melt fucking.

What a dream.

It had been fifteen years since Tia Belmont scoped a fertile Earth male—and that one hadn't been too interested in her. Boobs too big, hips too wide, tummy actually in existence—if a girl didn't look like a twig with tits, she didn't stand much of a chance with the flesh-and-blood-dick bunch.

And fertile-male sightings had dwindled to nil now, especially in big cities like Isis.

To ensure the viability of the human race for as long as possible, sperm donations from the FM's were picked up by the men's union, the Earth Male Association. EMA sent eunuchs (genetic "almosts"—hairless no-muscles who couldn't get a hard-on even with medical help) to retrieve vials and transport them to World Health Organization Masterbanks via air-shuttle. In exchange, EMA received hefty payments from WHO, which all of Earth's remaining men, FM's and "almosts" alike, used to support themselves and their mates. Consequently, Earth's males had no need to work traditional jobs.

Instead, EMA members hid in the millions of acres of protected wilderness with their chosen mate or mates. Otherwise, they'd have no peace. Women would pursue them wherever they went, eager to experience live-action fucking.

Tia slowly buttoned her blouse. Her breasts were so sensitive she gasped as fabric brushed them.

What would it feel like to have a real man suck my nipples until I couldn't stand it any longer?

The thought made her pussy twice as wet. Her self-stimulating thong hummed faster and faster.

"God." Tia leaned against the counter and closed her eyes.

The thong tightened and slid up and down her slit. It moved gently at first, then harder. Tia pinched her nipples through her shirt. The pressure between her legs felt just right. The fabric super-heated, doubling her pleasure. Her knees gave, and she pitched against the counter as she came.

This time she shouted, despite her best effort to be quiet.

Clamping one hand over her mouth, Tia forced herself to stand upright in case some well-meaning night staffer ran in to make sure she was okay.

No one did. Thank the universe for small favors.

Once more, with determined effort, Tia straightened her rumpled clothes.

"Enough fooling around for one night," she said. "I have work to do."

Still basking in the relaxation from her orgasms, Tia padded across the wide expanse of tile to her desk in the lab's north corner, near the entry doors. Her cloth lab-boots barely made a whisper as she walked the length of the room, and the only other sound was the distant, incessant thrum of SETI-WHO's giant satellite array. There were 130 high-powered dishes in all now, linked to 360 Hubble 10-strength telescopic visual and sonic monitoring ports above Earth's atmosphere.

The dishes were searching. Which was, of course, the point of the SEARCH program. To search for, find, and contact new worlds, in hopes of righting Earth's dearth of viable males.

Tia, SEARCH's scientific director, opened her upper left-hand drawer and tossed the egg vibrator inside, next to the tempting full-length, solar-powered *Fleshcock* and the spare access card to her *BigMan 3010*. Good old "Mike" was at home, of course. Masturbating on the clock was one thing, but bringing an android sex unit into the lab would be in poor taste.

Still thinking about her fantasy man, Tia returned to her array of computer screens on the far side of the lab. The machines were soft to the touch, like satin-wrapped foam, and created in the latest aesthetically pleasing colors.

Robin's egg blue.

Soft moss green.

Dove gray.

That much comfort, SETI-WHO offered their employees without hesitation.

"A new satellite dish would just kill 'em, though." Tia settled in her chair. She often worked all night, hoping for a miracle. Nothing like the charge of finding a new planet with humanoid life forms.

Unfortunately, the 68 worlds SEARCH had catalogued and contacted thus far hadn't been able to help Earth. Many had their own reproductive problems. Some weren't biologically compatible. A few had difficulties with Earth viral strains, and another group, known as the Hostiles, were too dangerous to approach beyond first contact.

The Hostiles were typically male-dominated societies. All-female cultures — or mostly female worlds — certainly had their perks, even though they lacked in some obvious areas. Earth's natural resources had been reclaimed and protected. Global warming had been arrested. Weapons had been eliminated, and there hadn't been a war in nearly 700 years. Science, research, healthcare, food production — everything was now a worldwide cooperative effort. The advances in women's healthcare were astounding. Menstrual problems, eliminated. Cervical, ovarian, and breast cancer, cured. Osteoporosis an ailment of the distant past, like sexually transmitted diseases and pre-term births.

Yes, women and society on Earth had been reformed in the image of the Goddess. Even childrearing was a cooperative effort. And yet, without men, Earth's energy lacked a certain charge. Women had become arrogant and complacent, like their male counterparts in the late 21st century. Scientific advances slowed from inertia and lethargy. Thousands and thousands of women had never known sex beyond vibrators, *BigMan* androids, and the pleasures women could offer each other. Some little girls had never even seen a male, and ran screaming if they passed an EMA donor shuttle full of "almosts" on the streets.

Worst of all, the Search for Extraterrestrial Intelligence-World Health Organization joint projects received almost monthly funding cuts.

Tia tapped <*scan*> on the main screen and meticulously studied the pictures and soundprints fed to the mainframes by the monitor disks.

It was less than three weeks to Eostre, the modern festival that had once been Easter. Most people celebrated Eostre on the second day of Spring Solstice, during the balance, when night and day were of equal length. It was a time of cleansing and renewal, when women prepared for the lighter days of the year. Millions of women would be lighting yellow candles on yellow altars marked with images of the wild hare. Celebrations of spring and fertility would abound. They would dance and sing to the Goddess, place wildflowers on hearth and sill, and say their own silent prayers for the salvation of Earth.

Maybe this Eostre, during the time when sexuality rekindled and young girls reached maturity, the Goddess would bless them all.

Tia still clung to a basic faith, though she shunned the magical aspects of Wicca and Paganism. Unlike her many foremothers, who proudly practiced healing and mystical arts, Tia was a stone-cold scientist. An experimental geneticist with cross-training in astrophysics and computer engineering. If it couldn't be broken down into karyotypes, RNA, DNA, bits, bytes, or algorithms, she wasn't interested.

Still, Tia knew how to hope.

And sometimes, she prayed.

In those rare moments of connecting to the greater energies, Tia conjured images of her mother, her grandmother, her great grandmother—and many more ancestors across the centuries. From holograms, digital images, ancient photographs, and even paintings rendered by one of her crazier aunts, Tia could see these women in her mind. Some had hair darker than night or whiter than the moon. Some had cropped locks the nut-brown of Earth's ground. A few were redheaded, like she was. At times, the women wore modern clothes. Other times, ceremonial drapes and dresses adorned their ample figures, or they were naked. Every now and then, Tia's prayer-visions danced about fires, chanted deep in primeval forests, or conducted ceremonies on ancient altars of stone or wood, with daggers of glittering silver.

Well, to be truthful, one dagger. An *athame*, blessed and consecrated for spellwork and ritual.

"A-tham-ay." Tia said the lyrical word aloud, lost in thoughts of her mother's colorful stories.

The *athame* seemed like a disturbing weapon. Tia had dubbed it "Widowmaker," because of its thick silver handle, irregular jewel-tipped hilt, powerful down-turning guards on either side of a centered—and strange—red stone...and that long, menacing double-edged blade.

Widowmaker glinted in moonlight or firelight when wielded by the foremothers in Tia's daydreams and prayer meditations. The knife never did damage, though. Summoning, soothing, empowering—those seemed to be its primary purpose. Still, if Widowmaker chose to do harm, Tia had no doubt she could.

She. As if the stupid dagger were alive.

"*Athame.*" Tia had seen the dagger in person only once, when she was near the age of six. After that, it disappeared.

"That's the way of things, sweetheart." Tia's mother had smiled when Tia asked what happened to the silver knife with the flickering red stone. "Our family athame *comes when she's needed, and leaves when she's finished changing everything. Don't worry. She's been with us for millennia. She won't let you down.*

Tia shook her head and sighed.

If only such magic and nonsense were true, beyond the simple comforts of spiritual ritual. Tia was aging quickly. Earth was dying. Eostre was coming. If ever her mother's fabled *athame* could make an appearance and change everything, now would be the time.

Get a grip, Tia. That's ridiculous.

Gazing into the depths of the robin's egg, moss green, and dove gray monitors, Tia dismissed thoughts of foremothers, magic, and ceremonial daggers. Instead, she offered a new, logical, and scientific request to the Goddess.

"Please. Let this be the year. Let number 69 be the planet we need."

As if in response, a gentle buzzing echoed through the quiet lab.

Tia startled and examined her computer screens. No indicator lights flashed—and the computers would have spoken if they made a hit.

No…

That buzz came from the other side of the room. From around her desk.

"What the hell?" Tia pushed away from her consoles, got up, and walked toward the source of the irritating sound.

Yep. Her desk. More specifically, the drawer where she kept her vibrators and spare *BigMan* access card. The metal was…well, vibrating.

Tia's heart gave a strange lurch, and she opened the drawer in a hurry.

The egg she had so recently enjoyed hummed softly against the sides and bottom of its prison.

"Must have forgotten to turn it off," she muttered.

The egg's velocity increased.

As Tia watched, too stunned to move, the tiny vibrator slammed against the metal drawer like a thing possessed. Tia's hands started to shake. Instinct kicked in, and she glanced around to see if any magnetic containment fields had been breached.

All lights were green. Intact. The lab was secure.

And yet the egg ignored reality and bashed the drawer hard enough to leave a dent.

Tia jumped to the side.

Just in time.

The vibrator exploded with a loud *bang*, spewing a cloud of white, sparkling dust. Lab filters hissed, and the sparkles quickly floated up into the ventilation system.

Swallowing hard, Tia eased forward and gazed into the drawer.

Her brand-new solar-powered *Fleshcock* was a melted pink puddle. The spare card to Mike had been rendered to a twisted mass of metal and plastic. In the scorched oval spot where the insane egg had done its final dance lay — oh, no.

"No!"

Tia shied away again. She rubbed her eyes, counted to ten, and then pinched her arm to be certain she was awake. Her experimental-genetic-astrophysical brain made a fizzling sound, like her organic circuits couldn't comprehend what she had seen.

But when she steeled herself, took that eternal step back to the drawer, and compelled herself to gaze once more at the blackened metal cavern, there it was.

Widowmaker.

Chapter Two

"*Athame.*" Tia's voice seemed small and distant to her ears. "*Athame!*"

Her mother's ceremonial dagger. And her grandmother's, and who knew how many great-mothers before them.

Tia pinched her arm again, just for good measure. But she knew she wasn't dreaming or imagining things.

"My vibrator exploded, and now there's a dagger in my drawer."

Somewhere in the recesses of her mind, Tia heard a sound like her foremothers chanting. Quietly at first, and then more urgently. Like they might be a little ticked.

"Okay, okay. Damn." Tia rubbed the side of her head. "You know I don't believe in this stuff, but...it looks like our *athame*, all right."

The chanting in her mind intensified. As if compelling her to touch the thing. Tia would have preferred spending a week with any of the Hostiles.

And yet her foremothers would *not* leave her mind in peace.

"I'm crazy. I'm losing it all, right here, right now." Tia chewed the inside of her cheek to gain control of her shaking. If she didn't stop the noise in her head, her brain might break.

Before she could second-guess herself, Tia reached out and grasped Widowmaker.

Tingles rattled her fingers, hand and wrist. The silvery metal burned with an unnatural but not unpleasant warmth. Unable to help her actions, Tia lifted the dagger and caressed its hilt—*her* hilt—and its warmth seeped into her skin, her breasts, her pussy.

In seconds, Tia's thong hummed in response to growing moisture. She didn't bother to shut off the toy panties. Her gaze was drawn inexorably to the irregular polished stone centered above the *athame's* formidable double-edged blade.

Red. It was red—and yet, more than red. Like a blazing fire, trapped in one drop of precious crystal. It didn't seem natural, or at least, not natural to Earth. Light played in and out of its carved surface, and Tia fought a backwash of dizziness.

She blinked, and the fire-images passed—but not the disorientation. Tia couldn't fight a sudden urge to hold the *athame* to her chest. Her heart pounded so hard she thought she could feel it strike the knife's silver hilt.

Your essence, commanded a voice not unlike her mother's.

But was it?

Daughter of the Goddess, child of the Earth and star, of sun and moon. Wind and water…

The chants went on and on, filling Tia's senses. She felt compelled to listen. Commanded to obey.

Hands shaking, she held Widowmaker away from her, turned up the two-edged blade, and pricked her finger on the sharp, silver metal.

It didn't hurt. Not really.

A trickle of blood marred the dagger's polished perfection, then disappeared.

As if the *athame* drank it.

Tia chilled. Her rational mind attempted to reassert itself—and then, without warning, her vision blurred.

The floor beneath her buckled. She dropped hard, but fell on something soft.

Naked. I'm naked.

No lab. No clothes. Not even the damned dagger, which would have given her a little comfort.

Fragrant moss tickled her skin, and moonlight splashed across her freckles.

Moonlight from three moons! I'm dreaming.

Gulping heavy, fragrant air, Tia sat up in slow motion and looked around enough to determine she was in a clearing of some sort, perched atop a stone table coated with thick, velvety moss. The scent of heavy spice and pine filled her nose, and the air felt warm and...sensual. A little ways from the table, a circle of bonfires blazed high into the night sky.

In the distance came a sound like the beating of a hundred drums, and Tia looked up. The star patterns were utterly foreign to her.

"Am I dreaming?" she asked aloud. "Where am I?"

Kaerad, answered a mind-voice so deep it wracked Tia's spine.

Shaking so hard she could barely move, Tia stayed on her butt but inched around on the table — and bit back a scream.

A man towered over the table's head, standing between two dagger-shaped columns spouting flames from giant gemstones on their hilts.

A real, live man.

Tia's shaking intensified. She wondered if she would explode like her egg vibrator, showering the man with silvery sparks as she disintegrated.

He had absolutely no clothes on his amazing body. And, he was aroused.

My god. Despite her mounting fear, Tia licked her lips. *His cock is bigger than my best vibrator — and twice as thick.*

Her pussy started a furious ache. She thought about drawing up her knees and hugging herself, but decided against sudden movements. With her arms propping her up and her legs stretched toward the man, she was completely open to his scrutiny.

The man leaned forward, as if to see her better.

Aided by the flames and the bright tri-moonlight, Tia could tell the hunk was humanoid and well over six feet tall. His muscles might have been carved out of smooth brown stone, and his shoulder-length hair was so dark it blended with the night. The man's eyes blazed as he surveyed Tia's naked body, and she thought they might be blue.

"H-Hello," Tia whispered.

The man didn't answer. His intense stare went from her freckled cheeks to her nipples. Shocks of pleasure rippled through Tia's body, as if the man had touched her—but he was only gazing at her breasts.

With undeniable desire.

Fear battled with excruciating arousal, leaving Tia pulled to bits between the two emotions.

The man's powerful hands flexed, then relaxed. Tia felt a feather-touch in her mind, not unlike the chanting of her foremothers. It startled her, but it didn't hurt. In fact, it eased her fear and increased the warmth traveling all over her skin.

Before she could speak again, the man's gaze dropped to the red bush of hair between her legs. Excited beyond reason, Tia slowly spread her thighs and drew up her knees to allow him a better view of her moist pussy.

The man clenched his teeth. His muscles strained like he was holding himself in check.

Tia's clit responded as the man's eyes touched her. Probed her. Pressed against her hot center, then explored the wet channel below.

The man leaned closer. His hard cock pulled against his belly, and Tia could feel how much he wanted to fuck her.

"Mmm. Yes, please." She raised her hips to give him easy access. "I wish I could have these dreams every night."

Once more, the man seemed to battle with himself. He pulled back, staying between the columns of fire.

Tia groaned in frustration. She had never seen a real cock live and in person, and she wanted more than anything to touch it. Taste it. Feel it ramming inside her pussy again and again, until she couldn't stop screaming with pleasure.

The man's intake of breath was audible.

He wanted her, but he stood still.

Why wouldn't he take her? She was offering herself, and this *was* her dream!

Impatient, Tia closed her thighs, swung her legs over the end of the table, and reached for the man.

He leaped away from her fingers, out of the column of flames — and Tia woke with a jolt.

She found herself in the lab, lying on the cold tile floor with her family's ceremonial dagger pressed against her left cheek. Her thong hummed out of control, tight and rubbing her pulsing clit with no mercy.

Sweat soaked Tia's clothes. She writhed as the thong stroked her pussy. Still dizzy and crazy with want from her dream, Tia ripped at the buttons on her shirt. Her breasts came free in an instant, and she grabbed her cherry-round nipples.

The tender flesh beaded as she rolled it between her fingers, and she heard herself moaning. Begging for release. A clear image of her dream man formed in her mind, and he lowered himself between her thighs. His thick cock parted the lips of her pussy, then sank deep inside her throbbing walls.

Tia cried out, lifting her hips to meet him.

At that moment, the console alarm beeped, and she heard the computerized announcement.

Hit in Sector 971. Hit in Sector 971. Incoming response. Open?

Tia groaned, needing to come too badly to stop.

Hit in Sector 971, the computer repeated. *Incoming response. Open?*

Pinching her nipples, thrusting against her hot thong and the dream man's incredible cock, Tia exploded with shouts and crying. Wave upon wave of a huge orgasm gripped her. She couldn't stop thrashing. Her legs spread as wide as she could get them, and still she could feel those hot, imaginary thrusts.

Across the room, the computer droned on.

Hit in Sector 971. Incoming response. Open?

There was a soft click.

Response opened.

Those two words jarred Tia back to reality faster than a cold bucket of water in the face—or between her legs.

She went still on the laboratory floor.

Someone was in the room with her.

Oh, god.

Someone had just watched her masturbate like a frenzied adolescent—all the while ignoring the monumental message from the computer. That a world had been found. A potential match.

This was likely the end. She would be fired, without a doubt.

Tia opened her eyes and swallowed hard. With trembling hands, she slipped her tender breasts into her torn blouse, then forced her skirt down over her hips.

Mustering a teeny ounce of dignity, she made herself sit up.

And then she screamed.

Languishing against the console was the giant man from her dream, clad only in a pair of tight black breeches. His dark hair hung loose about his brown shoulders, and his deep blue eyes were fixed on Tia. The bulge in his breeches announced his pleasure over her little show, as did the playful smile on his enticing lips.

His muscles rippled as he straightened to his full, impressive height.

Tia scrambled to her feet, managed to pick up the ancient dagger, and held it in front of her. The silver hilt almost burned her palm. She felt woozy and swayed, almost fell, but the man strode forward and caught her in arms like hot molded steel.

Sagging in his grasp, Tia inhaled his strong scent of earth, wood, and something like incense. The dagger slipped from her limp fingers and clattered to the floor.

I'm touching a real flesh-and-blood male.

She had never felt such a deep thrill, such consuming warmth. It was happening. A man had his arms around her. And not just any man. Her very own dream-hunk.

He handled her with infinite care, despite his overpowering size. Tia knew she should have fled in abject terror from this possibly dangerous stranger, but she felt completely safe in his embrace. And completely turned on.

The man lowered his head and brushed his lips across her forehead. At the same moment, feathers seemed to brush across her thoughts.

Tia realized the man was attempting to communicate telepathically.

With every bit of energy she could muster, she battled her fear and fatigue enough to open her brain to the possibility.

At first, she could hear the man's words, but she couldn't understand them. Then, like computers negotiating an interface, their languages mingled enough for her to pick out his repetitive greeting.

Tia, the man's deep mind-voice rumbled. *I am Brok of Kaerad.*

Tia nodded. She gazed up at him in absolute wonder.

Brok nodded toward the computer console and gave her a devastating smile.

You called on Kaerad. As First Priest of the People, I have come to respond.

Chapter Three

Brok cradled the alien female in his arms and drank deeply of her woman's scent. *Tala* blossoms and the sweet, sweet musk of her arousal. Her hair blazed like firelight, captured and worn. The curve of her lips and the rich fullness of her body intoxicated him. After watching her climax, Brok wanted to fling her to the strange, hard floor and couple with her until they could not walk.

Fuck. That was what this strange, enchanting woman called coupling. She seemed to get pleasure just from the word. *Fuck.*

And she seemed pleased by the feel of his hard staff against her lower belly. His . . . *cock.*

This word excited her, too.

If a few spoken letters could make her happy, Brok would certainly use them.

As First Priest of the People, Brok was trained in the history of all known alien species. These delectables, however, were new to Kaerad. Up until the moment Tia appeared on the vision table while Brok was performing the Rite of Aran, Kaerad's Council of Wisdom had never heard of *Aoert*.

"Earth," Tia corrected, her lips inches from his. She was still bonded to his thoughts. "E-a-r-t-h."

"Aoert." Brok couldn't make the strange hiss-sound at the end of the word, or the short growl at the beginning. Yet. This language was harsh when spoken, but it had a stark majesty.

A quick glance around Tia's shelter told Brok these were primitive people, still reliant on technology. The people of Aoert had not learned to blend science and ancient wisdom. They hadn't found their center, their heart. And they were in the infancy stages of true cultural advance.

Time and again, Kaerad's principle axiom had been confirmed across the galaxy: with knowledge comes true magic. Advanced societies worked *with* their planet's natural forces, and lived in a much simpler fashion.

"Why did you call on Kaerad?" Brok asked, doing his best to master the syllables he had imbibed through their psychic connection.

The beautiful woman in his arms opened her flawless mouth to say, "I—I—the computers. We're trying to make contact with other worlds."

"For exploration? Friendly purpose?" Brok's scrutiny of Tia's mind intensified, but he was careful to cause her no pain.

"Yes!" Her leaf-green eyes widened. "We want—we need—um, cultural exchange." And in seconds, the plight of Aoert was clear to Brok. The men of this planet were near to extinct.

His heart ached for Tia's planet, but thrilled for Kaerad.

Had he found what The People so desperately needed? Was their salvation at last within his grasp?

Tia's eyes held him spellbound as he struggled to subdue his excitement. *Slowly. Carefully. With proper precautions...*

And then she sighed, and moved against him ever so slightly.

With a growl, Brok joined his lips with hers.

Tia struggled, but only for a moment. The heat of her mouth fueled the heat in Brok's throbbing cock.

A female. A beautiful female.

It had been almost thirty *lunari* since Brok had known or even seen a woman. He had been but a strapling, then. Too foolish to appreciate what lay beneath him during the training rites.

But this woman—who could fail to appreciate her? Her intelligence ripped through him like electric storms. Her kindness, her gentle spirit, her exceptionally high desire to *fuck*—these things drove him to hold her more possessively.

Their psychic link was unusually strong, and Tia wasn't even of The People.

The People…

Have a care. Be cautious.

Swallowing a groan, Brok pulled back, keeping his prize in his arms.

Tia stared at him, breathless. Her lips were swollen and full from their kiss. Her lids drooped, and Brok understood this to be a sign of desire.

She feared him, but she wanted to fuck him. That thread gleamed brightest in the tapestry of her thoughts.

"How did you get here?" she asked.

"Our Council of Wisdom detected your signal. I was sent to vision, to explore the situation—and you came to the sacred table." Brok leaned forward and ran his lips across Tia's forehead. She tasted of sweetness and salt, all at once.

When next she spoke, around the time he was tasting her neck, her voice trembled. "But, how did you get here?"

Brok cursed himself for his ignorance. Of course, a technology-bound civilization would not understand a transfer of energies. It wasn't apparent to this beauty how he sampled her essence, or how he attached his essence to Aoert's communication beacon and rode that pathway to Aoert.

No.

These primitives would travel only by vehicle.

And so Brok murmured in her ear what he hoped she could comprehend. "After you visited, I followed you home."

This seemed to suit Tia, because she moaned softly and kissed him. Brok gloried in the petal-silk feel of her mouth, the sensation of her tongue begging entrance. He parted his lips and joined his tongue with hers, coupling in a small way. His animal instincts warred with his better sense even as his hands began to move.

First, a compatibility check, he reminded himself. *Without it, this is foolish!*

And yet Tia's hips filled his eager palms. He squeezed.

Tia groaned and eased back from their kiss. Once more, her verdant eyes fastened on his.

"Are you mated?" Brok forced himself to inquire, though his voice grated like the grunt of a beast.

"What?"

"Do you have a mate?"

Tia flushed. The pink beneath her freckles further charmed Brok. "No. On Earth, men—"

"I know from your thoughts." Brok handled the *-th* sound with more success. "But men yet live on this planet, and I cannot believe any fool would leave you unclaimed."

"Earth men don't *claim* females." Tia looked offended. "And they'd never claim me. I'm not their type."

"Then your men are bigger fools than I imagined. No wonder they fail to survive." Brok took Tia's chin firmly in his hand. He chose his next words carefully, due to the monumental import. "I must know—have you fucked a man recently?"

Tia's expression hardened another notch. "That question could get you slapped on Earth."

Brok frowned. He added this information to his mental files on Earth social rules. "Why?"

Tia shrugged in his embrace. "It's personal."

Brok leaned down and kissed Tia again, slowly, savoring her silken lips and the way she sighed into his mouth as he moved his hands over her many enticing curves. For a moment, his thoughts turned loose, and he came dangerously close to surrendering himself to the moment. In fact, it took all of his strength, mental and spiritual, to separate from this woman, this being worthy of Kaerad's most solemn of endearments. *Ban-ri.* Beautiful queen.

At last, he extracted himself from her dizzying essence long enough to ask, "And this is *not* personal?"

Tia shuddered in his embrace. From her thoughts, Brok learned she liked the deep timbre of his voice. His body. His cock. His man-ness.

By the Ten Gods, she *was* unmated, and that was all Brok needed to know. No man had fucked her, and thus no man would challenge his claim to her and disrupt the initial peace between Earth and Kaerad.

Brok had a clear chance to win her heart, her mind, her body — and her partnership in his heretofore lonely life. Even more shocking and exciting — and control-rattling — was this simple fact: Tia had *never* known a man's cock inside her.

Absently, Brok stroked her arms, her shoulders. The hard press of her nipples on his chest broke loose another of his mental restraints. Soon, he would have none left. The consequences could be disastrous for him, and indirectly for Kaerad and Earth.

The initial exchange of information had gone well, as had the first tests of energy and compatibility — mind-speaking, skin-to-skin contact, initial touching... But until the moment of penetration, of true joining — there was no way to know for certain.

Briefly, Brok considered explaining this complexity of Kaeradi mating to Tia, but she seemed beyond conversation. Her eyes had closed. She leaned into his touch. One of her breasts had eased out of the tear in her blouse.

Brok groaned.

In a fit of true dyscontrol, he dispensed with the atoms of fabric separating their bodies.

Tia's eyelids fluttered in surprise when their clothes disappeared.

Brok pulled her against him, naked flesh to naked flesh.

"So soft," he said, thinking of flower petals and the feel of hot breezes on cold-battered skin.

"So hard." Tia's thoughts spoke of his firm muscles—chest, arm, thigh—and his rigid cock, near-buried in the soft paradise of her belly. Below that, the wet, fragrant sanctuary...he dared not linger in those images.

Yet.

Il aka n'domna. Ma Angaei, Ma Angaei. Brok's mind acted on its own, speaking sacred words, invoking Kaerad's Goddess of blessed unions. Telling Angaei how he had found his beautiful queen, pleading for mercy and acceptance.

"*Ban-ri,*" he said aloud, as was custom. "I would have you as my own. Would you have me?"

Tia shifted in his embrace, rubbing her entire body against his. Lustful images tumbled from her unguarded psyche.

Brok used every technique of self-control to hold back until she responded.

"What do you mean?" Her voice was soft, husky, almost assenting in just the tone.

"I would choose you, my beauty." Brok gently captured one of Tia's roving hands and moved it to the base of his cock.

Her eyes opened wide then, and her gaze locked with his.

Gently, yet deliberately, Brok drove himself near to madness by moving her fingers along his pulsing length. Surprise flickered on her delightful freckled features, followed by curiosity, wonder, and then raw desire.

Brok's heart leapt. She might accept him. She might assent, and he might fuck her. And above all, this touch was going well, so he might not die in the process.

"*Ban-ri,*" he said again, speaking the formal invitation. "I would have you as my own. Would you have me?"

Tia gripped his cock, squeezing. Exploring from sac to tip. He knew she was thinking of pumping it with her hand, sucking it, sliding it into her woman's center—her *pussy.*

Strange, these Earth words, and how they pleased her.

Yet she would not speak the vows of claiming.

Brok felt like he would die of frustration or desire, right there on the odd, cold floor of Tia's technological shelter.

Unable to stop himself, he thrust his cock into her hand, groaning as she slid her fingers up and down, up and down.

With his last coherent thought and breath, Brok made one last attempt to satisfy the laws of his world and the demand of his Goddess.

"Do you choose me, Tia of Earth?" His voice was no more than a harsh rasp.

Tia squeezed his cock so hard he almost shouted, and used it to pull him closer to her.

"Yes," she said in firm, certain tones. "I choose you. Now quit babbling and fuck me."

Chapter Four

Some part of Tia's brain informed her that this alien god with the perfect cock had just performed some alien god ritual which, in his mind, bound her to him forever.

She didn't care.

And she didn't care that he would soon learn that Earth had many women more beautiful than her. For now, he was hers, and she planned to enjoy him to the fullest.

Brok's thoughts interlaced with hers, then untied, then laced again. Sometimes she understood the words, sometimes the images — but the untamed emotions — those came through without a hitch.

Brok's incredible erection felt splendid in her hand. She wanted it in her mouth. She wanted it in her pussy. She wondered if she could take him up the ass, since she had practiced with the *BigMan* unit so many times.

"Fuck me," she demanded again, and he separated her hand from his prick.

With cat-like grace, he stooped, retrieved her near-forgotten dagger from the floor, then grabbed Tia and lifted her like she weighed nothing.

Muttering to himself, he turned a circle, and then another.

Altar, he repeated in his thoughts.

For a moment, Tia wanted to tell him to forget it, to throw her on the floor and go to town — but she sensed this was important to Brok. He was intent on respecting her, on giving her the dignity and honor afforded to women in his culture.

Screw Earth's men — and not literally. Tia would take this sort of treatment any day.

Their psychic bond poured so much through her consciousness. This man's nobility, his gentle regard for life, his profound attraction to her. And duty, responsibility to his people—he was some sort of leader, very important on his planet.

And…he was worried.

As if he didn't know what would come of their joining.

I'm afraid, too, she said, taking his nervousness as a sweet form of insecurity. His uncertainty helped her relax, and she kissed his neck.

"Ah." Brok exhaled, and at last seemed to find direction. He held Tia against his bulging chest and strode across the lab floor.

Just as she realized where he was headed, guessed what he intended to do, he shifted her to a one-armed grip.

Crashes and clatters told her he had cleared the surface of his chosen "altar."

He was going to fuck her on her desk.

"Sweet goddess." Tia felt insanely aroused as he lowered her to the smooth, cool surface, leaving her ass near the edge and gently encouraging her to lay back.

Tia didn't resist. At least ten thousand of her finest fantasies involved being ravaged on her desk.

Her nipples turned to stones as Brok gently spread her legs and stepped between them.

The sensation of his muscled thighs against her own nearly made Tia come. His cock teased her pussy, sliding up the slick lips without entering, and that nearly made her scream.

A glint of silver caught her attention, and Tia realized Brok had raised the sharp, dangerous Widowmaker high above her prone form.

Her better sense told her to freak out, scream, get up, run— and yet she trusted him. Even when he chanted in a language she barely understood and used the dagger to prick his own finger, just as she had done before being swept away to his world.

Once more, as Tia watched with more fascination than disbelief, the *athame* absorbed the blood like an offering.

Brok intoned what sounded like a prayer, then with a quick, sudden motion, he drove the blade into Tia's desk, about an arm's length above her head.

Even this didn't frighten her, though she didn't want to think too much about the kind of strength it took to ram an ancient blade through solid metal alloy.

Once more showing his supple grace, Brok bent forward and kissed Tia, dragging her thoughts away from the ceremonial dagger. Slowly, agonizingly so, he moved his kisses down her neck, to her chest.

Tia raked her fingers against his iron-firm shoulders, hunching against his cock, holding it tight in her labia.

His lips—so hot on her skin. The feel of his flesh on hers…

Nothing like sex toys. So much better than an android unit. So warm, so alive.

And then his mouth fastened on one of her beaded nipples.

"Damn!" She let out a sharp breath.

This was better than she ever imagined. More than she ever dreamed.

Brok's hot breath, the nip of his teeth, the feel of his slight stubble on her tender skin—and his hard body everywhere, pressing against her. Possessing her. He wrapped her in his thoughts, drank of her very being with each suck, tasted her essence with each nibble—and all the while, his cock seemed to grow and grow, sliding up and down in her lathered vagina.

Do you choose me…

His words drifted through Tia's mind over and over.

Yes, she chose him. Oh, yeah.

New smells overwhelmed the canned lab air. Male smells. Salt and sweat. Strong, basic, almost forest-like—wild. A little dangerous.

An alien male is about to fuck me, her science-brain warned. *Virus checks, compatibility profiles…*

And then Brok's mind joined with hers again. Only this time, they really were like two computers, swapping data.

Tia's entire body hummed from the sensation, just like the satellite dishes outside the lab. Brok fed his genetic structure into her knowledge like a data dump, and accepted her images in return. In seconds, even as Tia squeezed and rubbed Brok's smooth biceps, they both understood they were of one species. Compatible. Safe.

For the most part.

And he wouldn't get her pregnant unless she asked him to.

Amazing.

Tia barely drew a breath. She was so excited by what just happened—and what was about to happen—she felt like a bowstring stretched tight to fire an arrow into the sun. One little strand of Brok's DNA troubled her, but she couldn't begin to think it through as he squeezed her breasts together and began to suck both nipples at once.

Heat consumed her.

The world condensed to that one sensation. His mouth. His teeth. His tongue, rubbing the hard, aching flesh.

"Yes, ah—damn. That's incred—ah!" Tia wriggled, barely able to stand the pleasure.

She felt like she was hurtling up a steep hill, body mobile and molten. She came before she even realized she was close to orgasm.

Only this orgasm wasn't short-lived and clit-numbing like the ones she had known from her fingers and her vibrators.

She seemed to come for entire minutes, wanting to push Brok away yet wanting to pull him closer and force his head down harder on her tits. He sucked and sucked, pushing her higher again, all the while rocking his hot cock against her clit.

Does this please you as it pleases me? His mental voice was as soft and hard and hot and tantalizing-teasing as his touch.

Yes. Yes. Yes. Tia came again, with shudders and gasps. She was so hot she thought she might faint.

So much for vocabulary. So much for sparkling sexual repartee and slow exploration. That could happen later.

For now, Tia was past wanting Brok. She *needed* him. If he didn't fuck her soon, she *would* explode like that egg vibrator.

Following her thoughts like some sexual bloodhound, Brok at last released her breathe-on-them-sore nipples and turned his attention lower. His hands eased down her belly, to her hips and thighs, stroking.

"You are too beautiful for words," he murmured, in almost unaccented English. "I want to enter you, but slowly. I am very large."

Tia spread her legs as he rubbed her thighs. "I'm ready. Please, Brok. I want you so much it hurts way deep inside."

Brok's response was a guttural purr.

Tia felt mild surprise at what she said. She meant to convey how her pussy ached for his cock, but the feeling *was* more than that. She wanted to be fucked, yes, but she also wanted him inside her—him, not any man. She wanted to be joined, body and mind.

The tip of his cock pushed against her swollen, soaked opening.

Her vaginal walls contracted, and she had a small orgasm just from that contact.

Too much. Tia's thoughts reeled. *Too good.*

Could a person go into shock from the sheer pleasure of sex?

Brok massaged her thighs and pushed deeper.

Tia gasped. There was some pain. Not much—but enough to know she had underestimated his fully aroused length and width.

Shivering from excitement, fear, the thrill of experience and discovery, she arched her hips, and Brok eased in, more and more.

Pain gave way to pleasure.

The sensation of firm, warm human flesh inside her—Tia moved her ass back and forth keeping her legs wide.

"I am halfway," Brok said, more grunts than words. "Can you take more?"

Halfway? Dear stars and moons. Tia's heart hammered. Her pussy ached. She wanted to take him—but this was only halfway? Damn!

Brok let go one of her thighs and put a finger on her swollen clit.

Tia actually banged her head on her desk. "Sweet goddess!"

Good?

Yes! Good! Do that again. Please!

Brok began a slow circular rub, slipping his cock out a bit, and then in to the point he had penetrated. His thoughts were calming, and Tia realized he was controlling himself.

She had a wild image of him releasing his inner beast and impaling her—and this image was not unpleasant.

Once more, her body tensed, coiled, prepared for ultimate pleasure.

Brok stroked her clit faster and faster.

"So lovely," he said over her ragged breathing. "Like the finest of flowers. *Ban-ri.*"

Tia suddenly understood that *Ban-ri* meant something like a queen, only different and more intimate. She liked the sound of it.

With a single near-scream, she came again—and at the moment of total openness, total relaxation, Brok sank the full length of his cock into her waiting pussy.

"Aaaah, yes, fuck yes!" Tia felt like he'd struck the center of her life force.

Impossibly long. Impossibly thick and hard. And yet, inside her, every inch.

For a moment, Brok rested there, once more holding her legs apart.

He looked surprised, relieved, thrilled—a hundred emotions, and Tia felt them all, too. Knew them from her own mind. His soft sac brushed against her ass, and his gaze hypnotized her. The same thoughts looped through her mind.

He's inside me. He's inside me. He's fucking me. I'm being fucked!

A strange red light flickered into existence, then spread like flames, bathing them both in a bright orange haze.

Tia had a sense of being inside a huge bonfire, with walls of flame surrounding her. It wasn't scary, not really—but unnerving.

With his face showing the same wonder and disquiet Tia felt, Brok began to move.

"Oh, my god." Tia moaned as he slid his cock out of her lubricated hole, then back in. Very slowly. Very gently.

Brok squeezed her thighs and eased out again. "Does this hurt you?"

Tia felt like a thousand birds were flying in her stomach. "No. No! Just build up easy."

Reflexively, her hands gripped the sides of her desk.

Like a skilled dancer, Brok rocked himself in and out of her pussy, never leaving, never plunging full ahead.

His gaze remained riveted on her face, and his mind grappled to hold her thoughts. Tia could see the intensity, feel how much he wanted to please her.

"A little faster now," she managed. "A little harder."

Brok responded immediately, picking up speed and depth. His breathing came in staccato bursts.

"Your pussy feels like hot...silk." His voice was so husky Tia barely understood him. And then she realized he was finding Earth words to convey his sensations, to please her all the more. Hearing him say *pussy,* talk about *her* pussy — damn. She arched off the table as her excitement and want doubled.

Could he sense the electric currents running over her skin?

Did he know his cock felt like a god's boon in her pulsing channel?

"You fill me up," she said. "So good. Fuck me. Yes. Please!"

Brok rammed into her, harder than she expected, harder than his thoughts indicated he intended — but Tia groaned and stretched her legs wide until she thought her muscles would burn in two.

"Take me. I can handle you now. Fuck me, and don't hold back."

Brok's desire-laden growl made Tia briefly wonder if she was crazy — and then he braced his steely arms on the desk beside her hips.

His next thrust rattled the desk, and Tia held on for dear life.

"Oh...my..."

All she could do was hang on to the desk and raise her hips again and again. Her mind turned off and her body had its way, opening, receiving as he pounded into her pussy.

Deeper. Harder.

"Faster!" Tia heard herself screaming.

Brok shouted things in his own language. His eyes never left hers, though. Tia caught snatches of thought — about a Goddess, about bonding, about sacred joining.

At the moment, it sounded fine. He felt more than fine.

Her vagina ached with the need to climax.

"Come," Brok demanded, once more using Earth words to excite her.

"Come when I do," she countered.

He groaned, and Tia knew he was close. Standing on the edge.

His cock hammered into her again and again, and Tia felt her entire body contract on his hard flesh.

She shouted as her orgasm swept away every thought, every sensation but the fire-kissing total ache, total explosion in her pussy. Convulsions seized her, earthquakes and aftershocks. Brok's burning essence spilled into her, filling, washing, sealing the bond that began with his first kiss.

"*Ban-ri.*" The words flowed like his seed, warm and satisfying, filling her thoughts and her heart. "*Ban-ri. Ban-ri!*"

As he collapsed forward, her arms received him like a long-time lover.

Tia had never felt anything so satisfying. His weight covering her like a shield, his spent cock still tight inside her pussy, the firm muscles of his back beneath her hands...she wanted the moment to last forever.

She wanted to catch her breath and start over. Do it all again. Then rest and try a bunch of new things.

"Brok," she whispered, and then at a loss for more words, she kissed the top of his head.

He kissed her chest, and once more opened his thoughts to her.

The content of images and barely-understood scientific formulas gave her a sudden chill.

The DNA, that one little strand she couldn't figure out or interpret. The one she chose to ignore—damn! And damn him!

Tia pushed at Brock's half-limp body. "Get off. Stand up. Why didn't you tell me that before? God! What if you—what if we hadn't been compatible?"

Brok eased himself up with a man-stupid grin, still keeping his hardening cock deep in her vagina.

Tia had half an urge to slap that expression right off his face, then pinch his dick off with a quick snap of her knees.

And then Brok said something she totally didn't expect. "If we had not been compatible in the final stage, after what I already felt—Tia, if I could not make love to you, I would rather die."

Anger melted to shock, which turned into a quiet stun.

Tia didn't know how to respond.

Brok had revealed the main problem Earthlings and Kaeradi would have in mating. An extreme genetic sensitivity, part of their intense telepathic abilities. Kaeradi males would be compatible with only a few Earth females each. If the energies matched, they could fuck like bunnies. If not, the Kaeradi male could quickly and easily die from shock.

And the worst part—in the most subtle cases of incompatibility, this couldn't be tested or known until the male entered the female. So, a couple could play and foreplay themselves into a frenzy, start to pound away, and the poor alien guy might just drop dead.

Brok had risked his life to fuck her. Without telling her. Damn him.

And then he went and said something so deep, so sweet—she couldn't even kill him for taking such a stupid chance.

"I want to fuck you again," he announced, already moving against her.

Tia groaned and met his gentle, exploring thrust.

"It is not as bad as you think," he told her, clearly tracking her thoughts as they strayed to the scientific problem at hand. "Most incompatibility is immediately known. Revulsion at the first touch. Pain early in the physical contact."

He pulled her hips to him, and Tia felt her ass slide half off the desk.

Brok held her there, fucking her with an easy rhythm, like he planned to do it all day. Tia closed her eyes. She had no objection. All day. All night. All year. For all time—"Oh, my god!"

Tia's eyes flew open. "Time!"

She hauled herself backward, up on the desk, forcing Brok to pull out.

"What is it?" he asked, the hurt obvious and palpable in his voice.

"Where are our clothes?" Tia's heart thundered as she stood. "Put them back on us. Hurry, Brok! The lab—"

But it was too late.

The lab doors opened, and the morning crew of seven chattering women bubbled right in, with Ms. Starched-Self-Righteous Colleen front and center.

Colleen froze.

They all pointed.

They all screamed.

And then as one, the wide-eyed, flush-faced women rushed Brok like an old-style rugby team.

"No! Wait!" Tia tried to throw herself across him, protect him from their possibly—probably—incompatible touches. "You could kill him! You'll hurt him!"

She had no chance. The man-crazed women shoved her aside like a sack of lightweight groceries. Her head struck the side of her desk as she fell, and the lab went dim.

The last thing she saw was Brok, falling, pawed by fourteen unwelcome, lethal hands.

The last thing she heard was her lover, bellowing like a dying bull.

Athame, her befuddled mind cried. *Brok! Athame...*

Chapter Five

Tia woke slowly, her mind grasping, reaching through cotton and fog and fighting pain like nails jabbing into her temples.

Someone was holding her up, on her feet. Strong arms. Muscled arms. Not female.

No. Not female at all.

Her own arms were draped around a man's neck. Tia convulsed and her eyes flew open—only to clamp shut against a brutal assault of light.

"Angaei, Ban-ri. Tu talla angaie."

Strange words, in a deep, spine-tickling voice. And yet she understood them. *Feel the earth, my beautiful beloved. Your own earth.*

And she did feel something beneath her bare feet. Tile. Cold, yet comforting.

Lips brushed the aching spot on her head, and Tia had the queer sense of vessels knitting, bruises easing. As if the contact erased her pain and dusted clean her senses.

"Brok." She tightened her embrace and opened her eyes.

Brok's stunningly handsome face filled her gaze. He smiled at her—that little quirk of lips she had seen when he first appeared in the lab. Her cheeks warmed. As she pressed against his hard bare chest, her nipples tightened. She wanted to fuck him again. Now. Forever.

"You will be fine. Yes." He kissed her mouth gently.

Tia became aware of a distant noise, like squawking birds and pellets striking faraway glass.

And then her memory rushed back.

Pussy-melting sex on the desk, the lab, Brok's vulnerable DNA, and the women, crushing in on him...she jerked back with a gasp.

"How did you get away from the lab techs? And where are we?"

But even as she asked, Tia knew the answer to one of her questions. They were still in the lab, right next to her desk.

Slowly, like rain drizzling down a windowpane, Tia's vision and hearing made a sluggish return. Light shimmered around them, like some sort of cocoon. And...

It came from Widowmaker, still lodged in her desk. Like a magical shell — and on the other side of that shell, Colleen and the other six lab workers shouted and knocked against the barrier. The shield blocked most of the sounds, but not all — and definitely not all of the sights.

Tia could make out Colleen's *drop-dead-you-bitch* expression as she glared from Brok to Tia and back to Brok again.

He gestured to the glimmer-shield without letting Tia go. "I had no choice. I had to throw off those women and create this to protect myself — so I could aid you. When you fell, you struck your head. I was concerned."

"Thank you." Tia snuggled closer to Brok, shutting out the reality of Colleen and the lab for a few long seconds. His arms felt so right around her. Tight, protective, and loving. As if he had always been beside her, and always would be.

Don't go there, she warned herself. *He hasn't had a chance to sample all the wares. He just* thinks *he wants to be with you forever.*

She let her hands stray down toward the small of his back, and her fingers brushed cloth. Brok had pants on again.

And...so did she. Tia glanced down at herself.

She was wearing a semblance of a dress — a leathery-feeling body hugger that barely covered her bare ass and pussy — with laces stretched across her breasts, revealing more cleavage than she thought possible without being naked. Tia also had silver bracelets clamped on her right forearm and left ankle, and something on her ear. She touched it carefully.

Some sort of long silver earring dangling from a cuff on her right ear. She wasn't certain, but she thought it might be a dagger on a chain.

Where did the clothes and jewelry come from? And where had her other clothes gone?

Matter surrounds us at all times, Brok patiently explained, as if seven rabid women weren't trying to pound down the energy field protecting them. *Clothing, some foods – these are simple objects to construct. Minimal skill is required to transform what you call atoms and molecules into such material.*

Tia leaned back and gazed into his all-consuming crystal blue eyes. "Magic?"

"Science." Brok kissed her deeply, continuing his casual disregard of the women outside the bubble.

Tia heard the bubble-pecking sounds intensify as Brok moved his hands over the hips Colleen had so recently pronounced "out of hand."

Well, not these hands, honey. Watch and wish.

Brok's soft mental laughter warmed Tia's soul. His every caress communicated his attachment, his joy in Tia's large body – and Tia knew Colleen would be half-insane by the time Brok released the shield.

A racy part of her wanted to fuck him again, right there, in front of all of the lab women. As if to announce her claim to this flesh-and-blood dream.

I am losing my mind, she decided, then lost herself in Brok's sensual tease of her mouth instead. He ran his larger, rougher lips across hers, keeping his eyes open.

You would claim me, then, before your People?

"You bet," Tia murmured as he moved his lips to her ear and neck. Warm breath tickled and thrilled her, just like his firm grip on her ass and the feel of his stiff cock against her belly.

Just before desire overwhelmed her, he asked, *Are you ready to speak to your sisters?*

"Sisters?" Tia felt confused, then realized he had used a cultural term. Sisters. Brothers. The People. She had picked these things out of his thoughts already, and now she assimilated them. "Oh. Yeah. I guess I should."

"Will they...harm you?" Brok's muscles tensed. "You must be honest with me. I do not wish to battle women who are not warriors by trade, but I will not allow these females to cause you hurt, sisters or no."

"They're pissed, but they won't hurt me." Tia smiled at him. "It's you they'll pull apart, just for the chance to touch a real man. Let me out of the shield, and I'll deal with them. It may take a while, though."

Brok grimaced. Tia could tell he didn't want to separate from her in any way. The possessive worry etched on his handsome features made her want to kiss him for a few hours without stopping to breathe.

At last, he grumbled, "I will keep the shield intact until you suggest otherwise, *Ban-ri.* While we are on opposite sides of the field, I will not be able to hear your thoughts, and you will not hear mine."

Tia gripped him tighter. It felt natural, like a reflex. She didn't want to release him, but she knew she had to do it. Grinding her teeth, she relaxed her arms and stepped away from Brok.

"Get it over with before I change my mind, okay?"

He smiled at her, melting more of her heart even as her skin tingled and a small *pop* made her jump.

And then she was outside the light. Disconnected from Brok.

Disconnected from life.

A hole opened in Tia's heart and mind. Tears jumped to her eyes, and she thought about knocking on the bubble, begging to be readmitted — until Colleen grabbed her arm and jerked her sideways.

Tia felt Brok's surge toward the bubble's wall more than she saw it.

"Let me go," Tia warned, cutting her eyes to Brok's towering, glowering figure. "If you don't, Brok might hurt you."

Colleen opened her mouth. Closed it.

She dropped Tia's arm.

Brok's tense readiness relaxed a fraction.

"What the hell is this?" Colleen whispered as if Brok could hear every word. Her sarcastic mutter cut beneath the mumbles and mutters of the rest of the staff as they circled around the field to Tia. "He's an alien. And you were fucking him! Are you out of your mind?"

Tia battled an urge to slap the woman cross-eyed. "We're compatible. And he's not hostile or carrying disease."

Colleen folded her arms and struck a pose of arrogant disdain. A show for the staff — most of whom were still ogling Brok. "And you know this *how*? Did you fold time and run a week's worth of protocols in eight hours?"

Bitch. Tia's hand itched to make that head-turning smack a reality. "No. He's telepathic. He downloaded the information — um, directly. To my brain."

If Colleen's lips pinched any tighter, Tia thought the twit might collapse like an air-deprived container. Meanwhile, six more sets of eyes studied Tia like she was the alien. And potentially hostile.

Inside the shield, Brok paced back and forth, keeping his steel-blue gaze fixed on the seven women surrounding Tia. His grim expression seemed highlighted by the shimmering yellow glow of his protective field. He knew what was happening, even though he wasn't reading her mind.

Tia figured he could tell from her expression, and the body language of all involved.

This was *not* going well.

Twelve hours later, Colleen and the six staffers had been banished (with great resistance) to other parts of the SEARCH compound, and the lab had been secured by five exceedingly humorless international guardswomen. In full uniform. With stun rifles. They were now stationed outside the door, barring entrance to all.

Brok remained in his cocoon, sitting cross-legged on Tia's desk. His eyes were closed, and Tia figured he was sleeping. "Renewing," he would call it. More than anything, she wanted to be next to him, feeling the easy rhythm of his breathing. Dozing against the warm iron of his muscles.

But, bleary-eyed and half-sick with emotional and actual hunger, she occupied a chair on the other side of the lab from Brok, at the polished steel table holding the grid consoles. The computers and satellites had been turned off for the first time in nearly five decades.

Beside Tia, way too close for comfort, one of the most powerful and intimidating women on Earth sat on the edge of the table, communicating displeasure with the bounce of a crossed ankle.

Dare Jenrette, M.D.

Six feet of polished black marble with close-cropped raven hair, eyes like ebony lasers, and teeth so white and perfect they looked almost predatory. The Chairwoman of SETI-WHO and Tia's direct supervisor, Dr. Jenrette was *not* a woman who enjoyed employees ignoring directives, protocols, precautions, and edicts from on high.

Keeping her acidic stare cranked to melt-diamonds mode, Dr. Jenrette waved a palm-reader in Tia's face. "Take it," she ordered, clenched teeth shining in the overdone lighting.

Tia knew if she looked around at the various metal surfaces, those teeth would reflect back at her like beacons of doom.

Tia accepted the small machine from Dr. Jenrette's long fingers and scrolled through what she expected to find. Newspapers. Headlines from all over the world.

The Hera Sun (Athens, Translated): *SEARCH FINALLY MAKES FIND*

La Femme (Paris, Translated): *BELMONT LOCATES PERSONAL STUD*

Isis Reader (Arizona):*KAERADI: FRIENDS OR FIENDS?*

Well, that leak certainly didn't take long.

An image of Colleen danced in Tia's brain, mocking her until she kicked it in the shins.

Before Tia could read more, Dr. Jenrette snatched the palm-reader back and crammed it in her lab coat pocket. The lab coat was pearl-white, just like her teeth, and it covered a one-piece black cotton jumpsuit.

Dr. Jenrette had on low spiked heels.

The better to stomp holes in your ass, my dear... Tia felt like groaning.

"Those headlines aren't the half of it." Dr. Jenrette clipped her words like an old-style military drill instructor. "The Purists are already screaming about mixing intergalactic bloodlines. Somebody leaked impressionist sketches of you fucking E.T.— the Mexicana Herald's already got 'em front page. The Antarctic Tattler says you're a witch conspiring with the aliens to take over earth and make yourself empress. And that space-slut outfit does not help the situation."

Tia fingered the strings and strips of leather barely covering her breasts. She had to work not to stare at the floor like a guilty child. Dare Jenrette had that effect on people. Community leaders, World Court judges, continental presidents, united planet prime ministers—it didn't matter. SETI-WHO'S Chairwoman had been a social class and force unto herself for almost ten years. More than once, Tia had told people Dare Jenrette could shame the Goddess with a single snort.

Only, Tia wasn't the Goddess, and Dr. Jenrette's snort more than overwhelmed her. To preserve a little dignity, she sat on her shaking hands and kept her gaze level.

No floors. Eye contact. Predators eat you if they smell fear...

Dr. Jenrette cut her dark eyes to Brok and shook her head. "Unbelievable. And you expect me to accept that he downloaded our safety and comparison protocols straight to your gray matter — in minutes?"

"Seconds." Tia somehow sounded calm, which almost surprised her into emotional collapse. "So much data I couldn't process it all right away. I'm still working things through."

Dr. Jenrette dissected Tia with another sharp glare. But, after a few unbearable moments of silence, she said, "And?"

"And —" Tia echoed her boss, taken aback by the simple question.

"And what have you learned?" Dr. Jenrette's impatience showed in the graceful tap of one pointed nail on the tabletop between them.

Shocked, stuttering, but grateful for the chance to share the information, Tia rattled off the facts she had managed to organize in her mind so far. About Kaerad's primarily male population. Their need for Earth's females. Their tribal social structure, how they had moved from an incredibly hostile and war-like race to a contemplative people through meditation and guidance from a council of elder-fathers, their advanced and almost magical science — and most importantly, their basic genetic similarity to Earth humans with one horrible twist: the compatibility risk.

Dr. Jenrette clicked her teeth. "Damn. It sounded perfect until that little quirk."

"I — I know." Tia risked getting off her hands, then rubbed her temples. "Mostly male planet, not Hostiles. No sneaky germs. No monster babies..."

Once more, Dr. Jenrette stared at Brok's meditative outline in the bubble. "And he risked dropping dead to make love to you?"

Tia teared up and nodded. Fatigue and near-starvation weakened her will to keep sitting, to keep "maintaining at all costs." She didn't care much about her job at that moment. All she could think about was Brok. Holding her. Kissing her. Sliding his cock in and out of her pussy until she finally had enough. If she ever had enough.

Desire rippled through her, causing a deep shudder.

Dr. Jenrette apparently misread Tia's trembling as nervousness.

"Honey, take it easy," she said with unusual lightness and humor. "Relax."

Shocked, Tia studied Dr. Jenrette's sharply-angled face. Was she smiling?

No. Surely not. Impossible.

"Damn, and ten damns." Dare Jenrette glanced at Brok once more and patted Tia's hand. "I'd have fucked his brains out, too. I'd still be fucking him. But enough of that shit. Where do we go from here?"

Tia had no idea what to say. She wanted breakfast, lunch, and dinner. She wanted a good night's sleep. She wanted — *needed* — Brok. But she had a job to do. And the meanest female in the universe had just gotten a little personal with her.

Some opportunities shouldn't be sacrificed.

Legs shaking, Tia got to her feet. She gestured toward Brok. "Would you…like to meet him?"

Dr. Jenrette's right eyebrow arched.

Bullseye. Tia chewed the inside of her mouth to keep from smiling.

Her boss, however, cracked a big grin as she stood and gazed at the glowing bubble around Tia's desk.

After taking one seriously deep breath, Tia led Dr. Jenrette across the lab. Just as they reached Brok's shield, Tia realized she had no idea how to rouse him—but she didn't have to. He sprang off the desk the moment she drew near, and placed both of his large hands on the inside of the bubble.

His bright sapphire eyes blazed as if asking, *Now?*

Tia nodded.

Brok's bubble dimmed as he yanked Widowmaker out of Tia's desk, and as he hooked the dagger into his waistband, the field of light disappeared with what sounded like a sigh.

Before Tia could say anything, Brok leaped forward, swept her into his arms, and fixed his lips on hers. His muscles felt like warm gold against her palms, firm and smooth, yet pliable even as she tried to push away. And gave up.

Right behind me. The woman. She's my boss...

Brok didn't understand the word. Ban-ri. *I was beginning to fear it would be forever before I could touch you again.*

His tongue plunged into her mouth, meeting her own. Tia moaned. Heat rose between their bodies like friction from scraping flints, ready to spark. Her nipples beaded in their scant prison, and beneath its minimal covering, her bare pussy moistened and ached all at once. Brok had a fierce hard-on, and his mind filled hers with images of him driving his cock deep into her wet well.

Dizzy, unmindful of her exhaustion but ever-mindful of her boss's eyes on her scantily clad back, Tia tried again. *This woman. Dr. Jenrette. She's like...one of Earth's main priests. We need to talk to her.*

Priests...The People. Duty penetrated Brok's thick desire. Tia felt him ease back, gain control of his lust—but barely. He let her go with a frustrated grimace, but kept a grip on her hand as she turned to face Dr. Jenrette.

"I am Brok of Kaerad," Brok began.

"First Priest of The People," Dare Jenrette finished. Her eyes drifted across his unbelievably crafted chest, then down to his pronounced erection. "You came to respond to our signal. I got that part from Tia. What I didn't get was a plan."

Brok fell silent, studying Dr. Jenrette. Tia felt a jolt as she realized the man dwarfed her boss, who was usually the largest and most prominent presence in any room.

Dr. Jenrette leaned forward, then came a step closer. She was less than an arm's length away now, facing both of them, but standing in front of Brok. Her hand twitched, and she looked at Tia. "Can I touch him?"

Tia's cheeks blazed. She wanted to scream her refusal, but her scientist's mind saw no problem with the request, as long as the touch wouldn't be painful.

Brok?

"I do not know," Brok said quietly to Dr. Jenrette. He studied her more intently than Tia wanted him to. "Move your hand toward me slowly. If I begin to experience adverse reactions, I will stop you."

Dr. Jenrette nodded. She reached for him in slow motion, like a digifilm cut to 1/10 speed. Her fingers were darker than his skin, midnight against earth-brown.

Brok closed his eyes. Tia held her breath, and her heart pattered faster as the millimeters disappeared between Brok's chest and Dr. Jenrette's extended hand.

Tia didn't feel jealous. More...fascinated. She wondered what it would be like to watch Dare fuck a hunk like Brok on the desk.

The urge to rub her clit nearly got the better of Tia as she imagined Dare screaming with pleasure at the whim of a real man's thick, hammering cock.

Damn. I'm going crazy. I'm a sex maniac.

Her clit felt too big, like it couldn't possibly fit inside her labia much longer.

And then Dare Jenrette touched Brok of Kaerad, right between his large pectorals.

The simple, minimal contact almost made Tia come.

"Oh, my," the doctor whispered, and for a split-second, Tia saw her boss as a woman. Not a powerful, strident world leader, but a female, lonely and longing, just as Tia had been just a day or so ago.

Brok didn't flinch or speak. When he opened his eyes, he said, "We have an initial compatibility, Dr. Jenrette. But we could not proceed beyond skin-to-skin contact."

Dr. Jenrette traced the outline of Brok's chest.

"Oh, my," she repeated, this time hoarse. "And...if we had been compatible beyond skin-to-skin?"

"We could kiss," Brok explained. "Then touch more intimately, taking our contact in stages, body to body, then genital to genital, until the point of penetration."

Dr. Jenrette swallowed and let her hand drop back to her side. "I see." Her eyes glistened, and Tia wondered if the woman might be close to tears. "Let me ask again. Since your planet's needs are similar to ours and you've been out looking as hard as we have, do you—does Kaerad have a plan for what to do next?"

Brok nodded. "We have a group of volunteers. Five young priests who have been fully initiated in the sexual arts."

Tia shivered when Brok said *sexual arts,* and so did Dr. Jenrette.

"When can they be here?" Dr. Jenrette asked.

"As soon as I retrieve them." Brok's tone was smooth and relaxed as his gaze shifted from the doctor to Tia. "However, I must eat and rest before transferring. I am very...tired."

"Of course you are." Dr. Jenrette didn't smile, but she sounded friendly. "We can arrange secure accommodations for you here at the compound."

"One Earth day. With Tia." A demand, not a request. Brok squeezed Tia's hand. "Those are my—my—terms. Yes. My terms. I will program your machines with genetic codes so you may screen your own candidates during that time."

Dr. Jenrette nodded. "Agreed. Dr. Belmont, you are hereby assigned to...er, him."

This instruction thrilled Tia, but she felt compelled to say, "The screening. One day isn't much time. I should help."

"Not a chance." Dr. Jenrette actually grinned at her a second time in one day. "You have your instructions. Do not leave this man's side. Colleen and the others are more than capable of running genetobank comparisons. Besides, it's high time they put in a few extra clock hours."

"From what I now know of your biology, I would suggest twenty females, under fifty Earth years of age, free of illness." Brok pulled Tia closer and held her against his side. "This will give the best odds for initial matching and success. Trials can be expanded later."

Dr. Jenrette's grin lingered. "Done. And now, let's get you two some food...and a little privacy."

Brok's smile would have melted glacial ice. "I will not forget this, Dare Jenrette. Favor given is favor returned."

Tia barely heard him. Her mind had gotten stuck on one word. *Privacy.* Every part of her body ached for that privacy. She wanted to be touched, to be kissed and treasured and exhausted anew.

God. And she had to wait until Brok finished downloading codes into the damned computers.

Maybe they could get rid of Jenrette and sneak a few fucks in between keystrokes.

Tia sighed.

Pleasant thought, but highly unlikely.

Chapter Six

Brok fought to finish his computer work before turning his attention back to Tia. It was no easy feat. His cock strained against his breeches, painful in its relentless demands. His *Banri's* nearness consumed him like ceremonial fires, leaving little energy for concentration.

And each time he managed to focus, he caught her sweet fragrance of *tala*, though from Tia's mind, he knew she called it *peach*. A lotion she enjoyed.

He made a mental note to bring her some *tala* extract back from Kaerad, to see if she liked it.

The codes. Focus. The sooner the codes are entered, the sooner she is yours.

He glanced across the room and saw Tia in deep conversation with her mysterious "boss," the woman Dare Jenrette. His sensitive ears picked up pieces of their discourse.

"...locked down the compound." This from Jenrette, referring to the laboratory and surrounding grounds. Brok saw an image of the giant enclosure in Tia's mind. He was relatively certain she would be safe here. And if not, he would be near her to protect her at all times.

"We need to shut off the leak," Tia added. "Find the person who's feeding information to the digipapers."

Jenrette's answering snort conveyed a cold, controlled rage, and indicated she planned to handle the culprit.

Brok smiled.

Every society had its treason and traitors—and those who dealt with them.

Dare Jenrette would make a fine warrior, and Brok couldn't help but think of Harad, his brother by blood. Kaerad's dark-tempered War Chief was physically similar to but emotionally opposite from Brok. And fiery Rad would no doubt find Jenrette perfect for his tastes. Brok felt certain of this, though he could not be certain of biological compatibility.

Best to run genetic comparisons first, before exposing Rad to such temptation. Brok had loaded data aplenty from Jenrette's touch. He smiled to himself. After his night with Tia, when he went back to Kaerad for the volunteers, he would need to have a brotherly chat—and data exchange—with Rad.

Fingers moving at eye-deceiving speed, Brok supplied the remainder of the genetic data on Kaerad's five volunteers.

Computers were so slow. So inferior to brain-to-brain interfaces. But they would be fast enough for this project.

He struck the last key, turned, and gazed at his *Ban-ri*.

Sensing his stare, Tia looked up from her conversation. Her cheeks flushed a pleasant pink, and her smile made Brok's cock all the harder.

"I am finished," he said aloud, for Dare Jenrette's benefit. "And now, please. Food and rest."

* * * * *

True to her word, the warrior-woman Jenrette provided an adequate meal for Brok and Tia in a large room with too many tables. Brok thought it looked like a ceremonial banquet hall, but the consecrated dagger at his side had no response to the space. No heat. No tremble. Not even a hum.

So much waste, here. Structures without energy or purpose. He consumed breads, slices of cheese, and green leaves with a pleasing sweet sauce splashed across them.

"We don't have any meat," Tia said as she finished her own coated leaves. She was sitting beside Brok, while Jenrette occupied a seat on the other side of the table. "The facility went vegetarian around the time I started working here. Most of our planet doesn't eat flesh."

Brok shrugged. Kaerad was different in that regard, but such trifles didn't matter to him. Those would be the smaller problems of blending two cultures. And for now, he didn't want to consider the larger issues. He desired nothing past a quiet room, Tia's eager embrace, and the sweet release of planting his cock in her hot core.

As this image crossed his thoughts, Tia coughed. Her skin flushed pink, all of it he could see, and he could well imagine the rest.

Brok used one of the cloths Jenrette had provided to wipe his mouth, meanwhile slipping his free hand beneath the table's edge.

Tia's leg felt hot to the touch, and to her credit, she didn't gasp or flinch when he touched her. Nothing to alert her "boss."

For all Jenrette could tell, Brok had placed his hand in his lap.

What are you doing?

Tia's mind-voice warmed Brok. Like light wind or soft rain. He slid his hand higher, beneath the edge of the short Kaeradi dress he had constructed for her. *One hunger has been satisfied, Ban-ri. The other hunger grows unbearable.*

Tia's eyes widened as he slid his fingers into the soft red hair between her legs. Like drenched *kier*. Or the Earth word, silk. Her lower lips and center were so swollen.

Brok grunted.

Jenrette's eyebrow shot up. "Are you okay, Brok?"

Keeping the muscles of his shoulder and arm still, Brok worked only with his finger, stroking Tia's engorged clit. "I am fine."

He almost groaned.

Tia did groan, but turned the sound into a cough as she used her own cloth and dabbed her lips.

Her free hand captured Brok's wrist and forced his hand out of paradise. *I'm not comfortable with this. Not in front of her.*

On Kaerad, the sexual arts are sacred. Beautiful. No one hides desire, or sex acts.

This isn't Kaerad.

You enjoyed watching Dare Jenrette touch me. Brok tried to inch his hand back into Tia's pussy, but she pinched him. *Would you not enjoy her observing our coupling? Our...fucking?*

Tia's shudder, both mental and physical, clearly communicated that she found that idea exciting, but she said, *No! At least, not now. I'm not that free. Yet.*

Very well. He squeezed her thigh. *But in a few minutes, we will be alone. And we will revisit this subject.*

Cheeks blazing like a midsummer bonfire, Tia nodded.

Jenrette's grin had a knowing edge.

Brok sensed that Tia thought of Jenrette as beautiful, but judged herself unattractive. Fat, oversized. As if her curves and ample figure somehow made her "less than" other women. He also sensed that the woman Colleen, one of the screaming clingers he had fought off in the lab, was partially responsible for this absurd perception.

His lips curled.

Then and there, he decided that he would convince Tia to live with him on Kaerad, where she would be openly appreciated. He would not have his beloved wounded, emotionally or physically.

Ever again. By anyone.

She deserved to be handled with care.

Brok's hand clenched on the ceramic cup holding a bitter liquid Tia and Jenrette called "coffee." Only his detailed ability to sense the increased movement of atomic particles kept him from crushing the cup to dust.

He had never felt such intense emotions, and many of the sensations confused him. One thing was atmospherically clear to him, however.

Tia was his woman, his *Ban-ri*. He respected her, and he would teach her to respect herself.

Jenrette led them from the dining hall to a set of apartments isolated near the back of the compound. "We had these constructed for situations like this," the warrior-woman explained. "Ten in all, with observation windows, complete computer and data links, and panic panels to summon assistance. Digifridges are stocked and restock themselves."

Much of this made no sense to Brok. He distilled that they would be given lodging and ample supplies. That others could watch their activities, though he heard Tia exact a promise that this would not be the case. Otherwise, his thoughts were on Tia's smaller hand in his, and the ease with which he could access her body the moment Jenrette departed.

Tomorrow, work.

Tonight, rewards, and sweet, sweet rest.

Jenrette opened the door to a corner room, and Brok saw essentials. One large square shelter with roof, chairs, and covered benches for sitting. To the left, a food preparation area. To the right, an open door revealing toileting facilities.

Most importantly, a large bed commanded the one-room shelter. The cloth covering was black.

"Will this do?" the warrior-woman asked Brok as she adjusted a round light switch to bathe the room in a low yellow glow.

Brok gave her a shallow bow. "Indeed. You have been most gracious. At 8:00 a.m. Earth standard time, I will return with Tia to the laboratory, and our next round of trials may commence."

To Tia, Jenrette said, "Good work. I expect more of the same tomorrow. And…tonight."

Tia covered her mouth and laughed into her hand.

And then Jenrette stepped out of the room, closing the door behind her. Tia locked it quickly, then hurried around the room closing the black curtains.

Her excitement flowed over Brok like ion showers, dancing on his skin, driving his lust to new levels. The time was now. He could wait no longer.

Striding forward, he captured Tia in his arms and gazed into the light of her green eyes. "Enough. If I do not take you now, I will explode."

As he studied Tia's thoughts, a strange image wiggled through her brain, of a white egg, a melted bunch of plastic, and her ceremonial dagger.

"It is here," Brok took her hand and tapped his hip, where the dagger remained. "You called it *athame*. Is that a name?"

Tia shook her head, rubbing her cloth-restricted nipples against his bare chest. "It's a function. Widowmaker is a family heirloom. My foremothers fancied themselves proficient at Wicca and Pagan ritual."

Brok considered these terms as he let Tia go, unhooked the dagger, and placed it gently on the counter separating the kitchen from the living area. "Dark arts?"

"Oh, not at all. Women's arts." Tia eyed the blade reverently. "Ways to respect the Goddess."

"*Angaie*. That is our name for her. Sometimes we use the name interchangeably with Kaerad. I suspect the universal mother has many names across the vast reaches of space."

The enormity of that statement rattled Tia. Brok could feel her amazement at the fact that a world light years from Earth shared similar spiritual beliefs — and that many worlds might.

Tia now realized the Goddess wasn't just an Earth concept.

My foremothers…their rituals and beliefs. Damn. Tia's shocked thoughts amused Brok, and charmed him. *That dagger — I wonder if it wasn't a coincidence. Did the* athame *take me to Brok?*

"The Goddess thrives in all women." Brok returned to Tia, interrupting her philosophical musings. He wrapped his arms around her and pulled her into a lip-tingling kiss. "Hopefully, she will be patient with me, a mere male, who needs to commune with her. Fully. Now."

Tia moaned and moved against him as he kissed her and rubbed her hips, her sides, and her bare ass beneath her Kaeradi tunic. Every part of her fit his palms as if made for his touch. Her mouth tasted sweet. The way she rubbed her hard nipples on his chest nearly took his control, but he held on, if only for a moment.

In seconds, his hand moved between her legs, hiking up her tunic and finding her damp, ready pussy once more. This time, however, he did not stop at her swollen button. He thrust first one, then two fingers straight inside her wet hole.

"More," she begged against his lips.

Brok jammed three fingers inside her, and as he flicked his tongue against hers, he fucked her slowly with his hand.

She raised one leg and wrapped it around him, then rode him easily, moving back, then forward, vaginal walls tightening on his hand with each undulation.

Brok slipped his thumb over her clit, and Tia cried out and shuddered. A small sudden orgasm.

"Incredible," Brok murmured. And he slid his fingers out, lifted Tia to his chest, and carried her to the bed.

She kissed his shoulders as he carried her, and when he laid her down, she spread her legs wide.

He untied the laces at the top of her tunic, then studied her as he had when she first appeared on Kaerad, during his vision. Her full, round nipples jutted toward him. Her large breasts seemed to beg for kneading, for kissing. The feminine outline of her shape pleased him to no end, as did the red triangle of her mons as it glistened, awaiting his hands, his tongue, his pulsing cock.

The smell of her woman's musk agitated Brok's desire. "You are so beautiful. I have never seen—never imagined a woman as perfect as you."

"I'm not—" Tia started to protest, but words degenerated to moans as Brok leaned forward, pulled the laces of her tunic, freed her breasts, and snared one hard nipple between his teeth.

In seconds, his fingers were back inside her pussy, pumping away as she writhed and thrust herself against him.

Every thought, every muscle—ready. She wanted this. She wanted Brok as she'd never wanted another person, and that pleased him.

"Fuck me." Tia's voice was heavy with desire. "Your hands, your tongue, your cock. Fuck me any way you want to."

Mine, he thought-whispered, again and again as he suckled her nipples until she screamed for him to stop, then begged him to do it forever.

Her mind told him what she wanted, and he gave it with no reservation. Moving down on the bed he opened her labia and ran his tongue through the wetness inside. Her juices tasted rich and sweet, like a heated wine.

She wriggled against his grasp on her hips. "Don't make me wait. Please."

Brok heard himself purr as he traced the outline of her pussy, stopping to kiss and suck anywhere that struck his fancy. Anywhere but her clit.

"Tease!" She beat his shoulder with her hand.

He laughed and inched closer to her swollen center. His tongue moved in slow circles, showing her what he would do. Making promises.

"Damn it, Brok." Tia's breath came in rough gasps. She thrust her hips higher and rubbed herself against his chin, his nose, his mouth.

Giving in to her delicious wanting, Brok slid his lips and tongue over Tia's clit.

She cried out, shivering, as he sucked it gently, nudging with his teeth, stroking with his tongue. His cock felt near to explosion as she came this time, and he didn't know how much longer he could ignore his own burgeoning desires.

With a shift of thought, he dispensed with the atomic structure of their clothing, all the while nursing Tia's clit through aftershock after aftershock.

"Stop," she pleaded, but he didn't. His training helped him, guiding him now as he respected her increased sensitivity, slowed his pace, eased his pressure, then gradually built Tia's excitement once again.

"Brok." She pulled at his hair, hard. "I can't come again. I can't!"

You can. You will. His mind-voice was more forceful than he intended, but it had the desired effect.

Tia let go her resistance and sank into the intense sensations he offered her. He sensed her insides coiling, tightening.

My Ban-ri. There is nothing I won't give you. No pleasure I won't offer.

And then Tia came with the force of a fire-spitting mountain. Her legs gripped the sides of his head as she convulsed, whimpering with release.

Brok felt a momentary satisfaction as his sucking became kissing and pressing, extending her delight as far as it could go, for as long as it could last.

Tia's body entered an intense state of relaxation, and Brok rested his face in her soft pubic hair. "The Goddess once more shows her infinite wisdom in uniting us. I love you, Tia Belmont."

Tia startled. A subtle shock rippled through her limp muscles, waking her from her sex-sated stupor.

Using more of the information she had assimilated about his culture, Tia shielded her thoughts without severing their mental connection completely. Rather like closing doors in a long hallway. Some stayed open, some cracked, and some closed for personal time and space.

Love.

Brok said he loved her.

That was silly. He didn't know her. Not really.

Another part of her brain argued that he knew her better, more intimately than anyone on Earth. And she knew him, too. At least his structure, from mind-sharing.

It was like knowing the foundation of a home, without the decorations.

Brok's angles were sound and solid. No serious flaws.

Their connection—just as solid.

Definitely something they could build on, but love?

Tia re-opened many of her mind-doors and reached for Brok's thoughts, wanting to talk about their relationship—but the moment she hooked into his inner world, the force of his need stunned her.

The man was near desperate.

He hoisted himself from between her legs and lay down beside her, and Tia knew he was intent on letting her rest.

And yet his want for her raged and burned. His cock ached.

Tia knew all this in seconds, and her own desires rekindled.

"You're an incredible lover," she told him, rolling to her side and gazing into his unnaturally blue eyes.

Like alien skies.

Brok ran his hand gently over her hips, down her thigh, and back up again. "Your body leads me. I could not have created a woman more perfect."

Wanting to believe, needing to believe what he said, but not quite reaching the mark, Tia massaged Brok's chest muscles. She contented herself with her luck in being the first woman on Earth who got to fuck him.

And briefly amused herself by remembering Colleen's maniacal expression when she saw them hard at it on the lab desk.

Later, when he saw what Earth had to offer—well, he probably wouldn't stick so close to her. A twinge of jealousy brought tears dangerously close, but Tia shoved them down. No need to ruin this night, this *now* they were sharing and enjoying.

Brok's gaze never wavered. There was no hint of deception or guile in his expression, though Tia had a sense of deep layers in this man. Things she couldn't begin to understand.

For the first time in her life, a person interested her more than science.

And, at the moment, his cock interested her most of all.

She moved her massage downward, toward the rigid tower of flesh.

"I had hoped you would relax, *Ban-ri*." The deep rumble of Brok's voice gave Tia gooseflesh along her shoulders and neck. She could listen to him forever. "I can wait for satisfaction. Sleep first. You are exhausted."

"I don't want you to wait." She eased her hand around his cock, marveling at how alive it felt. Hot, bulging, throbbing — from his velvety balls to the veins in the side to the moist red tip — no artificial dick could be this wonderful.

Her chest squeezed with happiness, with the rightness of Brok's natural arousal. She knew, without question, that a dildo would never satisfy her again. Not even a little bit.

She wanted to taste him, to experience his flavors and scents. Imprint them to her memory and never forget them.

He shuddered as she stroked him gently with her hand, then leaned down, trailing her red curls across his rock-firm stomach.

"It's so big. I never thought a real cock would be so...different from plastic." Tia kissed the rounded tip, sampling a salty drop of semen.

Brok groaned.

Your body guides me, he had told her.

Well, his body guided her, too.

She opened her lips and licked his sensitive tip, and listened happily as he groaned again.

God, he was so warm. So absolutely human and real. Slowly, gently, she stroked the rest of his shaft with her tongue, lingering on the sac at the base, because he groaned even more then.

When she raised up to look at him again, his erection had turned deep red, and swollen even more. As if it might explode at any moment.

Tia bent over and took his cock in her mouth, as far as she could.

"*Ban-ri!*" He gripped the black bedspread beneath them.

Moving her head up and down, Tia sucked his shaft like he had sucked her nipples and clit. She used her hands at the base, guiding it so she could take more, and more. After a few moments, she figured out how to regulate her breath and swallow at the same time, claiming his full length without choking.

This seemed to drive him to a frenzy. Tia could hear his thoughts, his words—all in Kaeradi. Some she understood. That she was beautiful. That her mouth was perfect. That she pleased him completely.

And she knew he was keeping tight rein on himself so he didn't go wild, grab her head, and pound into her mouth.

Restraint.

Admirable.

She wanted to blow it to bits.

Sucking deeply and massaging his balls, Tia let the world shrink to his salty, fleshy taste. The heavy, wonderful smell of his maleness. Her pussy got wet again, even though she thought he'd licked her dry earlier. And then her nipples turned to hard stones.

Her breasts bobbed with her head, brushing against Brok each time she had his cock fully in her mouth. His fingers tangled in her hair, pulling gently.

"Yes. Tia. So sweet. Yes!" He bucked beneath her, still gripping the bed with one hand.

Tia pumped harder and faster, like she wanted Brok to do in her pussy. All the while, she teased at his thoughts, urging him to turn loose. To go wild.

She wanted to know what wild felt like.

Brok moaned and came in her mouth, filling her throat with his warm, welcome seed. She drank it down, excited by the experience.

Drunk with it.

"I'm not finished," she said as soon as she released him. Her hand kept working his shaft. "I want you inside me. I want all of you, hard and heavy."

The flesh against her palm stiffened.

Do not tease me, Ban-ri. Brok's mind-voice held a dangerous edge. *Kaeradi males are not as tame as our Earth counterparts. I don't know if—*

"If what? If I can take it?" Tia squeezed his cock hard. "Let me worry about that. I'm not teasing. Not even a little bit."

Brok moved so quickly Tia barely had a chance to process that she was on her hands and knees, pinned with his hands on her wrists and his weight on her back. Brok drove his cock into her pussy, balls-deep, groaning even as she did. Another stroke, and Tia shouted with pleasure.

"You feel so damn good," she said aloud. And in her mind, *Don't stop. Give me everything. Fuck me. Fuck me hard.*

Growling like a wild animal, Brok pounded her pussy.

Tia slammed forward with each thrust, but Brok's grasp on her wrists kept her from falling off the bed. She struggled against his steel arms, but not because she wanted him to let her go. She wanted to challenge him, to make him hold her there forever.

"*Ban-ri*," he roared, rocking her beneath him. She felt his sweat. His urgency. It made her heart race.

Tia ground her teeth, then stopped holding back and screamed as she came once, then twice.

And still Brok plunged his cock deeper, harder. Pleading to his Goddess for release.

Dizziness swept Tia as he took her completely, totally. Her breasts jerked and bounced, sensitive nipples scraping the smooth cotton comforter.

"Fuck me!" she shrieked, unable to find other words. "Ah, damn!"

His balls slapped her pussy, and the heavy smell of sex claimed the very air Tia breathed.

She never wanted this to end. She wanted him to drill her straight into the bed, and keep going.

Minds locked, Tia felt his animal pleasure and made it hers.

Brok came with a bellow, and she came with him. Her pussy clamped against his cock, holding it hard and tight, as his heated essence poured into her core.

Almost at once, they both fell forward.

Tia loved the sensation of Brok's weight on top of her. She felt owned. Possessed in a splendid, freeing way.

He shifted to the side, keeping his hard chest on the side of her back and one leg over her thighs.

Guarding. Claiming.

"I love you," she whispered as they both drifted into black, dreamless sleep.

Chapter Seven

The next morning—and its many demands—came too quickly for Brok. He wanted desperately to be on Kaerad, with endless days and nights to get to know his *Ban-ri*. Her needs, wants, and appetites had become his purpose, his new study. Brok intended to satisfy her completely, every day, then every night. And then he intended to start all over again.

Nothing would ever be too good or too much for his beautiful queen.

And yet, duty called the First Priest of the People, as clearly as the chiming of festival bells.

He shifted in the bed, stretching his well-exercised muscles. Tia's warm body beside him made his cock stiff. His desire overflowed, but he didn't dare wake her and sate himself. He barely dared look at her. Transferring took significant energy, and a morning of sex wouldn't be conducive to a quick, safe trip back to Kaerad.

Brok forced himself to get up, heart aching, and he summoned his ritual robes from available free matter. White, with a trim of yellow, for the season fast approaching on Kaerad. In his rope belt, he hung Tia's dagger, the only truly magical inanimate Earth object he had thus far encountered. It would be a comfort to have it in her absence, and it might strengthen his connection to her in these earlier stages of knowing each other.

Then, before the planet's sun crested outside the SETI-WHO compound, Brok kissed Tia's exquisitely soft cheek, allowed himself one long moment to linger in her sweet scent, and took his leave.

The guardswomen outside the suite door failed to react to his departure. He knew that to their sluggish eyes, he was a brief flicker of light, fading through the door and away down the hall.

Kaeradi were, of course, solid by nature; however, their understanding of the basic composition of the universe allowed them to flow in and out of molecules and atoms much like a liquid. They could not take the shape or appearance of others, or of other objects and creatures—this was the province of shapeshifting species, of which Kaerad's Council of Wisdom knew many.

Not shapeshifting, no. Just…mattershifting.

When a Kaeradi chose not to be seen by any but another Kaeradi, he simply wasn't seen.

Brok had no difficulty returning to the laboratory. As easily as any of his kind, he stored great mental detail about simple things such as routes, sights, smells, and the psychic feel of the structure and land around him. He knew these things intimately from just one passage. In fact, if tested, he could detect the scent of the room or hallway or causeway, or even the large laboratory from great distances, or select it from many choices. He could do the same with the cast of the lighting, the texture of the walls and floors—even the atomic structure of most of the objects he blithely passed.

As for Tia, now that they had bonded, Brok could locate her genetic and molecular essence anywhere in the universe *from* anywhere in the universe.

She was, quite literally, a part of him.

This fact he repeated to himself over and over again, even as he readied his mind and body for transfer back to his home planet, so very many light years away from Earth.

If he hadn't believed he could find her, instantly, no matter what, he wouldn't have been able to leave her at all.

I will not be gone forever. Only long enough to gather the volunteers, convince Rad of his need to return with me – and then back to Earth. Back to Tia.

"Nothing will happen to her in my absence." He growled this last belief—almost a warning to any who might dare to listen — while he touched a pad with his fingertips and activated the sliding door to the laboratory.

Tia is a part of me. I am a part of Tia. We are one of spirit, heart, and body.

The pad was coded to admit only employees, but Brok easily used Tia's fingerprints.

Simple information. Great detail.

When he stepped inside, he was greeted by a chorus of gasps.

White-bright lighting revealed six women, very near the door, punching keys in front of lab machinery. These were the same females who had pawed at him the day before.

Brok tensed.

The women stared at him now, slack-jawed and wide-eyed, but they made no move to attack. The situation seemed...safer, somehow. As if some restraint had been placed on them by superiors.

The seventh female from yesterday's debacle made her appearance on Brok's left, sliding into his field of vision like a long-toothed serpent. *Colleen.* The tall, light-headed and too-thin-for-his-tastes female who attempted to damage Tia's opinion of herself and her reputation at every turn.

For her, Brok mustered a terrific frown.

Colleen narrowed her eyes. She seemed to read Brok's meaning, and despite her obvious interest in his physique, she offered a strange greeting with her middle finger.

Brok could only assume this was not a friendly salute.

He raised his hand to his chin and touched his index finger to the center.

The bitch gave him a quizzical look. If Brok had deemed her worthy of further communication, he would have told her the gesture's rough Earth translation:

Your parents must have been big-dicked hairy whores, and you bear their image well.

Behind the bitch, at the consoles where Brok first set foot on the planet, the exotic and attractive Dare Jenrette stood waiting — apparently for him. Brok strode past Colleen-bitch and the six gapers without so much as a sideways glance.

Jenrette straightened to her full height, an impressive stature for Earth females, as Brok came to a halt in front of her.

"Where's Tia?" she asked.

"Still asleep." Brok couldn't hold back a smile. "She is very, very tired this morning."

From behind him came a choking, coughing noise. Colleen's displeasure. Brok smiled all the more.

Jenrette shook her head. "Glad somebody was having a good time. Listen. There are some things you need to understand about Earth politics. Things may not be as straightforward here as they are on Kaerad."

Brok glanced around the complex laboratory. "I do not doubt you."

"Fear moves faster than any object on this planet." For a moment, Dare Jenrette looked chagrined, an expression Brok found most unnatural on Jenrette's face. "Digitechnology allows for information to lap the globe in seconds — and your arrival here is no secret. It was announced in a rather unceremonious fashion."

At this, Tia's "boss" cut her eyes in the general direction of Colleen.

If only the Colleen-bitch were a true fighter. Brok clenched and unclenched his hand. *No doubt this warrior Jenrette could take her quickly and without mercy.*

On a mostly-male planet, settling issues of treachery and deceit were infinitely simple.

Jenrette sighed. "We've got a real situation brewing already. The Purists, a bunch of nuts who fear mixing Earth blood with alien blood — they're doing their best to stir up terror, and they're winning some support. So, the faster we can pull off some success stories to shut them up, the better."

"Understood," Brok said, still curling and releasing his fist. "Will Tia be safe in my absence?"

A snort came from Colleen-bitch. Brok imagined feeding her to a cauldronite lizard. He wanted to find a way to deal with the unkind female at some point. It would not be easy, since Tia's heart was too true to return such meanness in kind, and Brok could not deal in meanness either. However, people like Colleen tended to draw meanness to them like twisted magnets.

An opportunity would present itself someday.

"I'll guarantee Tia's safety with my own life." Jenrette's serious stare stilled Brok's worry almost instantly. "Will that suffice?"

Rad is truly going to enjoy you, warrior Dare. "Yes. Without question."

"Well, then. I held up my end of this deal." Jenrette crossed her arms and looked twice as fierce. "Time for you to deliver."

"An honor." Brok bowed his head out of respect, then met the woman's unwavering gaze. "I will go to Kaerad, and before your sun sets, I will return with our volunteers. Will you be ready?"

More coughs and grunts behind Brok told him that the laboratory help, most especially the lazy Colleen, thought this wasn't enough time.

Jenrette, however, said, "You know it. Now, go home, big boy, and don't come back to me empty-handed."

Without another word of discussion, Brok closed his eyes and transferred away from Earth faster than human minds could comprehend.

* * * * *

Tia wanted to scream as she ran toward the lab, ignoring her sore muscles.

She had slept the day away, literally. Her stomach rumbled from hunger and nervousness.

Brok was gone. *Gone.* As in, not here. Not on Earth. She knew this with a dread certainty and rage.

Why didn't he wake me? He should have told me goodbye, damn it. A tear creased her cheek. *When will he be back?*

What if he doesn't come back?

That thought made her want to throw up. Anxiety chewed her like cruel metal jaws. Her brain tried to grasp whole images, complete ideas, but she felt too rattled.

She nearly poked her fingers through the lab entry pad.

The door slid open with a quiet whoosh. Tia hurried in and nearly bashed into a small crowd of civilians, lab workers, and guardswomen. Maybe thirty or forty people in all. All shapes, sizes, colors — but age-wise, fairly young. Most of the unfamiliar faces appeared to be in their twenties or thirties.

The strange sight snapped Tia clear of her self-absorbed freak-out, and she realized what was happening.

The code search. The matching! I should have been helping hours ago.

Dare Jenrette must have coordinated the retrieval of willing matches using international guard hoverjets. No other way to get the women here so fast from so many different places.

And Dr. Jenrette was in the lab, on the far side of the room, using one of the old satellite terminals. Colleen made her presence known with an ill-disguised sneer. The shithead was, for some inexplicable reason, sitting at Tia's desk, at Tia's personal use terminal.

"Didn't want to wake you." Colleen's nasty smile wormed through Tia's distress. "Figured you needed all the beauty sleep you could get."

Something in Tia's mind bent dangerously close to the breaking point. Brok's kisses, his embrace, the perfect feel of his cock deep in her pussy — these things flew through her thoughts.

"I'm beautiful enough to the people who matter," Tia fired back in a too-quiet voice that somehow quelled murmurs of conversation all over the room. Most of the women, familiar and unfamiliar, turned toward her.

Without really knowing why, Tia raised her index finger to the center of her chin and added, "Bitch. Get your bony ass up from my seat."

Two of the lab workers and even one of the stoic guardswomen snickered.

From across the room came Dr. Jenrette's icy-sweet, "Ladies, ladies. We're down to the wire. Keep your minds on strand three and strand four. We still have four potentials to find. Tia, get busy. And Colleen — find your own machine."

Colleen flushed an ugly shade of puce, shoved away from the desk, got up in a big huff, and elbowed her way toward the terminal bank.

Work it, baby, Tia thought, watching her nemesis perform. From the vantage point of her desk, she had a clear view of the entire lab. *No matter what, you still haven't had a real cock.*

She was still smiling to herself as she turned her focus to the database. Red, blue, and purple helix structures drifted across the screen, some comparing automatically, and others awaiting closer examination after preliminary hits.

Tia glanced at the work stats.

As usual, Colleen had been doing the hand-comps very, very slowly. And she had done her own strands first. Three times each, just to be sure.

Figures.

The familiarity of work gradually soothed Tia's panic. Brok stayed in the back of her mind…and the front, and the side. He was everywhere, from the lingering scents on her skin to the twinge of her muscles when she moved. Still, genetic strands and helixes consumed her eyes, her brain, and kept her hands busy. Her thoughts didn't stray again for another two hours, when she heard the twitter of a digiset.

One of the guardswomen tapped her ear in response to the wireless chip's hail — and then frowned. She raised her wrist and spoke into her watch chip. "Deploy Unit Two, main gates. Confirmed. Unit Four, reinforce laboratory quadrangle. Purists. Yeah. They're disrupting the EMA shuttle drop-off."

"I'll get the shuttle." Dr. Jenrette stood and headed for the door before the guard had time to react.

Tia was torn between following them and keeping at her comparison work. She decided comparisons were more important.

The matches spoke nervously amongst themselves, and far in the distance, Tia heard what sounded like a small swarm of bees. She hand-comped a few more strands, and chills broke out along her shoulders.

The buzzing sound disturbed her.

Because it isn't a swarm of bees.

She glanced up. The grim faces of the three guards remaining in the lab confirmed what she suspected.

The noise was coming from people. A crowd.

A very big, very angry crowd.

Getting bigger, angrier — and closer — every few seconds.

"I can't believe this," she muttered. "We've been trying for decades, finally get somewhere, and now the idiots come crawling out of the woodwork."

The muffled *zip-zip* of stun rifles brought Tia to her feet just as her terminal tweeted for a full-match.

The other lab techs, Colleen included, also stood.

"This is ridiculous," Colleen grumbled.

For once in history, Tia agreed with her.

The matches looked petrified, but the guardswomen remained calm, keeping their hands on the stocks of their weapons.

"Don't worry," one guard said. "They aren't that close yet. Our girls will handle them at the gates."

You hope. Tia's anxiety roared back with a major vengeance. Only, she wasn't worried for herself or even the other matches. Her first concern was Brok, and her second, the innocent Kaeradi males who might pop into the complex from outer space, completely innocent—and completely at risk.

She had to reach Brok on Kaerad and tell him to stay there. Not to come back to Earth right now. But how?

Tia sat down hard and stared at her terminal in desperation.

The dagger. Yes. But, I think I left it in the suite.

Outside, the bees buzzed and buzzed.

Zip-zip, zip-zip went the stun rifles.

And then the room sort of...rippled.

"Oh, my god!" one of the matches shrieked.

A split-second of silence ensued, followed by squeals and screams and shouts, and barked instructions from the guardswomen.

This time, when Tia looked up, she knew what she would see—and she was almost too happy to be terrified.

Brok and the Kaeradi volunteers had come to Earth. Only, not quite as Tia expected.

Chapter Eight

Tia's pulse quickened even as the guardswomen grew nervous. The nearest woman tapped her ear chip and notified headquarters.

The aliens are here, Tia imagined the woman whispering. *The aliens are here!*

Outside the lab, and Tia hoped outside of the SETI-WHO compound, the crowd made themselves heard. Stun rifles hummed and spat, raising the hairs on her arms.

"Holy goddess," Colleen muttered.

Tia had no urge to slap her, which felt surreal.

Inside the lab, along the back wall, a white-robed Brok stood beside not five volunteers, but a group of twenty Kaeradi males. Five of the men wore robes of muted sapphire. They looked clean-shaven, focused, youthful, and strong.

The other fifteen, however, had a rough, brutal appearance. Beard stubble, flashing blue eyes, smiles almost cruel...predatory. They were muscle-bound beyond what seemed possible, and dressed in what appeared to be red ceremonial robes. Worst of all, they had knife belts full of lethal-looking blades and daggers.

She was reminded of old movies about Saracens.

Aliens, she reminded herself, eying Brok—and the red-robed man nearest to him, who looked much like Brok, only edgier. Much edgier. *What if we underestimated their potential for hostility? What if I underestimated it?*

As if in response, Brok spied Tia, beamed, and strode toward her. His rougher double followed, and the other fourteen "extras" fanned out through the lab. Guardswomen, badly outnumbered, faced them with grim expressions.

The five clean-cut Kaeradi didn't move from the wall; however, they did eye the matches with great interest.

And boy, were the matches eying them.

"No touching," Tia reminded in a loud voice, just before Brok reached her and swept her into his arms.

Tia wanted to be angry, demand explanations for the rather scary guests. But for the moment, she melted into Brok's hard chest and gloried in the feel of his massive hand stroking her hair. His cock quickened as she leaned against him, and her pussy ached as if in answer.

"I'm trying to be mad at you for taking off this morning," she murmured. "Next time, wake me."

Forgive me for leaving at all. Brok's mind-rumble made her tremble with pleasure. *Even for a day. For an hour. I had to retrieve the volunteers.*

Tia pulled back far enough to look him in the eye—but she kept her hips settled against his delicious erection. "Who are the other goons?"

"Goon does not sound…polite," said the man beside Brok. His voice was hoarse and deep, and he seemed to talk through his teeth.

"*Ban-ri*, meet Harad, my brother by blood." Brok kept his warm arms around Tia. With a wink, he pressed his cock against her. "Harad is Kaerad's War Chief."

That title made no sense to Tia, but as she explored Brok's mental images, she quickly understood. Like ancient Earth tribes, Kaeradi believed that no one leader could govern both in peace and in war. A man suited for peace would not make good war, and a man suited for war would not make good peace.

And so, Brok was First Priest of the People. Kaerad's Peace Chief. The "White Chief." His younger brother Harad, of equal intellect and mental and physical power, but different temperament, was the Second Priest. The War Chief, or the "Red Chief."

Tia would have offered her hand to Harad, but Brok still had her tight against his now-throbbing erection. She settled for a quiet, "Hello."

"Pleasure." Harad gave her a small bow. "I had nearly surrendered hope of my brother finding a planet such as yours. We are grateful and pleased to make Earth's acquaintance."

It was all Tia could do to keep her expression even. *Then you brought the first battalion of an invading security force...why?*

"This is no invasion!" Brok laughed and gestured to the fourteen red-robed Kaeradi now ringing the lab. "These are our finest warriors. I brought them to reinforce the guards protecting this enclosure."

At this, the guardswomen relaxed almost as one, but their eyes remained wary.

"But, why?" Even as Tia spoke, the crowd noise escalated and the fire of stun rifles doubled.

Harad's frown made Tia draw closer to Brok. "Because chaos is rarely desirable. Where is...Dare Jenrette?"

Tia fought not to close her eyes as Brok kissed her ear and neck. "Outside with the perimeter guard."

"*Ilya ita dou,*" Harad growled to his red-robed companions.

Eight of them left the lab.

Tia blinked.

Eight of them left the lab...without using the door?

"Brok," she asked, even as the guardswomen and matches cried out in surprise.

"They moved quickly," Brok assured her. "Nothing unnatural. They have gone to help restore order — but they will harm no one without Harad's command."

"*Dinot!*" Harad barked at one of the blue-robed recruits, who had eased toward the clump of matches in the center of the lab floor. The muscle-hunk retreated, but kept his eyes fixed on one of Earth's volunteers.

Outside, crowd noise swelled, then pattered to silence as if squashed flat by some giant hand.

Tia realized the Kaeradi warriors probably shocked the protestors into speechlessness — and just the sight of those knife-wielding mega-men likely convinced the rabble to go home and plan for another day. That, or they were having a giant masturbation session, plotting ways to jump the warriors and fuck them to death.

Harad grumbled to himself.

The matches giggled and huddled, waving at the Kaeradi volunteers, who nodded back at them.

Tia noticed some of the Kaeradi red-robers leering at Colleen and the lab workers — and the guardswomen, too. The workers and guards looked nervous, but also highly interested.

"See?" Brok nibbled Tia's neck, rubbing his rigid cock against her until she stifled a groan. "Order."

Given the demonstrations and rapidly rising media hysteria, Tia knew time was of the essence. Dr. Jenrette would be back from the shuttle delivery soon, but until then, Tia had to move the project forward. If they had success…well, the photos, the reality of women with men, and plenty more men to choose from might silence even the loudest protester.

It took steady nerves, a loud voice, and the fierce backing of Harad and Brok, but Tia managed to move the guardswomen, lab workers (Bitch included), red-robers, matches and Kaeradi volunteers out of the lab, down the hall, across two corridors, and into the observation suites.

As outlined by Dr. Jenrette and suggested by Brok, Tia placed each volunteer and his four potential matches into one of the ten available efficiency rooms. The rooms were completely secure, and private except for the one-way glass facing each bed. Tia divided lab workers, Kaeradi guards, and human guards into the observation porticos.

The lab workers switched on dista-sensors to monitor the vital signs of all participants, and terminals began recording data. Guards of both races were present in case some nutcase made it into the lab—and in case something went wrong. According to Brok and Harad, the red-robers were fully trained healers, and they would assist should one of the volunteers show signs of illness.

Tia located herself in the portico of an empty room with Brok and Harad. The set-up was simple enough. A broad panel of one-way glass took up most of the inner wall opposite the door, a table with four chairs faced the glass, and on the table sat an integrated terminal. Doing her best to ignore the oddly matched set of Kaeradi gods on either side of her, Tia tapped her code on the screen, engaging a master program to monitor all five experiments at once—including a small digivideo bubble showing the actual activity in each room.

"These machines are useless." Harad smacked the top of Tia's terminal. "My warriors will mentally monitor the situation at twice the speed."

Brok opened his mouth, clearly intending to chastise his brother, but Tia silenced him with a glance. She knew she had a chance—one chance—to set the tone of her relationship with this man. And ultimately, with all the dominant males of Kaerad.

The women of Earth would have to hold their own. Might as well start now.

"You have your ways, we have ours, Harad." Tia gave him a nudge, just enough to move him away from the terminal. She sat down and treated him to her best icy stare. "At the moment, you're on Earth. So, we do it Earth style. Get over it."

Harad narrowed his eyes. His cheeks flushed, but he set his mouth and didn't say anything else. And he gave Tia wide berth at the console as she turned to set the baseline functions for the five monitors. Retreating to the portico shadows, Harad nearly faded into the corner beside the observation glass.

Brok's large hands rested on Tia's shoulders, and slowly, gently, began to massage.

His touch was just right. So gentle, yet strong. Powerful.

I wish we were having our own...experiment right this moment, he murmured in her mind.

Tia's pussy responded with a clenching wetness. *Yes. Damn.* She ground her teeth, and very nearly had to flog her brain to keep her attention on the monitor.

Brok continued the easy pressure of his massage, pausing only to move his hands lower or higher on her arms and neck. Shivers of pleasure traveled Tia's skin.

Concentrate.

So far, all contacts were in preliminary stages. Tia had sound hook-up to the other observation porticos, but not to the rooms themselves. From the porticos came the low rumble of conversation, punctuated by nervous laughter. It took Tia a second to realize what she found odd about that, but then it struck her.

Male voices.

The timbre of male voices in easy conversation with women.

Somewhere in the distant reaches of her mind, the chanting of her foremothers began. Tia's palm itched, as if she should be holding the dagger dangling from the belt of Brok's robe.

In Room 1, the first Kaeradi volunteer was naked. His four matches circled him, gazing at the definition of his muscles, at his stiffening prick. Some of the women were taking their shirts off.

Room 2, Room 3, and Room 4 were still in the staring-and-gaping phase.

Tia felt a new tingle in her pussy, this one from the sudden sensation of being a voyeur. By the time this experiment ended, she would have watched — hopefully — a *lot* of fucking.

Brok's hands eased over Tia's shoulders, hinting that with little effort, he could reach her breasts. Her nipples pressed hard against her cotton shirt, and Tia was grateful for her lab coat.

I'm a scientist, she reminded herself as her body temperature climbed. *And besides. Harad is still in the room.*

Behind Tia, the portico door opened.

The chanting in Tia's head grew louder.

"Where are we?" Dare Jenrette's voice overrode the piped voices from the other porticos.

"Phase one, as prescribed," Tia responded, mentally swearing at her foremothers to be quiet.

"Don't know why you brought the extras," Dr. Jenrette said to Brok. "But they were damned useful. Handled the crowd with just their presence. Amazing. The EMA shuttle made its drop off and—"

Without turning fully to see, Tia knew Dr. Jenrette had seen Harad.

Harad's low, dangerous growl suggested he had more than seen Dr. Jenrette, too.

In Tia's mind, the chanting swelled, then fell silent.

She blinked.

Harad was gone.

One minute he was in the corner, and the next minute, he simply...wasn't.

Brok's grip on Tia's shoulders tightened as a wild sexual energy filled the room. Tia's monitors jumped and wiggled in impossible ways—and the room's door opened and slammed shut.

This time, Tia did turn around. Dr. Jenrette was gone, too.

She whirled back to Brok. "What the hell is going on? What has he done? What have *you* done?"

Tia raised both fists to hit Brok in the chest, but he caught her hands and turned her toward the one-way glass.

Fear twisted her insides, and betrayal burned in her belly like hot oil.

This wasn't part of the experiment. Tia aimed her thoughts straight at Brok's brain, struggling as he held her from behind, hands firmly on her wrists. She thought about stomping his big foot. *Your wild brother kidnapping my boss...*

Ban-ri, he mind-spoke. *I would never betray you, or anyone you love. I am not, by nature, a betrayer. Trust me.*

Trust.

Whatever.

Tia questioned her sanity, fucking a total stranger and an alien, believing the pieces of information he psychically dumped in her mind. It could be a ruse, all of it. Perpetrated by a more crafty set of Hostiles. And yet her instinct warred against suspicion.

Hadn't she shared more with Brok than sex?

Yes.

Of course.

Or...had she?

Old doubt wormed in Tia's belly.

When the Kaeradi figured out how to mate safely with Earth's large selection of females, wouldn't Brok move on to something better?

Stop. Enjoy what you have while you have it.

Tia wriggled in Brock's arms. He kept her in place, but made no effort to dominate or hurt her.

"When I met Jenrette, I knew she was a temperament match for my brother." Brok kissed the top of Tia's head. "When she touched me in your laboratory — her genetic signature — I pray this works well."

A light came on in the efficiency, revealing two figures.

Tia went still in Brok's ever-tender embrace.

Her panic subsided, partly because she did trust Brok at a fundamental level, and partly because it was quite clear Dare Jenrette was *not* being forced to do anything against her will.

Annie Windsor

Harad carried her, cradled, as if the tall, powerful woman were no more than a little girl. Dr. Jenrette's long arms were wrapped tightly around the huge man's neck, and they were kissing.

Deeply.

Passionately.

Tia drew a slow breath, now twice as aware of Brok's hard body—and hard cock—pressed into her from behind.

The experiments. I have to…monitor…the data.

"Harad and Jenrette are now an experiment." Brok let go Tia's wrists and stroked her arms. "And we are their observers."

"I—uh…" Tia's thoughts melted into images of one of her earlier fantasies. The one about her boss fucking a hunk on the lab desk. Her nipples puckered. A full-body shiver covered her in delicious chills.

Brok's only response was a throaty grunt as he kissed Tia's neck, and then removed her lab coat. It fell over the terminal running the master program, and Tia barely noticed.

There were audio-alarms, if something really got out of hand.

I'm what's getting out of hand. In a big hurry. She was so wet between the legs she wondered if she would soak her pants—which wasn't an issue, really, because Brok was methodically taking those off.

In the efficiency, like a movie made just for Tia's enjoyment, Harad lowered Dr. Jenrette to her feet beside the large bed. Still kissing her. Now half-pulling, half-ripping her lab coat, her blouse, her gentle-support undershirt…

"Dr. Jenrette's skin is so perfect," Tia whispered. She had never seen her boss naked, but she wanted that now, in the worst way.

And then her cheeks blazed. *I shouldn't be watching this.*

They know we can see, Ban-ri. Brok's hands seemed to be everywhere at once. Massaging her arms, unbuttoning her shirt. *They do not care. In fact, they welcome us.*

Freed of fabric, Tia felt her nipples jut, fairly begging for attention. Brok didn't neglect them. The shock of his gentle pinches made her moan.

Harad had Dr. Jenrette — *Dare, I should call her Dare if I'm going to watch her fuck an alien god* — Dare naked from the waist up. Her breasts were full and round. Dare shoved Harad's red robe down over his shoulders, and it fell open, revealing carved muscles.

With a ferocious smile, Harad took one of Dare's huge nipples, the color of rich wine, into his mouth.

Tia gasped. *Too much. This is too much.*

"Nothing is too much, *Ban-ri*." Brok held her firmly against him, rolling both of her sensitive nubs in his skilled fingers. "When the universe offers such pleasure, should we not partake?"

Tia leaned against Brok and raised her arms over her head. When she bent her elbows, she could reach the sides of his face as he dipped to run his tongue across her ear. "You're incredible."

"Mmmm." Brok's purr gave Tia a new round of shivers.

Dare's head fell back. She plunged her graceful hands into Harad's long black hair, and Harad held his new prize in a fiercely possessive embrace.

Does Brok hold me like that?

Yes. He did.

Tia knew it was true, and the thought thrilled her. Her arousal climbed another notch. Between her legs, her clit ached so badly she thought it might burst.

Reading her desires, Brok let go of one nipple, moved his hand down, and cupped Tia's pussy. She almost shouted from need. Her eyes remained glued to the scene in front of her.

Dare, mouth open, screaming with pleasure…

Harad savaging one nipple, and then the other…

"Touch me," she begged Brok. "Please. Rub my clit."

Brok growled and bit her neck. He thrust one finger inside her wet folds, found the hot spot instantly, and pushed. And then he rubbed.

Tia moaned and rocked against the pressure.

In the efficiency, Harad tore off the remainder of Dare's clothing and let his robe fall to the floor. He had on nothing beneath it.

His prick, thick and long like Brok's—*are all Kaeradi hung like horses?*—stood out like a granite rod. Dare's eyes widened. For a split-second, she looked frightened, right before she grabbed that prick and used it to haul Harad closer to her.

Brok rubbed Tia's clit harder. With his other hand, he squeezed her nipple. Wave after wave of excitement shook her.

"Give in, *Ban-ri*." Brok's bass whisper filled her ear. "Watch it. Feel it."

Dare's well-sucked nipples seemed huge as they pressed into Harad's chest. She moved her hand up and down Harad's swollen rod. His muscles flexed, and Tia knew he was about to throw Dare on the bed.

In seconds, Harad would do as Brok had done—risk his life to fuck the woman he chose.

Harad chose Dare Jenrette.

"You chose me," Tia said breathlessly as she came, shaking in Brok's powerful grasp. He continued stroking her clit, pushing her to a second climax. Tia's whole body rocked. Heat spread through every inch, every muscle. She felt giddy.

"Then, now, and always, *Ban-ri*." Brok moved Tia forward, close to the one-way glass, and bent her over. She gripped the wooden lip holding the observation window. "Keep your eyes focused on Jenrette and my brother. The dangerous moment has arrived."

As if on cue, Harad swept Dare off her feet and laid her across the bed.

Dare spread her legs.

Tia felt the tip of Brok's cock teasing her pussy. She wanted to drive herself backward, fill herself with his hot, hard flesh — but she had to watch Dare and Harad. Harad could get sick. Die.

Eyes open, Tia told herself. She gripped the wooden sill. Her breasts hung down, her protruding nipples still throbbing from Brok's touch.

Through the one-way digilink to the other porticos, Tia heard moaning and grunting.

Masturbation? New experiments? God. No one's watching the watchers!

Harad studied Dare like Brok had studied Tia, and Tia knew the other woman could feel his eyes like fingers, hands…

The tip of Brok's cock pushed into Tia's moist opening.

She wanted him to fuck her, just as much as she wanted Harad to drill Dare — and live.

"Has he entered her yet?" Brok's question was quiet. Tia wondered why he didn't look for himself, then caught her breath at the truth. If it went poorly, Brok didn't want to watch his brother drop dead.

Her heart clutched. "Not yet," she managed. Despite her best effort to stay still, she moved against Brok's waiting cock. "He's saying something."

"Vows." Brok gripped Tia around the waist. "And Jenrette?"

"I think she just agreed." *Vows. Oh, my god. Back on the desk — vows.* Tia's heart pounded. *I want to keep this man so badly!*

And in the room before her, Harad of Kaerad, still standing, eased his massive cock into Dare's waiting pussy.

Dare gripped the bed with both hands, her expression a mix of ecstasy, pain, and fanatical desire.

My face looked like that. My face looks like that now.

Harad continued, and in moments, he was fully inside Dare's welcoming core.

And, he was still standing. No sign of illness.

Opening his mouth in what Tia could only assume was a roar of triumph, Harad pumped himself in and out of Dare's pussy.

"He's in!" Tia's fingers dug into the wooden lip. "It's fine. He's fucking her. Now please, stop teasing me!"

Brok entered her with a single, driving thrust.

"Yes!" Tia yelled, spreading her legs wider, pushing back to take every inch.

Harad found a rhythm with Dare. They moved like one being, up and down against the bedspread. Dare wrapped her thighs around her newfound warrior. He bent forward and captured her arms, holding her in place.

Behind Tia, Brok found that same rhythm. Holding her by her hips, he slammed in, pulled back, slammed in, pulled back.

"So good," he murmured. "So sweet."

Tia's breasts bounced as he rocked her against his groin.

She felt completed, whole. Her pussy felt full to the rim. Orgasm built like creeping fire, starting in her legs, moving through her hips and belly.

"I'm coming already. Damn. I'm going to come right now!"

"Surrender," Brok demanded, pounding into her throbbing channel.

In the room, Dare thrashed under Harad, and Tia knew she was coming, too.

Tia's vaginal walls constricted violently, holding tight to Brok as he hammered in and out. Giddy became dizzy. Dizzy became delirious. "Aaaah, yes. Yes!"

Brok plumbed her depths once more, then let loose with his own orgasm. He groaned loudly, spilling his hot seed in her center—while in the room, his brother had his mouth wide open again. Howling.

"Unbelievable," Tia gasped, wishing Brok could fuck her for hours. For days. With or without the incredible view before her.

And then the lab-coat covered console's audio alarms started ringing.

First one.

Then, a second.

Chapter Nine

SETI-WHO EXPERIMENTS TAKE HORRIBLE TURN
ONE DEAD, ONE INJURED AT SETI-WHO SEX FEST
S.E.A.R.C.H. DIRECTOR BELMONT UNDER SCRUTINY
HOLD THE ALIENS! EARTH WOMEN LETHAL!
WHO'S JENRETTE GUARANTEES RAPID SOLUTION

Tia dropped her palm-reader into the trash bin beside her desk.

A week had passed since the disaster, and still the digipapers raged and rehashed, then raged a little more.

The whole situation made her sick.

The lab was deserted except for Dare, Harad, Brok, Colleen, and the only two workers who hadn't quit or struck it rich selling stories to the press. They bent over consoles or gazed at stacks of paper data.

Outside, Kaeradi officers guarded the lab door. International guardswomen ringed the compound. After the experiment debacle, male and female troops were no longer mixed. At least not for the time being.

Members of the press grouped like ravenous crows, lighting at one entrance or another, rebuffed only by stun rifles and shows of force. Everyone wanted a glimpse of the aliens.

The *real men,* according to many headlines. The *wild men.* The *alien barbarians.*

Competing headlines called them *intruders, blights,* and *interlopers.*

Tia didn't know what was worse—the real headlines, the fanatic digigossips, the EMA press releases warning Earth to proceed with caution, or the Purist bullshit about a mutant bastard race.

Kaeradi were taking on the proportions of myth. Half of Earth thought a woman died at the compound, despite SETI-WHO'S careful press releases. Digigossips claimed the woman was fucked to death, and a big cover-up was underway.

The other half of Earth thought the men from Kaerad were sex machines, and planned to screw them all. Three at a time, if possible.

Tia sighed.

Truth was always less sexy than rumor.

And the truth was sad, indeed.

Four of five experiments, the unscheduled Dare-Harad tryst notwithstanding, had gone well. In the fifth, the Kaeradi volunteer had been sickened the moment he entered the third of four matches. Harad's red-robed officers had revived him and taken him back to Kaerad. He was expected to recover, but sexual relations might not be an option for him in the future.

Unfortunately, Tia, Dare, and everyone involved had underestimated the effects of cultural mingling and sexual deprivation. Unplanned "experiments" occurred in every observation portico, ranging from heavy petting to penetration, and one of those had gone so, so wrong.

Apparently, a Kaeradi guard had taken a fancy to an Earth international guardswoman. They made it through initial stages of touching through clothing, but moved too quickly in their passion. When the red-rober tried to thrust into his willing partner, the incompatibility shock killed him on the spot.

His body had been sent back to Kaerad. The guardswoman remained in protective custody in the compound holding section. Even after seven days of counseling, she was still suicidal.

And Tia still didn't have a clue how to make the couplings any safer.

The "fast solution" Dare promised the world…it just wouldn't happen. Tia could barely eat, barely sleep. She and Brok had been together a few times in the last six or seven days, but Tia felt guilty.

How could she fuck like the world wasn't blowing up around her?

Every time a new idea failed, she grew angrier with herself. A lifetime of insults flooded back, *fat* and *stupid* first on the list.

Brok seemed to understand, and yet he also seemed…sad. And worried. Even now, he was hovering.

After a minute or so, Brok circled around to Tia's desk and kissed the top of her head.

"Don't," she whispered, thinking of the suicidal guardswoman and her infinitely sad expression. Tears clouded Tia's vision. "Please, not now. I—I need to think."

Her Kaeradi hunk looked wounded, but she ignored him and turned back to her console.

There had to be some way to resolve this.

A small clatter on her desk made her look up, and she saw a well-polished Widowmaker resting beside her left hand.

Brok?

He had already walked away, toward the terminal bank where Harad and Dare were working. As she watched, he sat in a chair beside his brother, keeping his back to Tia.

Perhaps the athame *will help you think*, Ban-ri. His mind-words were warm, even though she'd been short with him. *She has not been speaking to me.*

Tia stared at the dagger.

Faintly, like the buzz of the crowd on that awful experiment day, Tia heard the combined singing of her foremothers.

She frowned.

Stop. I need to concentrate, and you aren't helping.

The buzz grew louder, more stubborn.

Tia imagined twenty or thirty crones, each an older likeness of herself, flipping her off and shouting their stupid chants around their stupid, useless fires.

In a fit of annoyance, she opened her desk door, dropped the *athame* inside, and slammed the drawer shut.

So much for rituals.

So much for magic.

"I'm a scientist, not a sorceress," she said to herself. "There *has* to be a way to do this."

"Bitch!"

Tia looked up sharply, just in time to see one of the lab workers push away from a terminal she had been sharing with Colleen.

Colleen almost fell getting up from her seat. "What's your problem, asshole?"

"We've done that test three times," the woman fumed. "Three! Why? Because it's your DNA? You *got* some strange nookie last week, baby. That Kaeradi guard had you wailin' like a cat in heat, just using his *fingers* — but he's not your match. You can't make him a match, no matter how many ways you run the program."

"Shut up." Colleen turned fluorescent pink. "I was just — "

"Just wasting time," the second remaining lab worker grumbled from a nearby terminal. "If you don't get over yourself, we'll never solve a bit of this."

"It's got to be in the sperm samples." Dare sat back in her chair and rubbed her eyes. "A way to make more direct — and definite — comparisons."

Tia looked from Colleen to the refrigerator beside the bitch. Inside were the one hundred Kaeradi sperm samples Dare referred to. Brok's included, and Harad's. Dare had them taken the day after the experiment mess. Since then, she and Tia had tried a few protocols with the samples to use, but overall, nothing worked. The sperm gave them no more information than the genetic codes.

Despite the brawn, Kaeradi males were fragile packages. She smiled and flexed her fingers. *Handle With Care. Indeed.*

"What are you staring at?" Colleen folded her arms and gave Tia the evil eye. "You think I'm being selfish for checking my own strands? What would you know? You already have a new Kaeradi husband!"

"He's not my husband," Tia said, surprised—though not unhappy with the idea of being Brok's wife. She was, sort of. For the moment. Until…until all the research they were doing came to fruition and Brok realized his many options.

Tia blinked at Colleen. *I'm just lucky enough to fuck him for now,* she almost said, and felt an odd compassion for her nemesis.

At the terminal bank, both Brok and Harad had stiffened in their seats. Even Dare sat up straighter. Yet, none of them turned around.

A loud buzz nearly made Tia have an out-of-body experience.

"EMA shuttle," Dare said absently. "Take this round, okay, Tia?"

"Sure. I'm useless here." Tia shut down her station and grabbed her lab coat. "But this is stupid. Nobody wants Earth sperm anymore—except the Purists."

* * * * *

Brok and Harad faced each other in Brok and Tia's private suite. They had left the laboratory just after Tia did, using Kaeradi atomic motion to slip undetected so they would not need guards.

"I hadn't believed you, Brother." Harad's tone was grim. "In truth, I still have difficulty believing Tia knows the level of pain she causes you."

"She agreed. Tia chose me." Brok paced back and forth in the small space. Pain poked his gut like spears. "She fucks me as if I am the only man in the galaxy—yet rejects our vows. She even closes me from her thoughts most of the time. 'You'll find better, Brok.' 'You'll leave soon, Brok.'"

Harad released a long breath. "Dare never says such things."

"Jenrette is a warrior. She believes in herself." Brok slowed and gazed out the room's single barred window. "Tia has spent many years considering herself ugly. Undesirable."

"Colleen does not help."

"No, she does not—but the bitch means nothing." Brok lowered his head. "I have tried, with every touch, every statement, to reach Tia. Nothing works."

"What are you saying?" Harad's tone was harsher than usual.

"I think I must face the obvious. My *Ban-ri* enjoys me. She rejoices in what the Earthers call flesh-and-blood sex, but she does not truly love me."

"Perhaps you were hasty in your choice?" Harad settled on the long blue couch. "You will match with other women on this planet. Three or four at least, if experience holds true."

Brok resisted an urge to punch his brother in the mouth. "Tia Belmont is the other half of my soul."

Harad kept up his maddeningly relaxed posture, goading Brok for reasons he couldn't articulate. "Time for truth. The half-soul you yet possess is distracted. Too distracted."

"I cannot prevent that." Brok frowned.

"You must. You are not helping our cause here, mooning after the woman." Harad placed his feet on the table in front of the couch. "Perhaps some time on Kaerad would ease you."

"I do not wish to leave Tia. The agitators—"

"My life for her life, Brother." Harad gave the sacred Kaeradi pledge that Harad's chosen wife, Dare Jenrette, had unwittingly given Brok just over one Earth week before. "Go home. Renew at the temples. Speak to the Council. Then you can return with a clear mind and a fresh heart."

Clear mind. Fresh heart. Brok bit the inside of his cheek, hard. Would he ever know those things again?

An image of Tia's soft, fragrant body filled his senses, and his cock grew hard and uncomfortable. He wanted to hold her. Suck her sweet, peach-scented nipples. Kiss her full lips. Fuck her until she screamed. Until they both shouted with total release.

Love me, Tia.

My Ban-ri.

Why do you allow me inside your body, yet keep me at arm's length from your heart?

Brok dreamed of taking Tia away from this pressure-filled laboratory, this unnatural clinical place, built with unnatural plastics and metals. Life's energy — it was scant here. Maybe that was the problem.

On Kaerad, he could teach her how true science crossed nature to make what she called magic. Tia had the mind for such learning. Unlike most of her Earth counterparts, Tia could absorb most of what Kaeradi wisdom had to offer.

Most of all, Brok wanted a full joining ceremony on Kaerad, before his people. He wanted to claim Tia before the Goddess again, formally.

And he wanted her to claim him.

Harad coughed loud enough to snap Brok's trance.

Brok glared at his brother, once more considering violence. Unusual, given Brok's vows against combat except for self-defense and the immediate protection of others.

"Contemplation will not force your hesitant bride to her senses." Harad stood. All teasing left his expression, and when he opened his mouth, Brok knew Harad would speak not as a man or a brother — but in his sacred role as Second Priest of the People, bringer of strength.

And indeed, he did.

In low, resonant syllables, he addressed Brok in the Kaeradi high tongue. Like a prayer. Like a chant.

"You are the White Chief of Kaerad. You are First Priest of the People, bringer of peace. Your responsibilities extend beyond your desires for one woman. Gather your wits. Go home, Brother. Return renewed, or not at all."

Brok closed his eyes.

Before Harad could goad him into sparring, he bled his essence into the atmosphere and transferred home at top speed.

As Tia helped four EMA eunuchs unload the last of the sperm canisters, she felt a tug deep inside. Like somebody tied a string around her heart and gave it a yank.

"That should get it," said Adam, the freckled EMA rep Tia knew the best. "Sign?"

He handed her a digipad.

Tia scribbled her initials without really thinking about it.

Adam took the pad, handed Tia a second digipad for the lab's records, glanced at the three men boarding the shuttle, and then leaned toward Tia. "So, tell me. Is it true? Did one of those monsters kill a woman in the big 'experiment?'"

"No." Tia heard the coldness in her response. It startled her, as did the urge to put her hands around Adam's throat and choke him until he apologized for calling her husband's people "monsters."

Husband. She winced. *Only for a little while.*

Adam gave her the once-over and shrugged. "Didn't figure we'd ever get the truth. Especially not from you."

"What's that supposed to mean?" Tia's shrill question brought the other three men right back out of the shuttle. They circled Adam and Tia, clearly ready to jump between them if necessary.

"Only that you're...compromised." Adam shook his head. "EMA Central warned us. You and Dr. Jenrette both. Hardly objective about all this, right?"

"That's enough, Adam." A brown-bearded man with an unusual amount of hair on his head grabbed his shuttlemate by the shoulder. Tia had never seen this man before, on deliveries or digivision, or anything.

"Not yet." Adam jerked away. "I'm not finished."

"Yes, you are." Brown-beard sounded authoritative, but Adam ignored him and approached Tia, shoulders squared.

Tia didn't give ground.

Adam kept moving until he stood toe to toe with her. Almost nose to nose. Tia was taller than he was.

"I think S.E.A.R.C.H. is sunk." Adam's mouth twisted in a cruel way. "I think you're all whores for opportunistic aliens now."

Tia couldn't help a mental comparison, holding Adam's puny physique and ugly attitude up against Brok's muscles and kindness.

No contest. Not even in the same league.

Good thing this little shit was an "almost." He didn't need to procreate.

"That's the problem with Earth males." Tia shook her head and nearly strangled the record-laden digipad she held. "Even in this day and age, you fuck whoever and however you want. But Goddess forbid the women get a little pleasure. Oh, no. Then we're compromised. Then we're whores."

Adam started to respond, but Tia cut him off. "Might want to cut down on the 'donations' for next month, boys. I'm not sure we'll be needing as much."

Tia turned her back on Adam. Scuffling sounds ensued, and she was fairly certain his friends were restraining him.

"Fat bitch!" he yelled.

"Rather be a fat bitch than a whiny bastard with a microdick." Tia strode past the guardswomen at the complex entry doors. They were smiling. "When's the last time you got laid, Adam? No, don't answer that. The poor girl probably didn't notice."

SETI-WHO's thick metal doors swung shut, muffling Adam's response.

Tia's fingers fisted around the EMA digipad. If it hadn't contained vital delivery statistics, she would have hurled it against the wall just on principle.

As it was, she didn't waste another thought on Adam the Jerk. Her mind reeled back on the sensation she had on the loading dock. That tug on her heart.

Had she felt it before?

Yes…and no. Oh, the hell with this. I need to find Brok and fuck him silly, then get back to work.

At that thought, her body responded like a plucked guitar string. Nipples vibrating. Pussy humming.

She was getting far too used to that man.

"God. Get it together, Tia." The empty halls echoed as she chastised herself. "No sex. No fantasies. Ideas, damn it. You need a new approach. A brainstorm. Two worlds are waiting for results."

Tia rounded the last corner on the way back to the lab — and nearly freaked when Harad appeared from nowhere.

"How — what —" Tia held the digipad to her chest, trying to breathe. "Don't *do* that, okay?"

"Matter transfer. It is a simple thing." Harad's sharp-featured face didn't change expressions. "We need to talk, Tia. About Brok, and you, and the future."

"I know. Later. I have to get back to my terminal and —"

"No," Harad said sternly. "Not later. Now."

"But Dare and Brok will —"

"Wait," Harad inserted.

Something in the alien's dark eyes made Tia nervous. She glanced toward the Kaeradi red-robers protecting the lab's inner doors. Like they'd help her against Harad.

"You will not need their assistance," Harad said in his characteristic rasp. "I intend you no harm."

Tia hugged herself. "You're making me really nervous. Brok never does that."

"My brother is a gentle, patient, and respectful man." Harad's frown gave Tia an unpleasant shiver. "I am not."

Once more, Tia glanced at the lab door. The digipad suddenly felt heavy in her grasp. "Where do you want to have our little chat?"

"Here." Harad flexed his massive biceps as he folded his arms.

Tia thought about that tug on her heart again. Her eyes kept straying to the lab door. To Brok. She felt a sudden, deep need to talk to him.

"What are your intentions toward Brok?" Harad asked.

"Excuse me?" Tia almost laughed at the antiquated question.

"Your intentions toward my brother." Harad's posture stiffened. "He claimed you, and you him. And yet you tear his heart at every opportunity, disrespecting that vow."

"I tear his—what?" Tia gaped at him. "What are you talking about?"

"I will try Earth terms." Harad spoke slowly, as if choosing phrases with great care. "You tell Brok you love him, yet deny the permanence of your relationship. You tell him he will leave you. That he will find interest in other women."

Tia's cheeks heated up. "So? I do love him. But once he sees what Earth has to offer, he'll move on."

Again, that hard, scary expression flashed over Harad's hawkish face. "Once mated, Kaeradi do not 'move on'. Brok claimed you before the Goddess."

"But he didn't know any other Earth women!"

"He didn't have to," Harad growled. "You are so blinded by negative feelings about your appearance. Reject before you can be rejected. Throw away before you lose. Your personal code, yes?"

White rage burned Tia from the inside out. She used the digipad like a giant finger, shaking it right in Harad's face. "What would you know about it? And that's stupid. It's not like I've gotten rejected a bunch of times. Hello? There are hardly any men here!"

Harad's face colored. "And now you have your pick of our planet. Did you act too quickly in choosing Brok?"

Tia thought about plugging her ears. This conversation sucked. She didn't want to have it. "Of course I didn't act too quickly! I love Brok. I really love him, and — oh, sweet goddess." Without warning, tears flooded her cheeks.

Harad's stern demeanor melted to concern in an instant. "What is it? Are you in pain?"

"He's gone again, isn't he?" That was it. The tug on her heart. The last time, she had been asleep, but she felt it nonetheless, especially after she woke up. An emptiness. A hollowness way down deep. "Brok went back to Kaerad. Without saying goodbye, and without taking me with him. And this time, he might not come back."

No response from Harad. The unnatural look of bewildered fear on his face confirmed at least one ancient male-related truth. Even bad-ass Kaeradi warriors had no idea what to do with a sobbing woman.

"Get out of my way," Tia whispered.

Without even a word of protest, Harad got out of her way.

Tia's walk to the lab felt surreal. She hugged the digipad like a teddy bear, tears flooding like a swollen stream.

Brok. She wanted Brok. But he wasn't in the lab. He wasn't on Earth at all.

He ran out on me. I'll kill him.

Tia slipped between the red-robed sentinels and pushed the door open.

Dare, Colleen, and the two lab workers didn't look up from their terminals. Dare had a set of sperm samples beside her.

He left me. Tia stared at the samples, wondering if one belonged to Brok. *But, what Harad said…did I leave Brok first?*

Her head ached, but worse than that, her heart ached so much she thought she would die on the spot.

I love him so much. And I told him, over and over – but Harad's right. I also kept telling him he'd take off once he found a prettier woman. I'd tell him I loved him, then take it back. Damn. Damn!

She had to talk to Brok, sooner rather than later. The worlds could wait fifteen minutes. An hour. Tia knew if she didn't clear this up, she'd be worthless for a lot longer than that.

Harad wasn't likely to help, but Tia knew she had one other option. Brok had given it back to her just a few hours ago.

She went straight to her desk, tossed the digipad beside her terminal, and yanked her drawer open. The dagger lay inside, beside the melted keys and dildos, right on top of the egg-shaped burn mark where Tia's vibrator had exploded. When she picked up Widowmaker, it tingled in her fingers.

Tia turned, intending to hold it up, just like she had done the day she first saw Brok—but the dagger seemed to have a mind of its own.

The *athame* pulled against her, back toward the drawer, until Tia looked down at the scorched place. Then it pulled her around once more, toward Dare and the sperm samples.

The burned-egg-mark. The sperm samples. Back and forth.

Chanting burst into Tia's mind this time. Female voices and male, singing, from two separate places. She saw shimmering flames reaching high into two very different skies. And different

Eostre altars, all honoring the same Goddess. Yes. And children. Hundreds. Thousands. Laughing gleefully as they searched for prizes and eggs.

The egg vibrator. Eggs in the hunt. Eggs for the sperm samples. It was the most natural thing in the world. In both worlds. How had she missed it?

"Eggs," Tia muttered, staring into the *athame*'s hypnotic firestone. She could almost sense Kaerad. Almost feel the lush moss beneath her. Almost sense Brok's piercing gaze. "Do you hear me? Eggs! That's it!"

Dare spun in her chair. Colleen looked up from her terminal. The other two lab workers stared. Harad entered in a rush, as if he sensed something urgent.

"Go tell Brok," Tia said. She knew her eyes were wide. Crazy. But she couldn't help it. "Tell him I love him more than anything, that I'm his wife now and forever — but I have to stay on Earth one more day. I have to make some eggs!"

Harad and the rest gave Tia cockeyed glances, but Harad nodded.

To Dare, he said, "By your leave, I will be back in a few Earth minutes."

Dare Jenrette stood, obviously concerned, both for Tia's sanity and Harad's impending departure.

"A few minutes," Harad repeated.

Dare came forward, almost to where Tia stood, and blew him a kiss.

Tia felt a shimmer in the room, and she knew Harad was about to transfer to Kaerad as she had requested.

At that moment, the world shook.

A loud *boom* — something forceful and hot blew Tia backward so hard she slammed right into the wall — a few inches deep.

Her last thoughts were of crumbling rocks and falling altars...and eggs, broken and scattered like old dreams across fields of dying grass.

Chapter Ten

A psychic dose of Tia's physical pain nearly brought Brok to his knees before the Council of Wisdom's great stone dais.

Bellowing like a wounded beast, he shook his head, turned a circle on the Council's rounded hallowed grounds, and would have transferred to Earth if five of the twenty Council elders had not stood and restrained his matter with a binding protection chant.

"Release me!" He pounded against the glittering energy strands hovering in five stacked circles around him. Visions of knives and blood and brutal revenge filled his mind. Someone had harmed Tia.

Brok knew he would kill that someone. Immediately.

Slay the bastard with his own hands in some tortuous fashion.

Peace be yours, young Brother, came the Council's Onevoice, firing down from the dais like honey-tipped arrows.

The gentle yet sharp intonation barely penetrated Brok's frenzy.

Peace. Wisdom. Peace. Wisdom. Peace...

The elders chanted without cease, working to restore Brok's inner balance.

All vows temporarily forgotten, Brok wanted to kill the Council, too.

The ancient morons dared to keep him from his *Ban-ri.* Tia was wounded. She needed him, and the Council was holding him hostage!

And yet, over the next long moments, their forceful calming efforts broke through the shield of his rage.

Bit by bit, Brok's front-mind rekindled. He remembered that with great age, wisdom, and experience came the ability to predict atomic patterns that *would* be, based on the patterns occurring in the present.

The Council could "see" something, or they would not have denied him.

Crumpling and prone figures appeared around him like lightning flashes on the Council grounds, bringing with them bits of fire and rubble. Moaning filled the air, growing with each arrival.

The bonds on Brok dropped away as the Council moved as one body, down from their stone table, off their stone platform, to the injured and dying.

Soldiers. Volunteers. Earth women bonded to the volunteers...and there!

Harad, bent and bloodied, clutching an unconscious Dare Jenrette in one arm and a broken, battered Tia in the other.

Brok's heart stuttered. Harad didn't...he couldn't have transferred both women. And yet, there he stood — barely — holding Dare and Tia against his obviously shattered body.

"No!" Brok was running toward his brother before he even understood he was moving.

Harad's pledge echoed like pealing bells through Brok's mind.

My life for her life...my life for her life...

Injured badly himself, Harad should have had only enough energy to move himself back to Kaerad.

But being Harad, he would not leave his wounded mate, nor forsake his brother's mate, whom he swore to protect with his own life.

Four Council elders reached Harad before Brok. One took Tia, and another swept Dare from Harad's failing arms.

Relieved of his burdens, Harad gave Brok a desperate, apologetic glance and croaked, "Explosion."

Then he toppled like a felled tree, face-first into Kaerad's loamy ground.

The next span of time held the longest and worst hours Brok of Kaerad, First Priest of the People, had ever experienced.

Two of the Kaeradi guard contingent—the two men stationed outside the lab door—never returned. Brok presumed they died on the spot, performing their assigned duty to the best of their ability. They couldn't even "home," or transfer their dying matter back to Kaerad for farewell ceremonies.

Three more guards did manage to "home." They expired on Council grounds before healing could begin. Burns, broken skeletons, smoke in the lungs—coupled with the energy drain of transferring—too much.

Harad's wounds were far beyond the healing talents of any but the eldest of elders. He had been taken to the Council house, forbidden to all Kaeradi but the Council of Wisdom themselves. Dare Jenrette and Tia had been carried to those sacred halls as well.

Tia. My love. My soul. Brok's muscles felt like stretched bands as he discharged his duties as First Priest, ministering to the lesser-wounded guards and the few Earth women who had transferred with their chosen mates.

Though he saw the people beneath his hands, Brok's *Ban-ri* held his thoughts. *Tia. Tia!* She had a wound to her head no human should have survived—and yet, when she arrived on Kaerad, clutching her ritual dagger in one pale hand, her heart beat as if to defy the bastards who would have her dead.

With all of his being, Brok wanted to storm the Council house, but he knew his very presence could kill Harad, Dare, and his precious Tia. The energies at the Council's most sacred of places—perfectly attuned, delicate, resonating only to the aged healers and their chosen charges. A "young one," as the elders called Brok, would do nothing but disrupt the flow.

Even if Brok would one day be an elder and walk those sanctified halls with knowing and careful grace, he could not enter today without tragic consequences. Not even to do the one thing he wished over all other wishes he had known: press his lips against the forehead of his *Ban-ri* and offer up his very life's force to save her.

Brok came to the next victim just as healers arrived from literally all over Kaerad, called by the freakish energy emanating from the Council grounds. He knelt by the woman, who was curled into a ball, and helped her turn over.

Burned white cheeks. Terrified blue eyes. Straw-like blonde hair. Long, reedy frame. Even soot-coated and superficially marred, Colleen was recognizable. One of the guards must have brought her out of compassion.

Great compassion, Brok decided as he flexed his fingers and readied himself to transfer energy. Two things crossed his mind while he worked, ignoring Colleen's unnecessary and theatrical screaming when he dispensed with her clothing.

First, the other two lab workers were likely about, somewhere on the body-littered grass, and they might have information about what occurred—from an Earther's perspective. Second, Colleen had no hand in the treachery, unless her stupidity exceeded Brok's original estimation. Which was, of course, a possibility.

Brok closed his eyes, calling down available and free atomic matter. Not too much. Just enough. With the rushing energy of the universe, he quickly healed Colleen's many cuts, and then went to work on her bruises. The burns, hardest and most delicate, came last—yet even these did not tax Brok.

Colleen's attempts to strike him, however, did.

"Monster!" she shouted. "Sex fiend! Are you going to screw me now? Give me back my clothes!"

And most of this was an act, Brok knew. The woman's broadcasted thoughts focused on nothing but fucking Kaeradi males. Brok, Harad, and every other one she had seen.

As bands of healers closed in on Colleen, Brok opened his eyes and sighed. "Be peaceful, Bitch. Your wishes are no doubt close to the granting."

By the time Kaerad's moon-trio rose in the eastern skies, the many victims of the SETI-WHO explosion were well-tended and mending comfortably in the homes of family — or, in the case of the Earthers — eager first-stage compatibility-tested hosts. To be safe, Brok had sent two healers to each of those homes, just for safety's sake. There would be no unmonitored, spontaneous sex on Kaerad this night.

Yes, all was well with everyone, except for the three who mattered most to Brok.

Tia. Harad. Dare.

No word had come from the Council house.

And so, Kaerad's White Chief paced alone, back and forth, in front of the formidable stone dais commanding the center of the Council's grounds.

"A bomb. On Tia's desk." This he repeated to himself over and over, retracing and regrouping what he had learned from the reports and wounds of the Kaeradi guards, the volunteers and their newly-bonded mates, and the lab workers (Colleen excluded, due to the screaming and hitting).

Why would anyone aim so directly to destroy his *Ban-ri?*

This made no sense to Brok. It seemed like war-strategy. More the province of Harad.

But Harad could be of no help.

And Tia is on Kaerad now. Unless one of the matches or lab workers means Tia harm, she is forever safe from such treachery.

Yet, even as he thought it, Brok knew the truth. If Tia recovered, she would go back to Earth to finish her mission.

To save her people.

Even if some of them wanted her dead.

"Brok."

The voice was so quiet Brok almost missed it amongst the whisper of leaves in Kaerad's new-fallen night.

Heart leaping, Brok turned.

The leader of the Council of Wisdom, Kaerad's oldest citizen, stood at the end of the dais. He looked like a gnarled everwood, newly sprung from ceremonial ground for some secret, frightening purpose.

Out of deference, Brok bowed.

When once more he raised his gaze to the elder, the man crooked one knobby finger. "This way."

And with that, the ancient turned and hobbled in the general direction of the forbidden Council house.

* * * * *

Tia woke before she opened her eyes.

Her first thought: *Oh, no. It was all a dream. Finding Kaerad, finding Brok...*

Her second thought: *I'm lying on the strangest bed.*

She raised her lids slowly, remembering another time when she moved too fast and felt the lab lights stab her pupils.

When I hit my head on the desk. Yeah. With Brok. But I woke up from that, right?

This time, sunlight made her squint. Warm rays stroked her cheeks, her arms. And a breeze cooled her right back down.

Golden leaves rustled overhead, and Tia blinked.

What trees had golden leaves? And golden fruit, and brown and golden bark with swirling green patterns?

Tia realized she was prone on a soft bed of moss, covered by those strange, magical leaves. The bed seemed to be raised, about waist-high. When she glanced to her left, she saw that it sloped down in a sculpted arc—to grass greener than any she had seen on Earth.

I'm on Kaerad. Or in some fairy tale.

For a wild minute, Tia felt like Sleeping Beauty, preserved for centuries, waiting for her prince to wake her with a kiss.

And then her prince bent over her.

Brok's crystalline eyes studied her with fervent concern, and his handsome face was tight with worry.

"Kiss me," she whispered, still lost in her fairy tale dream.

His firm lips pressed against her mouth. Gentle heat flowed between their bodies like a current.

Tia stirred as his tongue found hers, feeling an odd languish in her muscles.

I am Sleeping Beauty. *And he really is my prince.*

Brok held the kiss longer, then longer still.

Tia wrapped her arms around his neck, enjoying the hard, broad feel of his bare shoulders.

Oh, yes. Was the rest of him naked?

Savoring his lips, loving the taste of his tongue, Tia let one hand drift over Brok's well-defined back, down to his waist, his steel-firm hip, his ass...

Yes, yes, yes.

Naked.

She was already wet, already thinking of him mounting the strange bed, spreading her legs, and plunging his cock deep inside her pussy.

I want you, she mind-spoke, directing her wish at the center of Brok's head.

He eased back from their kiss, keeping his lips a breath from hers. With one large hand, he brushed the warm golden leaves off her right breast, and Tia realized she was naked, too.

Good. All the better.

I assumed you would be weak, Ban-ri. *Far too weak for what I wish to do.* Brok squeezed her breast, capturing the tip between his thumb and fingers. Meanwhile, he kissed her again. *The elders told me to leave the decision in your hands. That you would know what your body needs…*

Tia moaned as Brok pinched her pebbled nipple, and then she bit his lip.

"Aah," he said. But he didn't pull away.

I want you, Tia insisted, pushing her breast fully into his palm. With her other hand, she caressed his ass. *My pussy aches for you. I don't want to wait.*

Brok groaned and let go of her breast. Before Tia could protest, he moved his kisses down the line of her jaw, to her neck, to her chest.

Gripping his hair, Tia steered him toward one of her puckered nipples. His mouth felt like silky fire on her flesh as he claimed it, biting and sucking.

"So hot." She writhed on the earthen bed. "Don't stop."

Brok didn't stop.

He sampled her like a buffet. Her other nipple. Her belly. The soft strip of skin between her belly and mons.

Golden leaves drifted and shimmered each time Tia opened her eyes—but she couldn't keep them open. Her body trembled and hummed beneath Brok's mouth. She felt played like an instrument. Played by a master, with infinite care and precision.

Brok's mouth reached the top of her pussy, and Tia nearly came.

"Yes." She tugged at his hair. "There. There!"

His tongue moved around the triangle, then slowly back up, up, to her swollen labia.

Was he tasting each hair? Memorizing each inch of her sex?

You are worth taking the time, Ban-ri. *All my time, today and always.*

Brok's mind-words splashed over Tia like soft rain, making her clit ache all the more. With a frustrated gasp, she spread her legs, tempting him to go for the center.

She was close to begging.

And then she felt his finger slip into her wet, waiting core.

"Damn!" Her hips bucked against his hand.

Sweet surprise. Delicious surprise.

Growling his pleasure, Brok gave her another finger, and another, spreading her wide, then letting her clench as he moved his hand against her sensitive opening.

Not giving up, Tia pulled his hair again, and this time Brok gave in. His mouth fastened on her clit, sucking and licking at the same time.

Molten. Burning.

Tia grabbed the side of her moss-and-dirt pedestal. Her hips arched, grinding against his eager mouth, his pumping hand.

Her climax happened fast. Too fast. She thrashed under Brok's tender, torturing strokes. Tongue and hand, hand and tongue. He kept up his speed, his pressure, until the fire in her body eased.

But she wanted more. So much more.

Keeping his hand in her pussy, Brok rose and kissed her lips.

Tia tasted her juices on his mouth, his tongue. She felt her own heat on his flushed face.

"I would fuck you the rest of this day, and the next," he murmured. "But first, I must know your true heart. Here, now, before the Goddess. Do you truly love me?"

One last time, Tia rocked against his outstretched fingers. His hand felt so good inside her pussy like that. As if he owned her.

"I love you," she said, tears threatening. "I'm so sorry I made you doubt that. It's just—my body—I've never been comfortable with my size."

Brok slid his hand from Tia's wet core. "And now?"

Tia felt her cheeks flush. She gazed into Brok's eyes, and for the briefest moment, *saw* herself. As a whole person. A solid, intelligent, strong woman, with her very own beauty.

"Now I feel better," she whispered. "About me. About everything."

A look of relief passed over Brok's tense features, followed by a slow smile. A hungry smile. He moved beside her until he stood between her legs, hard thighs pushing hers apart. His rigid cock pressed against her bush, teasing her with possibilities.

"*Il aka n'domna. Ma Angaei, Ma Angaei.*" he said in a strong voice. "This is a sacred place, Tia. A healing altar of the Goddess. *Il aka n'domna. Ma Angaei, Ma Angaei. Ban-ri,* I would have you as my own. Would you have me?"

Fully understanding and accepting the vows, Tia said firmly, "Yes. I choose you."

My husband.

Brok closed his eyes, and Tia heard him praise the Goddess in his native language.

In her own mind, she heard her foremothers singing. "Thank you," she murmured, to them and to the Goddess they — and now she — trusted with their destinies.

And then Brok slid inside her, pushing his cock farther and farther, until Tia felt his rough hair rubbing against her mons.

For a breathless moment, they remained completely still, listening to the wind, feeling the brush of golden leaves — and the total joy of complete joining, mental and physical.

Then they groaned as one, and Brok slowly pumped his cock in and out of her ready, throbbing pussy.

He kept his startling blue eyes locked with hers, and Tia didn't consider looking away.

"Fuck me," she whispered, feeling the release of surrender, of trust, of her fledgling self-respect.

Brok placed his strong arms on either side of her, bracing on the altar as he dipped into her core.

Tia stroked his shoulders, his man's nipples — and then took hold of his black hair, as she always dreamed of doing in the days before men were real to her.

With a soft rumble of pleasure, Brok fucked her faster, harder, like he knew she wanted. Like he would fuck her each day of the rest of her life.

And each night, too.

Tia lost herself in the sway, moving back and forth on the Goddess's soft earth, light years from her own Earth.

"Yes," she moaned as tension built in every muscle, every fiber.

Her body rocked, nipples hard and sensitive to the breeze. Tia knew Brok enjoyed how her big breasts looked. The sight of them turned his hips into an engine, his cock into an incredible piston.

"I love you!" he shouted as he came, dragging Tia over the summit with him.

Orgasm seized her slowly, like hot flickers of fire spreading out from her pussy in wide circles. The only noise she could make was the same single word, over and over.

"Yours. Yours. Yours!"

Minutes later, or maybe it was hours, Brok lay on the Goddess's healing altar, cradling his *Ban-ri*. He would never cease to be grateful for her recovery, or for this beautiful moment of renewed claiming. Every day, he would make her glad she chose him.

And yet, any minute, she would remember what happened, and he would have to surrender her — at least for a time.

Brok sighed.

He would remain by her side. On this, he would insist. Though Tia's will was formidable — his was at least a match.

He hoped.

Tia snuggled closer, running her foot up and down the length of his leg. "I love you so much. After you left Earth, I was so scared you wouldn't come back. I told Harad…oh, my god. Harad! Dare!"

Brok let Tia go as she struggled to sit up, then captured her again, reading her thoughts as everything rushed back.

Loud. Fiery. An earthquake?

No. An explosion.

Tia's breath caught, and she started to cough.

"There was so much smoke! And my head, the rocks, crushing—"

Brok felt a scream building in her chest and held her closer.

"Easy. Stay calm, *Ban-ri*." He let his voice take on a low, even resonance. His Priest's cadence. "You are here with me now. Safe. Easy, Tia."

"But what about Harad and Dare?" She clawed at his arm. "And the rest of the guards. Damn! And the workers?"

"Kaeradi guards died. No Earthers. And the lab workers, even Colleen—they are here on Kaerad, and fine. Dare Jenrette is also awake, but my brother…"

His voice trickled to silence, feeling Tia's surge of anguish.

"Is he—did he—" She couldn't finish.

"Harad lives, but he remains near here, in a healing trance on the grounds of the Council of Wisdom."

At this, Tia pulled away from Brok and stood on shaking legs. Her eyes darted around the little clearing, taking in all the details now. The alien trees. The alien skies. Kaerad. Yes. She had known that when she woke—but now, she *knew* it so deeply Brok felt it like a hammer in his own mind.

Harad brought me here.

Yes.

"Will he be okay, Brok?"

"Yes." The answer was definite, but Brok couldn't banish a flicker of fear, of doubt.

Turning back to him, Tia asked, "How long have I been out?"

"An Earth week." Brok reached for her and drew her back into his embrace. "Please relax, *Ban-ri*."

"Has anyone contacted Earth?" Tia's agitation was mounting. Brok knew if he released her, she would pace. "Does SETI-WHO know what happened?"

"Yes." Brok kissed Tia's hair. "Dare Jenrette has been communicating through the links our under-priests established."

Relief washed through Tia, bathing Brok as well. "Good. Good. So, have they made the eggs?"

Brok went still. "I — do not know what you mean."

"Damn!" Tia banged her head against his chest. "I must have blacked out before I explained it. The eggs. I've got to talk to Dare. But — that can wait. First, are we allowed to see Harad?"

Yes. If you are calm and centered. Brok tailored his mind-voice to induce such a state. *Disruptive energy would be...draining for him.*

Tia stepped back and took Brok's hands. "Take me to him, please. I need to thank him."

Brok frowned, but he nodded.

As they left the clearing, Tia's thoughts filled his mind like a long, confused sigh.

Eggs. E-g-g-s, she was saying. *Eggs!*

Chapter Eleven

Earth, 3012

SETI-WHO Main Research Compound

Isis, Arizona

Eostre, Morning

Tia was so tired she could barely think—but she was finished.

Despite Brok's obvious discomfort with her being back on Earth. Despite Harad's continued coma and Dare Jenrette's absence. Despite Colleen's typically slow and grudging assistance. Despite the Kaeradi *Legio*, a special squad of thirty aliens in black robes who made Harad seem like a Paleo-Buddhist Pacifist—the psychic "police" Brok had brought to protect her and the lab. And, last but certainly not least, despite a virtual civil war raging in the digipress, in city streets all over the planet, and outside the SETI-WHO compound.

It was now or never for Earth and Kaerad.

If Dare and Tia's much publicized "solution" failed, the protestors would likely win out over scientific sense, and SEARCH would crank up the satellites again. Tia, Dare, and a few Earth women would live happily ever after on Kaerad—all the while knowing both of their worlds were dying.

Not an ideal solution.

So, inside the massive grounds of the enclosure, ninety-five blue-robed Kaeradi volunteers waited, along with twice that many healers. Four hundred potential Earth matches waited in another part of the compound.

Tia had kept five of the volunteers in her patched-up lab (missing one wall, her desk, and half the computer terminals) to help her with the last test, along with several healers.

If all went well, then at dusk, when the bonfires of Eostre blazed into the starlit sky, a new era would dawn on Earth.

Brok, Colleen, and Tia stood in a straight line, staring at the six sample eggs on the counter where the satellite terminals once rested.

"They look like — I don't know — freaky old-style footballs," Colleen muttered.

"Painted footballs," Tia agreed, annoyed at how often she had been civil to the bitch since they nearly got blown up together. "Only three times the size."

"I like the purple zig-zag design." Colleen nodded to the last egg in the row. "Nice touch."

"That is...mine," Brok said. He sounded wary.

Tia took a deep breath. She slipped her hand inside her lab coat pocket and rubbed the smooth surface of the *athame*. When they had returned from Kaerad, the dagger had been lying atop rubble untouched, as if it lifted itself for Tia to find.

"You two ready?" she asked.

Colleen nodded. Brok gestured to the first waiting volunteer, who stepped forward. Two healers shadowed him. Tia could see them on her left, from the corner of her eye.

She reached for the nearest egg — clone penile tissue created from a Kaeradi volunteer's genetic code and proteins from his sperm sample. Tia had stretched the created tissue around a tin alloy (an excellent conductor of psychic energy, according to Kaerad's wise), and coated with a thin acrylic to reduce shock from incompatible touches. They already knew from three pilot tests on Kaerad that volunteers could mind-link with their eggs. That if they handled their own eggs, they felt penile sensations. If other Kaeradi handled the eggs, the same sensations occurred.

But now, the true test. Thus far, the eggs had been created and handled through machinery and Kaeradi hands. Earth hands had not touched them at all.

It was time.

The purple one with green polka-dots (Colleen had painted it), had been created from a volunteer with "anticompatibility" to Tia. The worst possible match.

Tia held her breath. She had a sense that no one in the room was breathing.

Hand shaking, she brushed her fingers across the soft, slick surface.

The volunteer gasped.

Tia snatched her hand away. The healers grabbed the priest by the arms, but he shrugged them off.

"What happened?" Tia asked.

"I-I felt your touch," the priest admitted, cheeks flushing. "On my penis. It was not painful. Just—surprising. And I knew immediately the level of our incompatibility."

Brok cleared his throat. *I do not like this,* Ban-ri. *You…touching them like that.*

Tia glanced at him, surprised to find her husband irritated. *Jealous, sweetheart? It's just science—and a little magic.*

Brok frowned. *Get on with it.*

The second volunteer, a slightly closer match to Tia, stepped forward. Tia reached out and stroked his golden-colored egg.

Once more, the volunteer gasped—and this time, Tia felt a light sensation in her own pussy.

Odd.

It must have been a sort of psychic transfer. She hadn't planned on that happening, or even considered such a possibility. Would it get stronger with each successive match?

Reading her thoughts, Brok grumbled something to himself. It sounded like Kaeradi curses. His mood filled the room like a stray storm cloud, and Tia didn't even look at him as she handled the third egg, this one blue, and belonging to a neutral match to her genetic signature.

Definite tingle in the pussy from this one, right on her clit. Tia stared at the egg, breathing a little faster as she set it down.

"Very pleasant," the volunteer murmured. "Would you do that—"

"Silence," Brok growled. He didn't move toward the volunteer, but he didn't have to. The volunteer moved back in one big hurry.

Tia had to chew her lip to keep from smiling. Brok's possessiveness amused her, and pleased her. She rather liked being claimed.

The fourth egg, another Colleen paint job with red and green stripes, belonged to a probable match. The volunteer stepped forward, and Tia laid her palm against the rounded surface.

Her nipples snapped to attention as if struck by sex-lightning. Her pussy didn't just tingle, it ached and throbbed all at once. The rise to arousal felt so heady she almost shouted, and the volunteer groaned—not from pain.

Wisely, the healers led the young priest to the far end of the line, out of Brok's sight.

Colleen giggled.

Tia felt Brok's urge to knock the bitch-turned-decent-lab-partner through the back lab wall.

The fifth egg, this from a definite match, loomed in front of Tia like a bright yellow caution marker. She held her breath again, willing her body to relax, to refuse most of the response, and touched it quickly with three fingers.

Dear god! Tia pinched her knees together to contain the deep throb in her clit. The fifth volunteer bellowed, and Tia knew the man almost came. If she'd left her hand there long enough, stroked the egg with more deliberation, they would have reached orgasm in minutes, just like they were fucking.

Brok's expression turned murderous, and this time, Colleen didn't laugh.

"Get them out," she told the healers with unusual authority and insight. "The volunteers. Take them down to the search field now."

Tia recovered herself quickly, zeroing in on Brok's egg even as Brok moved to intercept and possibly behead the fifth volunteer. Before he reached the retreating priests and healers, she grabbed the purple zig-zag sphere with both hands.

Damn. Damn! Brok's egg vibrated beneath her touch, and she could feel his mouth sucking her nipples, his finger stroking her clit, and his cock plunging into her drenched pussy. The sensation of him all over her, everywhere—she came instantly.

The egg seemed to stick to her hands.

Orgasm after orgasm rattled her body.

From behind her, near the unhinged lab door, Brok groaned loud and low, and Tia heard a muffled sound. His thoughts—yes, he was coming, too. He had fallen to his knees, obsessed with her scent, the mental sensation of her wet channel and mouth and hands on his cock.

Put it down, Ban-ri. *Please...*

And then he added, *At least for now.*

Tia laughed in spite of her shaking, helpless body. The more she laughed, the more control she gained, until gradually, she was able to detach from the painted purple surface.

Colleen nudged Tia in the arm. "Stop, already. Fuck later. We have a shitload of Eostre eggs to finish and take to the volunteers."

Eostre, Early Evening

"Antimatch, no match, neutral match, compatible, definite match, and...perfect match," Tia explained to the teeming hoard of reporters surrounding the SETI-WHO press platform just outside the compound's main gate. The crowd included two contingents from EMA, "almosts" and fertile males, too, ringed by international guardswomen for their protection—although it seemed the women present were ignoring them.

For the moment, at least, Earth males were taking a drubbing in public opinion.

In the far distance, behind a human shield of guardswomen, Purists—some male, some female, some "almosts," shouted and protested and waved flashing digisigns.

Go Home Diseased Aliens

Keep Our Earth Sperm Pure

Kaerad=Crud

Tia didn't bother looking at the nuts for long.

The press corps kept a respectful distance from the platform, owing to Brok towering beside her and the Kaeradi *Legio* menacing all moving objects.

Even Tia didn't like to be too close to those guys.

At the moment, the Kaeradi psych-police stood like statues, arms folded, serrated knives clenched in their teeth. Tia knew they were scanning thoughts, intents. Woe be the idiot who planned treachery *now*.

The reporters piped up with questions, but Colleen quieted them with a short whistle into the bouquet of digimikes.

"Essentially," she said, sounding as important as possible, "neutral match and below should not attempt genital contact. Compatibles may f—um, have sex, but only with Kaeradi healers present for the first time. Definite matches are free to engage in genital contact without supervision, and perfect matches, well…" Colleen cut her eyes to Tia. "Perfect matches won't have to ask us any questions at all. Trust me."

Tia waited for the smatters of laughter, applause, and out-of-turn questions to die down. Already, bonfires burned inside and outside the complex grounds, paying homage to the

Goddess. Altars would be everywhere on Earth and Kaerad and who knew how many other worlds. The thought of such shared celebration made Tia warm inside. Earth seemed...less isolated. Connected now, to something greater than their blue sphere, turning about their single blazing star.

Chanting began, and this time, it wasn't only in Tia's mind. It was everywhere. On Earth. All through the universe. The *athame* vibrated in her pocket, picking up the resonance and warming Tia all the more. She reached for Brok's hand, and he gripped her fingers gently. His jealous thoughts were gone, replaced by concern, wariness — and ever-flowing love.

And Tia believed him now. Believed in their relationship and herself, with no reservations.

"Until we are able to make the technology smaller and more accessible, this will be the best way to determine compatibility," she said, smiling at the almost completely female crowd. "All interested parties from either planet will complete basic screenings and be entered into the Egg Database. This is the first of what we hope will be many, many hunts — though this first is certainly symbolic, in honor of the Goddess."

Then, she explained the process.

Inside the lush SETI-WHO acres, lit by bonfires and decorated with Eostre altars, Kaeradi volunteers stood beside their eggs. Earth matches would be released into the field to begin searching. It would be up to the couples and groups — since more than one woman might match a volunteer — what to do after they sampled each other. After all, some people might want sex and no relationship. Some might want to live as groups until more Kaeradi volunteers arrived. Some might find a perfect match.

And fuck on the spot, Tia thought, though she didn't say this aloud.

Brok mind-laughed.

Colleen once more took over the presentation, as agreed. "Special barred platforms have been established for the media. No digicams, please. Observation only."

Five of the *Legio* stepped forward and sheathed their knives.

"Those of you holding passes one through twenty, please accompany the soldiers to your box." Colleen smiled. Actually, she bared her teeth nervously, but Tia thought it passed for a smile at a distance.

The reporters holding passes one through twenty appeared less than thrilled by their escorts. In fact, many seemed downright terrified — though a few gave the musclebound psych-cops the once over as they headed into the SETI-WHO compound.

Tia tugged Brock's hand. "Are you sure your boys will control themselves if one of the digijournalists tries to jump his bones?"

"Positive." Brock's tone and the hard flash of his blue eyes left no room for doubt. "The *Legio* are trained in the sexual arts, but also trained in the higher art of self-denial. You could strip one naked and suck his staff, and he would not allow a physical response."

Colleen shot Brok and Tia a glance. "That's just...creepy. Now, hush. It's time for me to talk again."

Brok checked the Earth stars patterns and the position of the moon, which he had already memorized. About one hour had passed. Reporters were situated. Bonfires had been optimized, and fire cast a soft glow over the field where the volunteers waited.

It was time to release the matches.

And yet, unease stirred in Brok's gut.

Something seemed off. Wrong.

Dangerous, perhaps.

As he and Tia followed Colleen into the grounds, heading for their secured box, he kept one arm draped over Tia's shoulder. His eyes traveled in wide circles, but he could find nothing amiss. The five *Legio* accompanying them also seemed wary — but *Legio* were always wary. Most especially Talok, Harad's second in command and the leader of Kaerad's elite fighting force.

With Harad out of commission, Talok took on the protection of Brok and Tia as if they were his own blood. Kaeradi for Kaeradi. His life for theirs. As for Harad and Dare, ensconced in the safety of the Council grounds, protected by the Council of Wisdom's advanced mental powers — they were virtually beyond harm.

"I do not like this, Brother," Talok murmured where only Brok could hear him. "Something disturbs the air."

"Likely the scientific equipment," Brok told him quietly. "Or the barely leashed sexual energy."

"Hhhmmph." Talok kept walking, but Brok could tell he didn't want to proceed.

When they reached the SETI-WHO box, a barred, walled platform ringed with windows raised some twenty feet off the grounds, Colleen climbed straight up.

Tia placed her hands on the smooth wooden ladder to climb — and stopped.

Brok put his hands on her hips and his cock got hard despite the circumstances. Just touching his *Ban-ri* made him want to hold her closer. And if he held her closer, he'd want to fuck her here, now.

Should I help you up, Ban-ri?

"No." Tia's voice had an odd ring.

She pulled away from his touch and extracted her ceremonial dagger from her pocket. From her thoughts, Brok knew the blade had become unnaturally warm, and Tia thought she felt it vibrating.

From the ceremonies? she asked herself—and Brok thought he heard the chanting of ancients in his mate's mind.

He caught his breath.

"You have a lineage of powerful elders, Tia. More powerful than I believed possible for a planet such as Earth."

Absently, Tia nodded. She studied the dagger she called Widowmaker or the *athame*. "I just…never really believed. But now, I'm learning to believe in so many things."

Talok moved toward Tia like a shadow in the corner of Brok's eye. The *Legio* captain stopped an arm's length from her and asked, "What are they saying, honored wife? Speak the words of your elders to me."

"*Anna de sancto, perifie. Perifie!*" Tia echoed. And then she spouted a set of numbers.

Brok almost understood the words—something about an affront to life, terrible danger—but he knew immediately what those numbers were. Rage blazed in his brain. A killing rage.

He forced Tia behind him and whirled around, staring at the coordinates Tia's ancients had supplied.

Talok grabbed him by the arm. "Take her to the box. Guard her there. Let us handle these…animals."

Battling a rise of Kaerad's old blood, the battle fire that bent minds and twisted souls, Brok grunted.

He wheeled, grabbed his *Ban-ri* and urged her up the stairs.

Tia climbed fast in front of Brok, shocked by the violent images rushing through his mind.

Below them, Talok, the captain of the *Legio,* emitted a piercing cry. Something like Tia imagined ancient tribal warriors did just before attacking a hated enemy. Then, he ripped his knife from his belt, put it in his teeth, and ran—on all fours, like a dog!—faster than humanoids should be able to run.

From every direction came his companions. Red blurs, like splashes of blood on the grass.

Tia reached the box, jumped inside, and ran to a glassless window. Brok closed in behind her and moved her slightly to the side. "Out of harm's way," he growled, holding her close to his firm chest.

Beside them, across the small expanse of the box, Colleen cringed. "What is it? Did some nuts break through the guards?"

"I don't know," Tia admitted. Her heart slammed against her ribs, and yet, as Brok stroked her arms, she relaxed a little.

He wouldn't let anything or anyone hurt her. Ever. She knew that.

More howls and cries rose from the field below, and in moments, the *Legio* came back into view, herding five Earthmen. One "almost" and four fertiles. One of the Kaeradi held what was clearly a large explosive devise.

Tia pressed a button on her digiwatch, summoning the captain of the guardswomen.

And then, as the group below crossed in front of a bonfire, Tia knew the Earthers. The fertiles were high up in the EMA political structure.

Son of a bitch! What, Earth's men feel "threatened?" They don't want to have to work an honest job for a living because their sperm isn't worth a king's ransom now?

Fuming, Tia glared at the "almost." She realized it was Adam, the jerk from the loading dock.

Who insulted her during the last sperm drop-off.

Who handed her the digipad.

The digipad she threw on her desk.

"The digipad that blew up the lab," Tia and Brok said at the same time.

Brok literally disappeared from the box and reappeared in front of Adam.

Tia grabbed her chest. She'd seen matter transfer before, of course. She'd just never seen her husband do it.

The party below stopped short, and Brok spoke to Talok, pointing at Adam.

From the main gate, a troop of guardswomen came at a run, stun rifles at the ready.

"Is Brok going to kill that eunuch?" Colleen asked.

Tia gripped the windowsill. Her stomach clenched. "I hope not, but he might."

Won't the Legio *stop him?*

But even as she asked herself the question, Talok shoved the "almost" on the ground at Brok's feet and offered him a long, wicked-looking sword.

Brok took it and raised it high above Adam's scrawny neck.

"No!" Tia shouted.

From other boxes, press members screamed. The guardswomen closed in, but they'd never reach Brok in time!

Chapter Twelve

Tia felt a shimmer in the box—and suddenly Dare Jenrette stood beside her. Someone else was briefly there, then gone—and Tia saw Harad materialize beside Brok, catching his arm on the downswing.

Adam's neck was spared by inches.

The brothers spoke. Seemed to spar for a moment. And then Brok stepped away from the *Legio*.

The guardswomen arrived, and the Kaeradi psych-police allowed Earth's security force to take the fertiles. Harad said something to the captain of the guardswomen, and she paused, shrugged, and then nodded.

The unit moved out with their four prisoners.

Adam, however, was lifted by his elbows between two *Legio* members. One of them picked up the large, heavily wired case of explosives.

And then the three of them were gone, bomb and all.

Brok and Harad reappeared in the box.

Tia's first urge was to hug Harad, then kiss Brok.

Her second was to slap the snot out of both of them.

"What the hell was that about? And what did you do with Adam?" Tia folded her arms. "Good to see you, Harad, by the way. Great, in fact. Thanks for saving my life when the lab blew up."

Harad bowed, then grabbed Dare around the waist. "A-damn has been taken to Kaeradi labor prison, on the moon near a planet we call Bannadu. The translation is *Bandu-Mother*. We trade with the Bannadu. All female—but they are incompatible with our biology. And with most societies. A bit war-like. Very—as you would say—hostile."

"They will be most interested in A-damn," Brok added, putting his arm around Tia and turning back to the window. "Male laborers are always welcome on Bannadu."

You almost killed him, Tia mind-spoke.

Brok took a breath and let it out slowly. *Sometimes, my discipline weakens.*

"I'm scared," Colleen whined from the corner.

Dare Jenrette startled, noticing the lab worker for the first time. "Take her to another box," she told Harad, and he complied before Tia could speak to the contrary.

By the time he came back, Tia knew that Harad woke up a day ago, and had been raring to get to Earth. Even the elders could contain the War Chief for only so long.

"Is it time?" Dare leaned into Harad's embrace. A barely perceptible move, but one that made Tia smile. "I've been imagining this for days."

Tia allowed herself to relax beneath Brok's protective arm. After closing her eyes for a moment and listening to the now peaceful voices of her foremothers, Tia pressed the digicom button on her watch.

"Let the hunt begin."

A roar went up from the north side of SETI-WHO's compound, and women came pouring into the field, past altars and bonfires, to the waiting Kaeradi volunteers.

Tia's pulse quickened.

Brok's hand drifted down, toward her breast. She didn't stop him.

Out on the field below, matches were being made. She could tell by the excited cries of joy, of pleasure. By the energy change. As if the Goddess were paying a visit.

Bonfires brightened.

The stars seemed to brighten, too.

Just below their box, a buxom brunette picked up a green-painted egg. The volunteer groaned with pleasure.

Definite match, Tia thought as the couple laid the egg on the ground and began tearing each other's clothes off. *Maybe a perfect match.*

As the volunteer dropped to one knee and caught his match's breast in his mouth, Brok shifted his arm, slipped his hand beneath Tia's shirt, and pinched her pebbled nipples.

Without thinking, Tia groaned.

Beside her, Dare groaned, too. Tia glanced at her boss.

Harad had unbuttoned Dare's shirt. He stood behind her, fondling both of her swollen wine-colored nubs.

Warm thrills covered Tia's body. Her pussy throbbed in time with Brok's pinches and Harad's rhythmic rubbing.

Ban-ri, Brok sighed in her mind, tickling her spine with his low, sexy tone.

Tia let out another groan.

Screw it. She didn't care who saw, or who took offense.

This was Eostre. The festival of the Goddess, the renewal of sexuality itself.

Brok captured her other nipple, and she felt his iron cock hard against her ass.

Shifting her gaze between the Dare-Harad show and the volunteer and match now fucking like mad beside the bonfire, Tia rubbed her ass against Brok's hard-on as she unbuttoned her own pants and shirt.

God, she wanted to fuck him.

Another volunteer-match occurred nearby — this one with two women, then three. Sex began immediately as the women stripped the willing volunteer. Healers stood by in case of problems. One of them openly stroked himself.

Shouts of surprise, of excitement emanated from nearby press boxes. Tia figured the reporters were ready to jump out and start grabbing eggs. Hence, the bars and the *Legio.*

Not yet, ladies, Tia thought as her skin burned as hot as the fires on the grounds below. Her wet pussy ached for attention, for Brok's cock, buried deep, deep, deep. *But soon. Very soon.*

"Hurry up," Dare murmured, close enough for Tia to touch if she reached out a hand. The tall woman was naked now. She bent over, facing the window, and Harad ran his hands from her shoulders to her lean round ass. His prick stood straight out, and Dare pushed back toward him.

Sweat covered Tia as Brok shoved her pants and underwear down, over her hips. They fell to the box floor. Her shirt and lab coat he left in place, which felt deliciously naughty to Tia.

"You are so beautiful," he said. "I could fuck you all night."

"Won't stop you." Tia gasped as he reached into her bush and stroked her saturated lips. His cock, now bared, probably because Brok "disappeared" his pants, teased the crack of her ass like a huge finger, moving up and down.

Bonfires, burning and burning. Eggs, grabbed and stroked. Couples, matched.

Yes. Yes! Tia's mind swam. Sex was literally all around her. The smell of it. The sound of it. Moans and cries of pleasure. The ah-ah-ah of well-fucked women. The bellows of men coming in waiting channels and mouths and hands for the first time in years. Maybe decades.

And Brok's hands, one on her nipple, one in her slit, rubbing her swollen center.

Take care, she thought to all the new couples, all the new lovers. *Handle with care.*

And then Tia rocked back against Brok's man's chest, rubbing up and down against his man's nipples. She loved the firm, unyielding feel of his body. The roughness of his pubic hair on her back and ass. The pressure of his cock, pushing toward where she most wanted it to go.

"Sweet heaven," Dare moaned.

Tia looked at the other couple with no hesitation now. Harad held Dare much as Brok held her — pinching one of Dare's big nipples with one hand, rubbing Dare's clit with the other—except—

Oh, damn. Tia's insides clenched, and she had a small orgasm. Harad was in Dare's ass, pumping away.

Brok asked without asking, pushing harder against Tia's crack, but she shook her head, disengaged his hands, and turned around.

"I want to look at you," she murmured, raising one leg and stroking Brok's muscled hip.

He smiled at her, his face barely visible in the shadows of the box. Then he lifted her up, situated her ass in the open window, and spread her legs.

Tia used his nipples to keep her balance, drawing deep guttural purrs from Brok.

He grabbed her hips, kissed her, and entered her slowly. Teasingly slow. Deeper and deeper as Tia sighed into their kiss.

As Brok began to move, still slow, still teasing, he pulled back and looked down, to the place where they were joined in such pleasure.

Tia looked down, too. The sight of Brok's huge cock sliding in and out of her pussy brought her near to coming in two seconds flat.

"God, yes. Fuck me." She couldn't get enough of that sight. She would never get enough of that sight.

Brok pumped her harder. Tia watched, fascinated. Her breasts moved with the force of his thrusts. She grabbed her rock-hard nipples.

"I'm coming!" Dare shouted. "Big one. Big!"

Tia glanced at her. Harad looked like a giant machine, ramming his rod balls-deep in Dare's ass. All the while working her nipples. All the while working her clit. He gave a loud roar and clenched his teeth, coming with his chosen mate—and yet never slowing down.

Outside the box, matches and volunteers yelled and cried with orgasms.

Bonfire light flickered, shedding more light into the box, and Tia gazed at Brok. His fathomless blue eyes locked with hers, and then he became the machine, drilling her fast, drilling her deep.

Tia bucked against him, trying to draw out the moment. She felt like all the bonfires on SETI-WHO's sex-saturated grounds now burned her pussy. And the flames were growing, moving, through her belly, up to her nipples, to her throat.

Brok pulled her closer, barely allowing her body to move as he pounded her sensitive pussy. Tia felt an explosion the size of a supernova blooming at the center of her soul, and Brok kissed her.

They came together, moaning, jerking as their bodies scrubbed and rubbed and moved as one, kindling. Soothing. Kindling. Soothing.

Beside them, Harad and Dare moved to the box floor to continue.

"This could go on all night," Tia murmured in Brok's ear, feeling his cock harden in her hot pussy again.

"Eostre," Brok reminded her in his spine-melting bass. "The time of renewal. It is supposed to go on all night. Would you like to go outside?" He thrust once, making Tia's walls clench on his rigid flesh. "Dance and fuck beside the bonfires, or sample each other on an altar, like we should?"

"Why not?" Tia wrapped her legs around her husband, knowing he would transfer them in the blink of an eye. In her mind, her foremothers sang lustily, matching her own lusty thoughts.

She and Brok materialized together on the ground beside one of the blazing pillars of wood and two other couples, hard at fucking, still joined cock to pussy, already moving together again and moaning. Tia arched her back, closed her eyes, and resolved to study more about her ancestors. Learn more about their magic—and Earth's magic, and Kaerad's too.

"Eostre." She smiled, catching her breath as Brok began deeper, longer strokes. "This could definitely become my favorite festival."

It was hours later, near sunrise, when an orgasm-sated Tia discovered the one loss of her enchanted evening.

Somewhere in the heat and beauty of the best Eostre egg hunt Earth had ever known, Widowmaker had departed, leaving nothing but a perfectly charred dagger image on the pocket of Tia's lab coat.

That's the way of things, sweetheart...our family athame *comes when she's needed, and leaves when she's finished changing everything. Don't worry...She won't let you down...*

Epilogue

Kaeradearth, 3422

SETI-WHO Sacred Fields

Isis, Arizona

The young woman gazed at her soon-to-be lover as the bonfires of Eostre burned throughout the sacred fields.

Mia's heart swelled. To be honored by the Council of Wisdom, granted permission to join with her chosen mate at the place of First Consecration, where Kaeradearth was born – Mia felt special, indeed.

The concrete buildings and scientific equipment had long since been recycled in favor of true science, but a memorial yet remained. A strange, square altar called "Blessed Desk," on the spot where Mia's famed foremother Tia of Earth first knew Brok of Kaerad.

Mia and Kormond lay very close to that monument, each stroking the pendant of the other's necklace. A small painted Egg of Essence, awarded during the Eostre festival. They smiled as they touched each other's clone-tester, feeling the swell of passion and the deep knowledge of their compatibility.

Such pleasures were rare in these desperate times.

Even as Kormond drew Mia into his warm embrace, they both thought of the Alku. Of the advancing war. Kaeradearth had not faced such danger since the Time of Near Extinction. Everyone wanted to make a difference, yet no one had found a way to fight the Alku's vicious psychic assaults.

Please, *Mia thought, sending a simple prayer skyward to the Goddess.* On this Eostre, give us hope.

Kormond suddenly went still, gripping Mia tighter than she expected.

She struggled free, following his thoughts to what had startled him.

A bright light blazed from Blessed Desk.

Silver, with red in the center...

The young couple abandoned their joining, at least for the moment.

Holding hands, they rushed toward the anomaly, then stopped short at the edge of the memorial.

Kormond let go of Mia and leaned forward. "It – it looks like a battle blade. But what soldier would be fool enough to bury his weapon in Blessed Desk?"

Mia didn't answer.

Words left her in a great rush, and the fields and fires around her receded.

For the moment, there was only Blessed Desk, only her.

Only the dagger with the dancing red stone, buried deep center in its silver hilt.

And then, gradually regaining her breath and balance, Mia of Kaeradearth found her voice.

She reached for the blessing-curse-miracle with one trembling hand.

"Athame," *she whispered.*

"Athame."

About the author:

Annie Windsor is 37 years old and lives in Tennessee with her two children and nine pets (as of today's count).

Annie's a southern girl, though like most magnolias, she has steel around that soft heart. Does she have a drawl? Of course, though she'll deny it, y'all. She dreams of being a full-time writer, and looks forward to the day she can spend more time on her mountain farm. She loves animals, sunshine, and good fantasy novels.

On a perfect day, she writes, reads, spends time with her family, chats with friends, and discovers nothing torn, eaten, or trampled by her beloved puppies or crafty kitties.

ANNIE WINDSOR welcomes mail from readers. You can write to her c/o Ellora's Cave Publishing at P.O. Box 787, Hudson, Ohio 44236-0787.

Also by ANNIE WINDSOR:

- Arda: The Sailkeeper's Bride
- Arda: The Sailmaster's Woman
- Legacy of Prator 1: Cursed
- Legacy of Prator 2: Redemption
- Redevence: The Edge

Why an electronic book?

We live in the Information Age—an exciting time in the history of human civilization in which technology rules supreme and continues to progress in leaps and bounds every minute of every hour of every day. For a multitude of reasons, more and more avid literary fans are opting to purchase e-books instead of paperbacks. The question to those not yet initiated to the world of electronic reading is simply: *why?*

1. *Price.* An electronic title at Ellora's Cave Publishing runs anywhere from 40-75% less than the cover price of the <u>exact same title</u> in paperback format. Why? Cold mathematics. It is less expensive to publish an e-book than it is to publish a paperback, so the savings are passed along to the consumer.

2. *Space.* Running out of room to house your paperback books? That is one worry you will never have with electronic novels. For a low one-time cost, you can purchase a handheld computer designed specifically for e-reading purposes. Many e-readers are larger than the average handheld, giving you plenty of screen room. Better yet, hundreds of titles can be stored within your new library—a single microchip. (Please note that Ellora's Cave does not endorse any specific brands. You can check our website at www.ellorascave.com for customer recommendations we make available to new consumers.)

3. *Mobility.* Because your new library now consists of only a microchip, your entire cache of books can be taken with you wherever you go.

4. *Personal preferences are accounted for.* Are the words you are currently reading too small? Too large? Too...ANNOYING? Paperback books cannot be

modified according to personal preferences, but e-books can.

5. *Innovation.* The way you read a book is not the only advancement the Information Age has gifted the literary community with. There is also the factor of what you can read. Ellora's Cave Publishing will be introducing a new line of interactive titles that are available in e-book format only.

6. *Instant gratification.* Is it the middle of the night and all the bookstores are closed? Are you tired of waiting days — sometimes weeks — for online and offline bookstores to ship the novels you bought? Ellora's Cave Publishing sells instantaneous downloads 24 hours a day, 7 days a week, 365 days a year. Our e-book delivery system is 100% automated, meaning your order is filled as soon as you pay for it.

Those are a few of the top reasons why electronic novels are displacing paperbacks for many an avid reader. As always, Ellora's Cave Publishing welcomes your questions and comments. We invite you to email us at service@ellorascave.com or write to us directly at: P.O. Box 787, Hudson, Ohio 44236-0787.

Printed in the United States
24653LVS00001B/43-669